This book should be returned to any branch of the
Lancashire County Library on or before the date shown

SKELMERSDALE

FICTION RESERVE STOCK LL 60

Bowran Street
Preston PR1 2UX

AFG 13

Lancashire
County Council

www.lancashire.gov.uk/libraries

Lucy's Monster

Lucy's Monster

R L ROYLE

Dog Horn Publishing

Published 2006 by Dog Horn Publishing
PO Box 208, Dewsbury, WF12 8WS
www.doghorn.com

A CIP catalogue record for this book is available from
The British Library

ISBN 0-9550631-0-8

Cover design: Saima Nazir
Chapter images: R L Royle

Printed and bound in Finland by
WS Bookwell OY

For You

Acknowledgements

I would like to thank the following people for their time, help, support and patience:

Jon Appoo (The Meadows, Hertfordshire); Robert Heard (Senior Nurse Manager); Anonymous (District Hospital Consultant Pathologist); Dr M Hayes (Consultant Pathologist at Hereford Hospitals, NHS Trust); Elain Benfield (Counsellor); Saima; Sharron; Lauren; Jez; Jimmy; Twig; Karen; Mogwhiii; Julia; Dad; R'Kid; Mum; Michael Richardson; V; Jonathan; Claire; Dwayne; Kate; John; Mrs T; Jane and the many other friends and family members that inspired me with their belief and encouragement.

A special thank you to James –
for everything.

'…sick with guilt for the miserable life I'm too tripped to realise I don't actually have.'

-Unknown

Introduction

Dear Reader,

You and I are standing side by side in a dark corridor. Large windows echo misty daylight in places but it's not enough to calm your nerves. We stand in silence.

'C'mon,' I say: 'Let's go and look at her.'

You twitch your mouth slightly and look down to your day shoes. You're far from liking this I see, and as the shards of light parade dust in the air you look to me again and nod solemnly.

I'm sorry, I must try to take it into account that this is strange for you, being in the story like this. You opened this book to read about my victim's decent into madness; you never opened it to be dragged into it yourself. Let's establish where we are first; I'm guessing you're a little dazed...

We are standing in her hospital, on her ward, in my mind. I say nothing to you for a few moments as I assess you. I feel bad for not providing more windows or some light bulbs right now; I never meant for it to look so eerie and undeveloped. I feel how edgy you are and sense you mean no harm.

'Follow me; I'll show her to you.' I turn and begin walking, hearing you following anxiously.

I mentally scan you from head to toe, dear reader, but please understand I only do this to calm my own nerves. You are scared of me as you assume I have the power here but you must understand that I too am wary. At the moment I am crunching footsteps into something I created almost accidentally and I have you, a complete stranger, following me, almost whimpering with fear.

The further we walk, the dimmer it becomes. Only a matter of moments ago the windows were teasing us with what could have been a sunny afternoon – now we walk past glimpses of an outside world rapidly heading for dusk, with the sun sinking fast. We pass trolleys piled with empty plates, walk on shiny tiles past rooms with collapsed wheelchairs outside the doors. All so sharp and real as we pass them but if you'd have looked back after a few steps you would have noted an odd kind of glow around them as if they were only there for show and now they weren't needed they were in the process of disappearing.

I lead the way, for it is in my head. I brought you here and, scared or not, I must show you what you are here to see. You can't decide whether you like me or not yet; I sense you feel strangely honoured to be allowed down here, yet you are scared. You think surely if I really were your friend I'd take you to a garden or somewhere else that appears pleasant and smelling of roses; how nice.

I look surprisingly normal to you too, which was a bit of a shock when you first found yourself standing facing me, almost zapped into this dream like state. I sense you thinking *surely somebody sick enough to make me feel so uncomfortable in only the fourth paragraph must have hidden depths behind an average enough looking exterior.* I don't try to argue; at least Mr King leaves it until the tenth page.

As we walk further the corridor thins, becoming more and more claustrophobic with every step we take. The windows have ceased to exist now and we are walking in what feels like the dead of night. I hear you swallowing deep breaths, panicking ever so slightly at how moist and warm the air has become. I want to turn around and jump back into my computer chair but I can't leave you lost here. I am your blind guide, dear reader. We must carry on until we get there.

We have to hunch over slightly now as the ceiling has dropped. It becomes darker still and stingingly cold. You tail me close, looking behind you at all times, even though your darting eyes are met only by complete darkness. I stop hard and you walk into me, jerking and jumping *shit, please don't hurt me* as we make contact for a second. You look so afraid I want to comfort you, but that is not what we are here for.

I do not say anything or make any movement. I want you to be the first to acknowledge the reason why I slammed my mental brakes on. You do so almost within a second.

'Is this where she hides?' you ask, turning to the door directly right of us, which is now the only thing other than darkness that is evident except for the whites of our eyes.

I haven't seen what the door looks like... I can only sense it. I stare ahead, my grey-green eyes looking into the darkness while my mind unveils a projector screen onto which a quick memory can dance upon in full, bright colour. I call upon the memory I reserve for times of fear. I need to get this out of the way first, dear reader – then I will have the courage to open that heavy door for you.

I watch the whole thing in under a second when in real life all those years ago it was a full sunny morning.

But you, you can only try and mentally prepare yourself for meeting her behind this door; you are shaking from your soul outwards but also feel as if you could pass a small amount of urine with the build up of excitement this has given chase to.

I turn to face the door, take a deep breath *I was once in control here* and place my hand on the biting cold handle.

'Yeah,' I say at last. 'Let's get this over and done with.'

You are the first reader I have ever taken on this tour, and you will be the last. I'm not doing this again.

I squeeze the handle tight as I push it clicking and clanking downwards. It reaches its lowest point and the heavy metal door opens like a wooden one. It swings inwards and we step in...

We walk into a high security bedroom but we don't particularly register it as we both immediately fix our eyes on the main attraction, and within a moment I can sense we see the same thing but view it completely differently. I feel nothing but relief looking at the shrinkin' stinkin' woman that today sits still and silent, whereas you feel disappointed, almost disgusted at the whole mockery of it all shrivelled on the floor, blinking every time the bedside clock ticks.

At just about the same time we both take our eyes off the unfortunate victim of my imagination and scan the room that she occupies.

To the left of us is a hospital bed, the walls are white and the only window in the room faces us and is heavily netted so the patient cannot reach the glass. The window looks out on to the home's gardens. The beautiful landscapes that stretch acre upon acre are magnified by midday sunshine as I stand here yearning to be outside running in it. But I see you – you know the sunshine and the landscapes aren't real and the only thing that is real is why you're here. 'Fuck the sunshine,' you would say if you were bolder; 'I want to touch her hair.'

I glance at you staring at her then look back out of the window. The view is clear and its normality relaxes me.

To the right of us is a wardrobe, a chair and a locker. The woman is in a heap under the window; her face is vacant with dead eyes pointing at the vinyl floor to the left of her.

'She's dying,' you say, unable to believe how pathetic she looks.

'She's fine,' I reply.

I can feel her. She's happy enough in her own little world. I created this woman whom I still find beautiful. I understand her depths more than you can, dear reader, but I can't expect you to fully understand that at this early stage.

'Look at her, she makes me want to cry. Can't you re-write her or something?' you almost plead with me. I watch my character for a moment, she blinks twice within this time.

'I could,' I shrug.

'So why don't you?'

'Because then I'd be taking away what she is.' I pause for a moment and turn to you. 'Plus,' I add, 'there'd be nothing for you to read about.'

'I want to leave now,' you say sternly.

I did not mean to upset you but I can see your eyes glaze over. I think it's time to leave now, before I make you so uncomfortable you decide to disregard this book and go for something less involving. I ask you to look down to the floor – only when you do so you can't see anything, shock jolts you back into reality and you realise with a start that none of that was real. Within a second you are on the outside of the pages and you're not sure what just happened. *Was that a dream?* One line on now and it's even hazier still. *But I can still see her face!* You picture that face and don't forget it, because this is the story of the woman you just met and how she came to be there.

CHAPTER 1

'And the winner for best leading actress goes to....'

The hostess, Ms Amanda Turpin, had flashed her pretty white teeth at just the right time to end up dressed in red here tonight at the 1990 *Epic Awards*. She pushed scarlet fingernails under the shiny white envelope and then flicked them upwards to reveal the printed name of this year's golden girl. Ms Turpin's glossed lips twitched ever so slightly as she read who the lucky lady was to be, and she raised those beautiful bitch eyes back up to the baying crowd.

Five of the world's most respected actresses had been nominated for this award, each one naturally thinking themselves more talented and beautiful than the other, yet each one totally unaware of who the winner was going to be. All five of the nominated limelight ladies sat as cool as the morning breeze for the cameras, their true feelings of utter nervousness and unbearable anticipation hidden perfectly for their images' sakes.

You and I are about to embark on a watching game, a dark adventure. And I too am about to reveal something... our main character. You see, our personal leading lady just happens to be one of those five nominated women. It's mad, isn't it? It's not often we have the chance to watch someone so famous so intimately without having to depend on the Chinese whispers of the media. But, yep, we're in luck in this time of celebrity obsession and I'm telling ya, she's a peach too. My dear reader, I am honoured to present to you Lucy Denharden. Although Lucy is her christened name she is better known by her brand, her stage name: Autumn Leigh. We will call her that for now as that is what everyone else in the world calls her and I don't want to confuse things – I know, I know – she's a far cry from the woman you met in the introduction and I can see how it's hard to believe that it is the same woman at all, but I swear to God, at one point in her life that sad, disturbed person really did have all this...

Autumn Leigh was sitting in the front row at the eight-seater table fully occupied by the hot stuff of the late 80s and early 90s. Among them were her heartthrob English husband of five years, Anthony Denharden – also an A-list actor; her co-star and fellow nominee Jerry Tilsey; and the famous director, Bret Hancolm. All eyes were twitching towards Autumn as Amanda took as painstakingly long as she could about soaking up the attention for a few more seconds. Autumn pinched the skin of her firm neck with one hand and squeezed Anthony's hand with the other.

Autumn had been nominated for her leading role in *The Green Book,* a dramatic blockbuster that had topped the US charts for ten weeks and had remained in the top ten for seven months. She'd built up a string of successful films since 1985, but this was by far the breadwinner. Not half – *The Green Book* had been nominated for almost everything at the spectacular *Epic Awards*, held in Hollywood. Being by far that year's leading event, Autumn knew she couldn't get away with a lousy video taping saying 'thank you *so* much' while clutching the silver award greedily in both hands.

You better believe it; Autumn Leigh wouldn't have travelled all the way from her marital home in England for it if it weren't *the* place to be.

So who are we dealing with here? Let's take time out for a moment and I'll describe to you just how beautiful this woman is. I think now would be a good time for you to build up a solid image of this superstar at the height of her power. You see, not only is Ms Leigh Hollywood's dream acting-wise but she is also the world's hottest ass, pardon the term. Compared to the likes of Rita Heyworth on many occasions, Autumn has a timeless, mature look of pure sex. Her hair is shiny golden-red; locks and locks of it tumbling down curved, sultry shoulders, perfectly conditioned and enviously bouncy.

Her eyes are swimming pools of chocolate brown and the perfect feature for any photographer to work upon, blessed with long, thick lashes that hold mascara beautifully and well defined sockets framing perfectly applied eyeshadow.

Her cheekbones are just as prominent, showing up strong behind flawless snowflake skin. But it's her lips that the eye is drawn to automatically. Autumn Leigh possesses the fullest, most natural and gloriously shaped lips in the circuit and when lavishly coated with glossy red lipstick the finishing result is a face that is beautiful enough to make even grown men want to put a poster of her above their beds. Behind those lips are pearly white teeth, perfectly straight and always sparkling.

Ms Leigh was born and brought up in rural Nova Scotia and her soft Eastern Canadian accent still presents itself in her voice when she speaks naturally and without effort. No matter how often she spends in the US or how long she's had her feet planted in the UK, when she speaks to Anthony in bed, she speaks her roots. In public our girl expresses more than just a hint of her husband's English accent when such things as politics or anything else intellectual is on the agenda. But, unknowingly to herself, when Autumn laughs, the girl is pure Hollywood. Her smile could be frozen in time and she could be admired for that alone, never mind her amazing acting skills and career-minded attitude that's respected all over the globe.

Autumn has always worked on the fact that she is an attractive woman and had taken a liking to presenting herself as an icon of days gone by. It allows her to really dress up, flaunt her curvy figure and experiment with vintage clothing. She moves like Rita, she laughs like Marilyn... it gives her that edge that the other beautiful stars just don't have with their waif-like frames and bland dinner dresses.

All in all, sitting at that table with her heart in her throat is a true born fantasy figure... and she knows it.

'Well, no surprises here...' Amanda Turpin declared after letting the tension build for just a little too long: 'Autumn Leigh, for her role as Mandy in *The Green Book*!'

Autumn's hands flew up to her awe stricken face, then straight to embrace her husband who was laughing with joy for the woman that he loved so much.

The roar of the crowd was breathtaking and over her husband's shoulder she could see herself, with tears enlarging her wide eyes, filling the two big screens at either side of the stage.

I've done it! I've done it! And tonight, ladies and gentlemen, Autumn Leigh rows the boat! Tonight Autumn Leigh rows the fucking boat! I've done it! I've done it!

Autumn Leigh had arrived in Hollywood as plain old Lucy Cunningham in 1979, when she was just nineteen. She didn't exactly cause a storm upon first sight like she had planned and by the summer of 1982 still nothing major had happened on the acting front and our girl was still renting a room with no windows and working as a waitress. She had attended more auditions than she could remember, some being close, others complete disasters. Although Lucy had grown used to Hollywood in a way that she no longer felt like a lost child in the middle of a fast road, many of her nights were still spent considering going back to Nova Scotia.

But then what? The question was the only thing that kept her there in those first few years. ***Then what?*** After the hugs and the *told you so*'s, the *at least you tried*'s and the *waste of two years* had calmed down, what would she do then... *waitress* for the rest of her life? Lucy knew that if she was to give up and go back home then she would have lost, she would be wiping down tables back in some out-of-the-way café or bar, always thinking *what if I'd have stayed just one more year? What if? What if?* Always feeling like she was wasting her life.

So she stuck with it and in the fall of 1982 an audition for a hairspray advert came up. Lucy, now going by the name Autumn Leigh, got the part. The advert gave Lucy a new lease of life and confidence. She was back on the circuit and no longer were her dreams about going home, they were now of becoming a big, big star.

Two months and several adverts later she got a bit-part in *Roosters,* a low budget comedy about a hillbilly family winning the Lotto and coming to live in Hollywood. It was only a ten-second walk-on role with no lines but finally, little Lucy from Whites Lake was in a film.

That little walk-on role and her good looks got her recognised just enough to land the one line part in an action film called *Sea of Blood*, in which the film's muscle-ridden all-American star Al Torgher bumped into her while being chased by bad guys. Lucy's line was: 'Hey, watch it!' and she appeared in the credits as:

> Woman at store   Autumn Leigh

Al Torgher took a liking to the young, slim woman who went by the name of Autumn Leigh and they had a fling that hit the papers: her name was finally in the gossip pages. Autumn Leigh had fucked a massive movie-star – and that was where it all started. Her new found notoriety meant that Autumn was getting nearly every role she went for. She quit her job at the café and found herself a decent agent and, although she was still struggling to make ends meet, every single role she went for (although still small) paid that little bit extra each time.

This continued for two years and gradually, Autumn Leigh's name became recognised. Autumn's first major character role was in 1985, when she was twenty-six.

By now she was a streetwise Hollywood actress who had learnt how to pull the strings that mattered, and luckily for her she was blessed with staggering beauty that was intensifying with age.

The film that set the pace of what was to come was *Cruel Wisdom*. She starred alongside another rising star, Anthony Denharden – an English actor who was conquering Hollywood just that little bit faster than Autumn Leigh. It would turn out to be their major breaks. The chemistry between Autumn Leigh and Anthony Denharden was undeniable and they married three months after the film's release.

However, the film that grossed number one and shot her to big-time fame was the 1986 classic *Lower*, which earned Autumn Leigh massive acclaim and respect, turning her into Hollywood's darling practically overnight. In less than 10 years, the girl that was once nothing more than a pale face with wiry red hair had become the biggest thing to hit that place since plastic surgery. The casting directors were chasing her now and she was pruned and perfected until one day she woke up a twentieth century icon.

Back to the *Epic Awards* and Autumn was forced to stand up only a split second after her name was read out as the winner and the rest of her table jumped into the air and into her space to congratulate her. Autumn had faking modesty down to a tee in situations like this and she planned to show the world what a nice young lady she was once again with another, as usual, selfless speech.

Not that she walked like the girl next door, mind you. She emotionally left her table, side stepping past others, patting the shoulders of clapping acquaintances and ignoring the fake smiles from the four unsuccessful nominees. Finally free from holding in her stomach she reached the walkway and slinked her way up the stage stairs. Tonight she was dressed in off the shoulder green velvet, clinging to her curves like skin. The long flowing dress moved with her body and breezed around her dainty stilettos gracefully. Her hair was up in a twist with long ringlets shaping her face and the womanly bones around her shoulder area.

As Autumn approached the podium the roar of the crowd became louder. She laughed tearfully and waved to fans she couldn't see due to the tremendous stage lighting. Amanda and Autumn kissed each other on both sides of the face as movie-star etiquette says they should, then Amanda handed Autumn the award – a solid silver Pegasus just about to take flight – and stood back into the darkness, out of the limelight.

'I... wow, I'm lost for words!' Autumn cried into the five microphones, holding the award with one hand and placing the other shakily onto her lower neck. 'Um, I'd like to thank all my family and childhood friends in Canada, my wonderful husband Anthony,' – at the mention of his name the female audience screamed hysterically – 'all the cast and crew of *The Green Book*, I love you guys. But... y'know, we all get dolled up and spend hundreds of thousands of dollars on this night but I think I know someone who deserves this more.' Autumn looked in awe at her award then back into the darkness which was the audience, 'My mom. She's been a night nurse for over thirty years; she works so hard saving lives and caring for people and she doesn't get rewarded for it, so Mom, I know you're watching... this is for you. Next time I'm up there to visit I'll bring this award, so make some space on that shelf of yours!'

The crowd stood up in a mass standing ovation and you just know everyone watching on their televisions were saying things like: 'what a genuine woman' and 'fame has not affected her one bit'.

Her mother was crying into her apron and everyone was smiling. *When I grow up I want to be a beautiful princess, just like Autumn Leigh.*

A typical Autumn Leigh speech. Like I said, she knows how to work it.

She gave a slight bow and returned to her seat, cameras following her all the way. She was shaking and taking deep breaths when she returned to the table, eager for a cigarette to calm her nerves. Anthony lit the long awaited luxury and slipped it into his wife's genuine 1930s silver holder for her.

'Oh, thanks honey,' she sighed desperately with a nervy smile. 'How did I do?'

Anthony pinched his wife's face gently and whispered: 'You were terrible. They all hate you.'

Autumn laughed and kissed her husband.

'You stole it, sweetpea, you always do,' he continued seriously, still beaming. 'I'm so proud of you.'

Let's pause the two in their tender yet public mutual show of affection for a moment, as I want to introduce you to Anthony. The man we have in front of us right now, still-framed looking into his wife's eyes, is one of the few genuine good guys that you'll find in this industry.

Let's start on his exterior first and then I'll take you a little further in and skim over his background.

Anthony is a handsome man. Although he is not *stunning*, there's something about this guy that a lot of his celebrity peers, even the models, lack. There's more to this man than his looks, there's something evidently special about Anthony. Anthony's hair is a very normal thick brown mop with strands of grey unashamedly starting to show through, this shapes a kind yet average face with lips that are neither thin nor full and a nose that is neither small nor large. The one thing that makes Anthony's ordinary features stand out and make calendar material, other than his loveable persona and massive credibility, is how mesmerising his thoughtful, happy brown eyes are. Even then they're not particularly modelesque with their many laughter lines and bushy eyebrows but it's more a case of it being to see *through* them and gaze at the beautiful man that lays even deeper in there.

Anthony's eyes really are windows to his soul and the spirit this man possesses is amazing. You can't help but see how intelligent and deep he is and you can't help but long to know what he is thinking when you look into those eyes. They give him away so blatantly that you don't even have to know him or to be up close to be drawn in. This is why women and men from England to Australia are able to fall into them, as well as being the reason that he is perceived as dashingly handsome by teenage girls, their mothers and even *their* mothers… even though most would find it hard to describe what it is that makes him so attractive. Anthony knows he is nothing overtly special which is why he greets his admiration with his famous mildly flattered yet take-it-or-leave-it attitude.

This may seem hard to believe in this day and age of image obsession but the basic good nature of a person can still shine through and touch people, subconsciously overriding all that materialist shit of what he wears and how chiselled his jawline is. Anthony is living proof of that.

Anthony's personality is wise, optimistic and incredibly, *genuinely* down-to-earth. One of the major factors contributing to why Anthony is so modest even though he has such fame is because, although he deeply appreciates all he's got, in a way he will always resent it a little bit too. His situation as it is came about due to and during such tragic circumstances that part of him always associates his job with that time.

Anthony Denharden was brought up in the northern city of Leeds, before being chased down south with his mother to escape his violent father as a teen, and then left on his own when she died shortly after. If Anthony's mother hadn't have taken him down there he probably wouldn't be where he is today and he is eternally grateful for that now. But at the time it was the lowest point in his life.

At 15 years old, in 1968, Anthony and his mother Louise had been living in their rented back-to-back in Morley, Leeds, for twelve years. They'd been happy there, just the two of them, since Anthony's mother fled Manchester to escape living with her violent husband, Anthony's father, when he was a toddler.

It was a particularly hot summer's day and Anthony had been playing football with some older kids from the street in some farmer's land near by. Inevitably, they were chased off by the farmer, and by the time he got to his front door

Anthony was buzzing with adrenalin, red faced and out of breath. He went to open the door, but it was locked.

He knocked on it a few times while trying to get his breath back.

'Who is it?' a small voice asked nervously from inside.

'Mam? S'me… Anthony,' the broad-Yorkshire accent from the outside answered, confused.

Anthony heard the sound of a key turning and then the door opened slightly.

'Hurry up.' His mother ordered him into the house and then locked the door immediately behind him.

Before speaking Anthony noticed how dark the house was. The curtains were drawn and there were suitcases and bags piled up on the carpet in front of him. The house was almost bare and his mother's eyes were red and swollen from crying.

'Mam, what's going on?' he asked, the effort of the chase still causing him to inhale and exhale deeply. 'You alright?'

His mother did not answer, she simply began to cry. He had never seen her cry before; sure he had heard her sometimes, but the moment Anthony joined her she would usually stop. Anthony moved closer to his mother, loosely putting his half adult/half child arm around her. She began to shake her head and then fully embraced her son, weeping onto his shoulder.

'What's up? What's happened?' Anthony asked into his mother's long blonde hair.

'Oh Tony, we have to leave. I'm so sorry. I'm so sorry.'

Anthony's heart skipped a beat. *Leave?* ***Leave?*** *We can't leave! This is our home, this is everything we know!*

'Why do we have to leave?' Anthony asked, shocked.

For a moment there was no answer, only tears. His mother then unclenched herself from her only child, wiping her eyes with her arm and taking jerky breaths. After composing herself a little more, she cleared her throat and said one sentence, the only sentence she needed to say to make it all clear: 'It's yer Dad…'

'What about 'im?' Anthony asked shakily.

'I think he knows wi' here…'

'What?'

'Apparently he's been in Morley asking after us…'

'He's *here*?'

'Mrs Elmtree at the post office told me that…'

'Oh shit, Mam! What if 'e finds us?' Terror gripped the boy who had been as free as a bird only a few minutes ago. This was the first time in his life that he had been sure that he was dead meat, that there was no escape, and the look in his mother's eyes held exactly the same thought.

Anthony had always lived in fear of his father. He lived in fear of him tracking down where they were, he lived in fear of his mother getting beaten to death and shook at the thought of having to come face to face with the man whom he hated so much. Anthony saw his father as a maniac and knew he'd be running from the man for his entire life. And now, after twelve years of waiting, they'd been tracked down. Anthony's hopes of *it's been too long, surely he'll have given up by now* popped just as quickly as his mother's shoulder had when his dad threw her down the stairs just that little bit harder than usual all those years ago, just two months before the young, beautiful blonde ran away with her little boy in the middle of the night.

'…He got out a picture of me and asked 'er if she knew who I was, she said she dint but…'

'Oh shit! Oh shit!' Anthony cried, feeling hysterical. 'Mam…!'

Louise stared at her son with pleading eyes and said: 'The Leeds train is due on the hour.'

Seeing his mother's eyes so wide with fear and her forehead creased with desperation, Anthony knew what she was saying. He gave a thick gulp of tears and nodded his head sadly.

'Okay,' he said.

And that's it. It was literally as fast as that. Anthony wrote a letter to their landlady briefly explaining why they had left and placed it on the kitchen table with their house-keys. He cast his eyes over the room for one last time, picked up his bags of clothes, and then shut the door on his childhood forever.

If news of his dad on the prowl hadn't have reached him or his mother he would have continued living his carefree life and he would have continued enjoying his youth, like all his friends. Then he would probably have got a job working in a mill or factory somewhere in Morley, he would have found a nice local girl, married, had children. There. Happily ever after... unless of-course his father *was* actually there to reclaim his lost son and finish his estranged wife off. Then he would have been kidnapped, his mother would have been beaten, if not murdered, and Anthony would be plunged into a living Hell. Why risk it?

So, with fear and fate preventing a steady, safe life, by 8pm that same day Anthony and Louise found themselves boarding a London-bound train at Leeds Central Station, carrying what little belongings they had. From then on, Anthony was a man.

After two weeks in a bed and breakfast, they had rented a flat and both took the first jobs they could get. Louise fell quite lucky due to her typing skills, and landed a secretary job in a window manufacturers, and Anthony started out as a kitchen hand in a pub. Things stayed like that for a year until Anthony found an advertisement for volunteers to help at a local theatre. So, with a lack of anything better to do, he walked into the dusty theatre and found a hobby.

He started off helping the lighting technician, just two nights a week while local plays ran. Then, after only three months, the lighting technician transferred to a bigger theatre with better prospects and Anthony took over, now being paid for the pleasure.

At this point Anthony also made the first real friends he'd had in his new life and one actress in particular took a special liking to our boy, and asked him to go with her to one of her drama school classes. Seeing it as a date invitation, Anthony went along one evening and although he didn't get laid, he experienced his first ever role-play and was surprised to find that not only did he like it, but he was also good at it.

He enrolled in the drama school there and after only six months was appearing on the same stage he once pointed a bulb at. twelve months later Anthony was encouraged to audition to play the part of the son of a new tearaway family in a popular British soap opera. He didn't get the part but instead one of the judges informed him of a television company that were looking for unknown actors who could look drawn and menacing at the drop of a hat for a low budget film. This time Anthony was taken on straight away and from that moment on, at seventeen, the fiery eye of fame head-hunted him and made him into the one of the world's most sought after men.

A few hours after Anthony's beautiful wife won her award (and after *The Green Book* shone once more as Bret Hancolm had graced the stage as Best Director), the after show party began.

'Cheers!' everybody at Autumn and Anthony's table cried as they clinked glasses and congratulated each other on the success of the movie.

'Well, I don't know about you guys but I'm planning to end up *unconscious* tonight.' Jerry Tilsey, *The Green Book*'s male lead role laughed as he expertly threw another Marlboro into his mouth.

'Hear, hear!' Bret agreed.

'Why not? The drinks are free!' Autumn laughed.

Anthony touched his wife's lower arm to get her attention and whispered in her ear: 'I'm going to go over and talk to Martin, see if I can get him on my side for the big one. Don't... don't drink too much, okay?' (Martin Gate being Anthony's personal idol and 'the big one' he referred to being the un-named blockbuster he was working on, yet to find an appropriate lead actor).

'Okay sweetheart,' Autumn whispered back. 'But don't make it obvious how desperate you are to work with him. He'll respect you more.'

Anthony nodded, gave his wife a kiss and a 'remember what I said, sweetpea' before leaving the table. He was glad to leave – with the obvious exception of his wife he didn't like the company he was keeping there.

Autumn Leigh watched her husband walk away and lowered her eyes for just a moment.

Sometimes Anthony sounded too much like her father for her to like. The way he felt the need to look after her and keep her safe was something that Autumn resented but couldn't seem to stop. She couldn't just change his protective instincts towards her, so he went on safeguarding his sweetpea and she went on feeling mildly smothered, with the feeling growing every time he did it.

Lucy had been besieged with physical and mental health problems throughout her childhood and from the moment Anthony found out to what extent, especially after meeting and discussing it with her parents, he had taken it upon himself to constantly look out for her. In a way she was touched by his love and kindness, but that feeling was constantly quashed by the frustration of being treated like a fragile vase when she was trying her hardest to convince herself to be strong and move away from all that.

In the beginning it had been perfect. It was a classic love at first sight story between Autumn and Anthony; he had whisked her off her feet, given her a fairytale wedding and their careers boomed, with phenomenal fame falling upon them both at exactly the same time. Their lives had never looked as promising as they did in those first two years of marriage.

But 1987 brought a devastating blow to their blessed existence when Autumn gave birth to their son. He'd lost his heartbeat in the eighteenth week of pregnancy and came out thirteen days later, an entire twenty weeks early, deformed beyond recognition as a child. The doctors had told Anthony they highly recommended that he and his wife should not try for children again as they feared that due to her medical records, circumstances and past, this could be something of a recurrence in the Denharden household. Within the three months following that fateful day in October, Autumn Leigh crumbled a million times over with the guilt and loss and it was Anthony's selfless support that prevented his wife from falling victim to a full-scale meltdown.

That was the only time in their lives together that Autumn let Anthony look after her. But although her husband picking her up off the floor filled Autumn with massive respect and gratitude towards him, at the same time it pushed her away. She couldn't pretend to be that perfect person anymore; he had seen the side of her she preferred to keep hidden. Because of the misguided shame of having her husband witness her naked vulnerability, she has kept herself at an emotional distance from him from then on.

Anthony too came out a changed person for the worse after the death of his child and his wife's near breakdown. He had had to put his own feelings and emotions second to his wife's in order to remain strong for her sake, and in doing this he never allowed himself to grieve properly. On top of this, it also brought back all the memories and feelings that he had buried since his mother's death when he was nineteen. Losing his mum had been the hardest thing Anthony had ever had to go through in his life. She had been diagnosed with breast cancer and declined at such a pace that by the time she died her teenage son was left grieving and alone in the adult world. Anthony had tried his hardest not worry either his wife or his mother with his own emotions, desperate to hide the fact that he was a shell also. Unfortunately due to this selflessness there was a big weight of built-up emotion in the very depths of Anthony's heart; although it was not heavy enough to drown his spirit from swimming, it did place stones in the pockets to constantly weigh him down.

To this day there is a mushroom mobile nailed to the ceiling of the room that was supposed to be a nursery. Now it is just a dusty, un-used spare room at the far end of the hallway. The mobile gently swings and turns in the draught and, although everything else they had bought for their much-awaited child has gone, that's Anthony's last reminder of Alexander Denharden, his son. Other than that, and a tiny plaque in a crematorium, there is nothing else to mentally spike them of that hard time. Although often thought of, it is no longer mentioned.

Autumn watched her husband disappear into the crowds of celebrities and turned back to her co-star and director who were sitting opposite her at the table, which they could now spread out and claim as their own.

'Where's Tony going?' Jerry asked sarcastically, leaning over the table.

'He's gone to mingle, Jerry. I said I'd join him later,' was the unamused reply.

Autumn had slowly grown to dislike Jerry Tilsey during the last few months of working with him, but could just about stand him enough to be civil with him.

'Mingle, huh? Such a popular guy!' Jerry laughed, dying out his cigarette.

It was obvious to both Autumn and Bret that Jerry had an immense disliking of Anthony. It was also obvious that the only reason for it was complete envy. Autumn rolled her eyes and shook her head slightly while Bret uncomfortably cleared his throat.

Jerry Tilsey is well known for his drug, drink and brawling problems within the LA crowd. The rough-and-ready twenty-three-year-old is admired by teenage girls all over the world but, get this, not one person who knows that guy respects him. Jerry handles his fame as he does his money – terribly.

For the first six months of knowing him Autumn defended him whenever she could. The papers hated him and were always around to snap him beating the hell out of some poor guy outside a club, but she thought he was misunderstood, naïve, and was once even quoted as saying he was like a naughty toddler: so innocent. Bless him. The nasty public drove him to it.

Innocent little Jerry has already snorted a ridiculous amount of coke on this fine night and has drunk many waiters' trays dry. Fresh out of rehab he's hardly doing well, but on a night out with Bret Hancolm what can the good people expect?

Bret and Jerry have been getting elegantly wasted together since the beginning of filming *The Green Book*. Bret doesn't do as much of the hard stuff as Jerry but he loves to encourage his pal. He likes to see him have a good time see and when Jerry's rocketed out of his brains he's such a riot. Plus, of-course, Bret has never fucked as many famous models as he has now – hanging around with the man who has more 'get out of jail free' cards than a Monopoly board.

Bret, balding, married and divorced three times within two years and possibly suffering from an acute mid-life crisis, is actually an okay guy who just tries to act bad. Easy to work with and a sharp wit, Autumn enjoys his company, it's just tarnished when Jerry's around. Bret's got this amazingly convincing alter ego that can jump out and turn him into a prick whenever his best pal graces the scene.

A thundering voice broke the silence that had temporarily fallen over the table.

'I knew you'd win that award, baby! I knew it!' Mickey Black bellowed pointing at Autumn before standing from his table and walking over to hers, conveniently ignoring the looks he was receiving from Jerry and Bret.

'Mickey,' Autumn blushed, standing from her chair and politely embracing her ex-co-worker while saying: 'How you been?' as if she really cared.

'Oh, y'know.' Mickey laughed in his bulging tux, sweating and holding a shot glass as always. 'I've just been talking to Pete 'the man' Millar... you know him?'

'Pete Millar? No, no I don't.'

'Well anyway, he's a great guy and he's got me talking to one of his buddies. A buddy who just happens to be involved with a movie destined for the top. And guess who he wants to play lead...?'

'Can I take a guess?' Autumn faked a knowing smile.

'You got it babe! It's your old friend Mickey!' He was grinning from ear to ear but his eyes looked sad, lonely even.

Autumn stared at him for a moment then blinked away. Her blatant look of pity stopped Mickey in his tracks and he didn't continue with his efforts to impress her.

'I'm hunting for ya, Mickey. Good luck.' Autumn made eye contact again and gave him a smile that showed sympathy, mixed evenly with the need to get away from him.

He wiped his large, red forehead with a handkerchief from his pocket and said with fake humour: 'Well, thank you. I best be getting back to the guys so... you, you have a great night Autumn. Congratulations about the award.'

'Thank you. You have a good night too, Mickey.'

'Yeah, see you later.' Mickey turned from her, his large smile fading into an embarrassed, nervy frown.

Autumn sat back down and looked to Jerry and Bret, who were staring at her with a look of mock disgust.

'What the fuck you doin' talking to that dried up fat boy?' Jerry, more than a little drunk, piped up first, as usual.

'I feel sorry for him, and we have history,' Autumn replied calmly, sipping at her hardly touched champagne.

'You been screwing *that*?' Bret laughed.

'No! We worked together a few years back.'

Jerry pulled on his cigarette, looked over to Mickey, eyed him up and down and turned back to Autumn.

'I hear he's so used up he'd be better off being crushed down and thrown in a recycling bin,' he commented.

'That would take a hell of a lot of crushing!' Bret chortled, nudging Jerry.

They both laughed cruelly while Autumn just felt bad.

'Hey, leave it. He's down on his luck,' she scolded, not a smile in sight.

Bret held his hands up as a sorry then carried on asking Jerry for the details on the sexual performance of Amanda Turpin.

Autumn sighed heavily and scanned the room for Anthony. Failing to see him, she decided to go one step further and actively look for him.

As Autumn got up to leave the table Jerry cast sly eyes on that perfectly rounded backside.

'Jez?' Bret nudged him. They looked at each other knowingly and both began to laugh.

We freeze-frame Jerry Tilsey in mid-laughter now, my dear reader. We freeze him with his head tossed back and his amusement is showing his pearly white teeth. Now this boy really does have the looks of a model. His brown hair is soft and flowing, well groomed and shiny. His eyes are deep and capturing, greens and blues, his features smooth yet chiselled, sporting stubble and Hollywood tanned skin. Yeah, we look at him and we think what all those screaming girlies think; we think, 'wow, this is one lucky guy, one of life's winners'. I'll tell you, Jerry has been a Hollywood prince since the day he was born... the little darling.

You see, Jerry's father is Burt Tilsey and his momsy is Mandy Myers. Burt was the first star in his class to ever fully appreciate the word 'extreme' when he was the film industry's sweetheart all those years ago in the swingin' sixties. So while Jerry was dribbling and gargling in diapers, daddy was saving blond vixens from certain death at the hands of rubber model dinosaurs, before coming home to a lovingly prepared lethal cocktail of heroin and cocaine from his beautiful wife.

And, man, what an upbringing Jerry had! The kid knew Hollywood before he could even say 'acid'. His mother was a true wild-child; ah yes, the infamous Mandy Myers. She was a beautiful, stoned, fashionable model. It wasn't until 1967 though, that her name really did hit the papers and get the coverage she'd always dreamed of, and that was when she jacked up then led the police on a forty mile chase in her husband's Hot-Rod while pregnant with Jerry. It went down in history.

His parents had married young when Mandy, at eighteen, became pregnant the first time with Jerry's older sister, Luca. Three years after came little Jerry, and two years after that, in 1969, Mandy was found dead in a motel room, blue and bloated, after an overdose of the golden brown.

By the time Jerry was seven he was attending all the parties that his dad held, serving drinks and looking cute. And, inevitably, by the time he was ten he'd had more than one stiff drink and had sampled enough grass to make him sick (it was only two pulls on a joint, and when he went green and fell over it caused a riot of laughter within the room, overhanging the few people who had gasped and thought of it as bordering on child cruelty).

Jerry floated into Hollywood as easy as a river into the sea and the place lapped him up – the innocent, beautiful son of the dead wild-child and famous 60s movie-star. Hell, he's going to make it, isn't he! The cards were laid out for that boy from the day he was born.

At twelve he landed the part as 'Timmy Renolds' in the hit comedy series (Friday night slot, guys) *The Renolds*. He stuck with it for four years before giving it up for the bright lights of the film industry.

And my, my – the lights were bright for Jerry Tilsey. So, while daddy stayed indoors drinking and his sister concentrated on her porn career in the dirtier side of town,

Jerry rose to be one of the most sought after serious young actors on the circuit.

Maybe it was his difficult childhood (I hear you laugh, but you weren't there) that drove him to drug addiction and a taste for violence, or maybe it was just the scene he was in. But, whatever it was, the man we have freeze-framed at this moment has issues. *Serious* issues.

Here at the table we keep Bret and everybody else as still as statues but bring Jerry back into time and motion so we can talk to him a little. Just you and I. Jerry would rather die than say these things out loud, my dear friend, but because I created him and you watch him we both have privileges above everyone else... in this book anyway.

'So, Jerry. How are you?' I ask.

'I need some more of the good stuff,' he laughs. As he brings his hand up to wipe through his chocolate hair, we both notice a severe case of the shakes going on.

'You're shaking. Are you nervous?' you ask.

'No, no,' he replies, tensely laughing between his words again. 'My hands always do this, it's nothing.'

'Oh,' you say.

'Are you having a good time tonight, Jerry?' I ask.

'Yeah, great time, man. This is what this fuckin' thing is all about, y'know? Me and Bret, we been at it all day. Ah, it's been real fucked up, man. It's been crazy,' he laughs.

'Your eyes are red,' you observe, more to yourself than to him.

'Oh, yeah,' he says as he rubs them quickly. 'They get dry easily, they itch around smoke.'

'Congratulations about *The Green Book*. It's done well tonight,' I butter him up.

Jerry thanks me, agrees about its success and waits for the next question.

'What do you think to Autumn Leigh?' I ask, looking forward to the answer.

'Oh, Autumn Leigh,' he looks into the distance as he repeats her name, then looks back to the both of us. 'She's a fox, ain't she?'

We both nod in agreement.

'What else?' I persist.

He lets off a sigh and rubs his nose, and then he leans in closer to us and says: 'It's not just that I want to ride her, man. I really fuckin' dig her, you know? But she's fuckin' married to that shitbrick, *Anthony*.' He says the word 'Anthony' in a high pitched, mock voice and I see a flash of envious anger electrify his eyes for a brief moment. You spot it too. It looks menacing and violent and then it's gone and we're back to the movie-star good looks. We exchange glances.

'Have you been in love before?' you ask. I nod approvingly. That was a cracking question to ask; you're good at this!

'Yeah,' Jerry replies, sitting back. 'But she was a fuckin' gold brickin' whore.'

'Why, what did she do?'

'She tried to get me in trouble, man, tried to get a hold of my money and drag my name through the dirt. Fuckin' bitch. I showed her though, now it's her that's seen as nuthin' but a lying slut. The bitch took me to court but I won.'

'Why did she do all that?' you ask. We are both engrossed.

'She said I used to beat on her 'n shit.'

'Did you?'

'Maybe a couple of times but, jeeze, you didn't have to live with the bitch. Six months. *Six months* of Hell she was. I loved her to start with you know, but she changed, man, she turned into all the things that pissed me off. I had to fuckin' beat her just to get her to shut the fuck up sometimes.'

'But you told everyone she was lying!' you exclaim. 'The papers, the courts, everyone!'

'Yeah,' he snorts smugly. 'Revenge is sweet, huh?'

You sit back, shocked.

I sit forward: 'Do you like yourself, Jerry? Or do you think you're a bit of a prick?'

Jerry submits a vocal, shocked sigh, a kind of 'huh', and a sarcastic half smile.

'I'm alright,' he answers reluctantly, hardly moving his mouth. 'I'm successful and I always get what I want. I'd put that down to a strong character, wouldn't you?' Notice how he's dropped the Hollywood mannerisms and compulsive swearing now that he feels threatened.

I can't think of how to respond to that question because the fact of the matter is I detest the guy so I sit back in my chair and don't even attempt to answer him. Jerry fiddles with his lighter on the table with his tongue in his cheek. He looks offended.

'How's your dad?' you ask, uncomfortable with the situation.

'Fine.' Jerry does not look up from his lighter; he's sulking.

'Did you grow up around here?' you continue.

'*Yes*,' Jerry replies, speaking the answer as if you'd just asked the most ridiculous question in the history of questions, and now looking down at you as if you were the most idiotic person in the history of idiots. 'Where've *you* been? Don't you know who my dad is? Do you even know who *I* am? Of-course I grew up around here.' He then submits a cocky pig-laugh, one that he may not have submitted if I hadn't got his back up just a few moments ago. He's obviously intending to make you feel as foolish as he possibly can. But you're smarter than him; you know he's only doing this to make himself look better. You (just about) don't take any offence.

'Did you go to school around here?' you ask calmly.

'Where *else* would I go to school?'

You ignore it: 'Which school did you go to?'

Oh man this is cool, you really are something my friend! Come on! Keep it up! I can't believe that this is only your first chat to the characters and already you know how to work it. I'm so lucky to have you on the watch with me, we're like good-cop bad-cop or something.

'The EE Academy of Dramatic Arts. It's exclusive. You two won't know it.'

I roll my eyes, you carry on with the questions.

'Did you enjoy it?'

'Yeah, I guess. It was alright, I was popular, so…'

You give him time to finish but he doesn't. So you add: 'What's your favourite memory from the academy, Jerry?'

The famous Mr Tilsey finally puts his lighter down and thinks for a moment.

'One of my best memories is… oh man, this is fuckin' great…' Jerry is back to his normal self now, thanks to your quick thinking and patience. That momentary lapse of ego seems to have passed and we're back on with the interview. 'I was at school, right? And there was this fat girl; Amy – and I mean *huge* – she was so fuckin' big it made me want to be sick, y'know? Anyways, she was always fuckin' pickin' on me. Ah shit, I knew she was just jealous but I didn't fuckin' like it all the same. She'd talk about my mom, who was a world-famous model. Hell, her mom couldn't have been anything to look at if she gave birth to *that*… but yeah, my mom had died when I was, like, two, and Amy would always fuckin' go on at me, thinking she's so fuckin' above me… 'my dad says *this*, my dad says *that*' bitching about how she died, like it was any of her goddamn business. So anyways, she's all like anti-drugs and all and then one day I'm driving home and I see this fuckin' fat girl by the side of the road with her hand out, right? So I pull in and it's Amy, all fuckin' wet 'cause it's raining pretty hard and she's like, 'hey Jerry, can you give me a ride' and I say 'sure, get in' so she waddles 'round the bonnet with her fat fuckin' ass and jumps in the passenger seat, totally forgetting about how fuckin' mean she is to me all the time, just 'cause her dad is a judge or whatever. Anyways, I set off and wait until I get to about forty then I lean over, open her door and kick the fat fucker out! Next day she was all covered in bruises and cuts and she didn't say a goddamn word to me after that night. It was the best thing I ever did, showing that bitch who was boss. It made me feel great for weeks. Man, I fuckin' love revenge.'

He'd said the whole thing looking at you and made it blatantly obvious he wasn't speaking to me anymore, but I heard him all the same. He was laughing by the time he finished his story and, I don't know about you, but I don't know whether to dislike him or feel sorry for him. I mean, if that's the only 'favourite' memory of growing up he can think of, there's obviously something very wrong with this boy's life.

We have to go now so we thank Jerry for his time and he nods, still smiling at the thought of pulling one over on Amy. Winning. He won. Winner. Upon bringing the party back to life we are left pitying Jerry Tilsey. Poor, shallow Jerry Tilsey, the man whose favourite memory is of kicking a fat girl out of his car at forty in the rain.

The atmosphere is electrified again and a buzz of conversation and laughter fills the air. We note, now we're actually here and not just simply looking in, how this is nothing like we'd ever expect. You think of a Hollywood party, right? You think glamour and oh! the glitz of it all. All that money, all that luxury. My, my, that diamond necklace is simply *supreme* my *darling*, you must tell me where *did* you get it from? Oh and yes we're all beautiful people in the ballroom tonight ladies and gentlemen. Yes, yes, we are all winners.

That is how we portray these things, these things we know nothing about. I am sorry, maybe you do (I never thought to ask), but as we stand here at the 1990 Epic Awards after-show party, filled with the crème of the movie world, we share one thought and that's how pretentiously uncomfortable it is.

For mega-stars such as Autumn Leigh this party is an entirely different place than it is for us, us mere mortals. But standing amongst all this hype, all this kiss-ass, when you're not the star of the show is, well, a bit shit to be honest. You and I are not anybody at this event so we are completely ignored and our chances of getting anywhere close to one of the big leagues (not using our special powers and advantages) are pretty damn slim, being normal people and all.

Okay, so let's scan. Every single person in here is either a Hollywood star or a Hollywood wannabe. You can spot the difference. Take her over there for example, 2 o'clock to your right: shoulder-pad woman. She's in a circle of five plump men, her arm linked around one of them (the fattest and oldest one: the richest one). Her left hand holds a flute of champagne and her nails are over-manicured to give that soap opera bitch look. They're claw-long and painted dark plum, with chunky gold and diamonds on every finger. She's around fifty but will only admit to forty. Her face could be an advert for obvious plastic surgery and if the makers of that heavy eye shadow she is wearing were to know what they had created, they would sue themselves. Her suit is another giveaway of who she is: it's gold (drum roll).... it's sparkly (louder)... and it's padded (symbol crash)! Wow! Three corkers all on just the one body! She laughs overly loud at conversation and pouts too much because she thinks it brings out her cheekbones. As people are talking her eyes slightly wander off for a second to see if any of the Hollywood big shots are looking her way. They're not. Do you want to know who she is? Are you ready...? She is a wannabe; a classic example. You can spot them a mile off once you get the knack. Her name? I dunno. All I know is that she married the richest, softest man she could have dreamt of. He's not a star; he's just a millionaire. Millionaires tend to have bad taste in women.

Okay, bear with me a second while I search for a real star... aha! Here we are! There, over by the band stage talking to the brunette. That, my friend, is Taz Andrea. See, straight up, I know his name.

He doesn't try desperately to get attention; he doesn't have to, he gets it anyway. As he sits quietly chatting to the beautiful woman dozens of eyes are on him. He doesn't even notice. He wears a cream suit and black tie; his suit jacket is draped over the back of his chair, his tie loosened a little. See the difference? It's quite easy really, isn't it?

The atmosphere, as you can feel, is strained. As I said earlier, only the superstars can relax. Except for the odd few, no-one really knows each other and they sure as hell don't like each other. It's one big competition of who looks the best and who is doing the best. This is why wannabes put in so much more effort. Most people, though, are just sapping up the glory of being here and looking pretty. You and I feel out of place but do not try to seek attention. In fact, just before we leave and venture back into the real world, you get the nearest to a brush with fame than either of us have done since we've been standing here. Autumn Leigh treads on your toe as she barges past us looking for Anthony. She doesn't even look back, never mind apologise. Charming! I think it's time we left...

Sick of being purposely ignored, Autumn had left the table to begin looking for her husband. As she passed through the room there were polite words and waves all the way. Autumn simply mouthed 'thank you' every time and carried on walking. She weaved in and out of the nobodies, big stars and wish-they-weres. She even stood on someone's foot in her rushed bid to find Anthony but did not recognise the face and figured they'd be grateful that the marvellous Autumn Leigh had touched them, so she didn't bother apologising.

After a couple of minutes she spotted Anthony leaning against one of the many bars talking to Martin Gate. She gave an inward sigh of relief and began walking over to him.

After only two steps an unfamiliar face seemingly shot in front of her frantically.

'Autumn? Autumn Leigh?' the pretty young face of the stranger smiled.

'Yes?' Autumn nodded, quite taken aback.

'I'm sorry, I've been wanting to talk to you all night! Please, let me introduce myself. I'm Hannah Gate, Martin's wife.' The young brunette held out her hand and Autumn shook it.

'Oh, Martin, yeah. Anthony adores your husband.'

'Y'know that's great!' Hannah smiled overenthusiastically. 'I just wanted to tell you that I think you're fantastic! When I saw *The Green Book* I just cried and cried. You were terrific!'

'Oh, well thank you Hannah. I'm glad you enjoyed the film,' Autumn smiled. 'If you could please excuse me I'm on a bit of a mission to find Anthony. I do believe he's under your husband's charm at the moment.'

'Okay, great. I just had to congratulate you!' The woman was still smiling ecstatically.

'Thank you again. It's been nice meeting you Hannah; I'm sure I'll see you later on in the night.'

'Brilliant, that would be great!' Hannah beamed. *Wow! Autumn Leigh!*

Autumn turned her attention back to the bar, where her husband no longer stood. *Typical, I talk to someone for one minute and he's disappeared. Just typical.* She walked over to the now empty spot where Anthony had been moments ago and folded her arms for a moment, quietly praying no more annoying fans would force her to repeat the same old lines and thank you's over and over again in shallow conversation.

Within ten seconds a man slid over to her and wrapped tanned arms around her waist.

'Hey pretty lady!' he cried, startling her. She turned her head towards him as she jumped.

'For Christ's sake, Jerry,' she scolded, genuinely angry. 'I didn't even see you coming.'

'The ladies never do,' he smirked. 'Why'd ya leave us all, huh?'

'I'm looking for Anthony.' *And you and Bret are complete assholes when you're drunk or high or whatever it is that's making you slur your words and act like children.*

'Anthony…? No, can't see him.' Jerry glanced briefly around the room with one arm still around Autumn. 'Come back to the table, pretty lady. Anthony's gone home.'

'Gone home?'

'Maybe; I can't see him. How he could leave such a sexy woman all on her own is beyond me anyway. Come sit down, huh? Jerry'll take care of ya.'

'No, you go on back to your table,' Autumn sighed, moving his arm away from her as she started to feel his fingers moving up and down jerkily in a feeble attempt to caress her. 'I really do need to speak to him.'

'No, no, no. Don't go. Look! I have something interesting to show you.' Jerry winked, putting his hands in his trouser pockets.

'That's it. I'm going to find Anthony.'

'*Going to find Anthony,*' Jerry mimicked.

'How old are you?'

'Twenty-three... how old are *you,* sugar?' he laughed.

'Fuck off, Jerry,' she muttered while walking away from him.

After ten minutes of attempting to find her husband Autumn tired of her search, which was a nightmare anyway with almost everyone she walked past wanting to engage in a full-length conversation. Upon returning to her table to find it totally empty, she poured herself a fresh glass from the bottle on the table and took a moment to indulge in feeling the total glory and pride of what she had achieved.

Autumn had never wanted to be anything *but* an actress. It started when she was around five years old. Lucy would watch her mother put on lipstick and brush her hair and dream of one day being so beautiful. To Lucy, her mother was a princess and by the age of five, way back in 1964, Lucy had already decided that that was what she wanted to be too.

Lucy's mother worked nights at their local community hospital. When she left the house at seven-thirty, Lucy would watch her pull out of the driveway, wave sweetly and then bolt upstairs into her parents' room.

As her father watched television Lucy would be applying lipstick and running circular brushes through her strawberry-blond hair. She would be standing in oversized shiny heels, wearing her mother's starched skirts as dresses. Floppy hats and elegant gloves would be carefully slipped on and many of her mother's plastic bead necklaces and hollow pearls would be draped around her neck to make Lucy into a woman. Usually a sickly, pale girl would look back at her when she glanced into the mirror while brushing her teeth, but not in her mother's clothes. In her mother's clothes, a beautiful, elegant lady stared back at her from the dressing table mirror and Lucy was a princess.

By 1976 Lucy's ambition was still the same as it had been when she was a child: to be a princess, to be beautiful, to bask in attention and be admired by all. And what career promised all that glitz back in 1976? Why, a career in films of-course.

'...I *know* that, but what *job* do you want? What *real* job?' Mrs Smith questioned Lucy in front of what was going to be the class of '78.

'Like I just said,' Lucy replied cockily, slouched enough to look menacing in her chair. 'An actress.'

Mrs Smith did not follow it up. She blinked slowly to show her disapproval then focused on Paul Thornton, the boy sitting directly behind her, who had no choice but to work on his dad's fishing trawler like his other four brothers when he left school. *This* was seen as a proper job.

While lying in bed that night back in the summer of '76, Lucy made a decision. She figured Mrs Smith was like some kind of community voice and more than likely everybody's reaction would be the same. So to be taken seriously she would have to go to the place where acting was considered a *real* job, in fact, the *only* job. She would stick out school for another two years and then, at nineteen, she would storm Hollywood.

Telling her parents had been hard. Her mother and father were sitting around the clothed dinner table with their only daughter when she had said: 'I've got something to tell you.'

Her dad, an unemployed chef, rose his head sharply from his chicken breast, potatoes and vegetables. He, like his wife when she had been younger, had been suffering from depression. He had lost his job cooking for *Bobbie's* restaurant in downtown Halifax and now had to rely on his wife to pay the bills. Stewart spent his days watching television and sleeping, causing his marriage and bank balance to suffer immensely. Now his heart sank as he prepared himself for yet another blow to what used to be a happy house, for his little girl to utter those two dreaded words: *I'm pregnant.*

Stewart looked to his wife who was obviously thinking the same thing, only her face displayed a look of worry, not anger. After all, neither could deny that their daughter had blossomed into an extremely beautiful young woman. Boys and men dropped at her feet and it was no massive surprise that she had boyfriends. The wiry ginger curls her mother used to have so much trouble taming were now silky locks that bounced and glided all the way down to her tiny waist. Her face was doll-like with huge brown eyes and not a hint of acne.

He'd always worried that his only daughter would meet some punk that'd get her knocked up and then dump her, or some hippy freak with long hair.

'What is it, honey?' her mother asked.

Lucy looked up from her plate and took turns staring at both of her over-protective parents, they looked worried.

'You know I want to be an actress?'

'Yes, dear,' her mother nodded.

Lucy was about to continue when: 'Look,' her dad said sternly, making the women of the house turn to glare at him. He pointed his knife towards his daughter as he spoke. 'Don't mess your mother and I around, Lucy. Are you pregnant?'

'No!' Lucy cried in a high pitched voice, a surprised, almost comical half smile on her face. 'I don't want kids, Dad. I never want kids, you know that!'

A blanket of tension lifted from the table.

'Well, what is it? My supper's going cold and your mom has to get ready for work.' He spoke sternly, not even hinting at his overwhelming relief. 'Get on with it, Lucy.'

'Okay. I'm moving to Hollywood.'

Silence.

Then: 'No you're not, young lady.' Again, the air ripped by her father's voice.

Her mother had widened her eyes then looked to her husband. He was shaking his head matter-of-factly. Lucy had expected this, *of-course* she had expected this. Her parents would keep her in bubble wrap if they could.

However, the speech had been prepared: 'Dad, I'd make a really great actress, everyone says so, but I just can't do it here. Nobody makes movies here. Mom, I need to go there to do what I want to do with my life. I've already got it all planned. I'll get a part time job now, weekends and evenings, then by the time I leave school I'll have enough money to get down there, then...'

'You are not going anywhere, Lucy,' her father interrupted. 'Do you have any idea what goes on in that filthy place? You'd be into porno movies and drugs within a year.'

'Stewart!' her mother scolded, quietening him, before turning to her fragile little daughter. 'Honey, I know it seems like a good idea now but have you thought all this through? Where would you live? How would you get down there? Thousands of people arrive in that place every day, all thinking the same thing, but they end up running out of money then coming back home with their tails between their legs. Would you want that? Even if you did get into a film I'm sure the work would be very gruelling and your body just isn't made for...'

'Mom, you can't mollycoddle me my entire life! Any job I get will be gruelling. Acting's easy. Anyway, when was the last time I was ill? It was months ago. You can't keep me here forever. I'm bigger than this place. I want to see the world and...'

'Go to your room Lucy, and don't ever waste our time like this again,' her father cut in, delving back into lukewarm chicken with his knife and fork, not even looking at his daughter anymore.

After searching her mother's face for some sympathetic support and not finding it, Lucy pushed her chair back harshly and left the table with heavy steps.

She did mention it again, however. She mentioned it when she got a part-time job waitressing in the café near her school. She mentioned it every time another wage cheque was deposited into her savings and she mentioned it whenever a good film was on at the pictures. In fact, she mentioned it so often her parents had stopped arguing back and just pretended they didn't hear her.

By 1978, Lucy had $1000 and the connecting coach times to get her to Hollywood. Her father had got a job filling cars at a local gas station the summer before and her mother still worked nights, looking older each time she came home. They had given her the porn and drugs speech several times, but it had not worked and they were forced to let her go.

The morning she left had been hard and for the first time Lucy actually did think *Christ what am I doing* but, although she was going against her parents' wishes, she knew there would always be a place for her back home and that added comfort. She had packed all her trendy clothes and the other basics she would need to get herself set up: it all amounted to one heavy suitcase and a bursting rucksack. Now, bags in the hall, parents talking in hushed tones downstairs, she looked around her childhood bedroom. She ran a finger over the wooden top of her old dressing table (complete with stickers stuck on randomly and half peeled from when she was a girl) and it made her heart race knowing that from this day forward she would never be applying lipstick in that mirror again. She felt her eyes filling and was suddenly painfully aware of what this was doing to her parents. But still, with a heart full of uncertainty, she closed the door to her bedroom and ventured downstairs. Scared or not, it was time to leave.

'What time is the bus?' her mother asked quietly, both parents standing up from the sofa where they had been talking.

'Eleven-thirty.' Lucy replied, her voice high and cracked by building tears.

Mr and Mrs Cunningham stood facing their only child, both of them looking old and beaten. Lucy's childhood, despite her constant random illnesses and several deeper, more worrying secrets, had been a good one and the resentment their girl had held for being so cushioned disappeared temporarily as she stood facing them, taking in how upset they looked, knowing how much they loved her.

'Mom, I'll be fine. I'll call you as soon as I get there, it'll be in a couple of days. I'm a big girl now, I'll be fine.' *I'll be fine, I'll be fine, I'll be fine.*

Her mother ran towards her, held her only child tightly, and began to weep onto her shoulder. Lucy began to cry and reassured her mother (and herself?) a few more times that everything was going to turn out well.

Her father – hiding his emotions of love, worry and sorrow – came second, hugged her powerfully and said: 'You be careful, Lucy. If you want us for anything, we'll be here. Don't get into trouble and don't be stupid, okay?'

'Okay, Dad,' Lucy smiled.

Just as she turned to leave she heard her mother say: 'Here, Lucy.'

Lucy turned around to her mother pulling a wad of bills from her pocket and holding it out to her.

'Oh, Mom, you don't have to do that. I've got lots of money – you keep that.'

'No, no, we've been saving it for you. You take it and keep it safe,' her mother said through tears.

Lucy took the money, feeling worse than ever, said thank you, goodbye, I'll call you, and then left her family home for good.

A faint smile passed Autumn's lips as she proudly recalled the fact that she had got here all on her own and everyone, especially her parents, had told her she'd never make it and would be back waiting tables in Nova Scotia within six months. And to think that there were times, before she met Anthony and became known, when she nearly did go back and give up. But she *didn't*. She *had* made it, big-time at that. All her teachers, Mrs Smith especially, would be eating their words. *I bet she refused to watch this tonight. She'll be as sick as a dog when she realises I won after she told me acting wasn't a 'real' job.*

Autumn nearly laughed out loud she felt so excited. She'd done it. She'd really done it. Best Actress of the 1990 Epic Awards. Jeeze. It was just beginning to sink in…

'Hey! Hey! Look who's back!' Bret laughed whilst getting his feet tangled in the chair opposite in his attempt trying to sit down.

Jerry, finding this hysterical, lamely helped Bret into his seat then sat down next to him, wiping his red eyes with his fists.

Autumn laughed along and lit another cigarette. The feelings she had just experienced had calmed her down from the frustrations of failing to find her partner, the annoyance of strangers wanting to speak to her, and the irritation factor of Jerry's sleazing just a few moments ago. By now Autumn had remembered how great she was and was feeling relaxed and beautiful again.

'I see you two have been drinking plenty,' she observed light-heartedly.

The two men looked at each other comically.

'Drinking? Why, we've hardly touched a drop, sweetheart,' Jerry replied. The two men burst out laughing again.

'Okay, I see you two have been *taking* plenty,' she mused.

Both men looked down temporarily at this.

'Just a little coke. You point me someone in here who ain't doin' it,' Bret said dryly.

Autumn pointed at herself with the hand that was holding her cigarette.

'Fuck off, you do coke!' Jerry laughed.

The calm feeling evaporated just as fast as it had started: 'No I don't! I did a couple of times when I was your age but not for the past ten years or so. Why the hell did you say that?' Autumn snapped back angrily.

'About three months ago, man,' Jerry laughed. 'You were tripping in your dressing room, I saw you. It was so fuckin' cool. Bret, she was going fuckin' nuts! It was when we were doin' The Street Show, you were in Mexico with Gillian.'

'Andrea,' Bret corrected.

'Whatever,' Jerry shrugged.

Bret turned his attention to Autumn, playing upon the information he'd just heard, eyeing her accusingly and raising an eyebrow: 'Well, well. You managed to keep that one quiet.'

Within the time that Jerry had been speaking Autumn Leigh's heart rate had soared and she could feel the heat of humiliation on her face. It had been three months ago when she had her last bad attack. This was the *last* thing she wanted to think about or be forced into discussing even on her most honest days, let alone have it creeping in on what was supposed to be her night of glory.

Those fucking attacks were the absolute bane of her life and up until Jerry had obviously seen her she'd managed to keep the true effects they had on her secret from everyone, including the hundreds of doctors she was passed through as a child. Medically, it was noted that she sometimes suffered from panic attacks… nothing more. The truth behind them was a lot darker, but Autumn would rather die than let anyone know exactly what was happening to her to cause the attacks and what really went on during them. On the odd occasion she had company when they came on, she could control them to the point where they didn't arouse suspicion and then she'd hide herself away to fully recover as soon as she felt steady enough to walk. But they engulfed her when she was alone; she lost all control of her surroundings and allowed them to eat her up. That day in her dressing room before the show, she had let it consume her. She hadn't known Jerry had seen her when she was in the throws of a fit. She didn't know until now.

'She was screeching and thrashing her fuckin' arms around like a fuckin' nutcase!' Jerry laughed, even going as far as to do an impression.

Autumn Leigh could not speak. She suddenly felt like the smallest person in the world again, the way she had felt throughout her whole childhood, the entire reason she took such pleasure in being admired whenever possible.

As Jerry glanced at Autumn to check her reaction to his impression of her, he noticed a strange kind of look on her face, one he'd never seen before. She looked like she was about to cry, she looked like a little girl... so suddenly, just like that. Jerry stopped with his arms and said light-heartedly: 'Hey, Autumn, I'm sorry. I'm only joking. You know that, right?'

'I was rehearsing,' Autumn said in a tiny, mortified voice with her chest heaving.

'Yeah, I know. I was only trying to wind Bret up.' Jerry shrugged casually to try to cover up his mistake of speaking and *shit* laughing at her. Jerry realised he'd hit a raw spot and something, maybe the look of sheer horror on her face, was telling him that he really shouldn't have mentioned that.

Autumn didn't speak. She left the table clumsily and went to the nearest restroom, locking herself in and immediately checking in the mirror to see if her eyes had puffed while trying to hold her tears in. They hadn't. She lowered her head, took a deep, slow breath then exhaled. Jerry had seen her having one of her bad attacks. It had come on suddenly in her dressing room when she had upset herself thinking about Alex, but she had thought nobody had seen her. She felt physically sick at the thought of Jerry seeing her, and, oh God, *telling* people about it.

She'd had the attacks a lot as a child, a few as a teenager and then they'd stopped for years and years and she thought she was finally free of the horrors once and for all. Only, after the trauma of giving birth to far-from-the-blue-eyed-and-blonde-haired child she was expecting, they'd come back. And they'd come back with an obsessive phobia of doctors and hospitals too. Although her husband and parents had witnessed the physical effects of the mild ones that they thought were panic attacks, she would never, *ever* let them know exactly what brought them on because of her immense fear of them and what they might mean. Instead, for years on end, she simply blocked them and pretended that yes, she may be physically fragile but not mentally. Oh no, not mentally. Mentally she was *fine*. Mentally she was normal. *Normal*. She wasn't mentally fucked up too.

The reality of Autumn's fits were that they were a lot more than the physical anxiety bursts she made them out to be. Although indeed they were acutely panic induced, they were actually brought about by mass confusion and terror following booming voices and images that would invade her head and cause her body to convulse. The voices came without warning if she thought too much about anything remotely upsetting for too long, and the images followed if she was having a particularly bad attack.

Other than the months following her baby's death the attacks had never happened often enough for them to interfere with her life in general. But nonetheless, what Autumn Leigh sometimes suffered from were untreated schizophrenic attacks, and she was convinced they would take over her mind forever if she didn't fight them away. Autumn Leigh had a mental illness. Doctors would know this in an instant if she told them the truth and somewhere deep down, Autumn knew this too. The fear of been thrown away into an asylum had stuck and even now, in adulthood, Autumn saw her mental problems as her dirty secret, unaware of the fact that problems of such nature are incredibly common and highly treatable. In the frightened mind of our small-town-girl it was shameful, rare and something that she had no choice but to take with her to her grave. *Sometimes, Anthony, I hear voices and they tell me to do things. I see things; mad, flashing images. They scare me so much my body starts to convulse and by the time I've come around I don't remember what I heard or saw but I know it was something.* He'd tell her to see a doctor and that she was *not* doing. She had been afraid of being taken away by doctors her entire life and unfortunately for her she had to visit them more than the average kid because of circumstances concerning her birth and her health. However, the experience of the premature birth of her blue-eyed-blonde-haired-monster turned her fear into a fully-fledged phobia and she would not set foot in a hospital ever again.

Staring into the mirror again Autumn Leigh forced herself to be calm, and, with much experience said boldly: 'That didn't happen.' She slapped herself hard across the face, waited for the redness to fade and then went back to her table, composing herself on the way, hoping Anthony might be sat back there.

'Hey, hey! You're back!' Bret shouted as Autumn approached the table of the two adult-children and sat down. Anthony was still nowhere to be seen.

'I had to use the restroom.' Autumn took a sip of champagne and lit up another cigarette. She sat back in her chair and felt comfortable and relieved in the knowledge that the last five minutes or so never happened.

'You alright?' Jerry asked in a soft tone. Genuinely soft, so much so it surprised Autumn a little.

'I'm fine, Jerry, thank you… I've just won an award. Of-course I'm fine!' Autumn laughed.

'Good,' he nodded. Then the serious side of Jerry disappeared into thin air and he returned to normal. He flicked a cigarette into his mouth and naturally allowed his eyes to follow a skimpily clad backside that was strutting past their table. He nudged Bret to look, muttered something through his cigarette just quiet enough for Autumn not to hear, then fell about laughing. All forgotten.

Autumn studied him a little and for the first time realised how much of a shame it was that he'd been brought up the way he had, and that now he was so screwed up with drugs that his true, decent personality only surfaced once in a while. She imagined he cried when he was alone at night. Autumn also knew, just as everyone else did, that his system had let the guy pump it for all it was worth so many times that it wouldn't be long until it gave in.

Yeah, his body took it alright. Jerry could do coke and God knows what else all night and still be able to act spot on at six the next morning. Whereas Autumn, on the other hand, would do one line and be wide-awake for a week then asleep for a month.

As I have touched upon, Autumn was an incredibly ill child and her mother had always said her weak system was the reason she had to eat three solid, healthy meals every day and: 'promise me Lucy, promise me you'll never smoke or drink a lot. It's not good… especially not for you.'

'Have another glass,' Jerry ordered, patronisingly clicking his fingers for a waiter (many a chef and bartender had the pleasure of listening to waiters tear strips off Jerry behind his back over the years, because of the way Jerry spoke to them). 'Bret, you want one?'

Bret had begun rubbing his temples and did not answer, but when the waiter arrived Jerry took three flutes from his tray anyway, spilling each one a little.

'Not for me, thank you. I'll just finish this one then I better not drink anymore,' Autumn declined politely.

'Oh c'mon, Autumn. We're celebrating here! You've just won first prize, treat yourself,' Jerry pushed it, the unlit Marlboro still hanging in limbo between his lips. He thrust the drink towards her and she took it for argument's sake and placed near another stale half-empty flute, with no intention of drinking both. Anthony would be back soon and they would be going back to their hotel suite for soft music and celebratory sex.

Autumn lit a cigarette while Bret stumbled from the table, his skin looking green, without saying a word.

Jerry fidgeted a bit, removed his Marlboro from his lips, took three large gulps of champagne to finish his flute, put the cig back in his mouth then turned to view the beauty queen sat opposite him.

She was expelling smoke thoughtfully, her full, moist lips slightly parted. He felt a tingle down his spine. Finally the two of them were alone. She had obviously forgiven him for pointing out that she was lying when she had said she hadn't touched drugs for years but hey, some people don't like to talk about it. They were back on good terms: *excellent.*

Jerry leaned over towards her. 'Did you find Anthony?' he asked, although his sneer showed he wasn't interested in Anthony at all.

'No.' Autumn pulled at her menthol again, looking around the room. *Oh great! Just great! Now that Bret's left you try and flirt. Christ.*

'No? Shame. Nice man is… is…'

'Anthony.'

'Anthony! Of-course. Yeah, yeah. Nice man.' Jerry clumsily lit his Marlboro on one of the two candles on the table, burning low in their holders.

'He is, that's why I married him,' Autumn replied dryly.

'Yeah but, you gotta admit… He's a bit, bit…'

'A bit what?' Autumn mused, turning to eye Jerry sharply, who was still leant over the table like a prowling cat – an unhealthy prowling cat.

'Well, y'know… square.' The sneer was still on Jerry's face.

'Jerry! He's thirty-seven! Ten years ago he was a livewire but everyone matures.'

'Bret's nearly forty,' was the quick response.

'… Except for Bret.'

Jerry stretched back in his chair and said: 'Yeah, well I think it's rubbing off on you, sweetheart.'

'What the hell are you talking about?' Autumn laughed, slightly amused at his insolence.

'Squareness, honey!' Jerry cried, wildly shrugging his shoulders and sitting up straight.

'Squareness?' Autumn repeated, astounded.

'Yeah, it's like a disease, you marry a square then you become one. Dominoes.'

'Domi..? I could give you a run for your money any day,' Autumn laughed, enjoying the conversation yet ever-so-slightly offended at the same time. Jerry was the only person in the world that would dare talk to the marvellous Autumn Leigh like this. In a way it was refreshing, but it was also quite foreign.

'Is this a challenge, pretty lady?'

'What?' Autumn asked, cringing a little.

'You just said you could give me a run for my money. Is it a challenge?' Okay, he was pushing it now. Jerry had a tendency to over-step the mark.

'Oh for fuck's sake Jerry, I'm past trying to prove myself to people.'

'So you *can't* give me a run for my money,' Jerry said matter-of-factly.

And just like that the enjoyment was gone and Autumn suddenly felt the need to defend herself.

'What?' Autumn said seriously. 'Maybe I just don't *want* to pump myself full of shit every night. Does that make me boring to you?'

Jerry made a special effort to look exasperated and replied: 'Whoa there! I'm not asking you to pump yourself full of shit, sweetheart. I'm asking you to fuckin' relax every once in a while. Jeeze. Woo!' Jerry wasn't going to continue but her smile had faded and she shook her head with a familiar look of disgust that he couldn't resist adding comment to: 'I mean, look at you; you've just achieved something millions of people can only fuckin' dream about… yet you don't seem to be having any fun at all. What's all that about?'

Although the conversation started off as light-hearted banter, it was collecting serious undertones at a deafening speed.

Conversations with Jerry often head this way, which is why he finds it hard to make and ultimately keep friends. The sad thing is, the guy doesn't mean to constantly rub people up the wrong way; he just can't help observing (and pointing out) things about people that they take offence to. Some would see that as not possessing very good social skills, others an honest yet brutal person, while others would see nothing but a through-and-through sociopath to be avoided at all costs. Which character you see him as is up to you.

'I don't have to listen to this. Yes Jerry, you're right. This is my night. *My* night. I don't have to spend it …'

'Exactly! It *is* your night! So come on, relax with me, have a few drinks,' Jerry interrupted in a spirited, friendly manner, not keen on the way this discussion was heading.

Autumn Leigh looked annoyed and flustered. She looked like she was going to get up and leave. Jerry had to turn this ship around.

'Babe,' he said softly, 'I'm not saying you never have any fun. I'm just saying that you don't seem to be having any fun *tonight*… and you *should* be. You shouldn't be worrying about where your fuckin' husband is, you should be thinking about *you.*'

The line seemed to work and Autumn's expression of anger morphed into one of self-pity. He could work with that. Actresses were easy to manipulate when you got them feeling sorry for themselves.

Jerry turned on the charm and said: 'Are you going to have a drink with your old buddy Jerry?'

Autumn didn't answer but he could tell she was considering it.

'Come on you, we did a fuckin' great job, you and I. We made that film what it was. Cheers?' Jerry held up his glass, inviting her to join him.

He'd got her back up, there was no doubt about that. But then, Autumn knew Jerry well enough; she knew what he was like. Was sulking all night really worth it, on tonight of all nights? Plus, he kind of did have a point now she thought about it, she *wasn't* having any fun. So Autumn joined him in a toast, prompting him to say: 'Atta girl!' which instantly made her loosen up again and for the second time tonight, the volatile co-star was forgiven and the tension was cleared just before it had chance to escalate.

Autumn clicked her glass with Jerry and smiled reassuringly to herself. *He's just a kid for fuck's sake. A cocky kid, but a kid. Plus, he's a welcome change from all the ass-kissers in here I suppose.*

Before she knew it, an hour had passed. Anthony had briefly showed up to let Autumn know he was at Martin's table over in the far corner, and: 'Hey sweetpea don't drink any more, okay?' Bret never returned and Autumn and Jerry were genuinely enjoying each other's company for the first time outside work. The two were going through bottle after bottle; Autumn sipping, Jerry downing. She realised that Jerry was capable of being very entertaining, funny, flattering and serious all at the same time. In fact, the more she drunk, the more she felt bad about never giving him a proper chance before.

'How can you get away with shit like that?!' Autumn screamed with laughter, almost blushing, after Jerry had finished telling her the climax of one of his exploits. She'd had around four glasses of champagne in all, and was well on her way to being absolutely wasted. The feeling was intensified by the total blast she was having with this bright young thing. Autumn hardly ever drank because her body was so fragile but tonight she had taken Jerry's advice and let herself go for once. And, do you know what? She felt fucking great for it and even kind of hoped Anthony wouldn't come back for a while.

'Because I'm a superstar!' Jerry laughed. 'Just like you, sugar!'

'Hey Jerry,' Autumn slurred, her eyes alight with confidence. 'C'mere…'

She leaned over the table sluggishly and signalled for Jerry to do the same. Jerry leaned so far over his head was above the ashtray in the middle of the table.

'You're alright, y'know,' she said. 'I always thought you were an asshole but you're actually alright. But still, I'm not going to fuck you.' Autumn then giggled and sat back, the movement causing her to feel unhealthily drunk and a little sick for a moment.

Jerry sat back too – a genuinely surprised expression seemed to flaunt itself on his face just long enough for it to be visible.

'Oh, don't look like that, Jerry. I know you like me.' She giggled hollowly again.

Jerry downed his glass then filled it straight back up again.

'It never crossed my mind. You're a married lady,' he lied.

'*Married*. And don't you forget it!' Autumn pointed her finger towards him lazily but as she pulled her hand back she knocked an empty glass off the table, sending it smashing to the floor. She placed her hand over her mouth and looked around the room for witnesses – of which there were plenty.

Jerry snorted then said seriously: 'Maybe we should stop now.'

Autumn glanced around with her eyes half open and it fully dawned on her just how wasted she actually was. Oh God, I feel sorry for her right now, award or not. I hate that feeling of having overdone it and can fully empathise with her. You know what it's like, right? I don't know, you might not, but every now and again there comes a horrible moment when you realise you've drunk too much. It's even worse when it's in a public place because it's almost like there's no way out;

you just have to ride it through and hold down sickness. If it's chronic then you'll find yourself listening into conversations to take your mind off the urge to curl up into a ball. It's the kind of drunk that makes you wonder why the hell you do this to yourself. I remember the feeling clearly from my teenage years. Autumn Leigh, the famous, the fabulous, is only two drinks away from the white flag, only two drinks away from the buzz of conversation hurting her ears, only two drinks away from the walls closing in and out.

With her intoxication on her mind, Autumn's blurry thoughts turned to Jerry and how he was handling himself. Autumn crooked her head over to him and was shocked to see two things. One, he was looking right at her, and two, he looked sober! He was flicking his cigarette, swigging his drink and sitting up straight like he hadn't touched a drop. *And he's been drinking more and at a faster pace... **and** he's been on the Rush as well! Wow, he really has got a body of steel, just like he said!*

In her current state, Autumn found Jerry's drinking capabilities hugely impressive. He looked almost sober. But Autumn? Autumn hadn't felt this close to leaving a party so early in years. Anthony turns his back for an hour and look at her, right?

As I said before, Autumn was a sickly child. She was a twin, but while her mother was pregnant the babies caught an infection and developed dangerously low heartbeats and stunted internal growth.

Alice and Stewart were informed there was a chance of both babies dying unless they were induced prematurely so, six weeks earlier than planned, little Lucy entered the world along with her twin brother, who died two hours later. Alice and Stewart's baby girl was kept in the hospital for nine weeks and there were several times the doctors thought she wasn't going to pull through at all... but she made it out of the woods eventually and was allowed home.

The suffering didn't end there though; in fact that was just the beginning. Lucy's childhood was besieged with constant health problems over the years, due to her incredibly low immune system and weak make-up. On top of it all, her parents became obsessed with the fear of losing her so their little girl wasn't allowed to do anything that involved risk or activity. This continued right up until she had had enough and left for Hollywood at nineteen. When Autumn hit Hollywood it didn't take her long to realise maybe her parents did have a point after all. She would get drunk on two Martinis and her hangover would last days. She only tried grass once, vowing never to do it again as it brought on the voices. By the age of twenty-one Autumn Leigh had decided to keep just the one vice: smoking. The rest she left to the people who could take it and had only been tipsy a handful of times since.

'I don't think you should drink any more Autumn. Anthony will not be happy at you behaving badly will he, huh?' Jerry sneered subtly.

'Anthony? What does he know? He's left me all night, Jez! I can drink as much as I want. I never usually drink. I don't know why, it's so much *fun!*'

'Yeah. I'm cool, y'know, you're fully grown and all, but I don't think you should let Anthony boss you around as much. That's just my opinion. You're a beautiful woman, why let him ruin your fun?'

'Exactly!' Autumn cried. 'I should be able to do anything, whether he likes it or not.' *until I keel.*

'Go girl!' Jerry laughed.

Autumn laughed back as much as she could without having to tense her stomach.

Jerry trailed off his sound and eyed Autumn. *She's dying for it yeah she's flirting with me. Autumn Leigh is flirting with me. If anyone can tempt her to a dessert other than vanilla ice-cream then it's me – and it's now.*

'Look at me, Autumn,' Jerry commanded, his heart racing, going in for the kill.

Autumn turned her laughter into a faint smile and did as he said, accidentally focusing on his eyes: electric pits of deep blue mixed like paint with emerald green. Realising that Jerry had beautiful eyes like Anthony Autumn felt a little better. Concentrating on discovering an attractive feature for the first time was better than concentrating on how inebriated she felt, and Autumn was enjoying the change of track. In fact, Autumn realised, Jerry really *did* have gorgeous eyes, but in a completely different (better?) way than Anthony's. Anthony's eyes were deep but Jerry's were the stuff of hunks – no wrinkles of age in the way, no greying eyebrows. Autumn's sudden realisation and fascination with Jerry's looks forced her eyes to flick to his floppy brown hair. And my, my, what nice hair you have to boot, longing for manicured fingernails to scratch and pull at it… and then those lips! Full, passionate lips that beg to be kissed and gently nipped at by pearly white teeth. *You've drunk too much, Autumn, that's the only reason you find him attractive. Find Anthony and go home! People are looking!*

Yeah, yeah whatever. But… she'd known he was good looking but the irritation factor always blurred it. But looking at him *now* he gave a different impression, he gave her something she'd reserved and kept private for Anthony… until now. *Go home!* He gave her the feeling of passion, she wanted his hands on her body *No, No, No! You love Anthony! Anthony!* and she wanted it now, she wanted to feel him breathing heavily onto her neck, she wanted…

'What are you thinking?' Jerry asked quietly.

'I'm thinking you're good.' *I shouldn't be saying this but it's fun and I…I…what was I thinking…oh, yeah, he's so sexy…*

'Good at what?' Jerry almost couldn't believe it had worked. *It only took a bottle and she's wet for me! Gee, who'd have thought it took so little for her to stray? Not so high and mighty now, Autumn. Not after you've felt me inside you,*

*you'll feel bad and fess' up to Anthony, Anthony will leave
you, I'll be front page headlines – wham, bam, another lead
role ma'am –* **and** *I get to fuck the world's most beautiful
woman. Can't lose! Goddamn. Daddy will be proud.*

'I'm thinking you're good at satisfying a woman.' Autumn
was far too drunk to care about consequences, to care about
the fact that she was in the middle of a party where all eyes
were on her, about the fact Anthony was somewhere in the
same room... about anything really. The only thing that was
important to her state of mind at that moment was turning
Jerry on. To feel desired on a one to one basis, not just a
crowd of faceless fans. *I feel a bit sick, I feel a bit sick. No I
don't, I feel fine. I feel sick but look into those eyes and think
about sex and ignore it.*

Jerry drew in a deep breath and felt a stirring in his
trousers. He had to do it now or he'd miss his chance with her.
*She's smart, she'll realise what she's doing soon. She won't
do it if I wait around too long.*

'Is this a challenge, pretty lady?' Jerry whispered.

Autumn didn't think; she spoke. 'I think it is,' she found
herself whispering back.

Her focus blurred for a moment, causing her to see double
but after blinking it returned to normal – no need to worry
folks, everything's sharp again.

'Follow me in two minutes. I'm going into the very end
room of the second left stage-maintenance corridor, okay?'
Jerry instructed slowly.

'Okay.' *This is not the right thing, what the hell am I
agreeing to? Oh fuck it, it'll be alright. No-one has to know.*

Jerry winked slyly and left. Autumn sat back and watched
him casually sift through the crowds of people and disappear
down the dark, forgotten corridors at the far left of the stage.
Once he was out of sight she groaned to herself and stared at
the flute of bubbles, half full. Just the thought of drinking one
more sip made Autumn's head feel heavy and tired. But still
there overriding that was an excited tingling. If she followed
Jerry that tingling would be satisfied and no-one would ever

57

have to find out... if she didn't she'd end up feeling frustrated all night, having to fantasise to herself all the way home while Anthony talked about how far he got brown-nosing Martin Gate.

The very end room.

Autumn left the table slowly, trying to maintain her balance. She heard some distant blurred voices asking her if she was alright but she just nodded them off and concentrated on getting to that dark little side corridor. It seemed to take forever but eventually she was there, slipping behind the staging first so she was out of sight then opening the second door down in the hall. It was well hidden away and if she hadn't have watched Jerry carefully and guessed the rest then she'd never even have known it existed. That excited feeling took over again and as the closed the door behind her she found herself holding her breath and feeling like a naughty schoolgirl.

Each step she took down the corridor made her feel even more desperate for satisfaction to start with. The corridor was narrow and dimly lit, housing white doors that led to different storage rooms and cupboards. The walk was long and cold but the end door was in sight.

However, the further Autumn walked towards it the heavier her breathing became and closer still, she realised she was shaking and the sick feeling was back. Unable to carry on walking, Autumn was forced to sit down to suppress the sickness, using her time to desperately convince herself that she was alright.

As she forced herself to inhale and exhale slowly, her common-sense slightly tugged on her conscious thoughts. *If I go in I can't turn back.* Autumn stared at the plain wall opposite her for a moment then massaged her forehead with her hand and slowly began to realise how overwhelmingly ill she felt. *Oh God, I feel sick. I want to go home. What am I doing? This is stupid. Harmless flirting, that's all it was. Anthony is my husband and he is the only man I share myself with. And anyway, my life is far from private; if I go into that*

room the entire world will find out one way or another.
Starting to feel a bit embarrassed by herself Autumn began to
take time to think as straight as she could in the state that she
was in.

Five minutes earlier Jerry had basically run down the corridor
to his special little room. He had discovered it while trying to
find a good place to hide his collection of goodies at last
year's party. It was a disused store cupboard with several fold-
up chairs and two shelves stocking glass-cleaning fluid left
and forgotten. Everything was exactly the same as it was last
year. When he switched on the light it became evident how
much dust there was in there. No windows, no carpet, nothing.
The perfect hiding place.

Jerry rubbed his hands together and went straight for his
belt and flies. He took down his black trousers so fast he
almost stumbled, then with care rolled up the right inside leg
of his Calvin's. At this precise moment Autumn was forgotten
as he viewed the sewn on lump of cotton with love.

He had designed it so the drug of his choice could be
slotted into his crotch area comfortably. It was invisible on the
outside of the garment and hard to spot even on the inside.
Jerry was ever so proud of his handy-work. He'd used the
initiative to cut up a matching pair of briefs to supply the
material needed, then spent half an hour stitching it in such a
manner so it held a small amount of drugs upright, secure and
discreet.

He delved into it now, removing a small plastic bag
containing a remaining line of coke and the mother of all
highs, the brand new wonder drug that Jerry and his close
associates referred to as The Servant, as it was a mind altering
drug that would do whatever you wanted it to do – if you were
in the right frame of mind. He placed The Servant on the
bottom shelf and removed his wallet from the inside pocket of
his dinner suit.

While flipping it open and removing a credit card and a $20 note he became overcome with a feeling of sudden urgency to get this done as quickly as possible. He couldn't risk Autumn bursting in and ruining the egocentric pleasure he experienced for a few moments after snorting coke. He unfolded one of the wooden chairs and placed his Visa on it; then, he knelt down on the floor and popped open the top of the plastic bag his coke was kept in. This was the crucial part of the ritual and having a steady hand helped – which unfortunately Jerry never seemed to have these days.

He transferred the $20 note to his mouth and gripped it with his lips, allowing him to use his left hand to pour the coke onto the chair seat, and his right hand to steady it. A few grains fell astray but no sudden jerks or twitches, so that was okay. He expertly brushed it into a perfect line with the card then rolled up the $20 note. Jerry tended to have an erection at this point due only to the arousing build up with the feeling of what he was due to experience in only a few seconds. He held the note up to his nose *perfect* then bent his head over the substance, savoured the feeling, and then snorted the chemical. He groaned immediately afterwards and cleaned around his nose with his finger, sniffing constantly.

'Hell yeah,' he said to himself, wiping his face with both hands. 'Hell yeah!' he repeated louder. *I am Superman. I am the Walrus. Hell yeah.* Now for The Servant.

The Servant was actually a precarious form of d-Lysergic Acid Diethylamide-25, more commonly known as LSD.

A drug not recognised yet as even having arrived in Hollywood, it was picked up in gelatin-tab form from Japan by Marone Scott, one of Jerry's pretend best friends and upper-class suppliers on the drug scene.

Marone had called Jerry over to see him in private as he had something he wouldn't want to miss out on. Half an hour later the two of them were strolling down the marble hall of

Marone's eleven bedroom mansion situated fashionably in the Hollywood Hills.

'What is it?' Jerry asked with greed in his eyes.

'It's called The Servant,' was the reply.

Marone possessed just enough body fat to be overweight evenly mixed with enough muscle to crush your head. To put it plainly, you wouldn't fuck his wife. Jerry wouldn't fuck his wife... now *that's* fear. Marone wasn't even the top dog in their quaint little gun toting, dope smuggling family. He was the go-getter, the tester, the dealer, the people's man, the sorter. Many more were ranked higher. But Marone was good at his job; in fact he was among the best and he knew the drug industry better than anyone else in LA... which was why his house had three swimming pools. Marone also knew how much information to give in these circumstances. Tell Jerry too much and Jerry will double cross you; everybody is a backstabber. Especially jumped-up pricks like Jerry Tilsey.

'The Servant? Why's it called that?' Jerry and Marone were walking slowly towards the recreation room, a heavily secured room where Marone did his dealing.

'It's called that because if you want somethin' it gets it. It's an hallucinogen, but a more lethal form of acid, and better than Peyote. This shit is the business, man. It makes dreams a reality.'

'Where did you get it from?'

'The east.' Marone was cooler than any actor could ever be. His thick, cushiony lips moved as he spoke, not his eyes.

'So it's basically just really good Sunshine?'

'The Servant pisses all over Sunshine. Your average dose of the Californian contains between fifty and one-hundred-and-fifty micrograms per hit,' Marone then stopped Jerry and said; 'It's always two-hundred when you get it from me.' He then began to walk again as he continued: 'The Servant has around four-hundred micrograms to start with and, although the structure's the same, it has different chemical balances which affect the brain in a way that your Sunshine never could. Once you've had this, man, that shit's candy.'

'Yeah? Sounds good,' Jerry nodded.

Marone didn't move a muscle other than to walk.

'How much for each hit?' Jerry could feel his fingers twitching already.

'Twenty hits for $20,000.'

'$20,000? Is that a joke?' Jerry spluttered. 'No fuckin' way, Marone. I can get twenty hits of LSD for a hundred... less, if I see the right people.'

Marone stopped walking and turned to Jerry: 'You're a good friend of mine Jerry, and an important client,' he bullshitted. 'I'd hate to think of you scoring your party prescriptions off some cheap bitch in a crack den. So I tell you what: I'll arrange you a free sample of my personal favourite, then if you like the high, you buy your hits from me. How's that for fair?'

'Okay,' Jerry shrugged, enjoying the feeling of being in the driving seat of a gangster's car. 'But you've gotta let me take it home to try out. I have better trips when I'm surrounded by my own shit, y'know?' he pushed.

'No problem,' Marone agreed.

Ha! Jerry couldn't believe his skill with the situation. *I've actually conned one of LA's top men into giving me free shit! Ha! Unbelievable! Marone values my custom so much he's actually giving top shit to me for free... and he's letting me take it home! Ha!*

Marone had found, over the years, that this one works best. Let the client think that they are manipulating you, give them a teaser of what you're trying to sell them, let it be on their own terms. It works a treat for business, because after they've had their freebie and they come back for more, they still think they've got the upper hand. The foolish bastards sometimes could actually go as far as thinking that you're soft... but not for long. If they keep on buyin', they keep on smilin'. When they stop buying, it's time for the payment of that freebie. Marone always wins in the end. And, I mean, come on, Jerry Tilsey is cotton wool compared to the power of some of his more distinguished clients.

62

LSD's effects last anything between five and fourteen hours, whereas the high off the mysterious Servant's effects were said to last between twenty and twenty-four hours, but because this was such a new drug no long term effects were known. Marone had seen a handful of Japanese prostitutes die and observed several of the hand-picked test people jammed in fairyland, the effects not wearing off them the whole two weeks Marone was there – they were still in the same state when he left back for the US.

Originally the manufacturers there tried to avoid telling Marone what extras were actually in this so called 'wonder drug', but Marone got it out of them and when he did he decided it would be best never to tell anyone much about it and never take it himself.

Marone knew from the very beginning this could kill and ruin people but he didn't get where he was today being compassionate. This could turn out to be his biggest job yet and the profit from this thing would be huge. Plus, according to the manufacturers, the chances of having these effects were decreased dramatically if the user was healthy, mentally stable and relatively young – which Marone would only sell to anyway.

This is how Jerry came to be standing in a dim storeroom looking at a little bag containing one square of The Servant. He had bought 40 and had 38 left. They were the best high he'd ever had and the last one he took kept him occupied with the most intense, real hallucinations he had ever experienced. It's not just that he'd see things, y'know? He could *feel* them. Like, *really* feel them, as if they were there. He'd taken his freebie back to his apartment, and tried it out straight away. Rule number 1: Whenever trying out a new high, do it alone. See, Jerry couldn't risk anybody else being there the first time he took a new, relatively unexplored drug. He never knew how he would react to them if he hadn't tried them before and he had to be careful for his reputation's sake.

The day he'd first tried it, he had slipped it in his mouth, washed it down with mineral water and waited. For half an hour he sat and smoked cigarettes, read through some lines of his latest film, flicked through television channels, tapped his feet on the floor. But slowly, as each second tick-tocked away on the clock on one of his side walls, Jerry could feel his attention wavering from reality. As the minutes passed, his anticipation grew stronger and stronger for the onset of this marvellous high Marone had gushed about. He turned the television off, put the script down and waited for that familiar feeling of numbness and tingling to devour him.

Imagine the good people of New York or London being disturbed from their rushing around by an odd noise approaching overhead, from the skies. So they all stop still, waiting to see what the noise is bringing with it, or what is bringing the noise. Their cappuccinos go cold, their cigarettes die out, they all wait, nearly spraying their pants with expectancy, they all wait to see what is casting a shadow over their city...

Jerry continued feeling more and more excitable, clambering up to the top of his sofa, giggling and panting like a dog. It was coming. It didn't take long before he started to experience heightened senses along the same lines as what he had felt in the past, with his much loved Sunshine. Except for, this time, on this sunny afternoon, all alone in his apartment, under the influence of a freebie from the scariest motherfucker this side of the Atlantic, it felt... *more*.

Colours began to seep into each other and make love, creating a harmony that nearly made Jerry come. Greens sparkled and fizzed, reds erupted and moved like lava, yellows glowed and pulsated, and looking at them was like looking into the eyes of God Himself. One colour especially had Jerry transfixed. It was the beautiful, rich colour of the stripped and waxed wood that was his side-table. It was the most seductive, smooth colour he had ever seen. And as he worshiped the table, the grains within it began to flow like water, an endless steady flow that would go on forever in its own little world. Jerry reached out to touch it and when he did, the grain waves began steadily flowing over his fingers. He could feel them, they felt like silk... no, no, no, they felt more than silk...it felt like a silk-worm had just flown its cocoon and the silk had drifted in the wind and landed on the thigh of a fairy virgin. Jerry had tears in his eyes. He could have stroked that fairy's thigh forever but the tick-tock of the clock suddenly alerted Jerry's attention. His head spun to face it, his ears pricked up and his body froze. The boy concentrated on it more than he ever had on anything before.

Within a few moments Jerry was utterly transfixed on this sprayed metal brand-red Coca-Cola clock, his eyes moving and widening each time the ticking hand moved along its endless circle. He suddenly realised how amazing this contraption was, and couldn't believe he'd hardly paid any attention to it in the past.

Jerry began to trip, eyes and ears fixed on the clock. Each tick and each tock became the loudest, most important thing in Jerry's life. He could taste each echoing click; it tasted of rusty water and scrap-metal yards. The colours from the clock, all reds and whites, now overpowered the sound. The colour formed a living, moving aura, as if the clock had just been blessed from Heaven and given a halo. Jerry could hear the colours singing to him. It was angelic. It was... *beautiful*. Within a second of that astounding red teasing its voice around him, a lot of things, in fact *everything* – time and existence itself – became clear to Jerry. He opened his eyes for the first time in his life. Jerry was re-born: A handsome embryo, if you may.

This machine, this machine was communicating with him, and he felt, no, no, he was *certain* that, if this machine stopped Enjoying Coca-Cola, then time itself would cease up too. Jerry had never felt so alive, so blessed. Each second that passed was a marvel, a wonder.

I live in time, I live in this clock, and this clock is my heartbeat, the very reason I exist. All these machines, they are my bloodline. This beautiful glowing red clock is my heart and soul and I'm living it. **I am living it.**

Jerry closed his eyes to taste the clock's beating. It no longer tick-tocked, it pulsed. It pulsed through Jerry and filled his mouth with a glorious metallic taste. He had shut his eyes but the clock was still there, at the forefront of his mind, but now it was bigger, and when he opened his eyes again it filled the room. Jerry was in the clock – the sound of red surrounded him and sang to him in the most beautiful chorus voice he had ever heard, or thought possible to hear. It was as if the entire army of Heaven's angels was embracing our boy and passing all their love and warmth through him, showing him the meaning of beauty, singing and humming him the meaning of life.

Jerry was in ecstasy. He stayed that way for the rest of the day, safe in the knowledge that if he fell, the angels would catch him, and that as long as the clock kept pulsing then so would he. Jerry did not panic over what would happen if the clock did stop pulsing; he knew it would not, he was in the company of God's angels. Jerry was surrounded by those holy winged creatures right through to when he woke up on that same sofa that he had been perched on, at midday the next day. He woke up knowing that that was the best trip he had experienced in his entire life.

…And Marone was right! There was no downside to it, no repressed memories, no vomiting, no paranoia… none of it, just plain old good time. Anyway, Jerry knew this beforehand because that's what Marone had told him and as far as Jerry was concerned Marone never lied. Marone even told Jerry there were no long-term effects whatsoever. 'It's totally short term. You'll be in this perfect dream world but when you come out of it you come out of it. It doesn't fuck your life up and it doesn't send you mad. It's the best shit on the market, man.'

How such a man-about-town like Jerry could believe such utter lies is completely beyond me; I guess that's what blind faith and copious amounts of hard drugs do to you. But yeah, Jerry was reeled in hook, line and sinker while Marone had his cut of an extra, if not measly, $40,000 to play around with for the week.

Jerry had just delicately torn off and put aside a pane, placing the rest of them and his tools back inside his Calvins, when he heard the footsteps. *Ah, and now for my second favourite pleasure...*

When the footsteps stopped Jerry looked towards the door. They hadn't stopped near enough to be just outside. Jerry's mouth twitched slightly and he rubbed his nose with his free hand. *Now, now Autumn. You made a promise to Jerry here... don't you go backing out on me now.*

Jerry thought for a few seconds, picked the hit off the side, placed it on the tip of his finger, then went to the door. He opened it to find the award-winning actress Autumn Leigh leant drunkenly against the wall about four doors away down the corridor.

'Hey,' he said softly, walking towards her. She looked up, sighed heavily, and then lowered her head to look at her feet.

'Hey,' she replied finally. Jerry approached her with The Servant still steady on his finger, out of her sight.

'You... um, you comin' to join me?' he asked in his caring voice, hiding the immense disappointment that she had obviously sobered up a bit and that the answer was going to be...

'No. It's stupid, Jerry. I just got a little carried away. I could never hurt Anthony like that. I'm sorry but... you know what I mean, right?'

'Sure. Yeah. Sure. But you did want to?' He could feel his anger biting into him already, and he hadn't even begun to persuade her yet.

'Jerry, I was engulfed in the moment…'

'But you did want to, didn't you?' *You did, didn't you? You prick tease bitch. You did, didn't you?*

'Yeah I did, for like thirty seconds. But…'

'So what's changed? You're attracted to me, I'm attracted to you. No-one will find out and c'mon, we both get our rocks off.' *Don't let me down Autumn, don't let me down like this…*

'No.' Autumn found herself talking like she would to a disobedient dog.

Jerry's fingers were starting to twitch slightly.

'You were more than willing to about five minutes ago.' Jerry could feel his teeth grinding against one another. *What the hell is this you fucking bitch?!*

Autumn continued: 'I'm not attracted to you, I never have been and I never will be. I'm sorry to sound harsh, Jerry, but I'm a grown woman with a happy marriage and a career in the spotlight for Christ's sake. Do you honestly think I'd throw all that away for you? Just for like, ten minutes in a dingy room?'

He'd never been so let down in his life. Poor Jerry. Crushed by Autumn Leigh. Hell, poor guy.

'I'm sorry for leading you on, Jerry. 'Scuse me, I have to get back now.' Autumn turned to leave when Jerry's thoughts took control of his vocal chords.

'No!' he shouted, grabbing her arm.

Autumn inhaled sharply, suddenly shocked and eyes wide open. Within a split-second this had sobered Autumn up enough to understand that he was being aggressive towards her and within that same second she had become afraid of 'innocent lamb' Jerry.

'Don't fucking lead me on like that, Autumn. No-one leads me on like that, you *fucking cunt!*'

'Jerry?' she almost screamed, causing his grip to tighten. He pushed her up against the wall and pressed his weight onto her, his eyes bearing demons of humiliation and anger.

'Get the hell off me!' Autumn screeched.

In response to this Jerry tensed up his face then turned to inspect his right hand as best as he could. His left hand had her arm pinned to the wall and his body weight controlled the rest of her. She had placed her left arm over her stomach for protection originally and now he crushed it there. The almost invisible square was still there, still on the tip of his finger – despite the struggle and his shakes. His heart was racing and his breaths were shallow to match Autumn's.

'Open your mouth,' he instructed, looking back to her. *Not so big and tall now, are ya?*

Autumn automatically shut her lips tight and shook her head vigorously. *You're a movie-star Jerry, you can't get away with this! What the hell are you thinking? I'm gonna get you three to five for this. Anthony will be looking for me now and he'll find you and he'll kick your ass. This is your life over with, this is…*

'Open your goddamn mouth!' he yelled. At that moment she opened it to sob as not only he was scaring her so much, but also because of the shock that this was somebody she had worked alongside for nearly thirteen months. This was her co-worker and this guy was world famous.

Before she'd had chance to even realise what was happening, he'd stuck the index finger on his right hand down her throat. Autumn thought he was trying to choke her so her mouth instinctively tensed around his finger, making her retch. She could do nothing but stare at him like a rabbit in headlights.

Jerry at this point was looking far from blank. He looked as if he was almost smiling, getting one over on her. He removed his finger to check The Servant had gone, then clasped his hand firmly around her neck. She had no idea she'd just been slipped, the poor girl – she had no idea it had smoothly glided down her throat as she swallowed back heavy tears straight afterwards.

Autumn was coughing now, with tears smudging heavy makeup down her frightened face. There was nothing she could do about the situation; she couldn't move to kick him and she couldn't reach to bite him. She couldn't even think – it seemed far too unreal.

'Now,' he whispered. 'You're gonna give me what you fuckin' promised me, okay?'

'No!' Autumn cried. 'What are you doing Jerry? This isn't you! Think of the consequences! You'll get a life sentence for this. This is *rape*!'

Autumn felt a sudden, strange queasy sickness wash over her but put it down to the shock and carried on pleading with the man she was close to having an affair with only ten minutes ago.

'You're gonna get so busted for this. If you stop now I won't say a word I pro…'

He slapped her hard across the face for that, so hard her head banged against the wall and her eyes showed the whites for a moment afterwards. He then tightened his grip around her neck and drew his face so close to hers their noses touched.

'Don't insult my intelligence, you fuckin' bitch. *I won't say a word,*' he mocked. 'You'd run screaming into the middle of the fuckin' hall if you could.' He blinked twice then pulled his face away from hers. 'But you can't… boo fuckin' hoo.'

With that he pulled her away from the wall and twisted her arm up her back. She screamed out in pain so he quickly covered her mouth, told her to shut up and pulled hard on her hair as a threat. She obeyed the throbbing and stopped screaming as he led her jerkily into the storeroom.

Autumn at this point was finding it hard to focus and was experiencing acute pains in her stomach and chest, the sickness making her want to keel over and cry.

'Sit down,' he commanded as he threw her towards the chair he had previously been snorting from.

Autumn stumbled and fell onto it. She painfully twisted her body around to an upright position, only when she attempted to sit up she found she couldn't do it. Her whole body felt like it was someone else's and her thoughts became muddled and blunt.

Jerry stood blocking the door, arms folded, watching her.

'Maybe this will teach you a lesson not to lead people on, you fuckin' prick tease whore.'

Autumn glanced up at him and realised that this was too much for her to take, she knew she wouldn't be able to refrain from passing out soon and then she wouldn't be able to defend herself in the slightest. She felt a surge of heat rise up from her stomach and she began to dribble sick down the left corner of her mouth. She couldn't even find the energy to open it.

'You look fuckin' pathetic,' Jerry sneered. 'What a mess.'

Autumn tried to ask 'why am I like this?' or 'what have you done to me?' but she couldn't even muster a noise now. She was deteriorating fast and Jerry was just watching and waiting for her to pass out so he could get what she promised him.

Jerry knew it would knock her out for a couple of hours instead of giving her a high because she'd never done acid or anything this hard before, so he figured it would just make her really ill for a week or so *and* she would be so shocked by it all it would be highly unlikely that she would even remember what happened. Tonight would be a blur to her, a blur that she could never discuss with Anthony because Jerry would tell Autumn they fucked in a back room then she passed out. Try telling Anthony *that*.

Finally, Autumn gave up the fight to function and slid off the chair into a heap on the floor. Jerry smiled, walked over and crouched down next to her. This felt like revenge for him now because she thought so fucking highly of herself and made him feel a fool. This was the ultimate power trip, making Autumn Leigh dribble sick down her lovely long dress then pass out looking ridiculous on the floor. He lifted her head by her hair and made sure she wasn't about to choke to death. Nope, all clear.

He carefully turned her over and stroked her face, moving his hand down her sore, red neck, slowly over her breasts and stomach, and that was it – he didn't need any more foreplay. He roughly threw her dress up past her waistline and hastily removed her black lace teasers... The rest, as you can probably guess, was a sickening act that was over in two minutes. He let out a loud gasp and then collapsed sweating onto her limp body. She could have been dead for all he knew. He stayed inside her for a moment then pulled out, positioned her as if she had fallen over drunk, straightened up, and left.

Not a single feeling of shame passed through that boy's head as he left her there. He just felt relieved and refreshed, even proud. *Jerry wants a red Jag, Jerry gets a red Jag, Jerry wants Autumn Leigh, and Jerry gets Autumn Leigh*. He didn't even think of it as rape – after all, she had agreed to follow him down there. And the best bit was, and wait for it... she would not remember any of it! The perfect crime, Jerry! *Perfect*! Ha, ha, ha! Yee-ha!

Yeah, okay, there was a chance she would remember him slapping her but the chance was very thin, she was in so much shock and so desperately drunk all night – he'd figure that one out if it came to it. Jerry thought Autumn was still blind drunk when she was leant up against the wall. People don't remember things when they've drunk that much, do they?

Now for the act that, if it had have been a film, he would have won an Oscar for...

'Jerry, hi! Where have you been, you rascal?' An associate of his slapped him on the shoulder as he was exiting the party hall, still full of shallow laughs and overpaid stars.

'Oh, y'know, sneaking off to powder my nose,' he replied chirpily with a wink.

'Ho, Jerry!' the man laughed. 'You'll never change!'

Jerry laughed back and put his hand up as a goodbye, then left the party.

At one o'clock that morning the ambulance services received an anonymous phone call stating that the actress Autumn Leigh was unconscious in one of the back-stage store rooms where the award party was being held. The caller then hung up.

CHAPTER 2

Something was burning into her eyes. It hurt and it made everything look purple. She managed to slowly flicker them open and realised the bright thing was sunlight.

Her fingers twitched and she turned over to avoid having to look at it. The bed she was in was so warm and soft, she wasn't ready to wake up yet. Her eyes remained shut and she began to drift back off to sleep...

'Open your mouth.'

Autumn suddenly jumped up in confusion of hearing a male voice shout this strange sentence into her dreams. She darted her eyes across the room with her heart beating almost out of her chest. A few moments later she realised she was in the presidential suite of the hotel they'd booked for after the awards. They'd stayed in this room a couple of times before and had spent the night before the party here too. Once she had established that she was in familiar surroundings she began to relax her shoulders.

After that brief moment of panic was over she tuned into the fact that she had a beating migraine and was sweating ice-cold beads down her face and chest. *Oh God, last night. What the hell happened? How did I get here? Did I go somewhere with someone? Everything aches...Anthony.*

'Anthony!' Autumn called out the loudest she could. It was a smoky, hoarse attempt.

'Anthony?' she called again. This time she heard footsteps walking towards the room and the door clicked open.

'Hi, baby,' she smiled, despite the pain, as he walked in looking distressed.

'Morning Lucy. How are you feeling?' he asked flatly.

'Terrible. My head hurts and my eyes are fuzzy. Don't call me Lucy.'

Anthony nodded slowly and ran his hand through his hair. His wife never liked him calling her by her real name, not even when they were alone. Why, he didn't know.

'Are you going to tell me what happened last night?'

His voice raised alarms in Autumn's head. *Why does he sound so angry?*

'I drank far too much. I think you'll have more of an idea than I do,' she answered wearily, eyeing him. 'Why? I didn't do anything stupid did I?'

'Well, let's see...' Anthony looked at his wife. 'I go talk to Martin Gate for an hour or so, within that time I see you getting a bit too merry with that notorious arse Jerry Tilsey.' Anthony sat slowly onto the foot of the bed. 'So I come over and tell you not to drink too much more because you were already arseholed and it's not good for you. The next time my attention is drawn is when four people wearing green suits rush down the other side of the room carrying a stretcher heading for the stage corridor. I go over to your table, only it's empty. A minute or so after I see you been held up by two of the ambulance crew after apparently someone had called them to say you were unconscious in the bottom storeroom there. We arrive here in an ambulance and I've had to get a taxi back to the bloody place this morning to pick up the car. Now, what were you doing in that room? Where was Jerry... and am I suppose to believe all you were doing was drinking?'

Gob-smacked.

'W... what?' Autumn shook her head, her face contorted into total disbelief. 'Ambulance? You're joking, right?'

Anthony shook his head, studying Autumn's puzzled look.

'But... I don't remember any of that. I tell you what I do know though, Anthony, I know I don't like you talking to me as if I've done something wrong here. What, do you think I've been up to something?'

Feelings of embarrassment surged though Autumn's body, imagining how she must have looked – and in front of Hollywood's top clientele. *Oh Jesus.*

'I was fucking humiliated.' Anthony stared at his wife as he spoke. 'You must remember how you got into that room.'

Autumn desperately tried to jog her memory but all she could remember was Anthony leaving to talk to Martin Gate. She shook her head and shrugged her shoulders. 'I don't know. I can't remember anything.'

'Well then in that case I suggest we ring Jerry, because he disappeared sharpish and I have a feeling it was him that called the ambulance. I also want to ask him what he was doing in a hidden away room with you in the first place.'

Oh yeah, this was just what she needed, Anthony acting suspicious and pissed off with her as soon as she woke up, feeling ill and upset. Does he not have *any* understanding?

Anthony, honestly, *never* got angry with his wife. He got upset, but he talked to her usually; no shouting, no swearing, no trouble.

Between you and I, my dear, the marvellous Autumn Leigh saw her husband as been a bit of a soft touch in general. She liked him for that in a way though; his coolness complimented her fire. She did get mad with him, a bit too much if she really had her nails out and was in the mood for some whining, but this… *this*, the way he was looking at her, the tone of his voice, the fact that he said 'fucking'. *This*, this wasn't good. This meant she'd really done it this time.

Autumn's back was up by this point. 'Anthony, you can't just assume he was in there with me,' she said, 'for all we know I drunkenly wondered in there looking for you – he saw me go in, found me unconscious then ran off 'cause he was scared.' The words tumbled out of Autumn's mouth although she wasn't fully aware of what she was saying.

Anthony shook his head slowly and looked down to the carpet.

'Well, we'll see.' Ice.

She was not in the mood for soul-searching but they talked for a further fifteen minutes anyway, both of them trying to find answers. Not surprisingly, they didn't accomplish anything. Anthony left to get the phone, knowing something had definitely happened, while Autumn just felt weak and frustrated. Will this be in the papers? Could this ruin her career? The questions were endless but the one thing that was blatantly obvious was that Anthony suspected none of this was innocent: he blamed her.

Anthony appeared a few moments later with his organiser and the phone.

'Do you want to call him or shall I?' he asked, eyeing her.

'I'll call him. But first I want a shower. I feel like shit.'

Anthony sighed and put the phone and organiser on the floor near the bed.

Autumn tried to move but everything ached so much she needed help standing up.

'I don't like this,' Anthony stated.

'Yeah? Well neither do I,' was the honest reply.

Anthony opened the ensuite door outwards and touched Autumn's back as she was walking in. Only Autumn didn't walk in, she stopped with a jerk.

Her mouth dropped and her hand slid heavily from Anthony's shoulder to hang limply at her side. The headache disappeared.

'Lucy?' he asked.

But she didn't hear her husband. She stared at the tiles on the floor and felt as if her eyes were drying up in their sockets, she had to run but she could not tear her eyes away from what she was looking at. This was impossible.

'Anthony? Anthony?' she whispered, stiff like a mannequin, eyes fixated on the floor.

'What's wrong?' Anthony asked, placing both his hands on her to steady her swaying. 'Have you remembered something?'

'Anthony, look at the floor.' As Autumn spoke, her words seemed to echo in her head.

Anthony looked down to the blue and white tiles and shrugged. 'What am I looking for?' he asked.

'How... can you not see them?' Autumn spoke in a daze, entirely in one tone.

The entire bathroom floor was littered with muddy, slithering worms, knotted up together in mud and puddle water. There were hundreds of them, foul and writhing together in filth, some moving fast and alone, others in bundles, strangling themselves. They were everywhere. They were... beyond words. It was like someone had dug them up from a garden in the rain and just dumped them in there.

'See what?' Utter confusion darted between Anthony's words as he spoke.

She had several under her feet and crawling over her toes, but she could not feel them with the numbness of Anthony not being able to see them. *He can't see them.* The need to be sick was immense but she was so transfixed not even her insides could move.

He can't see them he can't see them but they're here. I can see them the dirty worms he can't see them...

'Lucy!' he yelled, shaking her shoulder once: 'What can't I see?'

'Worms!' she cried, suddenly grabbing at her hair and trying not to cry or be sick. *I'm not going mad, I'm not going mad. He's not looking right, he's just not looking.*

Anthony stayed silent for a moment, eyes darting from his wife's and the floor.

'Worms?' He spoke in a low, worried tone.

The look on his wife's face was of pure disgust and terror. He swallowed and took a deep breath.

'They're everywhere!' she wailed. 'How can you not see them! Oh God!'

'Lucy, look at me!' he commanded, spinning her towards him. 'The floor is clean, okay? What the hell did you take last night? No more bullshit, alright?'

She viewed him through watery, red eyes. The tears had arrived silently and were falling down her face like acid, making her sockets sting. All she could do was shake her head, unable to speak for bewilderment and fright.

'What did you take?' he repeated.

'Nothing!' she screamed. 'I didn't take anything! They're just *here*! I can't believe you'd think that!'

Anthony didn't know whether to feel angry with her or sorry. She seemed so genuine, yet this was far too strange to have a simple explanation. Her eyes looked so void that the thought of a mental breakdown flashed through his head. Drugs were the main thought in his mind, obviously. *But she knows, she knows not to touch them. Why would she when she knows what they do to her? She's always said no. Why would she do it when she knows what she's in for afterwards... unless she's been slipped? It may not be her fault.* With this in his thoughts he tried to think and speak a little more rationally, although panicking and not knowing what to do on the inside. *Is she going mad?*

'What do you expect me to think, Lucy? We're standing outside a clean bathroom and you're telling me that there're bloody *worms* on the floor!'

'Oh my *God*!' she cried, distraught. 'What do I *do*?!'

Anthony picked up on the pleading in his wife's voice and his tone became softer.

'Why don't you try to pick some up? That way you'll see they're not real.'

Touch them? He wants me to actually touch them? They're dirty they're dirty they're dirty Autumn shook her head vigorously and submitted small whines from her throat.

'C'mon, do it Lucy, seriously. You're hallucinating for some reason and I bet if you go to touch them they'll go straight through your hands, then they'll go away. Just remember they're not real.'

Autumn turned back around to them. They were so real she could smell them, foisty and warm. For the love of her husband and lack of any better ideas (except running away), she reluctantly squatted down and held out shaking hands. *They'll go, they'll go...*

Anthony watched as his love screwed up her face and turned away in torment, her hands hovering above shiny, clean bathroom floor.

'It's okay, I'm here,' he whispered.

With that he watched as she plunged her hands onto the floor and picked up piles of nothing. She then turned to them and retched, her body convulsing in horror.

80

'Anthony,' she whimpered. 'Anthony, I'm touching them. They're real.'

Anthony was speechless, unable to take in what was happening. *Surely this kind of thing only happens to the mentally insane, locked behind some iron door with no key? This doesn't happen to people like us. This just doesn't happen. She was fine yesterday! What the fuck...?*

They wriggled in her hands and dirtied her fingers. After a moment of bewilderment Autumn threw the worms as far from her as she could. She heard them splat onto the inside of the tub then slide down. She couldn't hold it then; she screamed so loud it stung her throat and made Anthony jump backwards. She fell from her squat onto the bedroom floor and encased her face with her mucky hands.

The scream faded as Anthony bent down to cradle her, whispering 'shhh' in her ear and shaking deeply himself. She was rocking back and forth with him now, crying uncontrollably. Her thoughts had taken so much battering that they were now blank. Anthony's, of-course, were juddering on overdrive.

After a few minutes Autumn wiped her eyes and took a much-needed deep breath. She stared at her distraught husband for a while before looking back at the floor.

'Ah...' she gasped, scrambling towards it. 'I-I...' was all she could stammer.

The worms had gone – just like that. The tiles had magically been restored to their full crowning glory, sparkling and fresh.

Anthony touched her hair as she told him they'd disappeared.

His wife then stood up and rubbed her head. He followed and took her into his arms, causing her to cry again.

'Shhh, it's okay. We'll get this sorted, all right? Maybe someone spiked your drink. We'll find out. It's okay, sweetpea.'

She nodded into his shoulder and held him tight. *They were there, they were everywhere Anthony. Oh God, I knew this day*

would come, I knew I wasn't right. Now everyone's gonna
know, everyone's gonna know but I can't help it. I can't help
it, I swear. It wasn't me. This isn't me. Oh God...

The clock had passed three and Autumn was still in her
nightwear. The black silk dressing-gown that usually enhanced
her beauty just made her look old today. She stood with a
cigarette held between jittery fingers, looking out of the
hotel's bedroom window at the impressive LA skyline she was
due to leave behind tomorrow, to go back to their warm
mansion in the heart of southern England.

Autumn's eyes were red and swollen from the constant
stinging tears. Her head throbbed from thoughts that struck her
like blows.

The most frustrating point of the whole thing was that she
had no idea what had happened the night before – the attack
and the rape had left Autumn's mind on overload so, like a
computer, it had crashed.

'Autumn, can I talk to you on the balcony?' Anthony, just
a voice behind her, called.

Without saying a word Autumn turned and met him there.

Twenty floors up the sights were amazing. They were in the
penthouse suite facing downtown LA. From this height the
city looked clean and organised below an undisturbed,
cloudless sky.

The balcony was modest with a wooden table and four
chairs, not to forget the several pot plants scattered around for
effect.

Anthony sat facing her wearing shorts and sunglasses. His
chin was resting on his fingers in a prayer position and his face
looked almost grey with a look of stress that had not been
there twenty-four hours ago. Anthony and Autumn could
easily have passed for rundown trailer-home folk, the way
they looked right now. With Autumn's hair tied back loosely

and without care, her face tired and swollen, and Anthony's visible frown lines magnifying themselves each time he swallowed, they looked old.

He had set up an ashtray, a jug of coffee and his wife's cigarettes in the centre of the table.

'What's this?' she asked, maybe the first words she'd spoken to him in as much as three hours.

'Sit down, please,' was his reply.

Autumn did as he said. She sat facing him, putting out her used cigarette in the ashtray.

Anthony placed his hands on the table and spoke sharply to her: 'We fly back to England tomorrow. Martin Gate and his wife are in London on business so I invited them around for dinner on Saturday night. Before we fly back, and before they turn up, I want to know exactly what you did last night and I'm not going to leave until I find out why you saw worms on the bathroom floor this morning.'

Autumn leant forward and said her words strongly: 'Okay, first of all; you could have asked me first before inviting people to our house. Second; Anthony, I've told you already – I have no idea what happened last night and to be honest I'd rather just forget about it. I could have been dehydrated enough this morning to hallucinate, y'know?'

Anthony laughed hollowly and shook his head. This angered Autumn and upset her at the same time.

'Do I amuse you?' she asked, her face showing she was hurt.

Anthony dropped the sarcastic cackle but continued to shake his head while he spoke: 'Okay sweetpea, you're right. Let's pack up and leave this place and never think about it ever again. Let's ignore all the newspapers having a field-day over this whole thing and let's pretend it never happened – then it will all go away.' He spoke as if to a naughty child.

Autumn was holding back tears of boiling anger. 'Don't talk like…'

83

'What were you drinking with Jerry Tilsey last night?' he interrupted in his normal voice and tone, realising an argument was the last thing they needed right now.

Autumn stared at him momentarily, also deciding it would be wrong to argue, although her adrenalin wanted it.

'Champagne,' she finally answered.

'Anything else?'

'I think... I... I don't know, I can't remember.'

'What's the last thing you *do* remember?' Anthony quizzed.

Autumn's mind began racing and she tapped her fingernails on the table to try and in some way aid her thoughts. If something *did* happen last night, that could mean there was a reason for her seeing worms this morning, and not just that her blackouts were not just 'blackouts' anymore. Not just that she was going mad. Not that it was finally happening.

'I was sitting at the table again after looking for you. Jerry and Bret joined me. Erm... Bret left and then I had a couple of drinks, I remember feeling drunk... then you came up and told me where you were... and that's it. I can't remember anything else.' Autumn wasn't even sure if she'd said those events in the right order, it all seemed so hazy.

Anthony stayed silent for a moment, questioning himself whether or not he should get angry about her drinking and laughing with Jerry-fuckwit-Tilsey. He decided, once again, it was not the time and it would simply sidetrack them from getting to the bottom of her odd behaviour.

'So you've lost about an hour of last night then,' Anthony thought aloud.

'Did I make a scene?' Autumn asked the million dollar question, bracing herself for what the answer might be.

'You'll have got people talking, no doubt about that. But it's not a career threatening thing. Hollywood will have forgotten about it by next week. Everyone gets drunk.'

That was a huge weight from Autumn's shoulders. She was afraid she'd never be able to show her face again.

'So, what do we do now?' Autumn asked, her voice lighter at just knowing she was still adored and not ridiculed. She could have done anything that night and have woken up totally oblivious to it.

Anthony sat back in his chair and replied: 'Now we ring Jerry.'

The ring-out on his bedside telephone entered his dream as a fire alarm. This continued for several seconds before his conscious thoughts tugged a-hold of his eyelids and opened them briefly. *Phone.*

Jerry groaned, extended his right arm and patted his hand-carved bedside table for the ringing thing.

He grabbed the receiver and held it to his ear, his head and face still embedded in his feather pillow.

'Mh-hm?' he said feebly; lips and eyes still closed, more asleep than awake.

'Jerry?' A female voice. *Always a good sign.* 'Jerry, its Autumn Leigh.' *Okay, not always...*

Jerry bolted up in bed and his heart started thudding wildly against his chest. *No, no, no Jerry... she can't do you for nuthin'. It was her choice! You gave her the choice! You were so drunk you seduced me, Autumn. Yeah, yeah, full consent, you're a cheating whore. It's you, it's you...*

'Autumn Leigh? Hi, how are ya?' Jerry gritted his teeth after this question.

'Well, I'm okay I guess. I just need to ask you a couple of things about last night. You see, I can't remember all that much.'

Autumn was still sitting on the balcony, feeling Anthony's glare as she spoke.

'Um, okay. But, y'know, I can't remember all too much either. You and I can sure as hell drink, huh?' Jerry faked that toothy smile of his, although he was alone and worried.

While Autumn was stuttering words and sounding under pressure, Jerry rescued a bent cigarette from his pocket with his free hand and lit it with the lighter forever on his bedside table. He looked around his bedroom *what a mess, jeeze* then turned his attention back to the phone.

'Sorry, what was that?' he asked.

Autumn sighed and repeated: 'I said I just want to know what happened last night, Jerry. Did I take any drugs?'

'No, no you didn't take any drugs.'

'So what happened?'

'Nothing *happened* Autumn, you got very drunk, I left, story ends. Why are you sounding so worked up?'

'Because I'm worried. Wouldn't you be if you lost your memory?'

'I lose my memory all the time. Everyone does when they drink a lot. It's nothing to worry about. Chill out, gorgeous.'

Autumn gritted her teeth before swiftly concluding the conversation with: 'thanks anyway. Sorry to wake you at 3pm.' She then switched the phone off shaking her head. *What an asshole.*

'He doesn't know a thing,' Autumn informed her husband.

Anthony laughed on the inside, more an ironic snigger. *Surprise, surprise; Jerry doesn't know a thing. If someone asked Jerry what drugs were he'd flutter those lovely long eyelashes and say: 'drugs? I don't recognise it... is it a foreign word?' and the lovely lady asking would smile back and sleep with him.*

'I see. You believe, that do you?' was the acceptable sentence.

'For Christ's sake Anthony, why would he lie to me? Just because you don't like the guy...'

'Hey!' Anthony raised his voice. 'Let's not lose sight of what happened this morning. You were with him all night. He's a fucking addict and he's a loser, he's probably given you something.'

'Anthony;' Autumn rubbed her templates and shut her eyes temporarily. 'Do you honestly think Jerry would give me drugs?'

'I don't know. Maybe.'

She opened her eyes again. 'Jerry is harmless. He acts like he's tough but he's just a kid. He's not capable of hurting anyone.'

'That's not what the papers say.'

'Don't believe... look, I'm defending a guy I don't like. If I had the slightest inkling he had something to do with this, I'd have played up on it. But I *know*. I know it's got nothing to do with him.'

Anthony stayed silent for a while, talking himself into believing Autumn's hand-on-heart that Jerry was innocent to all this, despite his own feelings.

'I think you should have a drug test back in England, just to be sure,' was his meeting her halfway.

'No way,' was her decline to the offer. 'uh-uh. I'm not going anywhere near a hospital and I'm not going anywhere near a doctor.' Her tone was so passionate he could almost hear the lump forming in her dry throat.

He had been expecting an answer like that. His wife had been in and out of hospitals her entire childhood, and she had once told him that she had hated them since she could remember. But pushing a premature, stillborn, deformed baby boy out in one had been the breaker. For the first few months after it happened she had nightmares of being wheeled down a hospital ward, strapped to the bed with her baby crying from inside her. She woke up screaming once or twice when her little Alex was really giving it blue mercy. Other than that she would just weep in her sleep, the corridor lights stinging her eyes once every few seconds as her bed moved under them. There was no way she'd set foot in a hospital again, and forget a drug test from home, to Autumn that would be letting the demon in a white coat into her escape. Anthony understood this.

'Okay, okay. I'll make you a deal then. If you see anything else, any more worms, we have got to see someone about it, alright?' Anthony tried again, wishing, out of all the mental blocks in the world, his wife didn't have this one.

Autumn nodded emptily and falsely. Her thoughts turned bluntly to remembering the white walls and worried faces that were once surrounding her, fast and panicking.

When her eyes eventually turned glassy, her husband stood from his seat and embraced her with understanding arms. They didn't cry or speak a word they were thinking because they didn't need to. It was in the air.

He was taken, he was taken and now I'm going crazy I'm going crazy and the whole world will find out, they'll point their fingers they'll say Alex? Alex where's Alex, hey crazy fallen star where's your little boy today, huh? They'll laugh where's Alex, crazy cuckoo brains!

Shhh, don't let this happen Lucy. Don't make yourself so much worse. Please just go back to being happy and beautiful, Lucy. Shhh…

They stayed locked in silent conversation, both thinking sad thoughts and, man, this isn't good. They stayed locked for two minutes before Autumn pulled away and left the private balcony with her head down solemnly.

The flight back to England was quiet. Autumn and Anthony sat in near silence the whole way, trying to get their head's around such a strange weekend. By the time they landed at Heathrow the two of them just wanted to be back home, back to normality and to be able stop thinking about this whole disaster of a weekend… aside from the award of-course.

CHAPTER 3

We've been driving for a while now but don't get tired, my dear, we're nearly there. You see, our couple's house is set in the southern countryside away from the traffic and congestion of the big, lonely city. As we finally pull up to it we both look in awe at the enormous manor with several stained windows and acres of land.

Once through the electric security gates, the driveway is wide and circular with a fountain sporting a Greek God among lilies in the middle. You nod your head with approval and I like it too, it looks... ancient. This property has seen generations of the rich and famous pass through its rooms; some staying for years upon years, others fleeting by so fast the walls had not even had time to recognise the change. Anthony and Autumn have been here for only two years, my friend, which is nothing compared to the manor's vast history. Before this massive achievement, Anthony had lived in a London penthouse and Autumn had lived in LA. They were now settled down together and had chosen their spot wisely. You comment on how clean and fresh the air is and it makes me proud that you like it out here.

Can you see over to the far right of the grounds (you may have to stand back a bit) on the horizon? Can you see that old barn? The same family has owned that for two hundred years and it's still a working farm today. The only other houses are those of the equally rich, but of-course I don't need to tell you that, you saw them on the way in; the council don't rent out houses like *that*! Anthony and Autumn fit in to this part of society like a glove, and their plan is to keep it that way for a very long time.

The double doors at the front of the house are made of thick dark wood with black cast iron latches and spokes. They were put on in the 1940s and the owner at the time did a very good job of making the brand new addition look almost medieval. It was a marvellous idea and it ties up the style of the exterior nicely. The fountain in the middle of the driveway has been here as long as the house and was used in the past as a roundabout for carriages dropping off and picking up, but due to the fact Autumn and Anthony very rarely throw parties it is now used as an exquisite focal point, and that it is.

The house itself stands grandly boasting stone, dark brown exterior beams and white washed external walls. It has been renovated and changed a hundred times but respectfully its character has remained the same. To the left of the manor stands what used to be stables, but is now a garage able to hold six cars.

We both run laughing up to the front doors and push them open. *But wait! What's this? Immediately both reader and writer are stopped in their tracks! Holy moly! They didn't expect it to be **this** nice!*

The interior design of this place is immediately breathtaking.

We are faced with a vast reception area and hallway decorated expensively with oak, oil paintings and handmade Indian rugs. A grand staircase starts to our left but as it climbs to the first floor it winds over to our middle vision. Archways, cubby holes and half a dozen heavy oak doors also look back silently at our astonished faces.

You mutter something under your breath as you continue to take in the sights.

'Apparently Dino Egidio designed and remodelled the interiors for 'em just last year,' I inform. 'It didn't look owt like this before.'

'Who's he?' you inquire.

'He's an Italian interior designer. They flew him over and gave him full responsibility of the décor and budget.'

'They made a good decision,' you nod, aware of the obvious understatement. 'How much did it all cost?'

'I dread to think,' I reply.

We stand there admiring the décor for a little while before our curiosity gets the better of us and we walk through the nearest door to our left, wearing cheeky smiles, to explore a little.

We open the door inwards and are faced with a massive designer kitchen. Marble islands and breakfast bars break up the large floorspace this room boasts, and what used to be one of two utility rooms has been successfully converted into a cove that houses the largest stove system I have ever seen. We both gaze around in awe for a moment before you joke that you wouldn't mind living here and I laugh back: 'tell me about it.'

Walking through the extensive kitchen area we come to an archway that leads us to a large conservatory. This floor to ceiling glass room looks out to the manor's amazing back and side gardens which are tended to by Arnold Sanders, who has seen three families come and go during his forty years here. The autumn grass is cloaked with masses of orange, red and brown leaves. It looks beautiful and it makes me want to don Wellingtons like a child and go out and play in it.

You want to see what's next so you wander off over to the right hand side of the ground floor to roam around on your own. The first door you open leads to a full sized downstairs bathroom covered floor to ceiling in marble tiles. With an astounded shake of the head you then move over to and down the polished wood stairs that lead to the basement. Did you know this level used to be the maid's quarters? Yeah, I know. You'd never guess now! The entire lower level is now a fully functioning private bar furnished to mirror something you would walk into in New York. You wander around just long enough to consider pouring yourself a drink before making a swift exit to somewhere with a little less temptation.

Back up to the ground floor and you take in an old library now mostly used as an office, then an extension housing an indoor swimming pool, steam room and shower-block. Man, these people really know how to live. Finally you get to the two main rooms running the full length of the house – the rich lounge and tremendous dining room.

You walk around both rooms taking in the sights and admiring their taste before calling me back through to the hall to check out upstairs. I can tell you are pleased I left you to it for a bit there… although, I am too. Just after you wandered off I opened their larder fridge and found some squeezy cheese. I then accidentally came across some crackers and a knife. Oh well, at least one of us can resist temptation, eh?

With crumbs on my top and you talking incessantly about what you'd found I follow you up the winding staircase up to the top floor. We find six heavy doors all leading to different rooms ahead of us so we both instinctively pick a door and excitedly make our way to opening it. I walk into the elegantly decorated and massive master bedroom complete with ensuite and two walk-in wardrobes, while your first door leads you to a guest bedroom also with private bathroom.

We leave each other to our own devices again and go off exploring. I run for the far end door and open it to find a circuit training room with laminate flooring, mirrored walls and plenty of keep fit equipment.

'Whoa, they've got a gym!' I call to you. 'I wonder if they actually use this stuff!'

I hear you call back 'probably' and say you've just found another spare bedroom.

I leave the gym pretty sharpish 'cause the fitness equipment is out-phasing me, and move on to the family bathroom.

'Bloody hell,' I mutter, walking in.

This interior designers' wet dream would not look out of place in the modern day, and I forget we are in the year 1990 looking around me. The design is so perfect it still looks cutting edge, even though it is floor to ceiling in wood. I take in a wet room with four showerheads and sliding glass doors, a steam-room, a huge risen corner bath, two massive sinks, a toilet, and a bidet – that I can bet my bottom dollar they never use.

Imported Scandinavian pine is everywhere and the bathroom's style is so convincingly European that I'm sure if I opened one of the windows I would be looking out onto mountains. Wooden ceiling beams and split-levelled floors complement the whole feeling of luxury that this room creates.

The temptation to take a bath in this amazing room is so overwhelming my body begins to ache a little. To rid myself of the yearning I take a walk around the whole room, mess with the taps a bit, then over to a cupboard and open it to a blast of hot air. Ladies and gentlemen, you're not going to believe this but they even have a constantly heated towel room. I take out a warm fluffy towel and bury my face in it, breathing in the heat and smell of fabric conditioner it radiates.

From behind me I hear you enter the room and begin to walk over to me. I open my eyes and greet you. I am just about to hand you the towel when I clock your expression. Instead I ask you what's wrong and without much of a speech you make me put the towel back and lead me through to an empty blue room.

I can suddenly see what brought your spirits down so fast, for it's had that effect on me too. This sad space is seemingly forgotten about. The air feels heavy with dust... or is that just melancholy? We are in the doorway of what was once meant to be a nursery. We know that because near the window a wooden baby mobile hangs down from the ceiling in solitude. We both stand mesmerised by this poignant message although neither of us is inclined to venture in any further to get a better look. We can see from here that it is made up of several painted mushrooms on different lengths of string. What we can't see is that the mushrooms have huge smiles painted on them. The longer we stare at the mobile the more we understand the extent to which Autumn and Anthony are unable to let go, and suddenly this big, beautiful house seems empty and sad. Crushing feelings of pity wash over us and it doesn't take long until we are forced to leave by the emotion.

As we shut the door and make our way back downstairs we are quiet, but leave knowing that we still had fun. Despite the sadness of one baby boy, the house is amazing and I'm glad you came with me to see it before they got home.

CHAPTER 4

The five days following his arrival home dragged by in a haze of heavy feeling and anxiety for our man Anthony Denharden.

Building worry for his wife kept him occupied enough not to sleep and his upcoming attempt to woo Martin Gate was also biting at his nerves. Autumn had scared the shit out of him a few days ago and since then the two had behaved like strangers around one another. Anthony simply couldn't talk to her. He had so much he wanted to say, so many suggestions to make, so many theories to discuss... but he just couldn't. It was as though an invisible wall had built itself up around his wife and he could sense that there'd be no getting through. The feeling was all too familiar.

The subject of his concern on the other hand had passed the stage of anxiety and was now engulfed in a building sense of panic. Tiny black dots had planted themselves in Autumn's vision upon returning home and the night terrors she thought she'd seen the back of were distorting her sleep again. The knowledge of such disruptive tendencies reappearing, coupled with the brand new problem of troubled eyesight, were enough to whip Autumn Leigh's focus into a foamy lather of confusion and dread.

Have you ever experienced night terrors? If you have, you'll know why they pose acute concern to our girl. If not, let me fill you in. First off, I have never experienced night terrors myself, but I have seen several documentaries and read into their effects, as well as knowing a handful of people that suffer from the odd one themselves, and by all accounts it's not the most pleasant of experiences.

My friend Sally once told me of waking up to hands decorated in henna dancing around her bed. She was unable to move or turn away and the experience was terrifying for her.

For years as a child and young teenager Autumn would stare wide eyed at her bedside lamp, forcing away slumber, scared of what her subconscious would bring. Sometimes her night terrors were so real that Autumn would be sure that it was more than her imagination, that it was an actual attack. And maybe she was right, maybe on occasion they were attacks of schizophrenia and – in turn – panic. Like a mugger on the prowl, maybe they struck in the dark. We'll never know for sure, but what is certain is the fact that our leading lady suffered throughout the night consistently for one reason or another.

It was only when Autumn started fainting through lack of sleep at fourteen that her parents found out there was a problem and medication was swiftly prescribed. The tablets had eased the night terrors and they had remained under control for many years... up until now.

She had been plagued with them every night since the awards party and they weren't easing up. Last night she had scrambled from her bed and darted to the window, begging to be let out because the dust cloths were coming. It took about five seconds for Autumn to realise what she was doing but by then it had been too late. Anthony was bolt upright; she had been witnessed. Autumn began to make her way back to the bed, mumbling in embarrassed tones that she hadn't realised she wasn't dreaming anymore, and hoping Anthony would just go back to sleep. Instead he wrapped his body around hers and asked her if everything was okay, but Autumn refused to discuss the matter further, easing him off by dismissing it as another odd dream. Sorry for waking you, goodnight honey. *Holy shit I am getting worse. It's happening, madness is descending.*

And then, throughout her waking hours, were the dots. The dots were new and that's what scared Autumn the most. These were a step up on the scale, surely?

To start with there had only been one. She'd noticed it in the car on the way back from the airport. It was only about the size of a pinprick, near the bottom of the field of vision in her right eye. When she moved her head it moved with it, when she moved her eyeball away she could not see it and when it was on a black background it disappeared into it. It was only apparent on light backgrounds, like black text.

100

This odd dot had puzzled her but she had not connected it to the worms incident to start with. In fact she had thought that it was dirt or soot and asked Anthony to have a look. It was only when he found nothing out of the ordinary that the possibility of it being another illusion arose within her and she stopped mentioning it.

However, it was only after she had crawled exhausted up to bed at seven that evening and awoke at midday the next day that she began to think that something serious might be wrong. For there were now another two dots violating her vision, one to the right of the first dot in her right eye, and the other near the top of the sight capacity in her left eye. Autumn Leigh's concern was catapulted into horror at the thought of the dots continuing to grow and breed until she would eventually become blind. Luckily, the following seventy-two hours brought comfort with the fact that the dots did not multiply as she had feared, and her eye sight remained intact. But, on the same hand, nor did they fade as she had hoped.

So Autumn Leigh resigned herself to this new soiled view of the world and that from now on her landscapes would be discoloured with these three mysterious dots watching on too, stagnant and forbidding, with no amount of water or blinking washing them away.

Anthony was worried about the woman he loved; yes, in that sub-normal way he was always worried about her, but a lot more so now. Once tonight was over and done with, Anthony thought as he watched the Saturday sun cloud over, then he would dedicate his entire time to his wife. It was only this morning that he had noticed her blinking heavily and twitching her head to the side as she did so. He had asked her about it and she said she was tired. He chose to accept this as the truth, but deep down he did not believe it. There were little things, things that he had chosen to ignore over these past few days, which had started praying on his mind with force this morning.

I would like it, my friend, if we could talk to Anthony now; we don't have to but he's a nice enough guy and I know you'll like each other. It's just after midday and he's sitting in the conservatory reading through a script that his agent had forwarded just today by special delivery. It's nothing jaw-dropping and it would mean spending six months filming on location in Texas but, although his mind is made up to turn it down, it still makes interesting reading on a dreary afternoon. He's obviously a bit bored.

Let's go see him.

The first glance we get of him, a millisecond before he notices us, is of him looking troubled. His script is on the sofa seat next to him and he is looking out towards the garden, his eyes deep somewhere else. The garden is slippery and greasy with fine September rain; faint tip taps are softly evident upon the roof of this warm glass room. It's peaceful – inspiring even – and everything's tidy and neat. As we walk further in, Anthony snaps out of his deep-thought trance and stands up to shake our hands, before offering us the two wicker chairs facing him to sit on. As we do so he sits back down, throwing his right foot over his left thigh the way self-confident men do, then resting his right arm on the leg that's raised. He's not wearing any socks or shoes and it gives us the impression of informality. It's nice and all, but our man looks anxious and older in real life, up close.

'How are you?' I ask first, to break the ice.

Anthony shrugs, smiling. 'I'm not too bad, thanks. How are you two?'

We both say 'fine thanks' and you ask him if he's excited about tonight.

'Oh yeah. Well, it's an important night tonight. The rest of my career depends on getting this part. It's making me really, um,' he searches for the word, using his hands to draw circles through the air as he thinks. '…On edge.'

'And how is your wife?' you ask casually.

'She's great, thanks,' Anthony nods. He has got privacy down to a tee and I don't think he's going to share his personal feelings with us. 'She won an Epic Award last week. Did you see the awards?'

'We were there,' I reply, missing out the words 'kind of'. You snigger slightly at this.

'Oh, were you? Sorry, I didn't see you. But, yeah, she was thrilled. She really deserved it.'

Anthony goes quiet for a moment then grits his teeth like he's experiencing heartburn.

Before either of us has chance to ask him what was wrong he says: 'sorry if I seem distant. You have no idea how nerve-wracking it is trying to impress Martin Gate. Every time I think about tonight my stomach turns.'

'I thought you seemed worried about something,' I say.

'I'm not a natural worrier, don't think that, but Martin makes the epics, yeah? He makes the timeless blockbusters that go down in history. If I can be a part of that, then it will straight catapult me into the hall of fame. I spoke to him properly for the first time at the awards party. I'm not kidding, it took a lot of nerve to invite myself onto the table of the biggies, but as luck would have it, he seemed to like me. He loves England, you see, so we spent a lot of the time talking about my accent and where I grew up. We didn't get around to discussing the film though; that's why I asked him and his wife over for dinner tonight, because as luck would have it, he's over here on business…'

'Woah, that was lucky,' I say.

'Yeah,' he nods. 'It's just really important to me that I get a *chance* to work with him: I really look up to him. I think he likes me so I must be in with *some* sort of chance. Well, he likes my accent anyway. He's just… he's so influential. Do you know what I mean?'

We both nod.

'Where's your Lucy?' I ask, knowing he prefers her real name to her stage name when they're not in public.

'She's in yoga. No, no, I tell a lie. She was in yoga this morning, now she's having a facial or a massage or something,' Anthony replies. He smiles, then adds, pointing; 'I recognise your accent.'

'Yorkshire,' I smile.

'You too?' he laughs. 'I was brought up there, you know? I love the place. Love it. I'd like to move back but Lucy wants to stay near London – agents an' all. She likes the fast lane, I like the countryside. This is our compromise.' Anthony looks around the room, then finishes it with: 'Always will be a northern lad at heart, though.'

Anthony uses his hands constantly to express himself when he talks. It's cute. His speech is hinting the Yorkshire accent a little thicker than usual – he knows he doesn't have to put up a mask when talking with us. I can see how his entire face has lightened up; he obviously is feeling refreshingly comfortable with our presence.

'Anthony, this is hard to say…' You lean forward slightly as you begin speaking, your hunger for knowledge forcing you to repeat the question Anthony so quickly disregarded not one minute ago. 'But we both know about Lucy. So, come on, how is she really?'

'I'm sorry, I don't follow you,' Anthony lies, eyeing us carefully. I feel he has suddenly closed up again. 'Lucy won an incredibly prestigious award a few days ago… she's on top of the world.'

There's a strained silence and your eyes dart in my direction just long enough for me to catch.

'We're as much of you as you yourself are, Anthony,' I say softly. 'We know what's going on… it would just be good to hear your take on it. My friend and I are not here to dig: we're here to talk.'

Anthony is looking at us quite suspiciously now. He's not at all threatening or unpleasant towards us, just mildly bemused.

'Well,' he laughs hollowly, 'if *you* know so much about her, maybe you could enlighten *me* about it.'

You shift in your chair and look out at the garden. I get the impression that this is not the most comfortable you have ever felt. In fact, I get the impression that you think we should just leave him alone. Bear with me. Honestly, it'll be alright.

'I know only what you know,' I shrug. 'I just think it would be good for the story if we could…'

'Does Jerry Tilsey have anything to do with her behaving like this?' Anthony interrupts.

'I…' Now I'm put in it without a paddle. I scratch the back of my head, feeling awkward. 'Anthony,' I sigh. 'I can't talk to you about things like that. I'm sorry.'

Anthony nods, his teeth gritted.

'I *can't.*'

'Okay,' he murmurs.

I genuinely wish this were a short story so I could tell him and write *The End…* but it's not and there are still many more planes to crash into this ocean. If I tell him it will bugger everything up.

'Are you worried about her?' I ask.

He nods slowly and thoughtfully, and says 'yeah' through a deep sigh as he sits back in his chair.

'Why?' you join in again.

He pauses, as if to argue with himself about letting his guard down, then says: 'She's started twitching, blinking really heavy.'

He goes quiet again. He looks slightly uneasy and most definitely troubled. 'Without going too much into detail, she had this weird hallucination a few days ago and it scared the shit out of me, basically. Worst thing is she's being so unhelpful about sorting it – so it's causing tension. She thinks it's nothing, see, and I don't even know if she realises she's twitching yet. I haven't spoken to her about it. She's been different ever since I left her with some of her bloody cast members when I was talking with Martin at the party.'

'Different how?'

'It's weird, it's… hard to describe. She was found unconscious at the party, right? Then, the morning after, she starts seeing things that aren't there and now she's hardly talking to me.' Anthony rubs his face with his hands. 'Her night terrors have started up again too but she won't talk about that either.'

'Again?' you question.

'Well yeah, she used to suffer from them years ago but she got some pills to stop it. Well, anyway, I think they've started up again. It's frightening. She's fragile at the best of times, she always has been. I think she might be having some sort of a breakdown or something. She *needs* to see the doctor, but she just won't go.'

'Are you worried about her for tonight?' I ask.

'Tonight? God no. Don't forget, we're trained how to behave in public. Tonight Martin and his wife will have no idea of any trouble we might be having. Lucy's a full time actress; it's not just in front of a camera when the act comes on. It's in front of anyone.'

'Do you do it?'

''Course I do. Wish I didn't have to, like. But, that's the way it is. To be honest I was never bothered about fame or acting when I was a young 'un, but when we moved down to London I caught the bug. I kind of got into it by accident. But now I'm doing it, I want to take it all the way. To do that, you have to act constantly. You can't have an argument and then go down the shops and say the wife's been biting my head off this morning, you'd have massively exaggerated stories in the papers before you'd even realise what you'd said. Always wear a smile: that's the best way.'

'It's a shame you have to do that, though.'

'Yeah, but it's part and parcel of the job, int it? You can't be a successful actor without fame.'

'No, guess not,' we both say, agreeing with him.

'Are you glad you took this road?' you ask.

'Oh, well of-course I am,' Anthony answers. 'I wouldn't have met Lucy otherwise, and look at how I live. I don't regret choosing this way of life at all – it's been very good for me. I've had a very good life.'

'Do you ever hear anything of your dad?' you ask, not quite meaning the question to spike Anthony as it does.

His eyebrows fall a little and form wrinkles on the top of his nose. He then breaks off eye contact with us and fidgets a bit.

'He died,' he says plainly. 'He beat my mother, chased us away from our home, lied to the papers about me... and then he died.'

In a heart-stopping moment I realise that I haven't mentioned to you that Anthony's dad died not long after Anthony swept Hollywood off its feet. Shit, shit and more shit – I'm sorry!

Anthony found out because it was in the papers; the jilted father.

He had sold his story to all and sundry, claiming that Louise fled him over an affair and took his son with her – poor man. Poor forgotten daddy... and now his son is living in a mansion and poor old pa is still living in a tiny council flat in Moss Side. He had even let the press into his sordid little grief-hole to take pictures, so the papers could compare them to pictures of Anthony's mansion; just for that extra bit of sympathy and publicity. Of-course, Anthony did not comment; he let the old man have his way. He did not lower to his level. He could have, he could have pointed out things that his father could go to jail for. But he hid instead. He hid and blocked it. Christ, I can't believe I brought you here to talk to him without telling you that. I am soooo sorry. You must think I'm a right knob-jockey now.

A sudden awkward silence falls upon us and Anthony looks at his chrome watch. His eyes widen slightly and he says: 'Well, if you don't mind, I think Lucy should be finishing her beauty stuff soon, so I better start preparing the kitchen for our masterpiece.'

'You cook?' I ask, clearing my throat, glad of the change of subject.

'No, Lucy does all the cooking, I'm the apprentice. She prides herself on it, you know. She's a great cook, her dad's a chef.'

'You still seem very much in love,' you point out. Anthony is pleased you said this – the soft smile that forms on his face tells us so.

'We are. Everyone has their hard times, don't they? This is just one of them. I'll get her to a doctor and get her sorted. Everything will be fine soon.'

'Good, I hope so,' you nod as we both stand up, making the wicker furniture creak. 'It's been nice meeting you. Best of luck with the film part.'

'Thank you very much. I'm sorry we couldn't chat for longer,' Anthony smiles, standing also and holding out his hand for us to shake.

As we do so he says: 'It's been a pleasure talking to you both. It's nice to be able to talk sometimes. Lucy is the only friend I've got really, and sometimes I can't talk to her either. It builds up and… you know what I mean… it can get you down sometimes. I feel better having someone to talk to every now and again, even if it was only brief. Thank you.'

We nod, say goodbye and walk out of the room.

It occurs to me for the first time that Anthony is a very lonely man.

After attempting to relax with a morning of yoga and facials, Autumn Leigh had said goodbye to her trainer and beauty therapist and had run herself a bath. Her beauty therapist had asked why Autumn was blinking sporadically and after Autumn's believable excuse of tiredness, the woman covering the movie-star in cucumber oil pointed out that it would wrinkle her eyes, doing that. That was half an hour ago. Now instead of screwing her eyes tightly shut, Autumn closed them gently and carefully, like a day-to-day blink in slow motion. Wrinkles were the last thing she needed.

The bathroom was thick with steam as Autumn undressed, and getting into the tub, she realised she had run the water too hot.

Rather than running the cold tap and opening the window, Autumn simply clenched her teeth and lowered her entire body in.

Her skin was flushing crimson the second it made contact with the liquid and she could feel delicate pins and needles stinging her feet in protest to the sickeningly high temperatures. Autumn Leigh cringed and singed until eventually she was submerged in the semi-boiling water, unable to move because every time she did it hurt.

You are probably gathering – or if not, then you will soon – that there are many things about this woman that we will never be able to understand, so let's just painfully accept the fact that she's scalding herself and carry on.

Autumn Leigh lay with parched skin hanging from her bones and began thinking that she just could not be bothered entertaining tonight. In fact, if she was being honest with herself about it, it was the last thing she wanted to do. Her head had felt like a lead weight all morning and it was taking her jet lag longer than usual to wear off. Right now a long sleep was all she craved but she had to impress Martin and Hannah (*was it Hannah? Or was it Sarah? Hannah, Sarah, whatever*) tonight. The more Autumn lay thinking about it the more it riled her...

Anthony just goes right ahead and invites around Mr Big and his pretty little trophy wife and I have to pretend I'm interested in all Mr high-and-mighty's bullshit and pretend I like his wife's dress and pretend, pretend, pretend...

Come on, you must know the feeling – she's not exactly being out of order here. You know when sometimes you have plans that involve being social, yet a couple of hours before the event you feel tired or ill and you begin to wish that you were just staying in with a bowl of soup and a blanket? Well multiply that by ten and imagine how Autumn's feeling; fearing for both her physical *and* mental health!

I'm obviously fucking tired but all Anthony's bothered about is what we're cooking Martin for dinner, and whether Martin will be able to find the house alright, and what kind of music does Martin like? She shook her head with disgust, realised with a jolt how uncomfortable this bath was, and then forgot again, going back to her thoughts. *Sometimes Anthony can be so fucking dumb. He has no idea just how fucking pathetic he can be. Does he honestly think Martin will cast him in his film just because Anthony takes his coat off for him at the door and pours his wine and licks his fucking shoes clean?*

The very thought of her husband kissing Martin Gate's big white New Yawk ass caused Autumn's face to contort into an ugly display of revulsion.

...and while everyone's laughing at him I have to cringe back into the shadows, whereas in reality I should be laughing with them for my reputation's sake. I can't believe all this time I have just put up with that fucking embarrassment. What if people tarnish me with the same brush? What if they think that because I'm his wife I must be desperate and pitiable too? Oh God, why did I marry this loser?

Autumn Leigh began to despair with the sudden awareness that she had ruined her own life by marrying a guy that was nowhere near as great as her. However, at the same time, allowing herself to get her claws out and dig them into this excuse for a man was proving quite enjoyable...

I've married a loser. A winner like me should not associate with losers. If I hadn't have married him I'd be living in the city with a man the world looks up to, a man that is everything a real man should be, a man that could give me children, a man that I could be proud of. Why am I actually with this guy? Sympathy? Pity? Sometimes I just want to kill him to spare him of the mortification he causes himself and everyone around him. He's asking for it and one day someone might just have enough of his personality and shoot him in the street. I'd be upset but I could understand it, sometimes I myself could just wrap...

The bathroom door clicked open and blanked her thoughts. It was Anthony: her husband. The man she loved... one of life's good guys. Up until just now Autumn's heart had been beating fast with anger, her fists had been tightening themselves into little balls of bones, but the sound of the door opening stopped her rage like it would a masturbating teenager.

'Hello, you,' her loving husband said, peeking his head around the door. 'I just wondered when you were getting out?'

Autumn, forgetting her rage, asked what time it was then replied: 'I won't be long now. This water's too hot anyway, it's making me feel dizzy.'

'Okay, sweetpea. I love you.'

'I love you too, honey,' Autumn smiled genuinely.

Anthony shut the door and Autumn was left alone with her thoughts once more, only *what was I thinking about? Oh, yes, tonight. I need to get out now to start preparing the food, pick out my dress, although I think I'm going to go with my French red one... or what about the blue? No, no, that needs altering. Yes, the red. Definitely the red...*

The feelings of near hatred had disappeared without a trace and Autumn went back to feeling nothing but love for her husband, totally forgetting that she was just about to think about wrapping her hands around his neck and squeezing them tightly until he went purple and stopped gurgling, until he stopped kissing ass.

She had been on the verge of engulfing herself with extreme feelings of deep hatred and, if Anthony had have come through the door only ten minutes later, he would have found the beautiful love of his life thrashing around in the skin-scorching water. He would have found her cursing and pulling at her own hair and her eyes would be rolling back and forth into her head. He would have stood in the doorway and said 'sweetpea?' in a quiet, scared tone. He would have thought *my wife is possessed. She's possessed by the devil*. He would not have known what to do.

However both husband and wife were spared of such a scene and Autumn Leigh pulled herself out of the bath the very picture of calm. Autumn left the bathroom and journeyed into the bedroom, where she dropped all towels and her robe to take in her naked body in the full length mirror. It was then that the better side of this troubled woman fully returned to us, if not only for a few more hours. Just as quickly as our girl had left us just then in the bathroom *my wife is possessed by the devil* she returned in full Autumn Leigh power… and it would have been triumphant too if she had realised that she'd ever left us in the first place.

Staring at her beautiful body without the censorship of clothes was just what she needed to bring back the sanity that provides a pleasant environment for everyone.

The fuzziness that had covered her mind, like hands-over-eyes, over the past few days took a backseat and the sharpness and sexiness of Autumn Leigh walked to the front row and sat down in the chair with the best view, with the seat still warm from where insanity had been sitting. Autumn Leigh felt a slight, niggling suspicion that she had almost forgotten who she was for a day or two. And now, for the first time since she accepted the award, she saw herself for what she really was again: a beautiful, famous woman and icon to the world.

The cloud of sickness lifted from above Autumn's head and her face softened. She ran her fingers over the fine contours of her breasts and turned around slightly to view her backside: still perfect. She was still perfect. She stood in the mirror for several more minutes, performing soft poses. By now her mood had turned and the person that had been raging in the bath was now long gone. This is who she was, who she wanted to be: a movie-star, a woman who had just won an important award for being successful, a sex symbol, one half of a youthful and happy marriage: a winner.

Autumn never realised it at the time, or ever again for that matter, but the black dots that had been troubling her vision for the past couple of days had gone completely in the time that she had been looking at herself. She had already forgotten about them. The tiredness, headache and hangover feeling had faded too and for this short period of time Autumn Leigh was herself again, forgetting about the person that she had been since the morning after the award party. Autumn remembered gleefully that she had to get on with her second biggest passion to acting: cooking. She squealed almost like a teenager as she ran over to her closet, clapping her hands in excitement over getting dressed up.

What we just witnessed there was Autumn Leigh's personality showing its first large cracks, cracks that will eventually lead to her ultimate downfall. My dear friend, meet Jekyl: my dear friend, meet Hyde.

I know for a fact that if we were to ask Autumn: 'What was with those dots in your vision?' she would not have a clue what we were referring to.

'Dots? What are you talking about? Why would I have *dots* in my vision?'

If she really thought about it, the dots may have seemed vaguely familiar, like some sort of hazy dream from years ago, but she wouldn't allow her mind to think about it. *What dots?* Just like if she'd have known that she had been thinking such hateful thoughts about Anthony a moment ago. She would detest herself and feel bad about it for years if she realised that she was capable of thinking so terribly about the man she loved. So, without a care in the world, Autumn got into her cooking clothes; a t-shirt and denim shorts, before skipping down to the kitchen as happy as the day she got married. *What dots?*

'And what is on the platter tonight, Mrs Denharden?' Anthony asked in his best jolly good, yes, yes accent as he watched his wife bend over to the bottom compartment of their designer fridge. She had trotted downstairs in good humour, much to Anthony's surprise and relief, and he had decided to honour and encourage that. He had also noticed that the heavy blinking had gone completely. This made him think that she had been incredibly stressed out and after her treatments of this morning the tension had lifted and everything was back to normal now. He had to think that anyway – if he carried on feeling so wound up himself, he would surely appear nervy and odd to Martin Gate. That was not the impression he wanted to give. *Relax, man, relax.* He would think about all that just as soon as tonight was out of the way but at this very moment he could have kissed the feet of his temporarily estranged wife for stabilising herself just in time.

'Tonight, Sir Anthony of England,' Autumn mocked humorously as she displayed perfect legs while rooting around in the large fridge, still bent over; 'we have oysters au natural for starters, which are to be made with just in season Colchester oysters...' Autumn stood up out of the fridge as she spoke and placed an oversized 6Ib gammon joint onto the worktop, and counted on her fingers with each item she added, '...served with lemon and cayenne pepper. Main course will be spiced orange gammon, which is why I have got the gammon out now – to soak for two hours. That will be served with an orange caramel glaze and a refreshing claret wine. Dessert will be mandarin liqueur gateau, and the petit fours are brandy snaps and coffee éclairs, which I think will complement my fresh coffee marvellously. Would sir care for anything else?'

'Good grief darling, that sounds exquisite! You really are supreme!' Anthony beamed, keeping up the accent. Autumn laughed and returned to her joint of gammon, proud of herself for being able to make such fine sounding dishes. 'But really,' Anthony's voice returned to normal: 'That sounds brilliant.'

He wanted to talk to his wife about how she had been for the last five days, he wanted to thank her for being in such a good mood for a change and he wanted to tell her that she looked beautiful when she smiled. Only he couldn't, he couldn't go that deep with her.

Anthony likes to believe that his wife is his best friend and that they can talk about anything. But they can't. He can hardly talk to her at all, in the same way that she can't talk to him. Since their son was... erm, born... they barely scratched the surface of anything meaningful at all. They could never sit under the stars all night and discuss their thoughts on how the human race got here and they would never question anything regarding feelings or opinions. It was too deep. Of-course, in the beginning it was different. But now, well.

'If I hadn't have been an actress I'd have been a chef,' Autumn smiled truthfully. She loved cooking and was able to make a spellbinding dish out of almost anything put in front of her. She got it from her father. As Autumn opened another kitchen drawer to get the necessary utensils out, she pondered making her own cookery book. She decided she would mention it to her agent the next time they spoke.

The gate buzzer had sounded at seven-forty and Autumn had let Martin, Hannah and their driver into the grounds.

'See, I told you they wouldn't be long.' Anthony kissed his wife as they waited to greet their late guests at the front door.

'Well, the oysters au natural have to be served before eight, or else they won't be fresh.'

'Sweetpea.' Anthony gave Autumn a glance that urged *forget about it* and Autumn returned it with a glance that said a thousand things. He chose to ignore it as his guests approached them at the door.

'Anthony, Autumn. Sorry we're late. Nothing pleases this woman, she'd look beautiful in a potato sack, but she still has to try on every dress she's bought before she'll leave the hotel room,' Martin laughed in his gritty New York accent.

'No problem, Martin. How are you doing?' Anthony shook Mr Gate's hand powerfully as he and his wife entered the house for the first time.

After ten minutes of polite small talk, everyone had settled down to his or her seat with a drink.

Autumn brought through everybody's starters and, acting more like a housewife than an A-list movie-star, sat down and wished for her guests to enjoy their food.

'Anthony, your wife looks stunning tonight, as always,' Martin stated with a mouth full of succulent sea produce.

'Thank you Martin. She does look like a princess in that dress.' Anthony winked at his wife.

'Where did you get the dress from, if you don't mind me asking?' Hannah joined in, all smiles and nerves as usual.

'Oh, this? I bought it from France in a small boutique. I've had it for years now.' Autumn passed off the short red number she was wearing along with diamond earrings and her hair pinned up to complement it.

Oysters au natural got thumbs up from everyone. Well, let's be honest, if it had tasted like shit it would still have got thumbs up from everyone, we both know that.

Anthony helped Autumn clear the plates and bring through the solid silver dishes of sauces, brilliantly cut oranges and carefully arranged salads.

Autumn removed the spiced orange gammon from the oven and with the help of meat forks placed it on the base of the main presentation dish. It smelled like heaven and had been cooked to perfection. She arranged the lettuce around the edges and garnished it with oranges and a few herbs just to add decoration. *Perfect*. Autumn carefully placed the large silver dome lid onto it and picked it up with oven gloves, watching her step as she re-entered the dinning room.

'Ta-da!' she sang as Anthony helped clear space for it in the middle of the table.

'Well it sure as hell smells nice. Take the lid off!' Martin commanded in his jolly laugh.

Anthony gave a mock drum role as Autumn took off the oven gloves and removed the lid.

'Mm-mm!' everyone sang in chorus, looking at the beautiful meal, large enough to feed eight.

'Wow!' Hannah cried. 'It's making my mouth water just looking at it.'

These voices, from the moment Autumn had taken the lid off, had become a distant echo. Instead of the spiced orange gammon surrounded by dressings and oranges, there lay a half-developed embryo.

It was Alex. *My baby boy.*

He was curled up among the lettuce, his head twice as large as the rest of his little body, his eyes open and black, his fingers webbed.

He looked cold, stiff, waiting to be eaten. Clinical wards and the odour of death had replaced the aroma of gammon and it smelt so strong it almost stung Autumn's nose. She could do nothing but stare, her mind blank of thoughts until –

'Hell's bells Autumn, are you going to carve it or do I have to eat it whole?' Martin piped up.

That was all it took for Autumn to drop the silver lid crashing to the floor and dart out leaving her baby blue and dead on a serving dish. All three people stood up from their seats with confusion skipping on their faces.

'Excuse me…' Anthony said as he left his chair to follow his wife. 'Please, help yourselves and begin your dinners.'

Once the door was shut Martin and Hannah shot each other a glance.

'Maybe she's ill?' Hannah suggested.

Autumn had not known where to turn as she bolted out of the room. She tried to climb the stairs but the more her body and mind came to terms with what she'd just seen the less her joints would allow her to move. By the time she'd dragged herself to the forth step, retching and clinging onto the handrail, Anthony had emerged from the dining room and was gasping at the scene before him.

'Lucy!' he cried in a whisper, running up to her.

'Up, up,' was all she could muster, her face drained of colour and entire body shaking violently.

All the feelings that had been slowly penetrating Autumn over the past few days were now pummelling her with such sudden force that her physical being was a pawn to the might and could only crumple beneath its power.

'Okay,' Anthony said as he picked his wife up and took her upstairs to their bedroom. He laid her on the bed and felt her forehead.

'Jesus Christ, are you alright?' *What's wrong with my wife?!*

She couldn't hear her husband, all she could hear was Martin saying he could eat her baby whole, all she could see were her baby's veins through clear skin, all she could smell was the reek of hospital wards.

'Lucy, what happened? Did you see more worms? What?'

Anthony's words were desperate and pleading and she heard him that time but her dry mouth could not let him know. He'd send her to hospital and that's where it happened and she'd rather die than go back there, she'd rather die.

I saw my baby, I saw my baby all prepared and ready to serve. Martin could eat my baby whole. I saw my baby surrounded by salad foods. I want to say this Anthony with your worried face but you'll send me back there and they won't find any drugs in my blood and they'll say it's just madness and they'll commit me and they'll say 'hey it's you with the dead baby' he'd have been two now, all blue eyes and blond hair not black eyes he had black eyes and clear skin and he wants to carve my Alex!

Her head began to shake as pictures of a few moments ago tormented her already cowering mind. She had to scream, she *had* to scream but her vocal chords were too tight to produce any sound. Anthony was holding her shoulders and watching her blank eyes dart around the room.

Panic began to build up in his throat and work its way to his eyes, they filled up with water and he so much wanted to cry.

'Oh God, Lucy! Oh God what do I do?' he pleaded.

A thousand thoughts flashed past him but they were all too fast for him to catch, so he sat beside his wife and allowed tears to fall down his face. *Why this, Lucy? Why this?*

'Cramp,' was the murmur after a minute's strained silence.

'What?' Anthony opened his red eyes.

'Cramp.' The voice that came out of her mouth didn't even sound like hers. 'I'm fine. Go.'

This was so hard for her but she had to do it, she had to cry and scream and she was busting to get it out but she couldn't do it around Anthony. She was saying words without trying to let the scream out but it was on its way. *Just leave! Don't ask me why just leave just go so I can mourn and scream and explode for what I just saw.*

'Cramp?'

'Yes.'

'Not worms?'

'No.'

'So what…'

'Go. I need sleep.'

'I can't…'

'*Go!*'

'Are you sure it's only cramp?'

'*Yes!*' she strained. The tears trapped under her eyes were beginning to hurt now; they needed to surface so badly.

'Um… okay. I'll come up and check on you in ten minutes. Is that al…'

'Just *fuck off*!' Autumn screamed.

With that and much physical hesitation, Anthony said no more and reluctantly left to rejoin his guests downstairs.

The second the bedroom door clicked shut Autumn turned and buried her head into her pillow. Deep, heavy sobs began hurling themselves uncontrollably into the material.

She punched the mattress beneath her and stifled her screaming as best she could so no-one would hear her and send her to hospital. Her stomach began to convulse and she threw up violently onto the bed sheets. The fact that she was actually doing it made her throw up again.

After the sickness had passed Autumn fell back into the pillow which was now heavily stained with red lipstick, pink blusher, pale foundation and black mascara. Her eyes were forced closed by the tears and all she wanted for this feeling to pass. The sobs became sorrowful cries for Alex and for help. She began to sweat due to being face down in the pillow for so long but Autumn didn't even have the energy left to move. At this point her mind overloaded and fused, forcing her to experience a sudden need for sleep. Slowly her breathing began to calm down and the tortured wails turned to soft whimpers.

It was at this point Anthony clicked the door open to check on her and, luckily, the sick was hidden by a mass of quilt. She was fine. Asleep. Cramp. He shut the door and went back down stairs feeling guilty for straight away assuming she had experienced another hallucination. No wonder she had been mad at him, it had only been a cramp. A bad one maybe, but a cramp none the less.

'How is she now?' Hannah asked when Anthony returned to the table.

'She's asleep. I can't apologise enough for that earlier, she has a very weak stomach and some things just make her so poorly.'

'Don't worry about it, these things happen,' Martin said with a mouth full of gammon.

She could feel her skin trembling against the crisp blue gown as she was rushed down a long corridor in her hospital bed. Each area of her body was a mass of delicate pimples and every one brushed the material with just enough pressure to make it feel like sandpaper as her body writhed with pain. Doctors and nurses were running by her side, talking to each other in medical terms she did not understand. Despite their panicked voices, she could hear her own whimpering above everything else.

She could see her own face; her frightened eyes crying hard, her teeth clamped together, her expression twisted with pain and, just to add to the ghost-like horror of it, the corridor lights illuminating it all every time she passed under them. After what seemed like a lifetime, a doctor squeezed her hand and said something about it being alright, and they finally reached the emergency room. Lucy Denharden was at this point hysterical, shrieking at such a volume that patients in the wards close by were sending out their sympathies to whoever was submitting those blood-curdling noises.

She was four months pregnant, four months pregnant and having contractions every two minutes. She knew her baby was dead, she could feel it. They could not perform a caesarean as the baby had already travelled too far so she just had to push, push, push to get death out of her....

Autumn Leigh twisted and turned in her sleep, sweating beads of ice and shaking her head in subliminal horror while Anthony cut the mandarin liqueur gateau for his two important guests.

A gas mask was placed over Mrs Denharden's mouth and nose as she began to hyperventilate. The exhausted patient grabbed it with both hands and tried her damnedest to breathe...

Downstairs Anthony, Martin and Hannah had decided to relocate to the lounge to eat their gateau in front of the log fire.

'The food was wonderful, Anthony. It's such a shame Autumn couldn't be with us all night,' Hannah stated. *And how strange.*

'Thank you. I'm sure she'll feel better in a little while; she probably just needs half an hour's sleep. You know, she makes all the food herself.'

'Not only do you have an acquired taste for dining, Anthony, but I also see you have a fine collection of records,' Martin said, scanning the CD collection by his side.

'Well, how about a little Van Morrison?' Anthony asked with a smile.

'Brilliant idea. You know I saw him live….'

'You have to *push*, Mrs Denharden!' the doctor cried.

'No! My baby's not ready to come out yet, I don't want to!' the patient yelled back, still mustering the energy to scream and pull at her hair.

'It will cause more damage if you try and hold on! The baby is on its way, Lucy, you *have* to push!' the doctor repeated.

The contractions were forcing her to push anyway but the thought of helping cruel, laughing nature to bring her baby out five months early just felt wrong. *Surely there must be some way to keep my baby in an incubator until he's due? I'm Autumn Leigh for Christ's sake! You can't let my baby die! Why aren't you helping me? Why are you allowing my baby to be born so fucking early?*

However, Lucy Denharden did push and the baby began to inch closer to the world. With every contraction she felt emptier and emptier. Her child's little body was nearly exiting hers, yet she knew its heartbeat and lifeline would always remain buried deep inside her, and would be until the day Lucy herself died.

Autumn was crying and murmuring in her sleep, unable to wake up. She was stuck in the worst few hours of her life and re-living every single second so clear and vivid it was like watching a home video.

No…No…

'You have a wonderful house, Anthony,' Hannah said as she glanced around the lounge from the antique Italian chair she was sitting on.

'Thank you. More wine?'

'We've got a head, doctor!' the midwife called with a shaky, stunned voice.

The doctor joined her and drew a sorrowful breath.

'Okay Lucy, just one more push,' he instructed, unable to look this pale woman in the eyes.

The pale woman shrieked an anguished cry as she gave all that was left in her and pushed....

Autumn let go of the pillow she had been clinging to and cried out.

'...so I said to Barney; 'hey! What the hell do you expect me to do...? Pay them by the hour?''

Hannah, although able to repeat this story line by line laughed heartily, as did Anthony.

'Cheers!' She held up her glass.

'Cheers!' The men clinked.

Lucy Denharden tried to hold up her head to view her baby but she was so drained it felt like a ten tonne weight.

'How is my baby? I want to see my baby,' she demanded weakly.

The midwife cut the umbilical cord, wrapped the baby in a white blanket and carried it briskly out of the room. The hospital staff were silent.

The doctor in charge walked to Lucy Denharden's bedside and cupped her hands. He too was sombre.

'Was my baby a... a boy or a girl?' Lucy sobbed, her eyes red and desperate for information.

'A boy,' the doctor answered, still holding her shaky, clammy hands. 'I'm afraid that your baby was born too premature to survive. I'm sorry.'

Not as sorry as I am.

'Can… can I see him?'

'That's most unadvisable, Mrs Denharden.'

'W-why?'

'Your baby was not fully developed, Mrs Denharden. I'm sorry.' *Your baby had clear skin, Mrs Denharden. Your baby had black eyes, Mrs Denharden. The internal organs showed the makings of a penis but your baby did not have any external sexual organs, Mrs Denharden; only due to my knowledge could I tell you your baby was a boy. Your baby was severely deformed, Mrs Denharden. I am sorry from the deepest, deepest part of my heart, Mrs Denharden. If you were to see your baby you would not be able to sleep for a very long time. Lucy, I am so very sorry.*

Laid in the hospital bed at that very moment, she squeezed the kind doctor's hand, shut her eyes tight and screamed louder than what she thought possible. She screamed for her dead baby, she screamed for herself, she screamed for Anthony, she screamed for this cruel, cruel world… and then she collapsed within herself.

Autumn Leigh shot up, gasping for breath. She scrambled for the headboard and rocked back and forth.

Not even the night after Alex was born. Not even the night after his private funeral with his tiny white coffin did I ever dream about that moment. What's happening?

Autumn's mind searched rapidly and crazily for some kind of normality. She was rocking like a person deranged, her feet planted in the sick she had dispelled earlier. *Maybe… maybe it's a sign that Alex is watching me… maybe Alex… No, no Alex is dead… but what… what if he's alive? I…I never saw him…what if they stole my Alex and he's in a foster home… oh my God!* **They stole our baby!**

124

A twitchy smile carved itself on Autumn's face. How could she have never thought of it before?

Alex is alive! Autumn's heart filled with pure joy at the thought of being able to see her baby son at last.

My baby is alive, that's the only reason I'm having these dreams and hallucinations... of-course! He's two now, just old enough to speak! He's letting me know telepathically that he's ready for this lifestyle now. We can come and collect you, Alex! Worms, the worms! Two-year-olds play with worms! My darling, darling Alex, I can hear you, we'll bring you home; daddy and I. He'll be so pleased, he'll be so happy...

Autumn jumped from the bed so fast she nearly tripped over and had to stumble for her balance.

Our baby! Our baby! Our baby!

Anthony was giving his views on where he felt the film industry would be heading in the 90s and Martin was agreeing the whole way. He'd bagged it, it was obvious. They had not got on to talking about *Wondering* yet but Anthony had Martin in the palm of his hand. It was on the cards that Martin was thinking Anthony perfect for the lead. This would be his biggest film yet, a *blockbuster*. He could almost jump for joy at the thought.

Thud, thud, thud. The noise made all three jump and Hannah brought her hand up to cover her mouth as she drew a sharp breath of surprise. Someone was hurrying down the stairs and the crashing was so immense the CD was skipping.

Anthony stood up. *Is that her? Who else could it be? Why's she running? **Why is she running?***

Within a second Autumn had burst into the room and stood in the doorway, excited and smiling as if possessed.

Hannah and Martin could do nothing but stare, gob-smacked.

Here was the marvellous Autumn Leigh with makeup smeared all over her face and dress, her hair a tangled mass of fuzz, standing in front of them with sick on her feet, grinning neurotically. It was almost too much to believe. Hannah shot her husband a shocked glance but her husband did not see it, as he could not tear his eyes away from what was standing facing him.

Anthony walked over to his wife, searching for a sign on her face as for what it could be. He himself was unable to speak or move for the first few seconds after she had run, jumped almost, into the room. He looked blankly at her and shook his head a little.

...?...

There was no sign, no warning as to prepare him for what he was just about to hear.

'Anthony,' she grinned through tears, placing shaky hands on her confused husband's shoulders. 'Alexander is alive!'

Anthony's eyes widened to a horror filled realisation that his wife was suffering from some kind of mental breakdown and was dragging up the memory of their poor child in the process, in front of important guests no less. After the initial shock of what she had just claimed, all he could concentrate on was a tumbling feeling of anger. A lump instantly formed in his throat.

'Excuse me,' he said to his bewildered visitors, sat rigid and speechless.

'Who's Alexander?' Hannah whispered to Martin once Anthony had escorted Autumn out of their sight.

Martin shrugged and shook his head, lost for words.

Anthony had hold of Autumn's arm tight and led her through to the kitchen. Once in there and with the door firmly shut behind them, he stood only centimetres away from her, staring into her fluttering eyes.

'What?' was all he could manage to say.

'Alex! He's alive! He's communicated with me and... and he's been in a foster home but he's ready for us to collect him now and he likes to play with worms!' The words she spoke were blurred with laughter and tears of joy.

Anthony blinked back angry water and hissed: 'Alex is dead. He was born dead and he was buried dead.' *Don't give me this shit Lucy, don't hurt me like this...*

'No Anthony, listen to me!' She was still smiling madly. 'He never died, the doctors made it up. They lied to us!'

Anthony made for the stool at the breakfast bar and sat down heavily, his legs a mass of nerves unable to support a grown man of thirty-eight under such emotion.

'Why are you doing this to me?' he whispered, staring at his hands outstretched in front of him, fingers pressed hard on the marble surface.

'What's wrong with Autumn?' Hannah asked Martin another question he was unable to answer.

He finished his wine in one rushed gulp and said: 'I don't know, but I think we better leave now.'

Autumn was still stood smiling, hugging herself and twisting her upper body as if ecstatically happy.

Well of-course she was ecstatically happy – her only son, whom she had thought dead, was actually alive! A thousand prayers had been answered and Autumn was on top of the world. So many plans to make, toys to buy, parties to throw...

She had developed completely selective hearing and sight as well, it seemed. For her husband was sitting opposite her looking like he was ready to explode or kill someone but she just didn't register it.

What she did register, however, was the sound of rustling just outside the kitchen door. She darted for it and opened it hastily to find Martin and Hannah getting their jackets out of the cloakroom.

Martin swallowed deeply when he saw Autumn's face. He just wanted to get the hell out of there, no prying, no goodbyes, just maybe a phone call to Anthony later in the week.

'Martin, Hannah, are you leaving?' Even her voice sounded airy and unreal, about three octaves higher than how she usually spoke.

Martin put his hand on his wife's back *the girl looks like she could hurt someone* and gave a weak smile.

'We do have to be going now. Thank you for the lovely meal and please tell Anthony I will call him.' With that he gently pushed Hannah towards the doors.

She opened one and shakily said: 'Bye Autumn, thank you,' before walking out without looking back.

Martin gave another nervy, fake smile and began walking out but Autumn grabbed his arm and he turned to her.

Martin – an eighteen stone, large, powerful man – suddenly found himself feeling quite afraid of this woman whom the public claim to know so well.

'Do you have any children, Martin?' she asked while Anthony remained transfixed sat at the breakfast bar, too crushed to even cry or think straight and too scared to try and convince his guests with a lie to explain her embarrassing behaviour.

'Yes, I have a child from my first marriage,' Martin replied politely, desperate to leave.

'Oh! Boy or girl?'

'Boy.'

'Really? We have a boy too!' she screeched, laughing.

*Autumn and Anthony don't have kids! What **is** this? What the hell is she talking about?*

'Oh,' Martin nodded, not knowing what to say.

'How old is your boy?' she asked.

'He's twenty-seven, not really a boy any more.'

'Really? Our Alex is two. Maybe they could play together sometime!'

'Erm, okay. Goodbye.' *What the hell was **that**?*

Martin did not even entertain a fake smile – She was crazy. He left the house at a fast pace and jumped into the car.

'What happened?' Hannah asked, uneased by her husband's saddened face.

'Looks like we have another friend who will be paying a visit to rehab soon,' he replied, waving his driver to move away. 'Out of everyone in the business, I never thought Autumn Leigh would be ruined by drugs, but that's what fame can do to you, honey.'

Autumn opened and shut the gates via the security pad near the door and waved her guests goodbye.

Once they had rolled away into the English country darkness she returned to the kitchen.

'Oh that'll be great; when Alex comes back he'll have another boy to play with. But first we need to think about Alex's room, it needs updating. I don't think he'll...'

'Alex is dead.' Anthony whispered through gritted teeth to start with but it only took a second for the anger to penetrate his voice and scream: 'He's dead! He's fucking dead, you stupid woman!'

His eyes were still transfixed on his shaking hands, his fingers turning white at the ends from pressing his hands on the hard work surface.

He couldn't even look at her now. Alex was a subject nobody ever spoke about in the family *and she knows this, she knows this so why fucking do it to me? Why do this Lucy, why break me too? Why?*

'Anthony,' she sighed happily, correcting him almost in a sympathetic voice. 'He's not dead, you can stop being upset now. He's back.'

She sighed again and pulled up a chair opposite him at the breakfast bar. She went to place her hand on top of this but he withdrew quickly, causing Autumn's to hit the surface with an empty slap.

He finally looked at her. Her eyes were alive and sparkling with joy, her features were glowing, brimming with plans.

She believes it. She believes every word of shit she's speaking. She believes that our baby, who never even had the chance to breathe, is living in a fucking foster home.

129

'Lucy, I wish I knew what was going on with you.' His voice was high, a wave of tears ready to break.

'He came to me in a dream. I relived his birth; it's a sign.' She tilted her head to the side and smiled softly.

'In your dream did Alex live?' His eyes had lowered again, sending drops of pain for his dead son splashing onto the table, and drops of sorrow for his lost wife falling down his drained face.

'No, well, they said he'd died but we never got to see him so the doctors were obviously hiding him from us. You see?'

'So your dream, message, whatever, was replayed to you exactly how it happened?'

She nodded her head enthusiastically. 'Yes.'

'Exactly the same?' he repeated, leading her into his trap.

'Yes.'

'Well on that fucking awful day our baby was born so underdeveloped and, and... *deformed* that the doctors had to rush him out of the room so it wouldn't upset you!' he yelled and stood up, pointing and shaking his finger at his wife: 'He looked such a bloody mess the doctor wouldn't let *me* see him. He was dead! *Dead*! He never even had a chance to cry!'

Here he was, shouting and screaming the painful truth and the smile still didn't fade, she was just not listening, he could say anything and she would smile and rock and think Alex.

'You have no idea!' he wailed. 'You're killing me with this! What the fuck is wrong with you, Lucy? I just don't get it! I don't know what's going on! I don't know where all this shit's come from and what the fuck I'm suppose to do about it but you're scaring me! You're going mad! God took our baby away, not the doctors. Why can't you stop this?'

Anthony bursts here, dear reader. It's an unheard of occurrence.

His fist rose and smashed heavily down onto the worktop, immediately sending shooting pain right through his hand, his face a contorted vision of pent up anger and his body a rising, falling heap of helplessness.

'He died in your womb, Lucy! You know that! I can't believe you're doing this! Why?' he screamed at her – almost trying to be intimidating – anything to make her snap out of this madness and listen to him.

With this final outburst Autumn Leigh's crazy smile faded, and for the first time since running downstairs her head seemed to clear and she was able to listen and watch her husband as he stumbled from his chair and stormed out of the room, crying like a child, hurt like a victim.

As Autumn Leigh's eyes began to widen with horror and her mouth began to drop, the girl under it all, Lucy Denharden, suddenly found herself standing naked in a boxing ring. The dusty ring was freezing and floodlights were directed onto her from all four corners, illuminating her for the invisible crowd. She trembled on the spot as Reality stepped into the ring and took off its cloak.

'No,' she shuddered, her hands rising up to her face in slow motion.

Reality laughed and turned to the crowd: plastic shop dummies occupied every seat now and they did not make a sound. Through plastic skulls they watched Lucy Denharden, the girl under the mask, among the dust in the floodlights. Every whimper she submitted echoed around the entire hall for the dummies to marvel at.

Reality swarmed like plague and prodded at her.

'Lucy,' was the songlike word it whispered: 'Lucy.'

'No,' she repeated, backing into her corner, trying to swat at it like flies.

'Lucy…'

Reality leapt at her and engulfed the madness she was feeding off. It teased her for a moment then offered a swift punch into her stomach, forcing the girl to keel over with a cough of air.

It kicked and punched and beat her until she could no longer scream and she just had to take it. Then, only when

Reality could feel her mind was blank of thoughts, did it turn back to the crowd.

The dummies were gone. Only a jester sat crying in the front row; but that was acceptable. Reality could cope with a jester – the jester would always be there. It had won the round.

Satisfied, Reality gave her back her mask and sent her back to the kitchen….

She stood, eyes wide with dread, mouth open with shock.

What have I done?

She managed a slow blink and looked down to pale hands.

I just told my husband our stillborn baby was alive. Oh shit Martin Gate, I sent Martin Gate fleeing with his mouth still full of food. What have I done? What was I thinking?

Reality laughed silently and returned back into her mind.

Autumn tried to make sense of herself but all she could do was shake her head, wondering why she had honestly believed that Alex was alive, and why oh why she saw him on the presentation dish, so real. Why she could smell him.

She dare not face her husband. By now she knew he would be loathing her and pitying her and thinking his own wife insane.

She stayed in the kitchen and tried as hard as any smart woman could to make sense of this bizarre chain of events and try to explain it to herself. Her hands were shaking and pale to match the rest of her body, and when she placed them heavily onto the worktop they buckled and she fell onto her forearms with a sharp crack. Here she was, the woman that the world looked up to, with her body weight on her forearms, snivelling and shaking, scared for her own sanity, wondering who that was just then. Here she was, the marvellous Autumn Leigh.

They do not move now. He counts them; 1, 2, 3, 4, 5, 6, 7, 8. Eight still mushrooms dusty in the dark. When he had slammed the door shut and slid down onto the floor they had jingled and jangled with the draft, but now they hang dormant again. They're directly above him as he spreads himself out on his back like a starfish upon the blue carpet.

Sometimes he walks in here and wonders: *why don't we use this room?* But on days like today he's glad they don't, he's glad that they have left it detached and barren. This room is his comfort; it is just like him, empty and alone.

He stares and he wonders what has happened to his beautiful Lucy. She was never like this when it was fresh. No, Lucy was amazing. She would smile sex and she would laugh and laugh.

Even in public, when she was Autumn Leigh she was perfect. *Even a few sweet days ago, Anthony, your wife was perfect.*

He wonders if she is still hugging herself, or if maybe she has gone to sleep to wake up just fine again. He wonders if she realises she needs help, or is she maybe planning a homecoming party for a son that never really was? He thinks: *no, I don't want to speak to her for a long while* and he continues to stare at the mushroom mobile casting shadows upon the wall from the moonlight.

Autumn knew she'd find Anthony in that room, even now, half an hour after he left her. She knew he'd still be mourning in this room with no light on. She had clicked open the door and had found him laid on the floor, staring at the baby mobile they had bought in happier times. The sight was terrible. She had broken him and the most dominant feeling in her bones was guilt, with a big dose of self-hate thrown in there too for good measure. Her eyes had been watering for a while now and all she wanted to do was pretend it never happened, but of-course, she knew that wasn't possible.

Anthony was a strong and hardened man; she knew she must have opened some pretty raw scars to make him turn into a child again, weeping and bruised. She'd never seen him so distraught.

Even when Alex was born, he'd appeared stronger than this.

Looking at him ignoring her made her want to bang her head against the doorframe over and over, just so it would blur the sense of her feeling so bad. But instead, as a grown and mature woman, she had to sort this mess out the best she could.

'I'm sorry,' seemed the best starting point.

Anthony didn't even blink.

'I don't...' Autumn shrugged wildly and swallowed back the tears that were disabling her from completing the sentence. '...I don't know what happened, Anthony. I don't know why I did that. I can't help it,' she cried, snivelling and admitting defeat.

After a minute of silence, Anthony lifted his head to view his wife. *Either something has happened to her that I don't know about or she has an illness. I shouldn't be mad because no matter which it's obviously not her fault... but I can't help despising her for this. Oh God, oh God why is she doing this? Why, all of a sudden? She was **fine** this time last month – last week even! What's happening to my wife?*

'You need help,' he whispered.

I know I need help Anthony but please, please let us do it ourselves. We could buy books, watch videos, please don't make me go back into one of those death haunts so they can throw me away because I'm crazy, please don't let them stick cold, steel objects into me. Anthony please, please, please...

'You need to go to hospital before you do even more damage,' he continued, his eyes still looking to the dark ceiling. 'I don't care if you want to or not. You're ill. You have not been right ever since the *Epic*s and all I know is that it has got to stop, Lucy. If we don't get it sorted this could happen again and again. Monday morning I'm driving you down to...'

'No!' Autumn protested. 'I am not going to set foot in a hospital, Anthony. I will not do it!'

'I know. I'm hardly going to take you to the local NHS centre am I? I'll call Dr Linford on Monday and arrange a private meeting. Okay?' His voice was still soft and his eyes still blank.

Doctor Linford was the couple's private doctor. He had only been called upon during Autumn's pregnancy and once after when she wanted to re-boost her diet. He was a stern man who catered to many stars but Anthony knew with something like this he would refer her to somewhere else straight away; he'd probably suggest a rehab centre or relaxation farm and Autumn would turn up her nose and protest her sanity. But still, he had to do something.

'Okay. For you,' Autumn finally agreed.

Anthony eventually wiped his eyes, stood up and moved through the door, straight past Autumn.

'Where are you going?' she asked

'To bed,' was the answer, as he opened the door to the second guest room and clicked it shut behind him.

CHAPTER 5

Doctor Linford was a stubby, balding man. By looking at his suit and expression it was obvious he drove a big car and owned a big house. His surgery was private, large and plush.

'Worms?' he repeated back to them.

'Yes, all over the floor,' Anthony nodded, gripping Autumn's hand hard, sensing how embarrassing all this was for her.

'And this was the morning after you attended the party and had a considerable amount to drink?'

'Yes, it was.' Autumn clenched her teeth.

'Hmm.' The doctor brought his thumb up to cover his mouth like a button while he thought.

Dr Linford was trying his hardest to make Autumn and Anthony feel stupid, she just knew it. *People are supposed to kiss our asses. I don't know who he thinks he is!* She knew it would be like this, she just *knew* it.

'And you say you didn't take any sort of...ah...*substance* at this party, Mrs Denharden?' he asked again.

'Like I told you five minutes ago, doctor – no.' Autumn was beginning to get irate to the point where she was having to bite her tongue. She couldn't remember him being like this when she was pregnant.

'Is there a possibility you may have been given some sort of substance without your consent?'

'A slight possibility, maybe.'

'I want to give you a standard and extended drugs test, Mrs Denharden, as well as a separate urine test, as it may be possible that you have being experiencing hallucinations due to a hallucinogenic drug such as LSD.'

'Fine,' Autumn sighed. 'But my entire life I have been told if I take drugs my internals will just collapse. I think if I'd have had LSD I would have died straight away.'

'True, your records show a fragile body, but one never can tell what the outcome of such things will be. Unfortunately the detection period to find hallucinogens in a sample is usually between twenty-four and forty-eight hours so it may show up negative even if you were given such a drug. But I still recommend we have a look.'

Dr Linford gave Autumn a bottle and showed her to the bathroom, leaving him alone with Anthony. He leaned back in his leather chair while Anthony browsed his eyes across the vast sea of certificates hung proudly on the wall.

'Does she take drugs often?' the doctor asked.

Anthony turned his full attention to Dr Linford.

'She never takes drugs,' was the cold reply.

'In my profession I deal with hundreds of actors, singers, MPs and personalities. They all say the same thing. I'm not accusing Mrs Denharden of lying – I just have vast experience and knowledge with this sort of thing.'

'Let me assure you, just because she's in show-business doesn't mean she's a junkie, okay? I really don't like the way you're handling this, doctor. We pay you good money and you're not even listening to a word she's saying. She needs help and she needs to be believed. She could be having a breakdown of some kind, I don't know.'

'She's not having a breakdown, Mr Denharden. The vital signs are not there. However, they are there for hallucinogenic abuse.'

'I can see where you're coming from; I thought that myself. But she swears it, she swears she has not taken anything knowingly and I believe her. Why would she do that to herself when she knows it could kill her straight away? I mean, like she says, if she'd have been slipped something, wouldn't she just have died? Who… who would do that to her? Who would spike her like that?'

Dr Linford sighed heavily. 'Let's say a person has taken a tab of LSD, shall we?' he said. 'Now, the after-affects are different from person to person, obviously. But the average documented cases include pseudo-hallucinations, distorted perceptions of things, such as… um… time, distances and so forth; the re-living of buried memories, depression, fear, feelings of anxiety… it sounds to me like your wife is experiencing a majority of these classic signs.'

'But a week after she supposedly 'took' one?' Anthony questioned.

'Like I said, Mr Denharden,' Dr Linford made a patronising shrugging suggestion with his hands and leaned back in his chair.

'Everybody is different. Mrs Denharden, if you don't mind my saying, is most definitely different – due to her medical history, you understand. It would not be surprising to see her experiencing after-effects for a long time.'

'I thought you agreed that, by rights, she would have died if she'd have taken drugs.'

'I never said that. I said that one could not predict the outcome of such things.'

Anthony wanted to hit him right then.

'Look, I just want it sorted,' he said, abruptly and off tone. 'She has a lead role coming up soon and she'll have to spend a lot of time away from me. I want to know she's okay – whether it's medication, therapy… anything. I just want her back to normal.'

'I can understand that,' the doctor nodded. *But the only way she'll be back to normal is if your wife stops taking drugs. Sir.*

Every drug test that was carried out that day was sent to a lab then returned to the doctor's desk three days later stamped 'negative'.

This didn't surprise Dr Linford as the detection period for hallucinogens soured over a week ago. Although the doctor knew that drugs were so obviously to blame, he realised that this 'no I didn't, yes you did' argument could never be solved and, instead of losing his high profile, high paying patients, he told the sleep-deprived couple the illusions could be down to over-tiredness and stress, and to 'get away for a while, go on holiday, go back to Nova Scotia, book yourself in at a health farm. Relax a bit'

After Anthony had told and re-told Dr Linford it was more than that and getting away would not solve anything, he

141

eventually offered to refer her to London's top psychiatrist: Dr Hazel King.

Autumn Leigh took some convincing but, let's face it; doctor knows best. Later that day he arranged a meeting for the drug-using star that following Monday.

Autumn had spent all week worrying about people finding out about the way that she had acted at the dinner party, so when Martin eventually rang their house on the Friday night she sat listening in to her husband's awkward conversation in the lounge.

'Martin, I can't apologise enough for last Saturday. She's just been so stressed out lately.' He spoke quietly, shaking his head, ignoring his wife's presence.

There was silence for a little while.

'No, no. She doesn't.' A pause, then: 'I can understand you thinking that but it's nothing like that. She just needs to…Alex…? We lost our baby three years ago. We named the boy Alex, she's never really got over it… no, no, it's fine. You weren't to know.'

Martin then spoke for a long time, Autumn guessed it was about business judging by her husbands reactions and then eventually: 'Sure, I understand. Well, I wish you the best of luck with it. Erm, I'd appreciate it if this stayed between us because, you know, it wouldn't do her good if… okay, thanks, okay, yep, goodbye.' With that he clicked the phone off and left the room.

Anthony had spent that entire week trying to understand and comfort his wife but it was so hard when all he wanted to do was stay away from her. The weekend was the same; they'd gone about separate duties all day Saturday and when they sat down for their evening meal together it was strained and uncomfortable.

'I didn't get it,' he finally voiced.

'It's my fault, isn't it?' was Autumn's reply.

'Yes.' He looked up from his meal. She was sitting to the right of him. 'Yes, it is. He said it would be in my best interests to look after you rather than work on such a demanding role… he's right though.'

'But it should all blow over once I go to therapy; all I need to do is talk it out. You should have told him that.'

'How do you know that's all it will take? What, do you think you'll spend an hour with some woman nodding her head from time to time and then it will all be sorted?' Anthony asked, not satisfied with Autumn's response that her problems were nothing and will go away soon like a bout of the flu.

'No, of-course not Anthony,' she scolded. 'I'm aware it will take a while but I don't think it's worth quitting a film over.'

'I didn't quit, I was rejected – remember?' Anthony said angrily.

Autumn looked down to her food and was on the verge of apologising again when…

'Please tell me you're not still considering doing *Val's Girls*.'

'Why… why not?' Autumn said after a moment of eye contact.

'You're kidding, right?'

'No, shooting doesn't start until May now. I'll be fine by…' she didn't bother finishing. By this point her husband had stood up and walked out of the room.

Autumn sat alone staring at Anthony's plate still stacked with food. She tried to remain calm but everything was just going so wrong. She had spent her entire life creating this perfect fairytale world for herself, and now all that she had worked for was being destroyed blow by blow.

I feel that now, in this moment of vulnerability, we should talk to Autumn. Even an icon needs a little help from time to time and this is one of the rare moments throughout our adventure

143

where our leading lady really does need to open up to somebody. She needs the support and honesty that we can give her at a time when she can't let anybody else in. This is also one of the rare moments in the book where she will welcome our presence so, come on; let's make the most of it.

We walk into the dining room and sit down facing her. She flashes us a weak, sad smile then continues looking to Anthony's empty plate. Her eyes are red and tired; she looks either on the verge of crying or falling asleep.

'Are you okay?' I ask sympathetically.

'Yes,' she nods. It takes only two seconds for tears to break and she begins to cry.

'It's just, everyone's going to know,' she weeps, wiping tears as they fall, still avoiding eye contact. 'Everyone's going to find out that I'm not normal and I'll lose everything.'

'Do you think it's a good idea to do the film?' you ask.

'Continuing to work would be the best thing that I could do,' she replies, her sobs quietening. 'If I don't then I'll be giving in and that'll be the beginning of the end for me. What if Anthony is like this over *every* role from now on? My work distracts me from my problems – why can't he see that? What would happen to me if I didn't have any distractions and all I could think about was when the next attack's going to come? It would make me worse, I know it. How can nobody else see that?'

'Why don't you talk to Anthony about it?' you say, more as advice than a question.

Autumn laughs in a sorry kind of way then looks up to you with tears still falling.

'I can't,' she shrugs. 'I can't because then I'd have to tell him the truth and you've seen what he's like, he won't let it go. He thinks that by taking me to a doctor he's helping me but he's not. He's just making me more anxious. The more anxious I get, the worse the attacks get. It's always been the same. If I don't think about them, if I pretend there's nothing wrong then they go. I hadn't had one for years up until recently and I just don't know, I *don't know* what's brought

144

them on again but this sure isn't helping. Thinking of doctors and lying awake at night worrying about it all is just making me worse. But how can I let him know that without telling him I've always had them?'

'Well, why *not* tell him everything? He only wants to help you and, you never know, he could be right. Seeking help *might* be the best thing; it might make you better once and for all. They don't just throw people into padded rooms these days, you know. They'll give you medication and it could put a stop to the attacks completely,' I say.

'I can't… I just can't,' Autumn shook her head adamantly. She hunches her shoulders and speaks dramatically in a voice no louder than a whisper: 'I will not let it ruin me.'

After some silence she raised her head and spoke to us with full eye contact, for the first time.

'By admitting I have a problem I am also admitting defeat. Do you not see that? I've kept it a secret my entire life and have tackled it by proving to myself that I am not mad. If I openly let others know about my problems then I am admitting it to myself, and I can only see myself giving up… either that or my attacks would take me over.'

'But you're admitting to them now.'

'I know that but look at me!' Autumn Leigh cries, pointing a finger at her chest. 'Look at the state I'm in! I'm not usually like this! But because I am being like this, and because Anthony keeps pushing me into 'sorting it out', they're getting worse. Everything that I've done, look what I've achieved… all to put these attacks behind me. But now they're everywhere and they're taking over my life. They're getting worse because they're becoming a focus point. When I was a kid, the attacks would be in sleep form but now they're in waking form. The best thing would be to block them like I have always done – that way they stop. But now they haunt my every thought and they're getting worse because Anthony won't get off my case!'

'What is it like when you have an attack?' you ask once Autumn has calmed down a bit. 'Is it like you're drunk or something and you can't help it?'

'No, no, no. It's hard to put it into words,' Autumn is silent for a moment and then follows it with: 'When I was a kid I would just black out and then wake up knowing that something frightening had just happened, something that wasn't normal... and it would scare me. But I'd visualise pushing it to the very back of my mind and covering it up with a blanket, then I would tell myself it never happened and just get on with my day and forget about it until the next one came... but the few that I've had recently – I am still awake and walking around, and these visions intrude on me so real that I don't realise that they're visions, so I try to rationalise them in a way that seems normal at the time... and end up causing this. Like with Martin the other night; I saw my baby... I *saw* him. He was as real to me as this food here... can you *imagine* that?'

We both shake our heads.

'...so I rationalised it as meaning that Alex was alive. It seems crazy now and I can't believe I even thought it, but I did and I believed it to the point where it was fact and I remember not being able to understand why Anthony wasn't happy that our son was still alive. I remember thinking that he must not want his son back. So look, look what 'admitting' it is doing to me. I don't feel any better now, I feel worse. Am I going mad? I think so, I have always thought so... but I am better when I ignore that thought, not play on it like I am doing now.'

'What do you...' I begin.

'This is not helping me,' Autumn interrupts apologetically. 'I'm sorry, but I think I need to be alone now. I don't feel comfortable talking about this. I'd rather just forget about it.'

We both nod and stand up to leave. As we do so Autumn runs her hands through her hair and cups her face in her hands.

We walk out of the room as quietly as possible without saying goodbye. We both feel she has too much on her mind right now for small talk and would be more thankful if we just left.

How could she not cry now? *How did it get like this?* Her lips began to quiver again with sadness, guilt, fear and all the other feelings that a person experiences when their happiness is being dangled at a carrot's length away from them. Eventually she slipped back into silent tears.

She stayed in the dining room until 9pm when the emotion and worry had finally worn her down. She then continued crying in her bedroom with the bed all to herself, again.

Monday came nervously and her driver took her to Hazel King's office in her blacked out car for 1.30pm. She wore a scarf up to her nose and a baseball cap just in case she was spotted. She could picture the headlines now: 'AUTUMN LEIGH BREAKDOWN SHAME!' 'AUTUMN LEIGH – IS SHE CRAZY?'

The car rolled up just outside the old three story building in central London and the engine was killed. Autumn's heart was pounding as she stepped out and ran up the stairs. She pushed open the glass door and approached the receptionist, but before she'd even had chance to speak the heavily made-up lady told her to take the lift to the third floor and Dr King's office was the end door on the right, and to go straight in.

Dr King was watering her desk plant when Autumn opened the door.

'Hello,' she said in a sharp, educated voice, placing her watering jug on her polished wood crescent desk and dusting off the palm of one hand with the other. 'Please, sit down. I'll be with you in a second.'

Autumn experienced a feeling, standing at that door, that she hadn't felt for many years. The marvellous Autumn Leigh felt small.

Dr King's office was rich. It was rich in wood, rich in colour and rich with certificates. Dr King had power; the way she looked, spoke and dressed made it obvious even at this early stage.

Dr King herself looked like she was straight from a movie set: blonde hair bobbed around a serious and pointy face *she must love this,* carefully applied makeup colour coordinating perfectly with her navy blue, shoulder padded suit. She looked more like a ruthless lawyer than a doctor.

Straightaway Autumn felt envious of this woman and didn't even want to tell her what she had for breakfast never mind her fears of her deteriorating mental state. This was the kind of woman Autumn took great pleasure in walking past in the street after she'd just had her hair done or just won another award. *Not* the kind of woman she felt comfortable talking to about her personal issues.

Autumn was on the verge of apologising and making excuses but instead she simply turned around and left.

Autumn pressed for the lift, whispering: 'C'mon, c'mon,' under her breath.

Dr King's office door opened and the doctor rushed out saying:

'Ms Leigh. Ms Leigh?'

'I'm not interested any more,' Autumn muttered once the doctor had approached her. *For God-sake, leave me alone.*

'I can understand how this must feel for you...'

'How dare you!' Autumn snapped, her heart pounding as if she was going to have a panic attack. *I'm too good for this. I'm too good for this...*

'I don't mean to make you feel uncomfortable, Ms Leigh. I understand you're an extremely successful lady. This is not like you, you feel embarrassed – I know that. *Please.* Our sessions will be based on mutual respect and all we need to do now is talk informally... no deep dark secrets, no monsters, no reclining chair... if you don't feel comfortable with it then you don't have to come back, but please just give it a try. *Please.* I can help you.'

148

The doctor had been speaking frantically, but when the lift reached their floor silence fell upon the two women.

It pinged open and empty. Autumn stared at it for a moment and watched as it shut its doors again, before reluctantly returning back into Dr King's office with her. If it weren't for the doctor calling Autumn successful she'd have got in that lift then and there. *At least she is aware I still have the upper hand. I am still God here. I am still God.*

Autumn gave the doctor her coat, hat and scarf to hang up and then sat down in the leather chair facing Dr King's desk. The doctor walked around the desk and sat down, crossing her legs.

'Why did you feel the need to run away from this?' Dr King asked.

Autumn thought for a bit then said: 'It's hard for me to come to terms with recent events, but it's even harder for me to try and face them.'

Dr King nodded and began to explain the way she practised. She explained nothing would be written down or thought of too deeply in this session, and to think of it more as a consultation – a meeting.

'The next session will be two hours long and will be held in a separate room. This will continue for some weeks, possibly months,' the doctor informed her. 'Then, depending on general progress or how deep the root of the problem is, other methods may be introduced. By this I mean hypnosis, medication, relaxation therapy, light therapy, even colour therapy – basically, whatever we can tailor to help your individual needs. Some people feel better just by talking. Some people see me four times and then don't feel the need to come back, and then there are others that I have being seeing weekly for years. It all comes down to the patient, and no two people are the same. Do you have any questions?'

'To say you deal with such sensitive subjects, you're not in the most discreet of locations, are you?'

'You'd be surprised,' Hazel King smiled.

Autumn raised an eyebrow: 'Central London, doctor? It caused me a lot of trouble trying to get here. I'm surprised you don't give a more personal service to high-profile clients such as myself.'

Dr Hazel King was neither impressed nor intimidated by ego talk from the A-lists. In fact, she despised it.

'Let me point out first,' she began, being careful not to speak in an abrupt tone: 'I am a good doctor, and not a doctor exclusively to the stars. Celebrities come to me, I don't go to them. I am one of the best psychiatrists in England. Ms Leigh, please remember I deal with hundreds of clients and I don't rank any single one of them. As for our location; if you put a hundred thousand ten pound notes in a black bin-bag outside on the street, you have less chance of it getting stolen than if it was in a laser guarded room.'

She studied Autumn for a second to assess the reaction. Autumn nodded at the thought then finished the questions with: 'Can I smoke?'

'Sure,' the doctor replied with a smile, and slid the empty glass ashtray over to her.

Autumn briefly explained about her memory loss at the awards and how she had been feeling since, but nothing was analysed or broken down. Dr King just wanted to know the basics.

After a chat the two shook hands and finalised weekly meeting arrangements, which was to be Fridays, 2pm 'til 4pm, before Autumn left her office, feeling slightly better about herself than she had anticipated. She had, after all, faced her fears in a way. It wasn't exactly a hospital but it was Dr Hazel King... *Doctor* Hazel King. She hadn't hidden from it and, to her surprise, she didn't feel worse for it.

Anthony was pleased that his wife had gone to see a psychiatrist, but he still did not yet feel ready to sleep and cuddle up to her in the same bed. He told her this when she got home from her first meeting and she began to cry. He did hold her then and whispered that he was sorry, and don't feel alone because you're not alone, it's just that I know I won't sleep if I stay in the same bed as you right now. I need you to understand that I can't get over the other night that quickly, okay sweetpea? It broke my heart and I haven't slept since.

She nodded sorrowfully and he left her in the front room with the fire burning. She had been sitting in and out of thought for only a few minutes when the phone rang. It was by her side on the sofa and she picked it up mechanically, saying 'hello?' faintly and without effort.

'Autumn Leigh?' It was her UK agent, Louise Dean.

'Yes?'

'It's Louise, Autumn. I've got to talk to you.' The tone, usually the kiss-ass spillage Autumn had become accustomed to, tonight sounded urgent... worryingly urgent.

Autumn's eyes opened fully and she sat up straight, energy and anxiety flowing freely through a previously half-asleep body.

'What? What do we need to talk about at ten at night for fuck's sake, Louise?'

'Just... please tell me you didn't go to see Hazel King today, okay? Autumn, please tell me it was a rumour,' Louise coaxed hopefully. Surely her biggest client couldn't really be dangling her fingers seductively over the self-destruct button like that? The possibility of it being true severely worried Louise, because if her biggest client pressed that big red button provoking a media backlash, it indefinitely meant that Louise's career would go BANG! with it.

'What?' Autumn's disgusted, higher-than-thou, utterly embarrassed voice shrieked. 'That's none of your goddamn business!'

'Yes it bloody well is!' her agent shouted back – something unheard of from those that dealt with Autumn Leigh. 'I am your agent here, Autumn! That *does* make it my business!'

'Who told you?' Autumn asked after a moment, taken aback at having someone raise their voice at her.

'Aw shit.' The voice came sharp and Autumn heard something slamming in the background at the other end of the line.

'Why's it such a fucking big deal? Everyone has a shrink,' Autumn retaliated with a heart full of fear.

'Yeah, everyone has a shrink. And yeah, most of these saps don't even need one; they just like to talk about themselves. But Hazel King is... she's... she's the nut specialist, okay? Sorry Autumn, but everyone knows that Hazel King is big time. Pete Williamson was snapped walking out of there a few years ago, the media got their claws out and exposed his drug habits and, look, where is he now? So what do you think my reaction is going to be like when I get a call saying my biggest client has just been spotted walking out of her offices?'

Right at that point Autumn realised that Dr King's bag of notes theory was looking more like a bag of shit.

'And,' she continued, sounding more and more agitated, 'you've obviously been referred to her by your doctor because Hazel King only sees people on referral. Did you know that?'

'No, I didn't know that.' Autumn's voice was light now; she didn't have the energy to keep up the bitch act. She was in trouble.

'Well the media does, and that's all it takes from them to tear your career up in shreds.' Louise lit a cigarette down the other end of the phone. To Autumn it was like speaking to a completely different person. She always thought of Louise as quite a pushover.

'Louise, I think you're getting carried away with yourself and I don't appreciate your tone. I am among the most respected and popular actresses in the world at the moment – they couldn't, and wouldn't, destroy me just because they found out I was seeing a shrink.'

'Oh no?' Louise said, exasperated.

'No,' Autumn Leigh replied.

'Autumn,' *cut the crap. You're living in a dream-world, love.* 'I am telling you now the best piece of advice I can give, and I know this industry inside out, okay? Don't take your status for granted. The more respected you are, the harder you fall... the better the story. The public love to see a fall from grace and the press know that. All they care about is selling more papers, so the second they get a sniff at a story it will explode in your face before you even know what's happening. I'm sorry to be so blunt, but do you honestly think they give a shit about you? I don't mean to offend you, but I am telling you now that they will exaggerate your problems to the point of no return. It's happened hundreds of times before and it'll never stop happening. Don't set yourself up to be the next victim.'

Autumn sighed heavily. 'I know what you're saying,' she said.

'Was it your first time with her?'

'Yes.'

'Right. Just don't, *do not,* visit that woman again, okay?'

'Were any pictures taken?'

'Apparently not, but we won't know until tomorrow morning. Without pictures there's not much of a story, so fingers crossed. But we'll have to wait and see.' There was a pause before Louise took on her soft, better spoken voice, the voice Autumn was used to: 'Autumn, I'm sorry to bother you so late on and you know I love you, right? But you're a big, big star... and no matter what you do people will be watching you. Stay away from Hazel King, otherwise the press will turn their favourite girl into their latest prey. Trust me, okay?'

Tears had begun to fall down Autumn's face again. She made her excuses about not being able to speak any longer and Louise agreed to call her again tomorrow after she'd checked through the papers.

Louise Dean placed the phone back into the holder on her desk and stubbed out her cigarette. It was only then that it occurred to her that she had not even asked her biggest client why she felt the need to go to a psychiatrist and if she was alright. Louise felt like such a shit she had to take a valium.

As Autumn pressed the soft 'off' button on her phone she realised that this was yet another thing that would be going against what her husband wanted for her. Things were crumbling at a dramatic force for the brilliant Autumn Leigh, and she hadn't felt this low in a long, long time. She had two choices to make; both were urgent and both needed to be sorted out soon, although she couldn't bear thinking about either of them. She had to decide whether to please her husband and pull out of the film she was already highly anticipating next year, or whether to ignore him and go for it, thus earning her a cool ten million. She had to decide which one was more important, her scarily verging on out-of-control mental health, or some twat with a camera snapping her receiving treatment. Autumn didn't sleep much that night; the entire time her thoughts were swapping between self-pity and self-discipline, they wouldn't switch off. It reminded her of when she was in her late teens/early twenties and trying to make it in Hollywood. There were so many decisions to make back then. *Should I go home? Shall I give it another week? Another month? Just one more casting? How low should I go? How far should I go to get a part? Should I? Could I?*

The fact was that she had faced up to it then and she would have to face up to it now. As Autumn drifted in and out of a fitful sleep the sun began to rise. Finally, by 6.30am, Autumn Leigh had made a decision.

CHAPTER 6

AUTUMN LEIGH QUITS!

Hollywood bombshell Autumn Leigh has pulled out of the much awaited gangster flick *Val's Girls*, which was due to be released next summer. What started as a rumour has now being confirmed as true as Leigh's official spokeswoman confirmed yesterday: 'Autumn Leigh has been in talks for the past few days with *Val's Girls* producers and directors. It has been decided that she will not star in the forthcoming production due to health problems.

IS IT ALL OVER FOR AUTUMN AND ANTHONY?

In last week's gossip column we documented how US-turned-Brit star Autumn Leigh was spotted walking out of the offices of a famous psychiatrists in London. This week she quit her forthcoming film *Val's Girls*. So what exactly is going on with the world's favourite actress? Worries have been heightening that the star is suffering from exhaustion, and rumours are circulating that her famous marriage to Anthony Denharden is on the rocks, following reports that at this years *Epic Awards* they sat completely separately all night. Leigh was reportedly having more than a good time with the gorgeous Jerry Tilsey, who co-starred alongside her in *The Green Book*. Has the bubble burst in the Denharden household? Stay with us for weekly updates and all the top goss.

WORRY RISING OVER STAR'S HEALTH

Canadian born actress Autumn Leigh is at the centre of controversy after growing concern for the star's health. The award winning actress, who recently picked up an *Epic* for her lead role in *The Green Book*, was due to start filming the new feisty gangster motion picture *Val's Girls* in May but she pulled out yesterday due to health problems. Worry of Leigh's health began to escalate at the beginning of this month when the voluptuous personality collapsed at the spectacular *Epic*

Awards' after show party. Despite her curvy figure rumours of an eating disorder have been circulating and, as ever, a shroud of mystery surrounds Autumn Leigh and heartthrob husband Anthony Denharden as they refuse to make any public appearances or speak of the subject....

'Eating disorder, have you read this? Apparently now I have an eating disorder!' the fabulous Autumn Leigh scoffed, sliding the newspaper away from her at the breakfast bar. 'Unbelievable.'

'Yep,' Anthony looked up from his cereal. 'They'll jump to any conclusion, won't they? Ignore it. It'll die down in a week or so.'

'Yeah,' Autumn sighed.

He'd joined her in the same bed since Tuesday night when she had told him she was to quit *Val's Girls*. They had not made love for a long while, but he did hold himself tight against her and still nuzzled his nose in her hair as she slept. She had officially quit yesterday and now, on this bright and chilly Friday morning, things were a lot better. She now had time to rest and time to get better and now everything was going to be alright. He could talk to her again without feeling strained and resentful.

Autumn had almost got away with being spotted at Dr Hazel King's office by the look of things too, aside from a few small items in the gossip pages. Luckily, it wasn't to be a headliner as there was no photographic evidence. She had spoken to Dr King, who, going against what she had said earlier, agreed to visit Autumn at her house in future.

Quitting *Val's Girls* had been hard but, after much careful thought, she realised other films would come up but husbands like Anthony wouldn't. He had been different with her since she told him and the world of her decision. The ice had thawed from his voice.

'How are the press reporting it?' Anthony asked, spooning the milk from his bowl like he'd done since he was a kid.

'Not as bad as they could be, I suppose. They don't have all that much to go on, thank God, so they can't make that much of a deal about it just yet.'

'Hmm, they'll try though. We best lay low for a little while.' Anthony said through experience, painfully recalling his brush with negative media attention following his dad's fifteen minutes of fame.

'Yeah. We could always go to Nova Scotia for a bit, to see Mom and Dad?'

'Sure sweetpea, if that's what you want.'

They sat over breakfast talking for some time. It was nice. She appreciated it for maybe the first time ever.

She liked the fact that it was almost like he was the one in charge recently. She respected him more for it. Anthony didn't even notice the change; to him there was no change in his personality. He was just trying to sort out his wife.

'Hey, why don't we do something nice today… something different?' Autumn suggested.

'Sure, what do you fancy?' Anthony replied, gladdened by the idea.

'We could go for a walk in the countryside, if the reporters aren't still camping outside. What do you think?'

'Sounds good.'

'Great, I'll get a shower,' Autumn smiled, kissing her husband as she stood up to leave.

Autumn hummed as she undressed in their lavish bathroom, looking forward to their day out. Once naked she performed her daily ritual of taking herself in in the full length mirror. It was upon the first glance of herself that the humming stopped. She looked old. Her reason for looking in the mirror every day was to remind herself of the one thing she still had going for her: her looks. So she was somewhat disheartened to find that even they weren't all too convincing today. As the public wowed about her fabulous body, Autumn always wondered if somehow, they knew that under all that expensive material and tanning lotion there were more than a few hints of cellulite and sagging muscles.

No doubt the girl was beautiful and possessed a body of the Gods; she knew that she was incredibly lucky, but even the Gods couldn't stop Autumn Leigh from ageing. Sure, the surgeon could, and had done well where needed but she had decided enough was enough. Any more and people would find out, more than the mere speculation she had denied in the past.

Autumn moved closer to the mirror and examined the bags under her eyes. Her face looked to have lost that rosy glow she was once blessed with and, even though Autumn looked after herself almost to the point of being over the top, her skin looked dull. Of-course it could be covered up with the designer make-up Autumn possessed – but in the cold light of day she looked tired and, well, ill almost.

The showers were a kind relief though; beads of hot water spraying hard onto her face and body, massaging her tense muscles and warming her bones. She smiled with her eyes shut and began to hum again. She had admitted to her current attacks. She had admitted to them enough to see a doctor and quit a film but she was surprised to find that she did not feel like she had lost because of it. She genuinely felt like she was doing the right thing and it felt good. Maybe she could get better? The attacks she had as a child, though, she would keep them to herself. That *would* be dragging up old problems and there was no point. Nobody knew about them and nobody was going to know about them. The only things that she would talk about and try and get sorted, she decided, would be the things that were troubling her at this point in time. Anyway, just to have Anthony back to normal was a welcome relief. Even if the attacks did go back to being black-outs she could deal with it – at least her husband was sharing a bed with her again and talking to her about something other than her health. She was gladdened by that alone.

Meanwhile, Anthony had tired of the table and moved through into the front room to flick through the television stations. He was over the moon that his wife had decided to do the right thing. It had taken a lot of persuading and many tactics to get her to listen, but it had worked and Anthony had got the fullest night's sleep in the best part of a month last night. Time and time again, when Anthony was sleeping in the spare room, he had desperately wanted to creep back into his bed and snuggle up next to the woman he loved. But he had stopped himself, for he knew that she would have the upper hand on the situation if he did and then they would never get to the bottom of these strange delusions. So he had resisted temptation for her sake, had acted as hard-nosed as he possibly could, and it had been worth it. Lucy wore the trousers in their marriage and Anthony knew that. She didn't wear them because Anthony was the weaker of the two, she wore them because that suited them both perfectly, but that didn't mean to say Anthony didn't snatch them from her when need be.

After a few minutes lost in thought, Anthony's eyes focused on the television. He managed to keep concentration for only a matter of seconds before his mind strayed back to thinking about his beautiful wife again. He thought of his wife wearing red lipstick; he thought of the way she had looked on their wedding day.

As he sprawled on his sofa he thought of the way she smiled shyly and still blushed when signing autographs. He ignored the television and thought about the way her hair smelt of flowers and perfume. He thought of how lucky he was to be able to put his arms around such an amazing woman each night. He thought he should join her in the shower.

Autumn was still humming, facing the back of the large shower room, when the bathroom door creaked open. The glass screen doors were pulled to on this occasion and as she turned sharply, she could only see a figure standing at the door through the steam.

She let out a frightened gasp and dared not move.

*Calm down, calm down. It will be Anthony. But Anthony is still at the breakfast table. No he isn't he's finished. Why would he come into the bathroom though, why, why, **why**?*

A heart-stopping realisation hit Autumn like a blow, *I didn't hear him jogging up the staircase, I always hear him jogging up the staircase. It's an intruder, oh God, oh God. He must have got in through the upstairs window and now he's coming to kill me, oh dear God save me, save me.*

Anthony stood at the door and savoured the moment, looking around the room. His wife's dressing-gown was hung over the closed toilet seat, her knickers were puddled on the floor and her watch was over the sink ledge. He could see her naked, fleshy mist in the shower surrounded by warm steam. He smiled.

Anthony was still truly in love with this girl, no matter what she had thrown at him recently. He loved her with all his heart and he still lusted after her as much as he had when the two had first met.

The naked, fleshy mist that was Autumn Leigh was trembling now, her heart thudding so loud she was sure the intruder could her it. She squeezed her eyes tight and held back tears of fear.

If I scream he'll pounce, but if I scream Anthony will save me... what if he's already killed Anthony? Oh good Lord he's killed Anthony!

With her mind racing, visions of her dear beloved husband lying in a pool of messy blood downstairs haunted her thoughts. Oh, her dear, sweet prince with his eyes rolled back, deep red crawling like germs out of an axed gash and bloody hole in his head. His rich, thick hair matted like animal with slimy and deceased blood, her darling, darling husband. Now

Autumn could do nothing but hope that if she stayed silent the sick murderer would not come for her too…

The more Anthony watched his wife and thought of her undressed and shower-warm the more he wanted her. Anthony had a passion that wanted her raw. He couldn't waste any time taking his clothes off, he wanted her right now.

He's coming to get me, he's moving, he's moving. This is it. This is how I'm going to go, naked and vulnerable. This is it…

Anthony pulled back the screen door, planning to fall into Lucy's arms and let the shower beads soak his clothes as he pushed her up against the wall to make love to her… but his wife jumped as if electrocuted and pressed herself up against the side away from him, terrified. Her whole body was shaking as if freezing.

Anthony could do nothing but stare, bewildered. Her eyes were wide and watery, staring straight through him as though he were a ghost.

'Lucy? Are you alright?' he asked as she began to whimper.

The screen door opened allowing steam to escape out of the shower room, leaving Autumn exposed by her nakedness. At this moment Autumn wished it had been an intruder, but it was far, far worse.

Its eyes were sunken and dry; its face pale and rotting. The thing standing looking at her was obviously once human but had decayed and transformed into something from her nightmares.

It was standing staring right at her. It smelt of earth, soggy leaves and dead organs. Blue veins stuck hard like gristle out of its neck, disappearing under a coarse brown cloak. Its lips were cracked, surrounded by dried, white phlegm. Its head was scarred with brown liver marks and dead, bristly hair sticking out in places. The cloak it was wearing hung loose from what only could be skin and bones, dusty and murky.

The thing stood deadly silent, blocking her way out, with only the sound of the shower water hitting the wet area and Autumn's slight whimpering filling the humid air. Its expression matched hers: blank. It watched her with eyes that didn't blink and a bony, shaking hand still grasping the glass screen.

The feeling she had was beyond words, beyond terror. It was too much to be real. The utter trauma she was experiencing was disabling her; she couldn't move, scream or run. So she was left to just stare at it, stare at it and wait to die…

'Lucy…?' Anthony repeated, his eyes darting around hers for some clue as to what she must be thinking.

It hissed her name and exposed rotting, black teeth. It called her Lucy, bringing out her vulnerable real self, forcing her into forgetting about the stronger alter ego she preferred to be known by.

Lucy's shaking hand rose up to her mouth to stop her vomiting. She felt like a defenceless child again. It was toying with her, playing her weak mental state like a piano. She could feel hatred all around her in the sticky atmosphere. This demon was here to crush her – she knew that she wouldn't be leaving this shower room alive.

'Lucy, what's got into you?' Anthony asked as his wife covered her mouth with a trembling hand.

Her answer was liquid: she gagged and then was sick on to herself. She kept the vomit-filled hand over her mouth and let it trickle between her fingers, wide eyes fixed on him like she was in some sort of trance. Some lumps landed on her breasts, stomach and legs, others swam down the nearest plughole with the hard water.

Anthony yelped her name and jolted back in shock. *Is she dying? Has she tried to kill herself? Is she insane?*

He stops asking questions now because he knows the answer, he has known the answer for some time now. *She is ill she is mentally ill and I can't look after her anymore...*

Anthony had taken a step back and was staring at his wife, chewing on sick, with great sadness and pity. She was broken. He didn't know for sure why or, at least, what had triggered it – but it had happened and he had to stop denying it to himself. She was a shell now, something had gone. She didn't need denial, she needed help.

'I am going to phone an ambulance, Lucy. Okay?' he spoke slowly and clearly.

She stood petrified with her hand still smudged over her pale face. She was terrifying him and he felt she might even lunge if he made any sudden movements.

He was stepping backwards, confused and afraid, while he spoke: 'I won't be gone two minutes so you just stay there, okay? Don't move.'

He didn't want to turn around so he continued moving with his hands out in front of him. He wasn't sure if leaving his wife alone in the bathroom was the best thing to do... right up until he noticed that the beautiful woman he had married had shit herself and it was clogging up one of the plugholes.

He could not hide the tears that sprung into his eyes and if it was the right thing to do he would have hugged her tight and held her wet little head hard against his chest. But it was not the right thing to do. The right thing to do was to call an ambulance.

It had left but she was paralysed. She had even lost control of her bodily functions at one point, leaving her ashamed and dirty *you naughty, naughty little girl – you pooed and sicked in front of the monster* but she couldn't help it. It had not harmed her physically but mentally it had murdered her in the most horrific and torturous way possible, walking away with her stable mind in its hands. It had crawled like scum into the shower room, violated her conscious thoughts, raped her mind and finally left with her sanity kicking and screaming in its possession.

The monster had abandoned her body and ventured back into the underworld with her soul. Her hand slid limply from her face and slapped against her parched skin. The water was still beating down upon her but she could not feel it. She was lost.

Her eyes began to dryly gaze around the shower room, only it was no longer a shower room. It was a thing and it didn't matter anymore. Her body became the most relaxed it had been for years.

At that point her thoughts travelled beyond her surroundings and she sat down in her shit. Everything was in soft tone.

Her conscious mind began to work overtime to rid her of the terror. Eventually it found a way out and once there, it shut down and left her to her psychosis. Lucy's vision slowly became out of focus and then everything turned into candyfloss.

She is six now and she is in the travelling circus grounds. A clown on stilts is walking with ease, waving at her and laughing. She laughs back and the sounds of Hammond organs are slow and sinking in the background. Her laughter penetrates the hazy scene, representing vulgar innocence. On a film in the distance, a cameraman zooms in on a dead girl's doll in the rain and you hear her giggle for the last time. She laughs like the dead girl and a family walks past her wearing their Sunday clothes. They too turn towards her and wave, their eyeless faces smiling eerily wide. Blood is pouring into their mouths from the slashed up sockets where their eyes once were. She waves back and giggles.

She skips up to the burger bar *candyfloss mister, please* and the chef hands her a stick with fresh entrails wrapped around it. He smiles so wide the corners of his mouth begin to crack and burst open, revealing bloody flesh, yellow fat and several ants. *Thank you, mister* laughs the dead girl and Lucy is smiling in the pink candyfloss that was once her bathroom.

Yeah, that was Lucy Denharden's happy thought. A bit different from the kind of thing you or I would think about to calm us down I'm sure but hey, this girl's a bit different from us.

Funfairs are nice, she thinks.

Let her think it, my dear. Let her think whatever she wants, because her brain is trying desperately to save her soul from destructing within itself, and this is its last chance. Let's leave her to her happy place, let's go and watch somebody else…

Jean's youngest had been taken into hospital only the week before. Her little angel at seventeen had wasted to only four stone ten.

Even at the best of times these heartless bastards upset her, but now, with her daughter dying of malnutrition from anorexia, she couldn't help it. The sheer fact that she still had to drag herself in to work and could not be at her daughter's side caused her to scream at the prankster.

'We have a serious job to do, you piece of shit, and you are wasting my frigging time!' she cried, after listening to him speak for several seconds, leaving her co-workers gob-smacked and silent. They did not intervene. They hated the prank callers too.

'Listen to me for fuck's sake!' Anthony yelled, tears of anger and frustration stringing his voice. 'She's ill and I need someone here *now*!'

167

'Yeah right, I'm sure your wife, *Autumn Leigh*,' – she turned to her co-workers and shook her head with disbelief at this bit – '*is* stuck in the shower in a trance and I have some advice, *Anthony Denharden*, go out and nick a car, set your school on fire – but don't ever, *ever*, try to make a fool out of me and our ambulance services again. You may really need us some day but we'll be too busy dealing with so called jokers like yourself to answer your call. You'll be left dying in the gutter where you belong.'

With that she hung up and began to sob, enough so that her available co-workers dropped their work and cradled her.

England's youth had turned into heartless fiends and she fucking hated this place sometimes.

Anthony should have known better. He realised this when he heard the dialling tone. Of-course she wouldn't believe him if he used his real name. So he was left alone, his rational thinking to call again under a different name was as gone as his wife.

He looks back now and thinks *if only I'd have just picked up the phone again, if only I'd have called somebody, anybody*... but Anthony was panicking and afraid in a way that he could honestly say he'd never felt before, not even when he got that call, that call: 'Anthony, I'm sorry to call you so late. It's your mother…'

He could still hear the shower running and his thoughts were to be a man, go back in there to his shivering wife and deal with it himself.

Lucy had been sitting for what seemed like hours in her dream world, her happy place, when she felt its presence upon her again. Only this time she did not flinch as it approached her, she only stared back at it with disinterested eyes.

'What have you come back for? You've taken everything.' She spoke in one tone, sat in the shower that wasn't even a shower to her anymore. It was just a thing. And this monster? This monster is just a thing too, *just a thing* like the shower and no more frightening. Why should she be afraid of it anymore? It had nothing left to frighten. It had taken that already. *Stupid shower, stupid monster. It's a stupid, stupid monster. It's a thing, just a thing.*

'Lucy, why were you sick, sweetpea?' Anthony spoke sadly to his wife who, thankfully, was looking a lot less threatening and more, well, asleep with her eyes open.

'You made me sick. Dirty monster.' Her voice was so airy and asleep it made Anthony's blood run cold. She spoke like a child. 'I know,' she added.

'What do you know?' he asked carefully.

'That this is the end,' she replied after a probable pause.

Co-operation was a start; he could talk her out of this nonsense and then get her to a professional.

'The end of what?'

'The end of everything.'

'Why?'

'You've taken my candyfloss.'

'Cand…? When?'

'Just now at the funfair.'

'Lucy, do you know where you are now?'

'I am in the shower room.'

'Do you know who I am?'

'You've come to end it all. You're a messenger from Hell.'

'Lucy, it's me, Anthony, your husband.'

'Don't mock me,' she said calmly, raising her eyes to meet the monster's.

The mention of Anthony's name sparked her thinking brain into action again and sanity was once more on the horizon. Lucy's thoughts were turned away from her happy place and she was back in the real world. Suddenly, so suddenly the

169

shower became a shower again and so suddenly this monster was a monster again and it was laughing at her. It was laughing at her.

'Don't fucking mock me!' she screeched in a voice that was so high pitched and frantic that the words came out inaudible.

A second of realisation had made her recognise that this *thing* had come to take her *life* away from her and she had handed it to him on a plate. No questions asked. *Here monster, here's my soul, thank you for your time* ...and she had just *let* it. She had not put up any sort of fight as it tried to ruin her life, thereby ruining Anthony's too. After all, it may have even killed her husband so her life was destroyed anyway. So, thought the woman covered in vomit and faeces, if she was going to die a messy and undignified death, then she might as well try and save herself first. Nothing to lose and all that cal. So, with all this anger and her soul back with her temporarily, she lunged at it.

Anthony had been talking to her when she screamed at him and then, before he had chance to realise what was happening, she jumped at him. His arms crossed his body as an instant defence reaction but he didn't have time to do anything else.

Lucy pounced on Anthony with an energy he didn't think she possessed. The weight of her landing on him knocked him back into a towel rail and his spine hit it with a painful blow. From there she grabbed at Anthony's clothes and threw him over towards the bath before he'd even had a chance to react or defend himself.

Luckily he was still on his feet at the far end of the bathroom, where he managed to regain some of his space and wits.

His beautiful wife was panting like an animal, glaring at him like he was prey from the other end of the room. Her eyes full of hate, ready to do him some damage. Anthony could do nothing but look back at her. He'd never been so confused in his life. He didn't know what was going on, he didn't know how to handle her, he didn't want to hurt her but he couldn't just let her attack him either. He didn't know whether to try to help her or to run for his life.

His heart was pounding so hard he was half expecting to have a heart attack and drop dead right there on the floor, and the sheer fear and anticipation of what could be to come was causing this strong man to visibly shake. He was losing his nerve.

Lucy stood viewing the monster, mustering every ounce of hatred she could for ammunition to use in her onslaught. It was standing over near the bath so she had a good distance to gather speed over, her idea being to push it in, trap it somehow, and then pummel it to death. This was her last chance to save herself and steal her soul back once and for all, for even the tiniest chance of her ever being able to live a normal life again. So Lucy took a deep breath, thought of her poor husband, and darted like a bullet towards it, desperate to throttle it …

Here she comes… Anthony thought, getting ready to fend her off.

In a matter of seconds she was upon him but instead of throwing herself at him again like he expected, Lucy swiftly kicked him in the stomach, forcing him to fold over. Within a second of him keeling she punched him square in the face with the strength of a street fighter.

Anthony nearly fell backwards into the bath but managed to regain his balance at the last moment and perch on the edge, not able to stand or sit up straight due to the crippling pain in his stomach.

Again, his wife did not let up even for an instant, and before he knew it she had kicked him hard in the face, causing an explosion of blood to spill into his mouth. This time he did fall back and, because he'd instinctively brought his hands up to shield his mouth, he cracked his head hard on the far side of the bath, before falling fully into the acrylic death trap.

Lucy was literally fighting for her life. She knew that if she did not use all the force she could then it would beat her, so she was trying harder than she'd ever tried before to survive.

Lucy looked down at it for a moment and savoured the feeling of strength. She was winning, and this fact gave her even more might. Fired up with an adrenalin rush almost equal to a drug induced high, Lucy jumped over the rim of the bath and landed heavily, feet first, onto the rib cage of the monster. She felt several bones crack beneath her feet and the monster's body collapsed further into the empty bath.

Anthony's mind was blank at this point. The pain was too much.

He was aware that his wife had jumped on him and caused a ripping sensation so excruciating that he was fighting the urge to pass out. He was also aware how defenceless he was in this position but that, thank God, she had moved to the side of him and her weight was transferred to the bath.

Sick little Lucy had gone and the mighty Autumn Leigh was back and brought with her the confidence and self belief that she was going to fight until the end. *Oh yeah!* **Yeah!** *I'm gonna kick your **ass!***

She stood up and over it as it lay pathetically, funny almost, like a battered dummy. She had heard its bones crack a few moments earlier and she wanted to hear more, enough to stop it from getting up. She wanted to scare it back into the underworld forever. Maybe if she murdered it, it would undo everything it had done to her and Anthony and life would go back to the way it was this morning. She had never felt as powerful as the way she felt now. She was going to beat the demon and live to tell the tale.

'You,' she pointed at it over-dramatically, laughing slightly. 'You are going to die.'

With that she kicked it hard in the ribs again, making its entire frail body jump and twist. She kicked it again, not quite believing how easy this was.

'Oh yeah?!' she yelled at it. 'Oh yeah, who's the scary monster now, huh? Try to beat me you piece of shit? Try to hurt my family and me? This is what you get when you try to take *my* life!'

It had wrapped its bony arms around its rotting stomach, so she took this opportunity to stomp on its face. When she did this a satisfying amount of blood shot out from beneath her foot and when she brought it off again the monster cowered further away under its bony hands, which were doing nothing to protect it.

She was kicking him with a force he never knew she had. Before she'd stood on his face he had cried out: 'Get off me you crazy bitch!' but had swallowed a tooth trying to get the words out, nearly causing him to choke.

She had said she was going to kill him and he knew that she would. He knew that if he didn't fight back *my own **wife*** then she would beat him to death. The second after he made the active thought to knock her off her feet so he could try to escape, she crushed her body weight onto his face. The pain was indescribable.

As soon as she removed her foot from his broken face he clasped his hands around his head and began to weep with physical and mental pain. *She's killing me. The woman I have loved and cared for for all these years is beating me to death and I can't stop her because I can't move.*

Autumn Leigh continued to plummet her naked foot into its dusty body so hard that her toes were beginning to sting. She had to find a weapon. Looking around hastily, she spotted something out of the corner of her eye: the toilet brush.

The chrome handled brush stood at the far side of the room so Autumn leapt from her prisoner and moved quickly to get it, sparing a moment to turn back to the bloody bathtub to remind her of her gory glory. *My helpless monster ha, ha. You're my helpless monster I am in charge now, I row the boat. Today, ladies and gentlemen, Autumn Leigh rows the fucking boat.*

With a smile Autumn picked up her weapon and began to move back towards the object of her desire, batting the heavy handle against the palm of her free hand like a bent prison warden with a baton. Now it was more than fighting for her life. Now she was enjoying it.

As Autumn left him for a moment, disappearing out of sight, panting as if possessed, Anthony's eyes were rolling to the back of his head then returning. His body tensed with the sudden pain then numbed for a short time while on the verge of blacking out.

Anthony realised that if he passed out he could die. He didn't know what she was capable of now – she had lost her mind. So, using all the strength he had, he fought this notion and tried to scramble out from the bathtub. He had to at least change positions because his neck was twisting due to the way he had landed from the assault, and he had to do something from fear of it breaking.

Anthony tried to hoist himself out with his hands but they were covered in blood so he couldn't get a grip. Not even his upper arms would work because the bathtub was such a bloody mess of red smears and puddles; he kept slipping down. He was stuck and every time he tried to move his body the pain was excruciating, but he also knew that if he stayed she would kill him.

He used his last reserve of strength and managed to wrap his fingers around the bath's edge to get some leverage, but then Anthony saw what he thought was a flash of light and his extended hand, his saviour, went numb.

The marvellous Autumn Leigh knocked the monster back into the depths of the bathtub with a whacking crack of metal onto its bony hand, which was oh so temptingly gripped around the rim. As she had brought the heavy duty handle down on to its fingers, the shiny chrome had caught the light streaming through the window, causing it to reflect beautifully like a blade. To her pleasure she thought she might have heard each and every finger break as it quickly withdrew back into the tub.

Autumn Leigh then leant over and into its resin grave and proceeded in stabbing her monster repeatedly with the chrome handle of the toilet brush, using both hands for extra intensity, losing her breath due to the tremendous effort of the movement.

Hearing its gasps of raspy breath and imagining its struggling internals made her jab it harder, fuelling her need to kill it. With each thud she could almost see her soul seeping out of it and back into her, and it gave her the strength to hammer it and hammer it until... finally, it went limp.

His wife had beaten him to the point where his body had become numb to the blows. He had stopped struggling and simply covered his face with one arm, to prevent her knocking out more of his already broken teeth or taking out an eye. Every time she hit him his body jumped as if electrocuted yet the pain felt normal now. He had accepted that this was how he was going to die and his beautiful wife would be a murderer without even knowing it. She was not killing him in her eyes, he had gathered that now, she was killing someone or something else but unfortunately her mind had taken power over her sight and replaced it with whatever it was she was hammering to death.

As she beat him over and over, he felt desperately sorry for her.

He was sorry for the day her mind would clear and she would come to realise she had murdered her husband. If he had the time between blows he could have wept for that day.

She stood over the battered, blood-spattered mess in her beautiful bathroom. She had saved herself; she had defeated the demon. It had come to take her and she had won. Not just a pretty face.

Autumn Leigh stood proud over the bathtub and looked over it through sticky air. *Pathetic.* She kicked it once more and laughed. The winner. The champion. A golden medal for Ms Leigh please.

As he's beginning to feel no pain at all his mind calmly journeys back to his archives. Ladies and gentlemen – this good man, our friend Anthony, is dying.

His body feels the most relaxed that it has ever been. The murky shadow standing over him does not bother him anymore. The fact the humid air is making his wounds itch, and that the moisture is sticking to him like a second skin, does not matter now. Everything is okay. Everything is just fine indeed and *yeah. Yeah, I'm starting to feel a lot better now…*

Tell us what you see, Tony.

I am seven and it is raining and sunning in Leeds. It's the six weeks of the year I love the most, the six weeks in the summer I have off school. Mum is with me in Pudsey Park – the child

Heaven that lets us play and eat penny sweets and stroke petting goats. This is my favourite place, my friends. I can't imagine standing here now, as an adult. The possible threat of graffiti masking it would be too upsetting; the possibility that children dare not go there these days and what if needles scatter the floor? I like it like this; I like it in 1960 when this beautiful park spanned the world and I, as a child, would run like a king through it.

I am here now, watching myself play as if in a dream. Only I can smell. I smell the fresh cut grass, I smell cinnamon sticks and I smell my mother's perfume. Look at me so young. Look at me in my favourite striped top and brown cord, my favourite outfit. Look at me with my wispy, straight hair, just growing long enough to cover my collar.

Can we join you, Tony?

I don't see why not. Come with me.

Anthony Denharden is right – this place is dreamlike. In soft tone we stand in Pudsey Park, which is a concrete rectangle roughly the size of a netball pitch, surrounded by gardens and bright flowers. It houses swings, monkey bars, a roundabout, concrete carved animals and a helter-skelter slide.

We stand watching carefree children play and eat ice cream and queue up at the candy shack for sweets. The rain is fine and brushes the sunny, almost cloudless sky causing a rainbow of colours to arch over the park. I can see why Anthony has chosen to revisit this time, this beautiful memory of adolescence – it portrays the childhood we all wanted. He is beautiful and he is laughing.

We are stood next to the bench facing the park where his mother is sitting. To the right of us are the masses of green

177

gardens that she will take Anthony round once he has tired of the swings and slides.

She is beautiful and we are standing close enough to see her smiling, watching her only child, her little boy, and not minding that the light shower is landing quietly on her golden hair. She is where Anthony gets his compassion and good looks.

Anthony's adult self is not standing with us, his presence is everywhere. He surrounds the sky. He is in the rain. He is the gardens.

The little boy that grew up to be a Hollywood movie-star is trying his hardest to push the roundabout with three young boys and one eleven year old girl upon it. He is grinding his teeth and his arms are shaking with effort.

His mother is so proud of her little Anthony, named after her father because he was a good man. She laughs loud enough for us to hear and we both smile widely.

The children on the roundabout hang their feet down and try to help Anthony to push. The roundabout starts to move slightly and Anthony and the other children cheer and scream with fun and games within their voices. The struggle eases as a girl in a plastic rain-mac runs up and helps him to push. Within a few moments Anthony and the girl are running and the roundabout is travelling at speed. They both jump on and for a matter of seconds they enjoy the rain covering their skin that little bit faster, before the roundabout begins to slow again.

The memory was short but beautiful and he wants to go somewhere else now but we cannot go there. We have other places to be right now, so we leave the sixties and Pudsey Park behind.

Autumn Leigh abandoned the monster and ran down the staircase to try to find her husband. It had dawned on her to stop beating the monster and to think about Anthony, to find him and make sure he was okay. Wonderful images of her love being blissfully unaware of all this ran through her mind as she jumped frantically to the bottom step. She heard the television on and pictured him sitting watching it.

However, upon running through to the front room she was distressed to find BBC 1 news depressing only the furniture.

Anthony was not there. She ran through to the dinning room – empty, the kitchen – empty.

'Anthony!' she cried, darting into the entrance hall. 'Anthony!'

Why did I waste my time on the monster once I had killed it? What if Anthony has bled to death while I was pointlessly kicking the monster?

She stood in the middle of the house and screamed so hard her throat hurt and she had to stop. Horrific thoughts of her darling husband croaking her name while she was too busy getting off on murder made her hysterical and the famous Autumn Leigh pulled at her hair and began to wail.

Her mind was telling her to go and kick the monster some more for hiding her husband. *Kick it, kick it, kick it until your foot sinks into its gaping wounds, slice and slash until you can reach into its filthy cloak and pull out its heart with your own bare hands. You should cut out its fucking eyes for what it has done to Anthony. Your gorgeous prince could be dead and that scum creature is going to get away with a simple beating?! Go and bite its goddamn ears off Lucy. Go do it...*

Knock, knock... the noise interrupted Autumn's anger fit. Her fingers stood still in her shower steamed, frizzy hair. She stood and listened harder to make sure it wasn't a trick of the mind. She waited silently until... knock, knock. *Anthony!*

The noise had come from the kitchen, a sound like a fist tapping on window glass. Within a moment Autumn's face lit up and she was running through to hold her loved one tightly, to tell him: 'I thought you were dead! Oh I love you, baby! I love you, I love you, I love you!'

As she darted through, her hair now drying in rattails from the central-heated air, she called to him once more. Still not

179

finding him in the kitchen she ran through to the conservatory and found the hand which was tapping.

What she was faced with was not her darling husband but the gardener. Her heart sunk upon first seeing him, but she figured she could use him to assist her non-the-less; at least she wasn't on her own anymore. No, he wasn't Anthony, but he could help her find him and dispose of the monster.

Arnold, the gardener – with his face pressed up against the outside glass of the conservatory – had jumped back in shock when she appeared and didn't quite know how to react or where to look.

The naked American-sounding movie-star began shouting: 'Gardener! I've been attacked, you've gotta help me! Wait, I'll get the keys to let you in!'

After those words she ran back out of sight and Arnold's speechless mouth dropped open.

Arnold had worked on these magnificent gardens for as long as anybody could remember and not once, not even *once* my dear friend, did he ever get involved with the people who lived there for anything other than business reasons. He had heard the wildest arguments while going about his thrice-weekly chores. He had seen women and men come and go in floods of tears and anger – but it never made him look up for more than three seconds. He was a wise family man. Wise enough to know it was none of his business.

But once upon a time, children, Arnold the trusty gardener was hauling dead and dying leaves into the leaf morgue when he heard the most bloodcurdling shriek you could ever have imagined. It made the hairs on the back of his weathered neck stand up like brave little soldiers. And what did Arnold do? Why he threw down his rake and ran towards the big, big house....

After a few minutes Arnold's crazy Canadian ran back through to the conservatory, fumbled with some keys, and then finally let him in.

Arnold, overwhelmed, could only say: 'What's happened, love?'

The woman was hysterical, shaking and moving like frightened people do.

'I've been attacked, gardener. I've been fucking attacked and I've lost my husband!' She wailed the words like a spoilt seven-year-old who had dropped her ice cream before one single wonderful lick.

Not knowing what to make of this whole strange and frightening situation, Arnold found himself stammering like he did when he was just knee high to a grasshopper.

'N-n-now, now love,' Arnold held her shoulders in an attempt to comfort her. Staring at her he continued: 'Who's attack... who's attacked y-you, eh?'

'A monster!' she yelled, her eyes wide. 'I think I've killed it but I can't find my husband!'

Now when she had first said 'monster', Arnold automatically assumed monster was 'woman talk' for some evil man who'd somehow snuck in and gave her the fright of her life. But the words 'killed' and 'it' made him worried enough to step back to the outside of the house.

'Oh, ma'am...' he said, shaking his head. 'Oh n-no. H-have you... you cal-called the po-police...? I think we... shou-should... lea- lea...'

'*No!* Get back here!' the woman screamed at the gardener, making him cower back one-step further. 'Didn't you hear me, you pathetic piece of shit? I said my husband has gone missing! Are you fucking deaf?'

The words struck our nervous and quiet gardener like venom.

'N-no... bu-but...'

The naked movie-star tried to grab the old man and pull him back in to help her *why won't he help me? What's wrong with this man?* but Arnold was caught off guard and scared stiff. There was no way he was going in there with that deranged woman.

He had to leave. He stumbled first, then ran. Before he knew it he was running through the grounds in the direction of the nearest house. He would help her, yes, but he would do it by getting hold of the police, not by having a look at a dead 'monster' himself.

The only words that stood out in his mind from the shouting she was hurling at him as he ran were simply three: 'You're fucking *FIRED*!!!'

Well that piece of shit. That goddamned lousy old man. The one person within distance of you that could have made everything all right and help out a woman so desperately in need has gone running. He ran from you, Autumn. He has left you alone with the monster and a possibly dead husband. What are you going to do now?

Autumn Leigh screeched with frustration at the thought. Her throat stung again but this time she didn't care. She screamed until her voice cracked. The disloyalty of her employee had turned a panicked woman into a maddened woman and I can't put into words how excruciatingly close she was to chasing him through the garden, catching up with him and then beating him to death too. However, on this occasion her crazed anger bubbled under just enough for her to remember that she had bigger fish to fry: she had to find Anthony.

Autumn Leigh took the largest knife from the knife rack and began searching room to room for any sign of her husband.

However, there was no dead body to be found in the bar, no floating corpse in the swimming pool, and no severed head in the dining room. In fact, there was not a trace of him anywhere downstairs.

Autumn made her way back upstairs, fingers gripped tightly around the knife, trembling with the fear of what she might find.

The bathroom drew her attention almost immediately because the showers were still on and the sound of the water running had aroused her suspicions about whether she actually had killed the monster off. She checked out the showers first and then began to walk over to the bloodbath at the far end of the room.

Before even particularly noting the corpse itself, Autumn took in the scene as a whole and it made her wonder how she managed to get out of there alive. Any normal woman would have surely perished, if not died of fright alone. But Autumn Leigh had come back from that... laughed at it even. She had conquered all as always and despite staring at such a sad and tormenting scene, she felt an overwhelming surge of pride flush through her body.

She then walked forward further in to look closer at the monster, just to prove to herself that such a bizarre thing really had happened... and that's when she realised it. She realised something about this scene wasn't right.

The monster had been wearing a heavy, potato-sack like gown... the leg sticking out from the deep bath was wearing bloodstained jeans. Following an animated blink and customary drop of the mouth, her heart rose up into her throat.

Arnold had stuttered murder to Mrs Deaves and her five shocked children. In fact he had stuttered it so bad she had to guess what he was saying.

Once it was established that there might have been a murder at the house further down the road, Mrs Deaves quickly called the police and ambulance, before flicking the kettle on for the distressed gardener.

She stood. Stood like a statue, staring.

The monster wasn't wearing jeans, this body is. The monster wasn't wearing jeans this body is. The monster wasn't wearing jeans. She was trying to deny it to herself but it was obvious what had happened. The monster had left and replaced its body with Anthony's. It had tried to frame her and the man she loved was dead.

My Anthony is dead and I'm staring. I'm staring at my dead husband's body.

Then and there it hit her. The knife slid from her hand and landed with a clatter onto the wooden floor she was standing on. Everything numbed. Everything ended. The alter-ego that had allowed Lucy to function for all of her adult life disappeared with a puff of smoke and now she was on her own again.

Have you ever heard the sound of an entire world crumbling? If you have then you can understand and I am sorry; it's sad that you can identify with such utter trauma. If you haven't then let's just say you are lucky and you can do nothing but imagine what Lucy, who is hearing and feeling it now, is going through. A screeching, scratching sound of brittle nails engulfs her. Her entire world falls like the towers and leaves the same destruction. It is horrific. She is gone.

We both know that since the party things have worsened at a dramatic, almost unbelievable rate for our girl... but today, now, this is the final nail in the coffin. Seeing that monster so real, surviving the life or death struggle and now coming face to face with a bludgeoned corpse that is the mangled remains of her soul-mate were enough to pass the point of no return for Lucy.

Staring at her husband's body, she still believed, from the bottom of her heart, that the monster had put it there to frame her. It never once occurred to her that this had been another trip like the worms and her dead child and all the other bizarre things that had been occurring. It never once came to mind that she could have done this while being in some kind of delusional state, that she had never even really seen the monster, that it had been Anthony all along just like the dead embryo of Alexander was really just a meat platter. She never

184

once thought that she would be able to see a monster in the gentle man that she loved so much, so it never crossed her mind.

Standing like a gawping tourist looking into the debris of what once was a wonderful life was all that our movie-star could do now. It was over.

Oh how he must have suffered at the hands of that rotting messenger from Hell. Oh how he must have suffered. On the verge of mentally imploding, Lucy left the scene of carnage and made her way into the same bedroom that she had peacefully woken up in this morning, and once in there she hung herself.

•

The police and ambulances' access was harder than most due to the electric gate they had to conquer first. Once they had entered the grounds they ran into the house through the unlocked front door.

What they found was unbelievable.

Autumn Leigh, *the* Autumn Leigh hanging naked from a beam in her bedroom. Anthony Denharden, *the* Anthony Denharden, hardly recognisable with only the slightest trace of a heartbeat laying beaten and dying fast in a bathtub filled with blood.

Lucy was cut down from the dressing-gown robe she had used to commit suicide. Like Anthony, there was only a faint heartbeat, however she was successfully resuscitated on the spot. One minute longer hanging from expensive nightwear and she'd have been dead.

Anthony, unfortunately, was not as simple for the services. A broken neck or back was feared so he could not be moved until the right people and equipment had been brought in, seriously delaying aid for a matter of minutes. Luckily, neither were broken but both were severely damaged in several places.

He was carefully hoisted onto a stretcher and rushed off to hospital. He flat-lined once on the way there and the poor girl trying to bring him back had one hell of a job trying not to push her hands too hard into the sinking, bloody bruises on his chest.

Anthony was not expected to pull through as his beating had been so ferocious, and by the time he arrived at the hospital he was in a deep coma so the extent of his long-term injuries and possible brain damage were unknown. Unfortunately the staff nurses and doctors were used to this in their ward; innocent people would often turn up beaten within an inch of their life. Most of them died, the lucky ones recovered and the tragic ones spent the rest of their years in a vegetative state. Anthony was going to be one of these three, and it was just a case of waiting to see which one the Big Man had in store for him.

CHAPTER 7

'You seem withdrawn today, Anthony. Do you not want to talk?'

Anthony nods.

'Is it what we talked about on Monday?'

Anthony shakes his head.

'What are you feeling today?'

Anthony looks up.

A little less than thirteen dazed months had passed since the day Anthony had gone to join his beautiful wife in the shower. The man who once had the world at his feet was now nothing but a shadow of his former self.

The list of injuries Anthony sustained on that day was colossal and it was a medical miracle that he had survived at all, never mind come out of it as able-bodied as he had. Falling into the bath alone had fractured his skull and Lucy had then beat him so hard around the head that it had left him mildly brain damaged, affecting his concentration levels and leaving him no choice other than to retire from work. Along with mass internal bruising she'd also broken all the fingers in his right hand, his ribs, his left leg and both arms, as well as fracturing two vertebrae and puncturing a lung. Externally Anthony was left with physical scars that he'd have to live with for the rest of his life, as well as needing to undergo corrective surgery on his face and having to wear dentures to replace his many missing teeth. Mentally, Anthony had hit the very depths of reactive depression and spent most of his days either sleeping or contemplating ending it all.

Today Anthony is having a 'bad' day.

A bad day is the description his psychologist, Dr Nazir, has given to the days where Anthony simply can't handle what has happened, when the depression forces his eyes closed and she has to push him to stay awake and communicate with her. On bad days Anthony has to be wheeled around in a wheelchair

189

because he can't find the energy or will to walk. On bad days he can see no good in the future and why live when everything is black and nothing will ever get better? On bad days like today, his misery grows so fierce you can almost see the emotion rise up from him and darken the sky.

But Anthony has learnt something within the past few weeks that could provide him with his only chance of saving himself... he has learnt the importance of fighting the mighty depression by talking about it.

It had taken Dr Nazir a while to get this far though. At one point she thought that he would simply never communicate properly with anyone ever again, that he'd sleep and sleep until one day he just never woke up. At one point she had thought Anthony Denharden unsaveable.

She had been seeing Anthony four times a week for the past nine weeks, but he'd only been responding for three. It was frustratingly hard work and her heart broke for him over and over again. Here, sat in front of Dr Nazir was a broken man, truly and unbelievably broken.

She remembered him from the height of his fame. She was one of the thousands of women who would queue up in the cinema just to watch him larger than life; an eye wateringly handsome man dressed in Gucci and on the arm of the world's most envied and beautiful woman. Not only was Anthony a stunner but, to fit the perfect man bill down to a tee, he was also incredibly down-to-earth and amusing, funny even, in interviews. Autumn Leigh appeared the same; they were seen as being by far the perfect couple.

And now, sitting crumpled in her company was a scraggy, unshaven, soulless human, a man with nothing to live for. When the news first broke that there had been some kind of attack and Autumn and Anthony were involved, the entire country listened avidly. They listened to the rumours, the gossip and the speculation for days until the official statement was made.

190

When the statement had finished only the journalists carried on screaming and shouting and asking improvised questions. The rest of the world sat back in shock. Nothing like this had ever happened in the history of show-business before. Never have two of the most admired and beautiful people in the world been involved in such a tragic chain of events. Nobody could believe it.

For the next six months, Anthony and Autumn were front page news, but when all of the big stuff was out of the way they began slowly slipping to page two, then page four, then six... and now, they were old news.

What was once neat, chocolate brown hair was now greying, brittle and straggly. What were once designer suits were now replaced by loose jogging bottoms and big jumpers, and sometimes, like today, a wheelchair. What were once striking eyes now just looked empty and spent. Something else was taken from him that day over a year ago: his personality. The blaze within Anthony had long gone; he was now a victim in every sense of the word.

The house had gone. He hired an assistant from his hospital bed six months ago and told him to sell it and buy him a place back up in his birthplace of Leeds. *Take me back home.* These were as good as the first words he said when he had come out of intensive care. *Throw everything away, get rid of it all. I never want to be reminded of that place again. Buy me a house in the city where I grew up. Furnish it brand new. I don't want to see anything from before all this.*

His personal assistant found him an executive apartment right in the heart of the city, costing a mere half million. It blended in so well with the hustle and bustle of central Leeds that you wouldn't even be able to tell that there were apartments in the building unless you stopped and looked.

Although Anthony became a virtual recluse inside his new home, on the odd occasion that he did venture out he never got recognised. No shit, straight up. He was, as intended, totally anonymous in the city and that's one thing he appreciated.

Who'd expect a traumatised Hollywood movie-star to be quietly standing in line in your local sandwich shop, bearded and nervous?

All in all, Anthony came out of hospital to his friendly assistants and carers, a furnished flat, and a bank account with a stockpile of millions. Everything was set up for him to start his new life. His carers, advisers and assistants had been amazing. The only problem was that Anthony didn't want this new life, he didn't want anything at all anymore... except to turn back the clock.

The people that had nursed him back to health had also provided him with the best psychologist this side of England to help him deal with the mental effects that this was bound to have. She was the gifted and compassionate Dr Saima Nazir.

Saima was in her mid thirties and had never come across such a challenge in her entire life, professionally or personally. In reality she wanted to hug the poor man, she wanted to tell him how beautiful he was and that his wife deserved bad things for doing what she did to him – such a gentle, mild man. But she was a professional and this was her career. She was here to save this man, not mother him, although... if only she could.

Today, in their ninth week they are sitting in the study of Anthony's discreet and dark apartment. Built to be open plan, light and modern, Anthony uses it only to cocoon his darkness, preferring to keep his heavy curtains shut and his furniture dusty.

The place is still tasteful, however, and the study in particular is in good order, almost in the same condition as Dr Nazir's own office. She is sitting behind the same desk that Anthony's assistant uses to write out cheques and pay bills from once a week.

Anthony sees this as Dr Nazir's space even though it is his property in his flat. She is unaware of this but Anthony trusts her with his life; he knows that this patient and intelligent woman is his last chance of ever getting better and – I can't emphasise this enough – the effort he puts into their sessions is immense for a man so eaten by despair. If you and I tried to talk to him now he would either fall asleep or mentally shut down. He would not mean to, you know what Anthony's like, he'd never intentionally be rude and is as accommodating as they get, but he wouldn't be able to help it.

This is why every single time Anthony strings a sentence together it sets Dr Nazir's heart alight. She fully understands how excruciatingly difficult it is for Anthony to fight what his body is telling him he should do. *Goodnight Anthony, let's sleep it all away.*

The first time he ever properly responded to her three weeks ago she knew then that he had the strength to beat this eventually, and from that very first full sentence, *I only went up there to show her how much I still loved her,* she made it her life's ambition to get this man on his feet and laughing again.

Dr Nazir asked him what he was feeling and he focused on her.

He didn't know how to word it and if she'd have given him a little longer he would have begun, but she assumed by his lack of response that the sentence had flown through him, like a little bird, so she repeated herself.

'Anthony? What are you feeling today?'

Anthony was not an obstinate or irrational man. He was placid and did not mind that she had interrupted him seconds before he was about to speak.

'Today I feel that life is unfair.'

'Why?'

This is how Anthony has learnt to talk. He spoke almost mechanically, no longer using his hands to express himself, no longer full of movement and emotion and everything else that struck us two when we were speaking to him all that time ago.

However, in the weeks that Anthony had begun listening to Dr Nazir, concentrating and talking back had gone from being almost impossible to almost manageable. In a dusky sky of a

193

foreign land Anthony could see the first faint beams of hope emanating from the clouds. These beams were welcome relief from the dense fog that had fallen on him since the incident, making him determined to continue trying.

'Why not? Life *is* unfair.'

'Give me your reasons.'

'Where do I start?'

'Start with the thing that is bothering you the most this morning.'

'Alex,' Anthony whispered, dropping his eyes. 'It's unfair that Alex was a mis-shape. Things could have been so different.'

There was a short, comfortable silence.

'Three years ago last month,' Anthony continued, sighing. 'It feels like it happened in a different life now to two whole other people, it's so far away.' Anthony gave a faint, sad smile and looked Dr Nazir in the eyes. 'He'd be three now. He'd be saying daddy. I just wish... I just wish he'd have been born a full human being. He didn't even have sexual organs, Doctor. Did I tell you that already?'

Dr Nazir nodded slowly and Anthony shook his head to rid himself of the thought.

'Sorry. Everything just seems so unreal. I keep thinking of ways that this could have been avoided. Oh I don't know, if I'd have lived a life full of struggles and hard times then maybe this would be easier to take. But to see a life of fame and fortune slip through your hands and transform into this, it's...' Anthony shook his head and looked around the room trying to find the right word. It never came.

'Is today a bad day?' Dr. Nazir asked after several moments' silence.

Anthony was biting his bottom lip. 'Yes,' he nodded. *It certainly is.*

'You will continue to speak with me though, won't you? You're strong and you can do it.'

Anthony nodded. He *must* try. He would have to force himself into finding more energy to think let alone speak, but he could do it if he put all his will into it.

On the days when he is alone, Anthony sleeps. That's all he can do. Without Dr Nazir around to make an effort for, melancholy flattens him and nothing at all matters other than shutting those heavy eyes and drifting away. Today the feeling is applying with force but Anthony understands how important it is that he at least *tries* to stay awake.

Fighting against a thousand emotions trying to crash his mind leaves him physically exhausted but, like Dr Nazir had said, when an unfit person attends a gym for the first few weeks it's murder too, but after a while its gets easier until one day they're fit and exercise is easy. This is the same thing. *Keep walking on that treadmill and you may even be able to run on it one day.*

'How are you feeling about Lucy today?'

He had specifically requested Dr Nazir to call his wife Lucy. That was her name and now she could no longer ban him, or anyone else for that matter, from calling her it. Anthony thought for only a moment before speaking.

'I feel so sorry for her,' he said, drawing a deep breath. 'I wish I could help her but I can't. Look what she's done. What she's done to me is just… just too much.'

Anthony paused for a long, long while but Dr Nazir could tell that he was thinking, so she remained silent.

'Like mother like son,' he said sadly, not altering his gaze from the floor. 'Mam was beaten to unconsciousness by the one she loved too.'

This sentence sank Dr Nazir's heart. She was keen to keep Anthony away from relating his wife to his father, as it always ended up causing unnecessary upset and was the equivalent of taking two steps backwards on the road to acceptance.

'A few sessions ago we discussed your dad's temper, and you said what Lucy did was quite different. Do you not think that anymore?' Dr Nazir asked.

'My dad beat my mam up, Lucy beat me up. It all seems pretty similar to me,' Anthony said with a facial expression of lazy self-pity.

Dr Nazir was painfully aware that her opinions must be kept to herself in her profession, but she had to do something about Anthony's destructive thought patterns of comparing the two as this subject was a vicious circle that could not be laid to rest until he snapped out of that way of thinking completely.

Between you and I, Saima can't help but hint at her opinions from time to time, and believe it or not it is this trait that makes her such an excellent psychologist, as her ideas are wise and knowledgeable and almost always never occur to the person she's speaking to prior to her telling them. Do not repeat this to anybody though, as voicing opinions is not a psychologist's job and is greatly looked down upon. If she knew she was unintentionally doing it then she'd make a massive effort not to, thus lessening her skills to improve lives. But anyway, now we both know that let's forget I even mentioned it and listen to the doctor as Anthony is...

'But look at the reasons, Anthony. Your dad was a man of much rage, Lucy was deluded. Do you really think of Lucy in the same way as that man?'

Anthony wrestled with her words until eventually she won and his shoulders dropped.

'No. You're right, I'm sorry. I must sound like a broken record,' Anthony said eventually. 'I guess I wouldn't feel quite so resentful if I could find out exactly what happened to her, the reason why it happened. I don't for one minute accept this as a mental breakdown.'

'Why not?' Saima asked.

'Something odd happened to her. I just wish I had the ability to convince people to look into it. It was the morning after the awards when she started seeing things. Something happened to her that night and I'm sure Jerry Tilsey had something to do with it.' To the surprise of both of them, Anthony's answer was spoken in the strongest voice and quickest pace he'd used so far.

'The actor?'

'Yeah.'

'Why? What changed after that night?'

'Well, you know the story, right?' Anthony asked, enjoying the need to talk about this subject, the urge to sleep lessening ever so slightly, just enough to make a difference to his word pace.

'Yes, Lucy drank too much alcohol and collapsed, didn't she?'

'Well, she collapsed and yes she was drunk, but there was more to it than that. They spoke about it in court before they sent her away reckoning that the breakdown was natural and nothing to do with that night. There was *nothing* natural about that. And I swear to you, I swear this is the result of something she's taken or been given. I sent her for a drug test but it came up negative so they dismissed it just like that and found an easier answer: crazy. She's had a breakdown. She's gone *mad.*' Anthony wiggled his fingers and widened his eyes with sarcasm. Seeing him expressing himself in this way was new to Saima. 'I know her more than anyone but all of a sudden they all know better than I do. I really wish I had the energy to fight for her but I just can't. I can barely muster the energy to feed myself.'

'But look at you now, the change in your voice, your body language. You're passionate about this, I can tell. Would you consider having a serious think about taking your suspicions further?'

He didn't hear her. This was a regular occurrence. She repeated the question.

'I don't know,' Anthony answered. 'I doubt it. Who's going to listen now? They've got their answers.'

Dr Nazir left shortly after the conversation as Anthony was feeling drowsy following so much excitement. Anthony walked through to his bedroom and lay on his bed with his arms behind his head. He shut his eyes and allowed his vision to be enveloped in darkness. It was within that darkness that a memory was found and began to take over his waking thoughts, before submerging him completely in the past...

The evening had been perfect. The two of them had been running around like children, talking and laughing non stop, sipping champagne, making love. Having only been in their house a few days, boxes were still stacked up everywhere and they were still living with the previous occupants' decorating and layout mistakes. Their living room was still wallpapered with pale yellow and white flower patterns over it, with the colour intensified where old pictures had once been.

They didn't care about the amount of work that lay ahead of them though. This was their dream house, the place to start a big family. Life couldn't get any better.

Anthony grabbed his beautiful new bride's hand and pulled her up close to him. They staggered a slow waltz to the silence and laughed at first. Then he held her closer and she ran her strawberry and cream fingers through his hair and whispered how much she loved him...

'She was so passionate,' Anthony said as he slipped into his favourite subliminal pastime.

•

Meanwhile, Lucy Denharden was sitting on her bed, staring expressionlessly through the walls. Her eyes were tired and out of focus, her body motionless and calm. She hadn't blinked for so long her eyes stung but still she did not move them.

The Home Office had sent Lucy to Penford Psychiatric Hospital. They had wanted to send her to a prison secure unit, but due to administration complications she ended up here, a small psychiatric hospital in Warwickshire. She was detained under the Mental Health Act 1983, sections 37 and 41. In other words she's sectioned here until the big-wigs of the Home Office say she's safe enough to leave, and that will not be this side of Christmas, sonny Jim, I can tell you that for sure.

Mrs Denharden, the woman who used to laugh gracefully and give selfless speeches when accepting awards, was given her own little room complete with a square observation window in the door so the nurses there could keep tabs without disturbing her. Like every other patient, she was now living off the GP Fundholders money, and was feeding from the hand of the Department of Health. The marvellous Autumn Leigh had disappeared up in smoke the day Lucy had hung herself and the nurses treat her no differently than any of the other twenty-four patients on their ward.

Lucy couldn't stand in court because by this point our gal had been diagnosed as suffering from catatonic schizophrenia, and was physically and mentally unable to attend.

Since Lucy saw the monster that day, she couldn't do anything for herself. Her mind had just shut down what it couldn't cope with. It had seen far, far too much in that bathroom so it retracted upon itself and hid. Only, it hid so deep that it left those big eyes glassy and unfocused, it hid so deep that her conscious thoughts lay abandoned, her body limp and unresponsive. It hid so deep that it couldn't get back out again.

Lucy had been on suicide watch for the first few weeks at Penford, but it soon became obvious that it would be more therapeutic for Mrs Denharden to be moved down a notch. She didn't pose a threat to those around her or to herself so she was brought into the general ward. Lucy was treated with benzodiazepines and fed 5 milligrams of liquid Haloperidol twice a day; this kept her calm and quiet. She, like many other diagnosed schizophrenics, was also given courses of ECP, Electric Convulsive Therapy, three times a week for four weeks each time, in the hope that it would aid a gradual recovery and that she would be able to communicate again... but it wasn't to be. Alas, the big, bad world remained cut off from Lucy, and Lucy remained cut off from the big, bad world.

If you were to ask our favourite nurse here at Penford, Nurse Lindle, what she thought of her newest patient, she'd have said: 'As patients go, she's one of the better ones.' And she'd be right.

Lucy, like five others on Nurse Lindle's ward, barely spoke and barely moved. She was a hell of a lot easier to look after than the ones who attacked and punched and screamed.

The nurses had signed a confidentiality clause and were told that if they spoke to the newspapers they would be fired immediately.

At first the press would hang around the hospital gates but now the place was back to normal and the nurses had forgotten who their patient used to be and concentrated on who she was now – a highly disturbed and mentally ill woman who tried to kill her husband and herself.

So now, please, my friend, come with me and meet our new character, Nurse Alicia Lindle. I think it's important that you get to know Nurse Lindle from the start, as she is our Lucy's Named Nurse, coordinating Lucy's treatment and care during daytime hours. Nurse Lindle is also one of the two the most experienced and qualified on this ward, in charge of the four other assistant and student nurses working the day shift.

I place her standing directly in front of us in one of the rooming corridors on the general ward. Don't worry, it's not going to be as spooky as the floor you found yourself on in the introduction. I didn't like that either; places like that are too dangerous when there's only the two of us. Considering we got off to a bad start like that, I think we've managed to pull through together pretty well, don't you?

So, anyway, here she is. The kind and sympathetic nurse is, like magic, standing about twenty metres ahead of us down a well lit, shiny tiled and spotlessly clean corridor in her workplace. I know Nurse Lindle already as I invented her well before you and I found each other and embarked on this dark adventure, this slightly sadistic watching game, together. This lovely woman is based on my Aunt Maggie, my dad's sister, who I have known and loved for each one of the twenty-three years of my life. My aunt is also a nurse, you see, and also a good person for that matter so I just can't picture anyone else, fictional or real, when a 'good nurse' character comes up on the cards. I can't help it, just like one can't help laughing at the word 'mullet'. You know what I mean, right?

We are still standing some distance away from her, so let's begin walking. From here, we can see that she stands with good posture, we can see that her hands are effortlessly held together entwined by her fingers in front of her midriff, and that she is wearing a crisp white uniform and flat, white pumps.

We get closer still and are able to determine that she is in her early fifties and has kind features and short, mousy hair. She is no taller than 5'2 but holds it well and is in good shape for her small frame.

We are nearly up to her now and her face breaks out in a gentle, enduring smile. Nurse Lindle greets us with a handshake and I introduce you both. I am not surprised to see that you like her immediately.

'I'll be heading a group discussion in five minutes, actually,' she informs us in a well-spoken manner, as the three of us begin slowly walking down the corridor. 'I'm going take the last one of the ladies down into the community room, her name is Lucy. I think she's the girl that you're most interested in so I thought you might want to come with me... maybe even sit in on the discussion group?'

We both agree that that would be good and continue walking towards where the girl that we're most interested in resides.

'What exactly is your role, Nurse Lindle?' you ask out of curiosity.

'I am Key Nurse to six ladies on this ward, and I am supervisor of the four day staff. There are twenty-four inpatients on the general wing – some demanding constant attention – but we keep a good ship running.'

We are approaching Lucy's room now so the good nurse will not be able to answer the many questions I feel you want to know.

So I'll tell you…

Nurse Lindle has worked in this hospital since she was twenty, way back in 1960. She's seen the system change countless times and hundreds of patients come and go along with a few staff; some kind, some cruel. Only two patients remained on the ward throughout the entirety of Alicia's career at Penford and would probably continue to be there until they died. Denharden, one of their newest additions, was expected to make it three.

Nurse Lindle is a genuinely caring lady who has brought up three children into fine young adults. She now lives alone with her husband six miles away from Penford. The patients respect her and, although sometimes testing, she respects them too.

She treats the women who reside at Penford as adults and people, not as objects like some nurses have over the years.

The hospital is dedicated to helping the mentally ill and it has been used for that purpose since 1920, although back in 1920 the building was used only to keep them, not to help them. Before that it nursed the wounded and dying of the First World War, and before that it was a boarding school. In 1972 it had had an extra unit added so it could house up to one hundred and sixty mentally ill patients, which was considerably small compared to most hospitals. Now, in our present fictional date of the early nineties it's only filled to half its capacity anyway, due to most of the people they deal with these days been outpatients, not living in the hospital.

Penford at the moment consists of a men's wing and a women's wing, each consisting of different wards and sections. The women's general ward, where Lucy is happily passing time by staring beyond walls, is housed in the extension built in the early seventies. The extension is all on one level and is the one part of the hospital where the nurses feel the most comfortable, and the staff turnover is considerably less than in other parts of the building. If you ask why the women's general ward is preferable, your responses will vary from *it's a little less spooky* through to *it's the only part of the hospital that's not haunted.* But anyway, that's a whole other show.

Nurse Lindle stops outside a room that we both recognise, although this time it is in totally different surroundings, thank God.

It looks a lot better in sharp light doesn't it? It looks a lot better now that it's fully developed, on a proper ward in a proper hospital. Much better than when it was still swimming around, growing and forming in a murky, unknown back-alley somewhere in the depths of my mind.

There is a standard hospital wheelchair parked up next to the door in the corridor. The nurse takes hold of it, peers in and then opens the door, which is always unlocked. She walks into the room with the wheelchair and doesn't look back at us. Lucy has her back turned to us, sitting on the bed. The room is exactly as we saw it all that time ago in the introduction. It feels like a trip down memory lane, back to a time when we didn't know whether to trust each other or not. Gosh, it seems like so long ago.

Lucy would have been quite happy staring at that wall all day but somewhere in the back of her mind she recognises that she is no longer alone.

Nurse Lindle says good afternoon to Lucy as she enters her space with the wheelchair.

'Now, Lucy,' she begins, talking to the back of Mrs Denharden, while we just stand in the doorway and keep quiet. 'We have another group therapy session now and I want you to be there again. You could even tell us some of your views today. Okay?'

Knowing there wouldn't be an answer, Nurse Lindle doesn't wait around. She walks up to Lucy and touches her slightly on the back as not to startle her. Nurse Lindle has learnt the hard way that no patient is predictable. Violence in a patient is a rare occurrence but it does happen from time to time; usually if that person feels that their identity is threatened. When Nurse Lindle herself was attacked many years ago, she hadn't been expecting it at all.

She had been twenty-two the first and last time it happened. It was early 1962 and 'Mad' Millie McTayson had just been deemed safe enough to come out of maximum security and into the general ward. She had been in Nurse Lindle's care for only four hours when it happened. After the incident Mad Millie was swiftly transferred back to maximum security and the senior nurses of the time proceeded to drink lots of coffee and place the blame on each other for months to come.

Mad Millie had, like Lucy, been given her own low security room. She was a towering, butch woman. It was easy to confuse her with a man because she was made up almost entirely of masculine features, with her only feminine assets being her breasts – huge saggy mounds of flesh that looked plain offensive and out of place upon such a built body. The hospital had shaved Mad Millie's head after she'd ripped most of her hair out on her first few days of arriving there, and it simply added to her fierce looks.

Mad Millie had been sitting on the end of her new bed with her feet placed firmly on the floor. Her eyes were shut as if meditating and the big girl looked peaceful. Young Nurse Lindle had come to give Millie an extra pillow. She peered through the observation window, saw her new patient sitting peacefully on the end of her bed, and opened her room door. Mad Millie did not flinch once as the kind nurse puffed up the new pillow a bit and placed it on her bed.

The mistake Alica then made was that she didn't speak to Millie as she approached her, she simply put her hand on her shoulder to get her attention. The plan was to touch the troubled patient and say: 'Millie, I've brought you that extra pillow so your neck won't hurt tonight. It's on your bed, dear.'

But what actually happened was that Nurse Lindle touched Mad Millie's shoulder and within a second Millie's eyes shot open and her arm swung around and clamped onto the young nurse's neck.

Nurse Lindle took a sharp breath of shock and tried to pull away, but Millie's grip was strong and her hand squeezed tighter.

The two had eye contact for a moment, but it was long enough for Nurse Lindle to see that there was no anger in Millie's eyes, only confusion and fear. It matched her own.

Millie looked lost as to what to do with the struggling girl in her hand and let go. The nurse who had startled her, causing this little outburst, fell to the floor and immediately put her own hands over her delicate, pulsing neck.

Then the anger came to the patient, the patient who never should have been transferred onto a general ward in the first place. She stood up from her bed slowly with her fists clenched, facing the young nurse. Millie's lips tightened and the breathing through her nostrils became deep and heavy. The frightened nurse began pleading: 'Millie, I'm sorry, I'm sorry! Please, please just relax! I didn't mean to alarm you!'

Mad Millie responded by going for her hair, causing the nurse to back up quickly towards the open door, willing for another staff member to walk past and see the situation. Unfortunately the corridor was empty and at that point Mad Millie lost her footing and fell on top of her instead.

The sudden mass of body weight pressing down on Nurse Lindle's small frame had caused her to dispel air through her mouth like a kick in the stomach. She was trembling uncontrollably, praying for somebody, *anybody* to walk down the hall and save her.

Having the nurse totally trapped, Mad Millie smiled broadly at her before reaching over to her little scalp and tugging at her hair so hard a clump of it tore off into her hand with a satisfying *rrriiip*.

Nurse Lindle now found her voice and screamed in a way she'd never been faced with before. The pain from her hair being torn out was excruciating and she felt like she had been scalded with a cinder-iron. It only took a matter of seconds after the scream for echoing, frantic footfalls to be heard getting closer, accompanied by cries of: 'Get the valium! Hurry up! Get everyone down here, now!'

Mad Millie got off Nurse Lindle and backed up to the far corner of her room, Alicia's brown hair still clumped in her hand. The whimpering nurse fled frantically out into the corridor and, once she saw her back-up only metres away, cupped her head in her hands and began sobbing...

Now, whenever Nurse Lindle approaches a patient, she almost waits for it.

However, Lucy did not pounce at the nurse upon approach, she did what she has done ever since the day after she got into the shower; she moved as instructed and did as she was told without even realising it.

Within two minutes Lucy had been guided and seated into her chair and was being wheeled down the hall.

'She can walk,' Nurse Lindle informs us, 'but it takes her hours. We're practising walking with her every day, but until she can move on her own, it's best to use the chair.'

We walk alongside Lucy's wheelchair and are able to get our first good look at her, our first clear picture of how she is these days. We start with her bare feet. The left one is bent inwards, like you'd expect when having a muscle spasm, and the right one is placed on the footrest. Moving up to her legs now and, from the bits that are showing, we can gather that both are hairy and pale but still maintain their supple shape. She wears loose jogging bottoms and an off-white t-shirt retrieved from the massive house that she once owned. Other items from her 'lounging' wardrobe have been brought with her too, but these are her most common day clothes.

Both hands and arms hang limply from the sides of the chair, her fingers pointing motionless to the floor with not so much as a twitch. Her head is to the side as if she were dead and mouth hangs open. Despite being wiped just moments ago by Nurse Lindle, a line of saliva hangs down onto her chin.

Her eyes are glazed and stare at nothing. The way they're pointing you would think she was tracing the floor in front of her, but she barely even realises that she's in a chair, so the floor's not of any importance to her.

Her hair is brittle and dry, tied back with a thick bobble. It is a dull ginger now all the golden colour has washed out of it, it knots easily and is a nightmare for the nurses to wash and dry. Her complexion is still crystal clear, however, and there are no bags under her eyes.

We decide to watch the discussion group from the outside of the pages, and let the two carry on down the hall alone, entering the meeting area. Lucy Denharden attends therapy sessions here every other day. It's always the same bunch of women all sitting in the same places. They've got a nice little routine going on at Penford Hospital, y'know.

Eight women in all are sitting in a semicircle around the room, all facing the focal point that is Nurse Lindle. All eight of our girls are sectioned. Most of Penford hospital is made up of volunteers, people who come off their own back, and outpatients, those who live in the outside world but continue to report back to Old Joe, but every woman sitting here in this group therapy session is forced to stay until deemed fit to leave. Some, like Mrs Denharden herself, are highly unlikely to be ever deemed fit to leave. Some will be here until the day they die.

Upon the cold white walls are wax drawings and a laminated world map. On the front wall hangs a standard

207

office clock next to a clean blackboard behind Nurse Lindle's grey sponge-filled chair.

Lucy, only one of two not sitting on a similar chair, is wheeled to the left of Lizzie, who is also yet to fully master walking again. Like Lucy, she too is mentally hiding someplace better than the real world.

Lizzie is the name given to her by the nurses at Penford because nobody really knows what she's called. The police brought her in 1971 after she had turned up at the Trinity Methodist church in Codsall as bare as the day she was born. Nobody had ever seen her before and she certainly wasn't local; it was like she'd just appeared from nowhere. It only took a matter of days after the incident for her to be introduced to the fine building that is Penford Psychiatric Hospital and, y'know what? she's never uttered a word so far. Not one. It was once thought she may be dumb and deaf but recent tests have proved she can both speak and hear, she just chooses not to. It's guessed that she is in her fifties and has probably suffered some immense trauma that wiped away any possibility of a normal life; that's what the top docs reckon anyway. I know what she went through but it's not nice... so I won't tell you.

To Lizzie's left, distanced from her and facing the circle, is Nurse Lindle; to her right, the new girl Lucy Denharden. To the left of Lucy Denharden is Sara White. Sara's parents had brought her here in 1989 when she was twenty-one after her last and final apprehension by the police. Sara is a character, dear. My God, that she is. She is diagnosed as being a paranoid schizophrenic suffering from anorexia, but her paranoia all comes down to just the one theory she has, a theory that has ultimately ruined her life.

She believes that there is a single organisation that controls all the other superpowers in the world. According to Sara this corrupt authority, the Secret Circle, poisons food, water and air to cause cancer and keep the population down. She believes cigarettes are actually harmless, but because of fake health warnings and manipulative advertising, they act as a placebo causing the brain to bring out the cancer that they're fed, keeping the Secret Circle's spending costs down. She knows for a fact that they communicate by a secret code in the form of shapes to be seen behind newsreaders on certain national channels. Not only is that and everything else they're about bad enough, but they also have a personal vendetta against Ms White. If she eats their tumour-ridden comestibles she believes she will die, and if that doesn't kill her, their spies will reach her eventually.

Sara is actually among the most intelligent in the entire hospital, and that's including the doctors and nurses. Unfortunately that, my friend, turned out to be our Sara's downfall. Sara had been thinking too much too deeply at just the wrong time in her life and it turned the intelligent bookworm into what she is today.

To Sara's left is Mary Cheeda who seems like any run-of-the-mill person upon first meeting her. After a few minutes of talking to her, however, you would realise that there is something quite confusing about this greying forty-three year old. *Hang on – she was shot down and held hostage during World War Two? I didn't think women fought in the war... is she...? Is she **lying** to me... or am I just uneducated? Wait a second... she's only in her forties! She **must** be lying to me!*

As well being an embarrassingly convincing liar, Mary is a compulsive hoarder. She was brought in after police were alerted to her house by a neighbour because of a stench only six months ago. When the police beat the front door down several hours later, among other things they found five dead cats and Mary's own faeces piled up in sandwich bags all over the house. She'd been keeping them for nearly a year and the cats for eight weeks after they all caught diseases from the squalor and died off one by one.

However, Mary is in denial about her illness. A woman of her high stature does not belong with these crackpots. She was the brains behind NASA at one point, you know.

To Mary's left is another woman stuck in her own world of fear and silence. She is not in a wheelchair and can quite easily walk around without shuffling and bumping into things. Her full name is Norma Jagger but if she is called that she will literally try to bite and scratch you to death. Instead, upon Norma's request, the nurses call her 'Pookie' and none of the patients know this is not her real name. Pookie is thirty-four and has reached her ten year mark at Penford only this year. Her childhood was so traumatic that before she went quiet she was a ball of fire, trying to do herself in and running riot like an untamed animal due to the memories. Her back, buttocks and legs are a mass of scars from when her mother threw a boiling chip pan, loaded with bubbling fat, at her when she was seven. Her mother would beat her to the point of hospitalisation on a few occasions and, although the neighbours and teachers complained, she was left to it for another five years until she was imprisoned for cruelty. All the others were mental scars brought on by her foster father's live-in brother and the sexual assaults she was a victim of for years by him and his friends, without her foster parents ever finding out until it was too late. She would try to attack fellow patients and nurses every so often but she's been quiet for over a year now. Not a word and not a movement other to walk, eat and take her medication.

Next to Pookie is another Sarah: Sarah Martin, who was brought in slap bang on her eighteenth birthday by her parents back in September 1960 because the poor girl has split personality disorder and, with her parents being religious people, when an exorcism didn't work they had to get the demon out of the house and straight into a padded room. By the summer of 1960 they thoroughly believed their daughter was the devil and wasted no time in getting rid of her.

The last two to complete the semicircle were admitted to Penford even before Nurse Lindle was born. Flo and Maggie. Flo held the record at Penford Psychiatric Hospital and at a grand age of eighty-one could now boast to a full sixty-two years in confinement.

Maggie, closely following, had been here fifty-seven years and the two had been inseparable since they'd met.

Their problems, you're wondering? Flo had pleaded insane after been sent to court for stealing and prostitution at the age of eighteen back in 1929. She had put on one hell of an act to avoid prison but, unfortunately, she became institutionalised and remains here to this fine October day in the nineties. Sad thing was, she was only on the game (with her mother, may I add) to feed her four brothers and two sisters after their father died and they had no money or furniture left. The girl was only stealing money to buy bread and coal and when she was caught taking money from a punter's back pocket while doing her job, she knew she simply could not go to prison. She knew of the women and girls who died from all sorts in prison so she did her damned best to avoid it.

Her plan was to act crazy for while, spend a few weeks in the loony bin, then be back out helping her family, struggling to survive. However, it was never to be and those few months turned into sixty-two years.

Maggie O'Leary was thrown in by society at the young age of fourteen. The reason? 'Why, the little whore is pregnant! She's not part of our (wealthy and respected) family! Shame on you!'

As cruel fate would have it, she was kneed in the stomach by a nurse only three weeks later and lost the bastard child. Her family were informed but Maggie had disgraced them, and they thought it best if she was kept in. Maggie fell into depression and that was seen as madness. Keep her in, boys.

'So,' Nurse Lindle begun, skimming through the neat file on her lap that contained the notes from the last session. 'Yesterday we were talking about wintertime. Has anybody had any more thoughts on that?'

211

All was silent for a moment then the bony arm of Sara White was raised.

'Yes, Sara?' Nurse Lindle responded.

'Winters are getting warmer,' Sara said frantically. Before she continued she looked around the room to see if they were watching her. She couldn't see them but they'll have bugged her, they're always watching her. She could imagine them standing with their lasers, ready to zap her if she mentioned them. 'They... they put holes in the ozone layer. They do it to cause disasters. To keep the population down...'

'Oh please,' Mary (our upper class shit collecting friend) tutted.

Sara ignored her and continued: 'I know they do it, I've seen their lasers.'

'Where did you see their lasers, Sara?' Nurse Lindle asked.

'Outside the window. I saw them last night, eating the ozone layer. Destroying lives to keep the population down.'

'Did anybody else see lasers last night?' Nurse Lindle looked around the group.

'Nurse Lindle,' Mary spoke again. 'You know there're no lasers.'

'*Sara* saw them, Mary,' Nurse Lindle replied.

This is how she gained respect of the patients. Of-course she knew Sara didn't see lasers, but where would that get her? Arguing with the patients over their quirks wasn't going to do anything other than get them wound up. When things got serious, that's when she had to pinch them with reality but that was rare. Mostly, Nurse Lindle let them say what they wanted. She didn't go along with it, oh no, she just kept them calm and asked them the type of questions that they would respond to without getting upset.

'Sara did not see them for pete's sake. It's all in her head,' Mary continued, waving her left hand in Sara's direction as if to dismiss her.

Mary is the type of woman that, at a supermarket checkout, would tap her nails impatiently and start huffing and puffing if the checkout assistant took too long counting her money. You picture the type, right? You see them in large department stores don't you, the woman in a long coat, dispelling attitude like scent. The husband dithering behind; 'yes love, no love…'

Mary is the long coated woman, only she collects shit and lies so believably it's confusing.

Sara's head began twitching slightly and she brought shaking hands up to her temples.

'I saw them, Mary… you'll be sorry when they start poisoning the water in this area. You won't even notice it. They'll get you… they'll get all of us.' Her voice was even more jittery and nervous than usual. For a new nurse on the ward warning signs of aggressive behaviour would start flashing now and panic would begin to rise, but Nurse Lindle goes through this nearly every single session with Mary and Sara. She knew what to do.

'Maggie, tell us about wintertime in the air-raid shelters.' The subject was quickly moved on after a stern look at Mary. Most of the group looked at Maggie, Sara included, who within a second had stopped shaking and returned her hands to her lap, concentrating on what Maggie was about to say.

'Huh,' Maggie sniffed. She rolled her head before leaning forward and adapting a pained look of remembrance upon her face.

'Cold,' she finally nodded.

'Yes,' Flo agreed. 'My brother.' …*Went to fight. He was stationed in, oh I can't remember now, France, I think. He only lasted three weeks apparently; it was the only letter I was ever given here. They let me read it once then they threw it away. The letter was from my sister Elsie, she had to beg the wardens to let me read it. She must have walked twenty miles to get to this place, and twenty back. I can remember the basics of it, the news within it struck me like a bomb, my family, the people I had fought so hard to keep alive, were all in the workhouse. They could no longer survive on what the good Lord had given them. That's when I realised I had made a big mistake by feigning insanity and that I had been awfully naive thinking this was going to be an easy ride, thinking I'd be out by the end of '29. I knew then that my life was over.*

Of-course, Flo couldn't remember what that letter said now. But, as we have privileges even above the person of whom that letter was intended for, we might as well take advantage of them. Had we not?

Dearest Flo,

I hop yew r wel I want yew to now thah simon int cuming bac we got a leter thah ses he ded a hero for his cuntry I am sory I now yew wil be sad but flo hes an hero naw mum went up ta corts an wear al of ta workhuse end af this week she wus criing but we carnt sel anyfing els naw flo and sins yew went away weav ardly eten a fing itll be alrit so do not wory carnt wate to se yew agen hop its beta than prisan lik you sed mis you cum and get us owt as sune as yewcan elsie

'Yes, Flo?' Nurse Lindle asked. 'Your brother…?'

Flo didn't speak any more that session, she just nodded and shook her head to herself.

That night Lucy Denharden was sponged and put to bed. We make use of the fact that she's alone and go to join her for a few minutes in her room. But just our luck, *just our luck* that the one night we decide to peek in at her, another visitor decides to drop by too…

We're taking a few minutes out, watching Lucy sleep peacefully when out of the blue, totally un-programmed, Reality arrives.

I have a problem with Reality as Lucy does; there is no place for it in this book – especially not right now. Reality can spread like a disease in your imagination; Reality can kill off your optimism if you let it take advantage of you. In cases like

214

this, it's fair to say that Reality is almost demonic. It is invading our adventure and trying to cut it short. It is not welcome here. We don't notice it at first as it quietly seeps under the doorframe and into her room, but we are alerted to the fact that something isn't right soon enough, as a small sound emanates from somewhere near Lucy. A small sound like muffled words. We both stop suddenly.

'Did you here something?' I whisper.

'I think she just spoke,' you reply, unsure of yourself.

'She shouldn't be speaking,' I say with my heart palpitating slightly, not quite believing that that could be possible.

'What, didn't you write it in?' You turn to me sharply.

'No! Of-course I didn't. She's *catatonic*. That'd be ridiculous!'

We speak in strained whispers, our eyes darting from Lucy's horizontal body on the bed, and then back to each other.

'Can you make her do that again?'

'No! I didn't make her do it in the first place.'

Our eyes grow wider.

'Shit.'

'I know.'

We fall into silence once again and just as we try to contemplate the effects that this un-programmed murmur might have on the rest of the story and our privileges within it, the demon named Reality passes through us and stops our thoughts with a jolt. The shock is electric and for a moment every single nerve-ending in our bodies jump and scream. Our minds don't even have time to catch up but before we know it it has passed and we're back to normal, with the ends of our fingers and toes tingling. We know that it passed through us threateningly. We know it's more powerful than us and it did that to prove a point. It did that to remind us.

We take a moment to gather our thoughts and then you nudge me and silently instruct me to look over there, by the bed. I do so and my heart nearly stops. It has grown power since I had last encountered it. Its form looks fuller, stronger.

Reality has forced its way into the novel and we can but stand fixated, glued to the spot with fear. I always thought that if this fiend ever tried to ruin my work again I would give it what for, I would raise my voice and say *just fuck off, this is my territory!* But now it's come down to it I am petrified. It's come to try and take her just as the monster had in that bathroom so long ago. We can do nothing but watch and wait, too scared to breathe.

After a moment of standing over Lucy, taking in her physical being, her mental status and her scent, the disease we call Reality begins to lightly pick at Lucy's skin, dulling and greying at as it clings like a puppy to her bones. It dances in front of her numb eyes. We see it; it's making us both tremble.

All it takes is for you to look at me once and I can see your thoughts – they match mine – *let's get the hell out of here*. I nod and you quietly open the door. You walk out first and I follow, closing the door behind me and leaving our favourite woman alone in the dark with a murky creature that goes by the name of Reality.

Christ, we are relieved to be out of that atmosphere, and quite happy to say our goodbyes and jump to the outside of the pages again to watch from a safe, sane distance.

It's the dead of night and she registers the demon in her subconscious, but it is not strong enough to penetrate her conscious thoughts as intended. It runs its fingers through her limp, tangled hair but she does not feel it. The jester weeps in the front row of the auditorium but she does not see it. Reality laughs in her face but she does not hear it. Lucy is too deep in her catatonia to use her primary senses.

However, Lucy's dreams are affected by its power and she slowly begins to lift her weak right arm unknowingly in her sleep.

Reality experiences a jolt of intense excitement as it observes movement.

She feels me, she feels me and I'm coming. I'm coming.

But Lucy Denharden does not attempt to swat Reality away from her body. She does not, no, stick a finger up to the invisible demon. She simply holds her arm up straight into the dead air above her still silent head, filled with a million thoughts yet focussed on none.

Reality watches, disgusted, as she holds it there with no intention of moving. It can hardly believe it has wasted so much time toying with this cretin only for her to mock it. So, without further ado it leaves the girl and decides it will try again later with better tactics.

We both smile. It looks like our adventure is still on for now.

Autumn Leigh had raised her arm up high and mighty for two reasons. The main reason was to catch the waiter's attention while he still had flutes of champagne on his tray, the other was to show the other diners that, not only was she the most beautiful person in this room, but that she also got what ever she wanted at the click of a finger. And they saw, all right, they saw her. They all saw her painted red nails (especially the older ones), they saw her attitude (*do not double cross me, darling. I have more power than anyone in this room and I could crush you if I felt like it*) and they saw her sculptured body (the bust, the eyes, oh, the lips). The more that mighty arm stretched, the more they looked.

Autumn Leigh was dressed in silk. Black silk. Her skin was tanned enough to glow, but was far from the parched mistakes of the 80's soap-stars. The has-beens *ha, ha, ha*. Autumn Leigh sat with her arm in the air looking youthful, vibrant and beautiful.

The waiter looked over in her direction after a few moments and Autumn raised her head into a nod as he did so. *Come on, boy, I'm wanting a glass.* He looked over and saw the red-haired superstar wanting a drink. He saw she wanted one of the crystal flutes filled with alcohol that he was carrying elegantly on his tray. He saw that and then he looked away.

Autumn Leigh's arm bent slightly and her eyes widened with brief humiliation. *Is he **ignoring** me…? He is! The little runt is ignoring me on purpose!* She heard a quiet snigger coming from one of the tables near her, so the fabulous Autumn Leigh quickly glanced around the room to the other diners. They were all staring. They were all wearing grins and mock sympathetic looks. Autumn Leigh lowered her arm and cleared her throat. More sniggers.

Luckily Autumn then spotted her saving grace, a young waitress walking towards her table with a full tray. *Fuller than the runt's.*

Autumn Leigh smiled and held out her arm, ready to accept the drink when, unbelievably, the waitress walked straight past her, not even noticing she was there. Autumn Leigh withdrew her arm sharply and this time the entire room exploded with laughter, from the deep belly laugh of fat rich men, right through to the superficial horselaughs of their wives. They were all laughing and pointing at Autumn Leigh with her perfectly painted nails and pert, lightly tanned body.

She could stand it no more so she pushed her chair back, took the napkin off her lap and slammed it on her plate of unfinished food. This caused a fresh outburst of hilarity and Autumn observed that some people were now actually falling off their chairs laughing.

'You're all just jealous because I'm better than you!' she screamed to the diners, her face a picture of mortification and fury.

The occupants of the ballroom all chorused louder now; all the staff were laughing and the chefs had even come out from behind the scenes to catch a look.

Autumn Leigh ran from the room, hot tears building up and her provocation increasing with each table that she had to pass. Finally she reached the ballroom doors and swung them both open. Past the doors, and not to her surprise, was an

218

abyss. She ran straight into it. Blackness. Her feet were soon distant from any sort of floor and she began to fall with her arms flailing and legs thrashing wildly.

As she descended into the very pit of nothingness, she could still hear the entire room laughing at her. If she were to have looked up she would have seen several of the diners looking in at her over the top, their eyes watering with tears of laughter.

Lucy Denharden slowly lowered her arm. A single tear fell from her left eye and forced her back into her comfortable, numbing sleep.

CHAPTER 8

Two weeks passed in the world. Two weeks of your life, my life, millions of lives. Whatever we were up to during those two weeks, it was probably better than what our two characters were going through; Lucy staring at nothingness and occasionally lifting that left arm when no-one was around; Anthony sitting in his wheelchair staring out of his window onto the street below.

Both Anthony and Autumn were nobodies now. But lucky for Autumn, lucky for her that her mind had not yet realised how low she had sunk. It was Anthony that got it the worst. He knew.

But don't worry! Don't start feeling down! Not everybody was stuck in either madness or depression; many people were still having the time of their lives... and one of those many people was our old pal in the US of A, Jerry Tilsey.

Jerry had been happily drying up the bar with five of his equally pretentious friends on that clear, mid-November night. The handsome young things had gone to The Milk Bar, one of the elite in the way of trendy celebrity haunts. They were up on one of the three private balconies on the second floor, looking down on those who were cool enough to get in, but not cool enough to go VIP.

It had started with: 'Check out that fox in the red!' from Sean *my-daddy-owns-Telecom-International-what-does-your-daddy-do?'* Portello.

Jerry had followed Sean's pointing finger to a blonde strutting towards the female restrooms on the ground floor. The two swapped comments and laughed then turned the subject to other things once she was out of sight. Several moments later the young minx wearing red lycra reappeared and walked with a pout across the room. Jerry and Sean had to lean but they could see where she had sat that hot ass down and praise the Lord, she was sitting with two other girls, all smoking cigarettes and crossing long legs. Within a second Sean had called their personal waiter over and instructed him to go and get those hot girls and bring them upstairs to join us, and bring us some more bottles, would ya?

Within three minutes of that instruction, three young models were sitting on the VIP floor with five dashing, rich gentlemen.

Sean had claimed the fox in red lycra from the onset, because he liked them siliconed-up with blown up lips and massive tits.

Two of the other fine young gentlemen accompanying Jerry were sat on either side of a beautiful French brunette. They were listening to her story of how she got to America; they were stroking a leg each.

Carman was the girl who caught Jerry's eye. No, she wasn't massively pumped and no, she wasn't foreign, but she was beautiful. She was pure, a model trying to adjust to the high life, sponsored from winning a national catwalk competition when she was fifteen. She was a size six, cheek-boned, natural blonde. Only seventeen. Just seventeen.

Jerry's fingers were caressing the pert skin just under the material of Carman's see-through shirt. It was tanned and soft, and tonight, his. Jerry whispered into the young girl's ear and she giggled. She was basically a child. Jerry liked that innocence.

Yeah, she was the one that he wanted.

The fifth friend was trying to ignore this and trying not to look too left out by laughing along with bits of conversations, adding bits overenthusiastically. The fifth friend was Paul Craswell. His parents were entrepreneurs and he was a good friend of Sean's; they met through their parents when they were four. The difference between Sean and Paul, however, was that girls liked Sean. They liked his Mediterranean olive skin, they liked his brown eyes.

Unfortunately, they weren't so keen on Paul's features; his curly, mousy hair, his pointing chin and sharp nose. They *all* preferred Sean. Both lads knew this. One was more pleased than the other.

So, there they were. The eight of them. Then six, then five, then four, then two.

'So then, just the two of us,' Jerry smiled to his young piece after causally signalling goodbye to Sean and the glamour model.

'Yeah,' Carman nodded shyly, putting a strand of long hair back behind her ear with her hand.

'Are you happy, being here with me?' he asked.

'Yeah,' she giggled. 'It's just, you know, I've seen you in the movies and I can't believe I'm here next to you. It's hard to believe people like you are real, y'know?'

'It's hard to believe a girl as beautiful as you is real. You're stunning,' Jerry leered.

Oh, but he really did leer. He spoke with a half smile, his clammy fingers touching her skin. He was sliming in a way that, had he not have been young and hot, would be eligible for a drink thrown over him round about now. She felt it but Jerry got away with it. She giggled to impress him. He loved it.

'Is your momma expecting you home tonight?' he continued.

'Oh, don't live with her anymore... I live with the girls I was with tonight. My sponsor set us up with a flat together. We all do different types of modelling though, but they're okay, s'pose...'

'Well, are the *girls* expecting you back?' Jerry said impatiently.

'No.'

'So, come back to mine.'

'Um... sure, okay.'

Jerry lived on the eighteenth floor of the exclusive Hollywood Apartments on West Basely Street. It was pretentiously fashionable, a palace compared to Carman's apartment block on South Row.

They had been back at his apartment for just enough time for fresh glasses of spirits to be poured. Carman was so nervous that she was trying to visualise her happy place by this point (her folks; basement, curled up on the sofa watching *Roseanne* with her sister and a root beer). He had been stroking her thighs all the way back in the car and, although she knew what a high profile fuck could do for her career (just look what it did for the marvellous Autumn Leigh), she wasn't so sure it was the right thing to do now. Deep down, when she tucked away all the attitude and I'm-a-model bullshit, Carman still felt like a child and wished she could be back at school, gossiping with her girlfriends. But no, popular, smart Carman won a modelling competition and here she was with a big film star… one that was expecting sex some time soon.

She was sitting with one of the most handsome men you could ever wish to meet, a man that was unknowingly scaring her with his power. She looked down into the glass of clear liquid that he had just poured her; she would do anything to avoid drinking it.

'I have a rooftop Jacuzzi, you know,' Jerry smiled as he walked around the trendy, multi-levelled main room, turning on lamps.

The seventeen-year old squeeze was perched on one of the four orange leather sofas lighting up a cigarette, trying to act like a grownup around this highly intimidating movie-star. As she was sucking on the cigarette she was dreaming about when it would all over in twenty-four hours time, when she could go home to the girls and lie about what a great time she'd had with Jerry Tilsey.

'Oh, cool,' she replied, instantly regretting it and feeling more like a kid than ever.

The feeling of dread Carman was experiencing took her back to when she once did an underwear shoot on a beach in LA. It wasn't the secluded beach as promised and gangs of surfers gathered around and watched her, laughing as she posed.

Recalling that horrible day only proved to make her more nervous.

She knew Jerry wanted to sleep with her and she knew it would do her career a lot of good but... it's hard to explain... there was just something about him that made her uncomfortable. Since the rest of the gang left, something about him changed. He was that little bit too close to her face, always touching.

In front of the others, Carman too, was different. She had the pouts and the heavy eye movements going on but as soon as everyone left she stopped it all. She was too scared, felt too much like a child next to this big movie star.

'Well?' Jerry suddenly said, stopping next to a couple of glass sliding doors.

'What?' Carman asked.

'Get your glass and come outside. I'll turn it on.'

'Oh,' she giggled, feeling dumb as well as young now.

With the flick of a switch, the rooftop (which was on level with the main room floor) had lit up with fairy lights and outside lamps in the style of women holding balls of light.

'I'll take the top off the Jacuzzi while you get changed. Put your clothes on the bed. I'll be in here waiting for you.'

'Oh... okay.' Carman stood up and followed Jerry's loose, brief point towards a bedroom.

She entered and shut the door quickly behind her, breathing out a deep exhale of troubled air once she clicked it shut. She looked around the room. Like the rest of the apartment, wood was heavily featured. It truly did remind her of something out of a James Bond movie, and she wondered if he had done it up like that on-purpose, in that sleazy sort of way that she'd gathered Jerry tended to do everything.

The name's Tilsey. *Jerry* Tilsey.

Carman began to undress, wondering how many other women had experienced these same feeling of nervousness and discomfort while stood, getting naked, in this room. She folded her shirt and placed it on the bed, then took off her tight fitting black trousers and belt and placed them next to it.

Carman was stood in the movie-star's warm apartment in a red g-string and white bra, wishing like hell that she had put on a matching set. Looking in the mounted mirror in the room she decided that she couldn't go out looking like that. The bra had to go.

'Come on in, the water's hot,' Jerry commanded as a shy girl wearing only a thong walked towards him out on the deck.

As Jerry was holding a glass, spread out naked in the hot tub, she was covering her chest and looking sheepish.

Carman walked up to the hot tub and put her first foot in when Jerry sat up abruptly.

'What are you doing?' he asked, shocked.

'You just told me to get in!' Carman replied defensively.

'Yeah, but not in your panties! Take them off!'

Carman did as he said and pulled them down, baring her full body for the first time. She could feel Jerry's eyes on her.

As she stepped in and surrounded herself with hot bubbles, Jerry laughed quietly and put his glass down on the side.

'You don't have to sit so far away,' he grinned, after studying her for just enough time to make her hate him for a moment. He finished it with: 'Are you scared of me?'

Carman smiled and the nervous giggles emerged again. 'Um, a bit,' she replied.

'Why?' Jerry stretched the word out and spoke as if he was suppressing laughter.

'No, it doesn't matter,' Carman smiled falsely, looking down into the bubbles, allowing her hair to cover her face like some kind of protection.

'No, come on,' Jerry laughed again, nudging his feet onto her legs.

'No, really,' Carman was having to force the smile as if she was in a photo shoot now. Things were getting chronic.

'Okay then, why don't you just come over here so Jerry can put his arm around you, huh?'

Jerry was nodding his head slightly to himself as she did as she was told and moved over next to him.

'You're such a beautiful thing. How old are you again?'

'Seventeen,' she replied as he began to play with her hair, moving it back behind her ear as he had seen her do earlier.

Once her ear was exposed he leaned over even closer and whispered: 'Suck me off,' before breathing heavily and kissing her neck.

Carman's head swung around. She wasn't afraid of doing it, she'd done it before without wanting to, but... *but... he's underwater!*

'Do you want a hand job?' she asked, as seductively as she could muster.

'Hand job? No, I want you to suck my dick, pretty lady,' Jerry spluttered, a look of surprise spread mockingly across his face.

'But you're underwater,' she laughed, trying to sound light-hearted.

'So?'

'I'm sorry, Jerry, but I can't do it underwater. I'll do it on the bed if you want.'

'Fuck the bed!' Jerry replied, a bit too hastily, a bit too nastily.

He quickly changed his tone into a lighter one when he saw her face distort with shock: 'Do it here, Carman, all the other girls do. You don't want to be the only one who can't please me, do you?'

'No.'

'So, come on.' As he whispered he pressed the back of his hand onto her head, lowering it and pushing it slightly towards the direction he wanted it to be going in.

Embarrassed to have caused such bother, she followed the physical hint and ducked her face underwater to please him... only the bubbles went up her nose and straight away she was spluttering and sitting upright again.

'Fucking *hell*!' Jerry slammed both hands down into the water like a sulking child.

'Sorry, I'm sorry. I just can't do it. I'm sorry,' Carman whined, not quite believing how degrading this all was. She'd die if this ever got to the papers.

And then, before she could even realise what was happening, her head was forced underwater.

'Just fucking *do* it!' Jerry said threateningly, his strong hand on the back of her small head. 'Fucking *hell*! Is it such a task?!'

Her arms flared and her legs kicked, sending water splashing onto the deck. One of her hands lightly scraped Jerry's face and he let go of her, there was no point, he wasn't going to get hard now. The pathetic little girl had turned him right off.

Carman came up gasping; in a shot her mascara streaked face turned to Jerry, but when she couldn't find the words to say to him and realised how frighteningly irate he looked, plus of-course the basic fact that he'd just pushed her head underwater to try to get her to perform forced oral sex, she decided just to leave.

As she was getting out Jerry grabbed her leg. Before he could speak she cried: 'Get off me, I'm leaving!'

He realised then that he had to reverse this situation. He wished that he didn't lose his temper so fast with women but he couldn't help it.

'Hey, hey, hey. Come back, I was only messing wi'cha!' Jerry pleaded, still holding her leg. 'Come on babe, don't go.'

But she did the wrong thing. She did what no woman should ever do to Jerry Tilsey. She defied him again.

'Fuck off!' she screamed, loud enough for the neighbours to hear.

She tried to shake her leg away from him but he was too strong.

He gripped it harder and pulled her back into the Jacuzzi.

'Shut the fuck up then before I really give you something to cry about,' he sneered in a whisper through gritted teeth, the pumping anger back again.

Carman struggled to get back out again. Who was this madman? Was he even who he said he was? Was he some kind of psychotic lookalike? All that was certain was that she had to get the hell out of there. *Fast.*

They began to tussle in the water. He was holding her, grabbing at her and struggling to talk at the same time.

'Just-just… no… wait… no… what…? Stop it-just…'

'Get off!' she screamed again, crying now.

He had to silence her then. It was going all wrong, tonight was supposed to be fun, tonight was supposed to highlight the perks of being famous, that's why he brought her back to his place, for sex. Not this. Now the child was screaming and it wouldn't be long until the neighbours started banging on his door.

He had no choice: he *had* to shut her up. So, as quick as a flash he head-butted the back of her head, hard enough for his forehead to pulse wildly with pain. She jolted forward and stopped struggling.

When he untangled himself from her, he had to quickly grab her hair as her face had unconsciously slumped under the water. Jerry was cursing so often to himself that if I were to write it all down it would just seem crude and, you know, my mother's probably *already* horrified about the levels of swearing and violence going on.

He awkwardly lifted her out of the tub, suddenly realising how light she was. He held her like a fireman would a distressed damsel and took her through to his bedroom, laying her on the bed (*Jerry Tilsey, you're my hero*).

Carman was laid on her back, exposed in her barest form. Jerry stood over her and looked at her frail body. She looked like she would snap if she was fucked too hard, and this made Jerry breathe heavily. He took in her legs and her thighs; they were so skinny they didn't touch each other at all. Her pubic hair was neat and wispy, her stomach concave and her breasts tiny. Despite the streaks of mascara down it, her face looked angelic. Her hair was a wet mess but he imagined that this would be what she looks like after being thrown around in a shower for a bit, and in Jerry's eyes those rattails made her look even sexier.

He ran his fingers over the skin on her belly; it was like peaches and cream. He moved his fingers further down and then... the door to Jerry's room shuts us out. We really don't need to see what he did next.

Jerry had committed the most sickening act of his life with the unconscious seventeen-year-old. He was in there all of twenty minutes and she didn't stir once throughout, not even when he sat on her face at one point, not even when he flipped her over and took her in a way he was sure she'd never been taken before at another. Once he had relieved himself on her and cleaned up the semen and blood half heartily, he left her alone and ventured back into the front room to skin up.

It took her two hours to come around and by the time she had Jerry had had to smoke three joints just to stop himself from going back in there and doing it again. Three joints were nothing to him now, the giggly high of grass had worn off by the time he was thirteen, the eyes-open-sleep had built up such a resistance that, these days, the same amount of smoke that used to knock him out was just like another cigarette now. But, yes, it did calm him nicely tonight. The worrying thing also was that he'd taken a tab of his favourite drug of the moment, The Servant, the other night, and he didn't get high at all. He didn't feel anything whatsoever. Man, Jerry's body could sure hack it these days.

He heard the sound of something falling bluntly into one of the wardrobes that ran down the right hand side of his bedroom. He gathered that was her getting up so he put his glass down, put his homemade back in the ashtray and stood up.

He had not locked her in and hoped that this was the right thing to do as the door handle began to turn.

She stumbled out, holding the back of her head. Her hair had dried and she looked like a skinny, young child as opposed to the jaw-dropping model that had followed him to his place earlier on in the night.

Carman's mouth had a tinny taste in it, the top of her legs were bruised and her bottom hurt so much it pulsed with every step she took.

'Come on, I'll take you home,' Jerry said in his soothing voice.

Carman was dazed and just nodded, not sure where she was and not caring. She just wanted to be in her own bed.

Jerry grabbed his keys and made a formal decision to find out where she lived, drive her there, knock on the door and convince one of the girls that she had fallen over and had concussion.

Please take her to bed, sweetheart, because I think she had a little bit too much to drink. She wanted to stay with me but I thought it would be best for her if she woke up in familiar surroundings. Oh, no, no don't mention it – it was the right thing to do.

He helped to dress her, got her to sluggishly tell him where she lived, which was luckily South Row, which he was greatly familiar with, and bundled her into his 1990 Pontiac Firebird. He would have preferred to have taken out his four-seater but it was parked behind this one in his section of the underground garage, and right now he couldn't be bothered messing around even more. Tonight had been a total disaster and all he wanted to do was get the bitch home and go to bed.

She was strapped in next to him, with her head rolling heavily back and forth. Her body was pressed against the seat belt and he knew that if he were to click it open she would fall forward and probably just stay like that. Before he'd even started the engine he'd had to push her chest twice to prop her up. This girl was such a pain in the ass. He kicked himself for not picking the glamour model.

233

They were cruising along East Shore Avenue just fine, with hardly a car in sight at 4.30am. Jerry didn't push the car or himself hard.

His eyes were feeling heavy now that the rush had died down. He knew these roads like the back of his hand so his concentration was wondering away from them, away from the girl slumped next to him. *Drop the girl off, get to bed.* Jerry looked up into his rear-view mirror for reasons unknown, looked away for a second, then sharply looked back...

Through the reflection of the mirror Jerry saw with horror-filled eyes that a gigantic smoky shadow with spindly long legs was running not far behind his car. Jerry swallowed hard and turned his head to look out of the back window, but could see nothing.

Again, he turned to the mirror, and it was there. Jerry snapped his head back to the window; it was gone. Then hurriedly back to the mirror; it was catching up. Jerry's wondering mind cleared and his tiredness pealed to reveal adrenalin. Something was following him, something alien. Jerry's eyes became wide.

The half conscious girl by his side was none the wiser that the car she was in was being chased. She was blissfully ignorant that Jerry's throat was becoming tight and that his bones had begun to shake. Jerry's foot pressed onto the accelerator a little harder, but the scrambling shadow kept right up. The misty figure was colossal and had long, long legs – it almost looked like it was on stilts. It faded into the streetlights and sidewalk if he looked at it hard, but when he glanced out of the corner of his eye it was there, running behind him. He had to speed up.

A slight whimper escaped from his mouth as the shadow ran faster with the car. He pushed the car further, now up to sixty. It was still there. Jerry was checking it in his mirror every couple of seconds; it just would not let up. Luckily East Shore Avenue was straight and empty, and the red Firebird that he had bought last year could screw a Ferrari if pushed hard enough. Surely the stalker could not keep up with eighty?

Eighty it was and Jerry's imaginary shadow, the trick of his drug fuelled paranoia, followed him still. What had started off as a relaxing, sleep-happy drive was now a crazy race against ghosts. In sheer panic Jerry pushed the car further, his head swivelling between the road and his rear-view mirror like it was programmed.

This thing was going to catch him and kill him. He had to lose it. The seemingly endless lights he was going through were mostly on red but the streets were empty, there was no way he could stop.

Then suddenly the shadow upped its speed and was right next to his bumper. Jerry screamed and let his foot travel all the way down to the floor, taking the accelerator pedal with it. The girl stirred at the shriek but did not lift her head or open her eyes.

Jerry was physically falling apart with fear now, unable to catch a single thought. All he knew and all that mattered was that he had to get away from the shadow before it climbed onto his car. His accelerator leg was twitching and trying to push the pedal down even harder, through the floor of the car, he was so desperate to leave it behind. The car was going phenomenally fast, zipping through the air and down the four-lane road at speeds he had never done before. The car had past the 100 point long ago and was still creeping upwards.

The shadow's long, smoke-like arms were nearly touching the car as they moved in time with its legs. Jerry cried out again and kept his eye on the mirror for just that moment too long.

When his attention turned back to the road he had only one split second to realise that his car had curved from going in a straight line and was now heading directly towards the side of a mucky concrete building. A concrete building with a red and orange sun painted onto it years ago, the words *Sundog – The Bathers' Choice* written below it, peeling and forgotten. He didn't even have time to shit himself before it happened.

The Firebird disintegrated upon impact. It hit the wall at 120mph. Jerry and Carman were dead within milliseconds, their whole bodies smashed into a thousand pieces. The menacing shadow that had caused this accident disappeared the instant Jerry's mind ceased to exist, for that's all it was – Jerry's imagination, a pretend phantom representing his paranoia.

Jerry went to his grave thinking that maybe his sister was right, maybe there really *were* such things as aliens and ghosts after all... but in reality that thing chasing Jerry was nothing more than three joints, a night's worth of drinks and the build-up of years of drug abuse.

Carman would have gone on to be a famous catwalk model. She would have grown up to be respected and wise; she would have blossomed as an even more beautiful adult. But instead, because her head was hanging down in semi-consciousness, when the car hit the building she was jolted forward in a slouched position that broke her back and snapped her neck in half. When her head hit the crash-compacted metal in front of her, it caved in her skull and took off her face.

As for Jerry, the sheer speed at which he collided with the building caused the steering wheel to plunge straight into his chest and stomach, breaking every bone in his torso, puncturing his heart, lungs and stomach. They were just his injuries, however. The thing that killed him was much more sudden. A rogue shard of glass had separated our boy's head from the rest of his body. When the windscreen glass fell through, it didn't just shatter. It flew. It flew forwards and backwards and straight through Jerry Tilsey, decapitating him in an instant.

So now, on a deserted road not far from the Hollywood Hills at 4:38am, there is a smashed up car yet to be discovered. It will be discovered in thirty seconds time when the Hispanic family living above the convenience store the car had just ploughed into unlock all the doors and put on their clothes to see what the hell had just shook their shop and apartment enough to make them think it was an earthquake.

But for now, for thirty solitary seconds, nobody knows but us.

There is smoke coming out of the mess, and other than the hissing sound that it is making, the streets are silent again.

Grinding metal and breaking machinery has given way to the usual sounds of early morning; breeze hopping along the plants and trees, the engine of the odd car every now and again in distant streets, early birds calling out to each other in tune. The sights are beautiful and peaceful.

If you turn your back to the mangled metal and the bloody dead bodies you will see the sky is still, cloudless and dark. The sun will be lighting up our lives in a little over an hour and a half, but for now we have a clear view of the moon, which is lighting the rooftops a bluish white colour. We are near several other buildings – liquor stores, Dunkin' Donuts, laundry services, undertakers' (ironic, I know), motorbike shops, McDonalds – all are silent and closed, in waiting for another day of hustle and bustle.

The roads also are as quiet as they could ever be. The scene of normality is relaxing and inspiring... it's only when we turn back around to see the scattered remains of two dead kids surrounded by twisted metal that the grim truth hits us.

Everything is peaceful until the owner of shop turns the corner with a shotgun and starts screaming *Estampido! Estampido!* and using wild arm movements to whoever is behind him. Then the morning is no longer peaceful...

CHAPTER 9

'Have you heard?' she called through to the other room.

It was two days after the event that had left Hollywood shocked and mourning for one of their youngest and most promising stars.

We are back in England now at the beginning of another one of Anthony's therapy sessions.

'Have you heard?' Dr Nazir repeated as Anthony walked in and sat down. She blew on the cup of tea she had made for herself from the kettle in the office while she was waiting for her client to get changed. She asked the question in the most solemn voice she could, not quite knowing how Anthony would react to the subject.

'Heard what?' Anthony replied.

He was feeling better than usual today. He'd had a full nights sleep for a change.

'Jerry Tilsey's dead. He crashed his car.'

'You're joking?' Anthony's eyes were wide with shock. *Dead?*

Dr Nazir shook her head as a no, she wasn't joking, and said: 'I'm sorry, I don't want this to upset you.'

Anthony didn't hear her. He didn't even know that she spoke, it was one of the side effects of the beating coming back to haunt him. The shock triggered it this time.

'When did you hear about this?' he asked.

'This morning… it was on the news.'

Anthony muttered a shocked curse and sat back in his chair.

'Are you alright?'

'When did it happen?'

'About four-thirty yesterday morning.'

'What caused it? Do you know?'

'They say he may have been under the influence of drink and drugs, but they don't know for sure yet. On the news they said he died of massive head injuries.'

Anthony shook his head and sighed: 'What an arsehole. I knew he'd kill himself in the end.'

'Killed a girl too,' she informed him, knowing that there was no love lost between the two and no, he wasn't going to take it all back just because he was dead. 'She was in the car with him. He crashed into a building, they said they could have been going as fast as a hundred and forty miles per hour.'

Anthony's face contorted into shocked disgust.

'A hundred and forty? What the fuck was he thinking?'

Dr Nazir could only shrug. She had now told him all she knew.

They both fell into silence and Anthony took a moment to feel great sadness, not for the loss of Jerry's life, but for the loss of glory that had befallen their crowd. The three of them had been up there at the top. There were plenty of others obviously, but Autumn Leigh, Jerry Tilsey and Anthony Denharden had all been sitting at *the* table to be on. They were the icons of their era... now look at them. One is living in misery, one in a psychiatric hospital, and one dead. Sadness spread over Anthony as he realised that the whole bunch of them had had their heyday and now the whole scene was over. The lime-light had dimmed for Anthony, while his wife's flickered wildly in madness and Jerry's had gone out completely. They had to make way for new superstars now, ones a little less pathetic. They would never be household names for their work ever again and for some reason, Jerry's sudden and tragic death made him realise this all the more. People will no longer think *Oh, I remember them, they were so cool. I would love to see one of them act again.* The world would never think that. Now 'they' were the unfortunate ones all the more. The effigy of what drugs, fame and money can do to you if you mess up, the type of person that you would never want to be. Anthony's almost positive frame of mind sunk back into its usual pit of darkness at this thought.

Dr Nazir could see his face change. It went from shocked to thoughtful to dark to sad. Now he sat with his eyes focused on the floor, his hands slack and his shoulders hunched.

242

Again, Dr Nazir had an overwhelming urge to show him an almost motherly type of affection and cry with him, for him; but instead she asked him what he was thinking.

He did not reply.

She reached out over the desk and touched his arm to get his attention. His head shot up and she asked him again.

Anthony kept eye contact and answered with the thought that had just manifested in his head.

'I'm never going to know the truth about him now.'

'The truth about what?'

'Whether or not he was responsible for what's happened to Lucy.' Anthony sat upright in his chair and continued: 'The police have always known about him you know. If he wasn't from Tilsey blood then he would have been locked up a long time ago. But just because he was born *son of Hollywood* they let it go.'

The rest of the session was aimed at Jerry. Anthony spoke throughout in an angry voice. When Dr Nazir left, Anthony poured himself a whisky and spent the rest of the day staring out of his window.

The girl in the car was named the next day, but it took another forty-eight hours for more important information to leak out about that night in Hollywood, and this piece of information just happened to be the one thing that the people of this world were the most interested in. Police reports stated that they had found an unknown 'super drug' stitched into a homemade pouch in Jerry's underwear but, although not official, he hadn't been taking it on the night that he finally ended his wild ways for good. This did not put the public off, however. Within hours of this news being released, the media raised its social, political neck at the inquest and began...

...*What was the drug? Where did he get it? Who else is on it? Is that why he crashed his car? Was the model on it? Is it available in the UK? How much is it? Do you know what it is? Is it lethal? Is it a powder...?*

...and with all the scraps of information that they were fed, they all went back to their nests and devoured it. The next day, the 'mystery drug' was front page news.

Anthony had started watching the news only to hear about the Jerry saga, and he had asked his part-time assistant to bring him any papers that contained information about it. That day, when the papers piped up about the 'Hollywood Killer', as they were calling it, was the day when Anthony felt for the first time that he might have a solid explanation for his wife's behaviour. He could not believe the headings, all front page, regarding the drug that they had found in Jerry's underwear. He knew, he just *knew* that this was what Lucy had either taken or been slipped; he knew it even before reading the details. His eyes scanned each paper, four in all, with so much enthusiasm he couldn't actually take in what was in front of his eyes.

Until he saw a familiar name.

Autumn Leigh.

As Anthony read and then re-read that first sentence his heart slowly crept up into his throat. It was like some kind of a magical Christmas present that he had to savour. So before reading it any further he walked (with energy, leaving behind the usual old mans dither, or wheelchair) through to his study, sat behind his desk and put on his newly acquired reading glasses. Then he laid the paper down flat and tried the best he could to digest what lay before him.

...but is this drug more established stateside than we've been led to believe? It was just over a year ago when Autumn Leigh, still at the height of her fame, collapsed at The Epics after spending the entire night chatting with Tilsey. Then, within that same month, she was sent to spend the rest of her life in a psychiatric hospital after physically assaulting her husband, actor Anthony Denharden, under the impression that he was a 'monster'. Obviously, reports are yet to be made available about the true make-up of this drug, but it

has been loosely compared to LSD. So, although the case of Autumn Leigh was quickly swept under the carpet, is there some investigation missing here? Surely Tilsey can't be the only star in Hollywood to have experimented with this illegal substance? And if not, how many more have... and was Autumn Leigh one of them?

Anthony's heart was racing. He couldn't just sit around and keep this to himself, he had to ring someone, tell someone.

Finally, after an entire year in the dark, somebody other than himself was facing up to the fact that people just *don't* go mad like that. There *must* have been something else involved, and how only Anthony and this journalist could see it was ludicrous. Surely other people out there must think that the trial was a farce, and there must be conspiracy theories flying about all over the place.

Anthony, fingers shaking, picked up his desk phone and with a dry throat, called directory enquiries.

'Directory enquiries,' a voice answered.

'The... the, uh,' Anthony quickly flipped the paper to its front page to get the name. 'The National, please.'

'One moment please.'

Anthony grabbed a pen and when the voice returned to him wrote the number on the front cover of the paper, said thank you and then clicked his finger on the dialling tone button.

Without even hanging up again he dialled the number and, with jumbled thoughts, waited for the other end to pick up.

After a few moments, a friendly female voice said: 'National Publishers, good morning.'

'Can I speak to someone from your news team please?'

'For which publication?'

'Um...your paper.'

'Which one, sir?'

'The National.'

'Hold the line please.'

With that Anthony was listening to Ms Shirley Bassey for two minutes, until: 'Editorial,' a male voice sounded, as if Anthony had just interrupted his favourite TV programme.

'Hi, I've got to speak to the journalist who wrote the feature on Jerry Til…'

'I'm sorry, our journalists don't take calls. If you have a story, please run it through…'

'I'm Anthony Denharden!' Anthony interrupted quickly. 'I've got to speak to the guy who wrote the piece. Please let me speak to him, it's urgent.'

'You're Anthony Denharden?'

'Yes! I swear to God it's me. Please!'

'Um, I'll just put you on hold a second.'

Ms Bassey was back, but this time only for a matter of seconds.

'Nick Fowler.' This time a different male voice.

'Um, are you the guy who's written the article about Jerry Tilsey in today's paper?'

'Yep,' was the cocky reply.

'I'm Anthony Denharden. Listen, I want to meet up with you. I agree with you about my wife and I'm willing to conduct an interview with you to try to get people to see that she was given drugs…'

Total silence.

Anthony hesitated then continued: 'I believe she was slipped by Jerry Tilsey. I don't think she knew about it and I think she's been put away for the wrong thing. She's been treated for schizophrenia but I don't even think she has it. I want to make people aware of that, then maybe they can help her more.'

More silence, then…

'Are you pulling my leg, mate?'

'I swear to God I am who I say I am. Please, *please* listen to me!'

'Okay, come to the main desk of our offices this afternoon then.'

'I can't get to London this afternoon, I live in Leeds. How about tomorrow?'

'Well, surely if you are who you say you are, you'd be able to limo or jet down here in four hours, wouldn't you, mate?'

'No, no. Things aren't like that for me anymore. The earliest I can get down is tomorrow.'

'Okay. But I'm telling you now, mate, there is maximum security at our offices and if you're not Anthony Denharden and you try to do something stupid, they'll…'

'I am. Now, where are you based?'

CHAPTER 10

DENHARDEN EXCLUSIVE!
MOVIE-STAR TALKS FOR THE FIRST TIME
ABOUT HIS ORDEAL!
By Nick Fowler

When I arranged to interview Anthony Denharden, I was expecting to be led up to a penthouse suite in a five star hotel, to be surrounded by suits and solicitors. After all, it was only two years ago when Denharden had the world at his feet, acting in everything from gritty UK productions right through to big budget Hollywood blockbusters, married to arguably the most beautiful woman in the world: Ms Autumn Leigh.

What I got was possibly the most down-to-earth person I have ever met. Looking older and wiser than I can ever remember, Anthony caught the train down from Yorkshire, where he now lives, and took me to a greasy-spoon café for the interview.

He orders a coke and a bacon sandwich; the waitress doesn't even look twice at him. 'People just don't recognise me anymore,' he shrugs.

But maybe that's a good thing. Anthony has been through a lot within the past fourteen months. His actress wife Autumn Leigh suffered from a 'breakdown' in September 1990, which ended infamously with her beating Anthony into a coma and attempting suicide. Leigh is now sectioned in a psychiatric hospital after being unable to stand in court, and Anthony has been left to pick up the pieces of a perfect life.

He believes that there is more to Leigh's problems than people are willing to accept. And after reading my report on The Hollywood Killer, the new drug that was discovered to be in the possession of the late Jerry Tilsey, he is talking for the first time about the events which led up to today.

251

Anthony, what have you been doing for the past year?

I've been trying to get my head together, and basically recovering from my hospitalisation. It's been a long process, but every day gets easier.

Have you come to terms with what happened to you last year?

I still have bad days but I will get there one day. I have a great doctor who helps me tremendously, and I know that [Autumn] didn't attack me out of anger or hatred, she honestly didn't know that it was me. She was delusional.

What exactly happened the day that the attack took place?

Um, this is kind of hard to talk about… [Autumn] was under the notion that I was some kind of monster, or demon. At first she was quiet and trance-like, then she just flew off the handle. I didn't even have time to realise what she was doing… she just went for me. We were fine that morning; there was absolutely no reason for the attack. We had a great relationship and a happy marriage.

What injuries did you sustain from the attack?

Well, mentally, my short-term memory is shot and my concentration and energy levels are too low to be able to act anymore; the hearing in my right ear is also affected. Physically I had to endure corrective surgery on my face, I suffered a fractured skull, many broken bones, a punctured lung, plenty of cuts and bruises. I was so close to death it's a miracle that I'm alive, never mind sitting here talking. I'm thankful for that every day.

Is it true that you have been suffering from depression since the attack?

Yes. I am suffering from unipolar reactive depression. Depression is an awful thing; you don't want to be feeling so dead inside but there's nothing you can do about it. It's out of your control.

Do you believe the popular notion that Autumn suffered an extreme nervous breakdown, that she had been living with undiagnosed schizophrenia?

Not at all. [Autumn] has been diagnosed with schizophrenia but I have never believed that. From the very first day when her odd behaviour and delusions started [the day after the 1990 Epic Awards] I knew she had either taken or been slipped some sort of hallucinogenic or mind altering drug. People just don't turn like that. The things she saw; they were drug induced, I'm telling you. She was in perfect mental health before that morning.

Leigh spent all night at the awards with Jerry Tilsey. Do you think Tilsey may have had something to do with it, now that it's all emerged about his drug habits?

I've always thought that. Someone knew that she had collapsed, the ambulance men got an anonymous tip-off... from who? I don't think we'll ever know for sure now that Jerry's dead, if you know what I mean.

Were you close to Tilsey?

Jerry was a drug user more than what he was an actor. I felt sorry for him, like most people did. But, no, we weren't close at all.

Do you think Autumn Leigh was spiked or slipped a drug, such as the famously dubbed 'Hollywood Killer', maliciously?

I have no idea. I have no evidence to prove that [Autumn] didn't take some kind of substance off her own back, but she was my wife. I knew her. She had a very fragile body and never drank much or took illegal drugs because she just wasn't like that and she knew that her system just couldn't take it. It's not like she was a reckless teenager trying things out for the first time. She was a sensible adult and I know she just wouldn't have done it. I also know that what happened to my wife, and the reason she is sectioned at the moment, is suspicious.

Leigh was tested and re-tested for drugs in her blood, but none were found. How could you explain that?

I've been told that hallucinogenic drugs don't show up in urine tests after forty-eight hours. It was long after forty-eight hours when she went for her first test.

Why did she leave it so long?

She was afraid of doctors and hospitals. It was a phobia she had.

Have you been in contact with Autumn Leigh since the attack?

No.

Do you have any plans to reunite with her?

I would like to get her the proper help she deserves, and I would like to be able to somehow prove that she was given drugs without her consent, causing her to act like she did. But I would not like to see her, it would be too upsetting. I'd rather remember her how the rest of you remember her, as a beautiful person, inside and out.

Are you certain though that your comments are factual enough to prove?

No tests have proven that I am right, but I know I am. I have thought so from the morning after the awards. She was never the same after that night.

What if it was simply a breakdown and her schizophrenia has been diagnosed correctly?

Then I'll have to accept that. But only if it's proven to me, and I know it won't be. [Autumn] was in and out of hospitals her entire childhood due to her immune system, I think if she did have schizophrenic tendencies it would have been picked up on by now. People just don't turn schizophrenic for no reason one day. It was totally out of character and those that knew her must realise that.

What plans do you have for your own future?

At the moment my one goal is to make sure my wife has been diagnosed correctly. After that – who knows; whatever comes my way.

The American authorities are said to be going crazy to find out more about this drug, but so far it is still a bit of a mystery. Are you scared about it getting into this country?

Of-course. I just hope it never does. I want to do all I can to prevent it entering England, if it hasn't already.

You can send your letters of support to Anthony via our offices (address details on page 2). Please write 'Denharden Interview' on the envelope.

CHAPTER 11

The interview had been a breakthrough for the man who once had it all; even Dr Nazir noticed the immediate difference in his attitude and complexion. When he let her into his apartment she had to take a step back out of surprise. He greeted her with an enthusiastic smile, his voice excited and jumpy – a far cry from the usual dark mumbled hello. His skin looked a little less grey, a little less dull. His eyes had a coating of gloss; they looked wider and brighter. Mr Denharden had finally found the will to live again. He had a purpose once more.

'Hiya, come and look at this,' he grinned as he first let her in. As Anthony was leading Dr Nazir through to see the surprise, he continued: 'Did you read the interview? It was on Thursday in The National, did you see it? The guy, Nick, the journalist, he reckons she took drugs too. He says it's obvious and a lot of people think it. He said this could mean that there could be some treatment available for Lucy. He says she's being treated for the wrong thing, that's why she's still, well, like, asleep. Don't you think that's great news?'

How do you say 'no' to a good humoured question like that? Dr Nazir quickly asked herself.

Don't you think that's great news? *No Anthony, I don't. Journalists mean shit to the law.*

Don't you think that's great news? *No Anthony, the guy was using you for the story only.*

Don't you think that's great news? *No Anthony, this is a complete waste of time that will end only in frustration.*

Don't get our good doctor wrong, my dear. She was indeed over the moon with Anthony's new found enthusiasm for life, but she was also a little worried that the poor man was heading for one heck of a fall.

See, Dr Nazir never believed Lucy was given drugs. Of-course she did not express this belief with Anthony, but the way the doctor saw it from a professional point of view, and after studying her in the interest of helping Anthony, she could tell that Lucy had always had some sort of minor mental illness. Our favourite psychologist believed it was overwhelming emotion brought on by winning the award mixed with something a little more sinister that had tripped up Lucy's stability: not a drug. She would never dream of planting the idea into Anthony's head but, come *on*, what was the girl doing in a dingy back room that night? I mean, *hello!* That had affair-gone-wrong written all over it! Dr Nazir believed that it was definitely something a little less innocent than what Anthony could ever admit to himself that went on that night.

Dr Nazir was among the best psychologists in the country and she got there by proving people wrong on several occasions. This time, with Lucy Denharden's case, her instincts, research, knowledge, and experience all told her that her favourite client's wife went, pardon the term, nuts. She could even go as far as saying that Lucy herself didn't even believe the things she was seeing. Something told Dr Nazir that Lucy made the visions up. Why? Sympathy? Attention? The need to be mothered and have people sorry for her – judging by her smothered, sickly childhood? Who knows. Shrinks everywhere will look back to Mrs Denharden's overly protected upbringing, and point out the obvious effects that it would have had on her adult life, mainly the need to squeeze sympathy out of people. The fact that Lucy turned out to be an actress in the first place wasn't a big surprise. Lucy: the attention magnet. I hate to point out the obvious, my loyal friend and companion, but you've got to admit, here we have a drama queen if ever there was one.

Dr Nazir was led into the dining room and stopped in her tracks.

Three emptied post-bags lay in the corner. The table and floor were awash with letters, envelopes, and postcards. Anthony was grinning from ear to ear. It was the widest grin she'd ever seen him with in real life and it lit up his face, showing off his straight, white teeth. Perfect teeth in fact, which she hadn't noticed beyond the usual deafening frown.

'Nick told me he wishes he'd never told people to write in. They've received another five bags today. He said it's the biggest pain in the arse since they wrote the article claiming that the Pope was an alien. Don't you think that's brilliant?'

'Yep, that's a lot of mail. What exactly are people writing to you for?'

'That they think injustice has been done, that the case was unfair, telling me their fears about the drug, support, sympathy… all sorts. I'm so shocked, I had no idea people still cared. Nick says my interview hit a nerve with the entire nation.'

'Who's Nick again?'

'Nick? The journalist who brought it up in his article to start with. He's promised to follow me all the way with it.'

'Anthony, this is great news, but I think you should slow down a little bit. There's no proof yet or anything. You have no idea if this drug has got anything whatsoever to do with Lucy. I know we discussed building on your suspicions but this is too much, too public,' Dr Nazir said softly. 'I think we should go into the study and talk about it rationally.'

Anthony totally ignored her and found a letter.

'Listen,' he instructed, and began reading from the letter: 'Dear Anthony, your courage to speak out at such a panicking time is both amazing and inspirational. I agree that it's too much of a coincidence that Autumn Leigh got so ill in such a short space of time after she spent the evening with Jerry Tilsey. I think you should ask for the hearing to be reopened. If she is spending the rest of her life in a padded prison when she should be getting drug rehabilitation help then it proves just how bad our justice system is. My thoughts are with you, I would love to see you acting again. Have you thought about writing a biography? Yours sincerely, Mrs Jean Simpson.'

Anthony looked up to his psychologist and suddenly felt the need to convince her that he wasn't just being stupid.

'You see?' he stressed. 'It's not just me. I want to find out all about this drug. I'm gunna go to America.'

'*America*?' the good doctor exclaimed. 'Are you sure you've thought this through enough?'

Anthony put the letter back on the table and looked at her in anger.

'Come on,' she instructed. 'We're running into session time. Let's go into the study.'

She turned and Anthony followed.

The session was tense, full of enthusiasm on Anthony's part and realistic doubts on Dr Nazir's. To her, he was acting like a child with a crazy idea stuck in his head. She felt it was too much excitement too soon and, in the long run, it would only serve to damage him more. What did he think the authorities were going to do? She had been tested negative for drugs and that was that. What else was he expecting? She's serving her sentence now, they're not going to alter that just because someone that she knew has been rumbled taking drugs, are they? Hell, would they let Bronson off because they found out that an associate of his spent his life helping out charities?

The session went something like this:

(Five minutes in…)

Anthony Denharden: What are you trying to say? Are you telling me you think this happened naturally?

Dr Saima Nazir: Well, no, it's just… okay, where's the proof that it didn't happen naturally?

A.D (getting agitated): Look at her! Look at what happened! And now this about Jerry, when she was with him? I suspected him all along, before all this came out, you know I did! What… do… do you think this is all coincidence or something?

S.N (speaking sterner than normal): Listen, I'm a doctor; I know how doctors think. Even when something seems like a dead cert it doesn't mean it actually is. Proof is needed in things like this. Yes, there is a lot of circumstantial evidence but if there's no hard copy to back up the obvious then it will be dismissed… that's why it was dismissed in court…

A.D (Interrupting): I honestly can't believe a woman as smart as you is completely missing the truth here...

S.N: This is a pointless battle, Anthony. I'm not even sure what you're battling against. Your wife is serving her sentence so let her do it in peace. This isn't going to get you anywhere.

(Silence)

...cont' S.N: I'm sorry to sound harsh and I can see how passionate you are to prove drugs caused this, but even if that was somehow proven, it still wouldn't change anything. They'd just add drugs to the list of catalysts that caused her to do what she did to you. She's been analysed a thousand times for crying out loud. She's been diagnosed.

A.D: But they say the drug they found on Jerry is similar to LSD, so if she did take it, it would prove that it was the drug that was causing the hallucinations, not her mind.

S.N: Okay... and then what?

A.D: And then her name will be cleared...

S.N: How?

A.D: 'Cause then everyone will know that she was slipped drugs...

S.N: No. Everyone will know she *took* drugs. How do you know she was slipped?

A.D: She had absolutely no memory of taking drugs, and she never would.

S.N: You can't accuse Jerry of slipping drugs to her on those two weak points. The public would never believe she was slipped drugs just because she *said* she would never take them. River Phoenix *said* he never would either, so it's not exactly a reliable phrase in the celebrity world is it? Come on, Anthony, you know that. Plus, you could be accused of slander jumping to conclusions like that... you're skating on thin ice already by the sound of things.

A.D: How am I?

S.N: Anthony, you can't just go accusing Jerry of dealing drugs. It's slander. You have no proof whatsoever. It's like... it's like me telling the papers that you're gay just because I think you are.

263

A.D: You think I'm gay?

S.N: No, it's just an example. Basically, for your own good, Anthony, you've just got to stop all this.

A.D (using the doctor's first name for the first time): Saima, I think you're a tremendous doctor and I think you deserve every single award that you've won, but just because you help me mentally doesn't give you the right to tell me what to do with my life. I'm a grown man. Please don't put me down by forgetting that. (Shrugs)

S.N: I'm not telling you this as a doctor. I'm telling you this as a friend.

(Anthony shakes his head)

…cont' S.N: I'm looking in from the outside and I can see this leading to nothing but frustration. If you want to try occupying your time then why not write a biography, like that lady said?

A.D (Sarcastically): Oh yeah, I can see the reviews now: 'great beginning and middle, shame about the shitty ending though.'

S.N (Sighs deeply): Right, I'm going to leave you to think about this, Anthony. I won't bill you for your time today; it's hardly been a session, has it? I'll see you next week.

Dr Nazir collected her coat from the back of the chair, picked her briefcase-bag up from the desk and began walking from the room, only turning at the last minute to say: 'Before you go shouting your mouth off on television or booking flights, think about what I've said… for Lucy's sake.'

Anthony watched her through scowling eyes and listened to her heels click down the hallway. When the sound of his front door opening and shutting signalled that she had left, his shoulders dropped.

As he sat in a black cloud of thought, the rational little man in the back of his mind began whispering silently, making him even more annoyed:

She's right. She's right you know. Of-course you know. What are you and your nutzo wife going to get from all this searching? Please explain, Mr Denharden, exactly which

264

aspect of this little accusation spree will bring her back to you the way she was? Jesus, accept it, will you? You're making yourself look foolish. You know the doctor's right, that's why it stung you so much when she spoke. No offence mate, but she's the award winning professional and you're the failed actor. She's right and you're wrong. There's nothing left for you, Tony, my boy. You've spent it. Come on now, you're wasting the storyline, let the good people get on with it. Go back to your nest.

But there was also the optimistic, answer-seeking little man in the forefront of his mind, the one he'd spent his whole life listening to until the past year or so. But this time his voice was loud and booming, stronger than it had been in recent times:

What?! And quit now? I know you still care about your wife, Anthony. Are you going to stand by and watch her rot out the rest of her life in a psychiatric ward when she could be receiving drug counselling and getting better – possibly coming back to you and starting over again? Would you be able to live with yourself if you just left her? Come on lad, you know she was given drugs, don't you? Other people know it too so do something about it, eh? Show the world you're both not as trash-heaped as what everyone thinks. Show the world it wasn't her fault. If you really loved her then you'd help her. Anyway, what else are you going to do with your life now? What else is there to concentrate on?

Anthony wrestled with both these voices until he found he could fight no more and decided to get out of the flat to clear his head. Armed with a jumper, coat, beanie, and gloves, he left his stack of unopened mail and the depressing surroundings that half a mil' had bought him, and set off down the communal staircase that led him to mid-afternoon Leeds. There was a second before he opened the heavy front door linking the outside world to all six apartments, that he considered he might open it to a gang of photographers and screaming girls, cameras flashing and microphones being shoved in his face, just like old times. So he inhaled deeply, closed his eyes, and then went for it.

•

It was early December and bitingly cold already. No snow had fallen yet but as ever it was predicted that a white Christmas was upon the good people of England this year. Matthew Lowe had been warned by his fellow 'buddies' that this time of year was the hardest to get through. The money was better; guilt money, but the weather conditions were killers and sometimes the beatings from the pissed-up lads coming out of the clubs were even more ferocious due to them all drinking for free, or using their Christmas bonuses to really make a night of it.

Matthew used to get quite generous Christmas bonuses himself, you know. He got £500 from Howley & Co back in 1989; that was more than any other employee, and he'd still been a teenager then. They said that he was one of the best salesmen they'd ever had. They said he could probably sell a turd if he put his mind to it – and he could have done.

That might be why even now, homeless and forced to beg for money and food, that he seemed to make more per day than the other unfortunates of this city. It still hadn't quite sunk in as to how he'd ended up like this, how things went so wrong. He knew why, of-course, but it hadn't sunk in, it still seemed like a dream.

Even after four whole months of sitting in doorways and standing on the precinct begging through the day, and battling for beds and trying to ignore the disgusting things that went on at the hostel at night, it still escaped him as to how he'd become the person he was.

It had been heroin, basically – like it was with most of the other desperate, homeless people in and around the city, every city. If you'd have asked Matthew three years ago, when he was nineteen, if he'd ever try drugs he would have replied: 'Never have, never will. I'm not that sad, thanks.' If you'd have asked him two years ago, he would have said: 'I don't mind the odd toke on a joint, or a pill now and then, but none of that heavy shit, no.' And if you'd have asked him from last year onwards, you'd have found the answer to be: 'Why? What have you got?' It only went downhill from there.

Matthew had met her in The Majestyk, one of the biggest and most commercial nightclubs in Leeds. She was beautiful in that sulky, hard-life, mouthy kind of way that he always seemed to go for.

She had been standing by herself looking angry, smoking a cigarette and holding a vodka and lemonade. Matthew had gone to the club with a colleague from Howley & Co and lost him during the night, and it was while trying to find him that he stumbled upon her: Lisa. They had got talking and she had invited him back to her flat in Beeston (it's as easy as that in The Majestyk, guys!) and that's where he'd had his first joint. He was with her for two months and within that time she sent him down the brightly-lit path of searching for the real meaning of fun. Matthew could hardly believe he'd got to nearly twenty without experiencing the high of weed and pills. He'd met scores of new underclass friends through Lisa and began spending all of his time with them, getting cained in their grotty flats and having a laugh. His old friends gradually stopped calling and he had been pulled up by both his employers and his parents about the state of him recently. The more people said 'what's got into you, Matthew? You're changing', the more it pushed him away from them. His old friends just didn't know how to live. He was having the time of his life; it was hardly his fault they were all boring.

Things took a turn for the worse though when Lisa dumped Matthew after eight weeks, because he was never sober anymore. Although she liked to get high as much as the next girl, it was just too much. So Lisa went back to her vodka and lemonade, and Matthew continued on his quest for more fun.

It was Philip Thornton that first acquainted Matthew with heroin. It was in Sniff's flat, but Sniff was the only one who didn't do it, so he'd gone into another room to play on his computer. Philip placed a small amount of brown tar onto a neatly cut rectangle of foil and began to heat it from underneath while Matthew watched on in awe. Then, once the heroin had started to boil, Matthew was handed a toilet roll tube and told to inhale. That was a year and a half ago. Now Matthew sits homeless, jobless, penniless, and dreamless in a doorway, begging for money to feed his habit. Oh, and to buy food.

Today he'd found a new spot after been thrown out of his old one by Bill... or was it Bob...? Anyway, the scary ginger one whose downfall was cider, rather than heroin. But that had turned out to be a blessing in disguise as Matthew reckoned he had got it just right with this new place. He was on one of the main streets yet sheltered by a stepped, indented doorway housing a double door, providing a roof from rain. It even had given him enough space to spread his legs out and it didn't look like it was used anymore. It was part of a massive, five-story building that spanned the entirety of Park Row and this door fell between banks. Matthew thought it must be some sort of a fire exit to one of them.

The kid who was once the best salesman at Howley & Co had been sitting there for three hours when a smartly dressed Asian lady kindly asked him to move his legs, as she had to get past. She opened one of the heavy front double doors with a latchkey and entered what Matthew saw to be a porch area. She pressed a buzzer and then the door closed. *Ah, flats.* Not even half an hour later the same woman exited the building, this time giving him a pound, followed by an ill looking man overly dressed in woollies about ten minutes later. Matthew asked the sombre man if he had any change but the man replied that he hadn't and stepped over him. They always say that, even if they're the richest people in the world. They haven't even got 10p to spare. *What the fuck is the human race coming to?*

•

Anthony didn't open the door to a gaggle of press-reporters and fans, only a tramp. It took Anthony aback a little as this was the first time he'd ever seen one on his own doorstep, and the kid was spread out over the steps! Anthony had been stepping over his legs to get past when the tramp asked him for some money, but Anthony hadn't brought his wallet out with him so he'd replied: 'No mate, sorry.'

Not even a tramp realised who Anthony was, never mind a frantic group of women. The tramp shook his head a little but Anthony chose to ignore it.

Honestly! A bloody tramp hassling me for change on my own doorstep and then making me feel bad for not having any. What the fuck is the human race coming to?

CHAPTER 12

The December day was milder down south and Nurse Lindle was sitting outside on the hospital grounds with day nurses Steve Jones and Lotti Mack, talking of both work and personal matters. Mary Cheeda and Sara White were doing their love/hate relationship justice by winding each other up just an earshot from their carers.

'Duncan wants me to have Christmas Day off this year, Alicia. Do you think that would be alright?' Lotti asked her manager in her fading Scottish accent.

Nurse Lindle pulled a pained expression and sucked air through her teeth.

'Unlikely, to be honest,' she replied, watching her colleague's face drop. 'Evelyn and Rose have already booked time off and we can't afford to be any more nurses down. You could book now for next year though?'

'Ah, okay. Are you working this year?'

'I work every year,' Nurse Lindle, Alicia to her co-workers, laughed.

There was a comfortable silence and all three glanced over to Mary and Sara. They were sitting on the grass; Sara was using wild arm movements, sitting upright and alert, while Mary was shaking her head in disagreement to what ever it was that Sara was saying, but obviously listening all the same.

'I'm finding Sara more and more difficult to look after,' Steve – a nurse at Penford for only eighteen months – said, still looking over to his main patient.

'Hmm,' Nurse Lindle sighed.

Sara had become more of a problem recently. She'd always been, how can I put it… strung, but never showed any hints of violence or intimidation towards other patients or staff. But recently Sara's episodes of total panic and fear were getting frequent to the point of concern. It also appeared to be for no particular reason, which bothered the nurses and carers of Penford women's general ward immensely. There had been no change in her treatment, drugs, diet, or routine. Yet for some reason Miss White was starting to draw likeness to a bubble about to burst… a bubble of fear and energy and wildness.

'She casually threatened to kill me yesterday evening while I was changing her bed sheets,' Steve continued. 'She said she had her eye on me because she thinks I'm a spy.'

Nurse Lindle turned her head sharply to her co-worker.

'She's said that to me before too, when I was giving her her medication last week,' Lotti added.

'Is it the first time she's threatened you?' Nurse Lindle asked Steve.

'Yes,' he replied.

'How come you didn't tell me about this yesterday?'

Steve shrugged: 'I forgot.'

'What exactly happened? What did she say?'

'Just that really. She was sitting on her chair glaring at me as I was putting the sheets on and she just said that she knew I was a spy, and if I reported back to 'them' then she'd kill me for it. She said she's smarter than I think and she's got her eye on me.'

'How did you handle that?' Nurse Mack asked.

'Well, I just said I'm not a spy, I'm her carer and I'm here to look after her. She laughed and was like, of-course you'd say that.'

'I want you to tell Dr Smith about that straight away, before her next session. She's getting more paranoid and I think it's becoming dangerous for herself, the other patients and us. Go tell him now.'

'Is he in?'

'Yes, and as far as I know he's not in session. Knock first though just in-case.'

Steve said goodbye to his colleague and his manager and went to tell the hospital psychiatrist that his main patient had said she would kill him. He didn't plan to tell him, or anyone else for that matter, that she had also offered him her weekly allowance for sex, an offer he had quickly declined.

We focus on our troubled patient Sara now. She had stopped talking the second Steve had stood up and she watched him intently as he walked back into the building. Mary turned her head in the direction of Sara's suddenly panicked eyes and saw that she was studying the young man as he walked away.

'What are you watching *him* for?' Mary asked, upon turning back round to the girl that she couldn't decide whether to love or hate.

'He's going to tell them what we've been saying. He's going to report back. He's been listening to us,' Sara began, before stopping suddenly and snapping her eyes dead on Mary's. 'You knew about this, didn't you? You've trapped me. You've set me up. Are you working for them?'

'I beg your pardon?' Mary exclaimed in her best middle class accent. 'Sara, I don't work for the hospital.'

'Neither does Nurse Jones,' Sara whispered knowingly. 'They've sent him to keep tabs on me. They're increasing activity, they're getting scared. I'm the cog in their works.'

Mary laughed her special *Sara's-paranoid-again* laugh and said: 'My dear, you are so young and naive. Nurse Jones works here: for this place. He's not with the government, you silly girl.'

'Oh no, he's not government. The government means nothing, they're just the mask over the face that really calls the shots. It's bigger than that. He works for the Secret Circle.'

'Ah, the Secret Circle again,' Mary nodded. She'd heard this one a hundred times before. Sara had accused Mary of being in the Circle on several occasions. Mary never bit to it.

'He knows, though. He knows I'm on to him. I told him I'd get him if he continued working for them; his reaction told me everything. And now…'

'Sara, you can't tell the nurses here that you'll 'get' them. They'll send you back to maximum security. They don't like to be threatened.'

'It wasn't a threat, Mary. No, no, no. It was simply a warning.'

'Sara, don't say it again.'

'He doesn't even work here. You're just like everyone else, all the other lemmings. You're brainless, you're numbed. You don't know how the world runs. I do,' Sara replied, agitated.

'You don't. You're just a stupid girl. You're crazy: that's why you're in here.'

'No, no, no. I am in here because I know too much. They put me in here so I won't spread their secrets to the mindless public. Lemmings like *you*.'

Mary stood up and wiped grass off herself.

'You're in here because you're crazy,' she said, before walking off to watch television in the community room.

To Mary's surprise, Sara didn't follow. That's what usually happened; Mary would begin to leave and within seconds Sara would be on her feet too, jerkily and nervously continuing trying to convince Mary about whatever it was she happened to be talking about. But today, Mary entered the community room alone.

There was only Flo, Maggie, and the three catatonics in the small room. Flo and Maggie were both asleep across two of the sponge chairs and two of the catatonics had been pointed in the direction of the television in their wheelchairs. Pookie was standing against the far wall with her head hung down to her chest. All was silent except for the quiet sound from the television. The TV was playing cartoons that were of no interest to Mary so, with nobody able to kick up a fuss, Mary headed straight for the channel buttons and flicked through. She remained standing considering each channel until she settled on a film in mid-flow on BBC2. After turning the volume up slightly, Mary took the closest available seat to the screen – which was next to the ginger catatonic whom she hadn't seen flinch or make any movement in the few months since the girl had joined them.

Much to Mary's disgust, she had only been watching the film for thirty seconds or so when it was cut off for an advert break. Still, it enabled Mary to find out what the film's title was when the still came up. *All About Harry*, it read. *All About Harry*... starring Autumn Leigh.

Lucy Denharden's mind was a mouse; a little brown field mouse burrowing and sniffing out nuts and seeds on a moist forest floor.

The mouse that was Lucy's mind had been happily doing this for months. Every now and again it would find a succulent berry and oh boy, then it was a happy mouse indeed. So on this particular day, the sun was shining through the forest and our little rodent was collecting food to hibernate for the winter. Its fur was beginning to feel glossy and warm and its little black eyes shone and danced. We have here a beautiful, happy mouse.

While an advert for Scotchtape was being aired in a TV room very distant yet very near to the forest, our mouse was scampering across from one oak to another, sniffing out any traces of edible woodland and stopping to see if the teasing aroma provided the goods. By the time an advert for yoghurt had graced the television, our silky brown friend had found an entire stash of berries that had obviously been dropped or forgotten by another animal. Oh my, it was a thousand Christmases at once in the forest at that moment!

And so the film was back on. The returning scene from the adverts was focused on a busty, beautiful redhead who was sitting flicking maniacally through documents in a penthouse office, wearing reading glasses and looking powerful.

There was a knock on the office door and a handsome, dark-haired man entered the room.

The redhead didn't acknowledge him, only continued looking pissed off and frantic at the mess of paper in front of her.

'I just wanted to apologise for earlier,' the man, no doubt a famous actor somewhere, said smoothly.

The redhead slammed down her papers and looked up to him: 'I don't have time for this now, Scott,' she replied. 'I've got to find the Kinderman report before Roger realises it's missing...' and so the typically American scene continued.

Our mouse had got one berry in each cheek and was about to store the third when its attention was drawn away from food as suddenly as lightening. Its little ears pricked right up and it shifted onto its hind legs. A voice had swarmed through the denseness of the trees and distracted it, a voice of a thousand memories – a voice that the mouse had heard before.

Then there was silence. Wind rustled the leaves and birds flapped strong wings overhead. The mouse stood, listening. And sure enough, the voice leapt at it again. The mouse squealed this time and darted under a mound of twigs and dead leaves.

Mary had been watching the actress telling the handsome young man how much trouble they'd be in if they didn't find this report, when the ginger girl next to her spoke.

Mary snapped her head to the unfortunate lady and said: 'Pardon?' but the girl did not speak again.

Mary watched the girl cautiously. Her head was still in exactly the same position as it had been when Mary had entered the room, her body unmoved. Had she actually spoken? *She did just speak, didn't she?*

After studying the girl for a little longer, Mary's attention was turned back to the television as the woman in the film stood up from her desk and began shouting.

Mary had looked away from the mentally dead woman sat next to her for only a matter of seconds when she did it again. This time Mary *definitely* heard it, a distinct mumble from her lips. Maybe the woman sitting next to her was not as mentally dead as everyone thought? Maybe she wasn't mentally dead at all.

Mary was out of her chair and back out to Nurse Lindle within an instant. *She spoke! She spoke and I heard her!*

But nurse Lindle did not hear Mary, because Mary was a compulsive liar and that was why she was in there. She had been known to make several untrue claims regarding instances involving other patients before, but the nurses and doctors would not be fooled then and they would not be fooled now either.

Of-course, if Mary had happened to mention that they had been watching a film titled *All About Harry* then it would have been a different matter completely. Mary and the other patients had no idea of-course that the catatonic woman residing in Penford with them was in fact the world famous Autumn Leigh, but all the staff knew, and they also knew that she starred in the amazing flop of a film titled *All About Harry*. The fact that she may have murmured something would be far more believable if they'd have known the film in question was coincidentally showing when the incident happened.

But they didn't know, and the matter was dismissed. Mary went back to watching both the film and the patient, but much to her dismay the catatonic ginger girl did not speak again throughout the day. Lucy's mouse went back to collecting berries, and the dense trees in the forest that was her catatonia blocked out that familiar voice from frightening her any more.

CHAPTER 13

Anthony had not meant to end up where he did; he never planned to walk that far. But now, three hours after stepping over a homeless young man on his doorstep, he found himself standing staring at a solid object that felt like it was from a distant lifetime. Like he'd never really seen it or been there before.

Anthony was facing a small, soot covered terraced house on Peel Street, the place where he grew up with his mother.

The walk had given him time to soul search and some of the tension had lifted from his head, at least temporarily. He had taken turns listening to both voices and admittedly, standing here now, he was more inclined to go with the one that agreed with Dr Nazir.

He had to be careful. Up until this day of strained words between himself and the doctor, Anthony had been charging full steam ahead like a kid whacked up to his eyeballs with e-numbers. But now he had properly, rationally thought it through, he could see it like the adult he was and noticed how careless he was being with his thoughts. Throughout his entire journey here, the only thing that had distracted him from thinking about what the fuck he was doing with his life, was what stood before him now. At last his mind was cleared of confusion.

The windows were new, the front door was plastic now, and the yard had been decked out with gravel and plant pots. But Anthony saw it just as he had all those years ago, when he was a boy. And, in a glorious moment of nostalgia, Anthony wondered why it had taken him over two decades to return here. As he stood looking wondrously up to the house, his hidden eye saw a small, mousy boy in the early 1960s. He was throwing his bike down on the ground, out of breath and high on energy, as his mother, young and healthy, appeared in the doorway and handed him a glass of juice. The boy grabbed it with both hands and drank from it so hastily much of it went down his top. His mother laughed and said something about juice to match the grass stains on his clothes. The boy wiped his mouth with the back of his hand, handed his mother the glass back, yelled: 'Thanks Mam,' and – before she even had chance to say: 'Be back for five,' – was off on his bike for another adventure.

Nostalgia is a magical, unreal feeling, don't you think? When Anthony, as a man, looks up at this cramped damp property of his childhood, he doesn't see the fear that used to cloud his eyes whenever the thought of his father coming to find them would haunt him. He forgets to recall the rainy, dark days when the gas would run out and he and his mother would huddle under a rug around candles… and the tears that would stain his face as a child after been continuously being called a bastard by the local people (the people who only saw a young, single mother with a fatherless child) are forgotten about.

Yep indeedy, not only does nostalgia lovingly place rose-tinted spectacles over most people's eyes anyway, but Anthony's life was so black at the moment – everything previous was viewed as being uber-perfect. This little street would always be a hot summer's day in Anthony's eyes. It would always be a place of laughter, of a loving mother and friends that have never and will never be replaced.

Look at you now, for instance. Today you have gone about your day and you probably haven't even thought twice about it, because it's just what you do, isn't it? And tomorrow, and the next day, and the next, and the next few years you will be 'going about' things without giving it a second thought. But then one day – maybe years from now – you will look back on this period of your life with nostalgic thought. Your recollections may be disjointed and rose-tinted; they may be clear and painful, but they'll still be there.

This, your life right now, will become another memory in the file of your life and you won't even realise it. My mother says that if everyone clung on to the harsher experiences, then everyone would be messed up; that's why she's an optimist. Anthony, except for his current lapse into depression, is one of those lucky people that do tend to look on the bright side. It would be easy for the guy to be standing on this road remembering only the hiding, the poverty, and all the rest of the shit that comes with being a victim of a violent father – but instead he chooses to see a brilliant childhood and I reckon that's the way to be. At least his mind is giving the poor bloke a break for a change.

Anthony's mother is buried in Bruntcliffe Cemetery. It's a ten-minute walk from where he stands now. He's been back rarely, but today he thinks he should go. Although he never discussed it with his wife, or anyone for that matter, the reason Anthony doesn't visit it more often is because it reminds him that she's dead. I know, I know; that's probably not how you and I would handle it but hey, everyone's different. But now, after getting the curtains twitching on Peel Street by staring up at somebody else's house for ten minutes, he feels he owes it to her. Whether or not he believes in visiting gravestones, that's where the body of a wonderful woman lays.

Anthony takes three steps up the street to begin his short journey to his mother's grave when he stops and takes one last look at his childhood. Within that moment, gone are the new windows, the door is no longer plastic, and the yard is bare of plant pots. It hits him like a brick and without even expecting it Anthony is in a different time. He is back in the sixties...

She had given him money for spice that morning and he had taken it from her hand with thanks. Robert Millis, Andy Tanner and Stuart Robinson were all waiting impatiently on their bikes for him to emerge.

As he was leaving the house she said: 'Be home by five. Don't get into trouble and don't ruin your new trousers.'

'Yeah Mam, see 'ya,' was his response.

He leapt outside to Stuart shouting: 'Are you getting a kiss goodbye, Tony?' and his other two friends suppressing giggles.

'Shur' up, Stu!' was Anthony's playfully embarrassed retort as he picked up his bike.

He'd walked it out of the yard and was just mounting it when, horror upon horrors! His mother opened the window and called, right in front of his friends and the entire street: 'I love you Tony. Promise me you'll be careful!'

Of-course, Anthony's friends loved this and the fact that Anthony mumbled: 'Yes, Mam', from an apple red face went down a treat too.

The second his mother shut the window the three boys burst into laughter and, despite Anthony's order of 'bloody shur up', it gave them ammunition for the rest of the day to jokingly wind up mummy's boy.

Anthony, the greying man hitting forty with his hands in his pockets, watched the four small boys cycle past. He heard Robert saying 'I love you Tony!' in a mock-female voice and saw himself, as a child, shaking his head and laughing; embarrassed but unfazed. Anthony, as a man, did the same thing, just before the imaginary children and the heat of August 1963 disappeared with a passing car.

Isn't it odd going back somewhere you haven't seen for years? You know you're not expecting things to be the same yet you are eternally shocked and disheartened when you see it for your own eyes.

Anthony's walk up to the cemetery took him through the heart of the town and through a sports field. It took him a good five minutes to stop reeling at the fact that he hardly recognised the town centre. Once on the field he was greeted with a rugby stand and floodlights that had been little more than wastelands when he was a kid. It had worried him, upon approaching the cemetery, that it too might be unrecognisable. How much of a shit would he feel if it were nothing but a mass of weeds with the odd, forgotten gravestone popping out here and there? That's why, when he eventually reached the back entrance to it, from the field, he was pleased to find that it was still as well looked after as it had always been. There used to be a tiny church in the middle of the yard but that was just a concrete square now. But still, the place was quiet and pleasant.

His mother had died only a few years after moving to London and, as it was due to sickness and she had known it was coming, she had requested to be buried back up in Morley, her reasoning being that she never wanted to leave it in the first place and that maybe, yes, her cold-blooded husband could chase her all around the country in life, but in death she didn't want to hide. She died just as Anthony was getting his break into acting.

She was buried alongside a row of eight, near the back of the vast graveyard. Heartbreakingly, hers was the only one of the nine that didn't have either dead or alive flowers on it. After he had recovered from that horrible realisation, Anthony sat down on the grass at the foot of it and stared at the marble calmly. It wasn't so bad being here, Anthony thought. He was expecting... well, he wasn't sure what he was expecting. Not this. He thought he'd be so filled with emotion he would break down and not be able to take it. But to his surprise he found that he actually felt strangely at peace here. The winter breeze was biting and the grass was damp but Anthony didn't feel any of it. He was in a warm place.

Just before her death, while Louise was still able to talk, she had told her son about his father. She spoke frankly and in depth about the man that had carved their distorted path. Anthony's mother had never hidden anything from her boy about what life was like before they'd ran away from Manchester when Anthony was three, but it was the way in which she spoke to him that made it different this final time.

It was one week before she died and Anthony had been at her hospital bedside more hours than you'd have thought humanly possible. She slept most of the time but when she woke and he saw the look of love and pride on her face once she realised her boy was there, it was magic. Obviously, what with Anthony being nineteen and already becoming an underground British film star, he had a lot of mixed up things going on and didn't always know what to say or how to say it. The words just never flowed right in those final months. Except the last day he ever spoke to her…

It was around 1pm on a damp autumn day. He had been there since seven in the morning, reading to her as she slept and drinking constant cups of plastic tasting machine coffee, when she eventually woke.

'Mam?' Anthony put the paper down and got down on one knee by the side of her.

Her eyes fluttered open sleepily and that beautiful smile that disease couldn't kill lit up her puffy skin.

'Tony. How are you?' she asked, still coming around. She lifted a tube-infested hand up and Anthony clasped it with his own.

'It doesn't matter about me, Mam. How are you feeling? Are you comfortable? Do you want a nurse?'

'No,' she laughed weakly. 'I would like to sit up though.'

Anthony gently helped move his mother into as much of an upright position as she could manage, and sat back down.

'How are you feeling?' he asked, with an obvious look of concern on his face, and a deeper one of exhaustion that he was trying to hide.

'I'm feeling a lot better, thanks. How are you?' Louise spoke softly and with heartbreakingly transparent weakness.

'I'm fine, Mam.'

'How long have you been here?'

'Not long.'

'Enough to go through five cups of coffee, though,' she smiled.

Anthony looked over to the seven empty cups on the table in the corner and laughed softly.

'Not too poorly to catch me out then, eh?' he said.

They both looked at each other and smiled, before their faces dropped into sorrow at exactly the same time.

'Are you managing the rent okay?' Louise asked her child, with pangs of guilt stabbing her heart that she couldn't be there to pay it anymore.

'Yeah, it's no problem,' Anthony smiled reassuringly. 'I'm up to date with the rent, the bills, everything. We don't owe a penny of debt.'

'You're such a good lad,' she smiled, squeezing her hand as tight around his as she could. 'Are you eating properly? You're not just living off junk are you?'

'Three square meals a day, Mam,' Anthony lied dutifully.

Anthony had been visiting his mother nearly every evening but she'd been so whacked out with drugs she'd hardly ever had the energy to open her eyes, never mind talk.

Anthony stroked the skin of his mother's hand, observant of how paper-fine it felt, of how devastatingly pellucid it looked.

'You've had to grow up pretty fast these last few months,' Louise perceived, studying her child – proud and sorry at the same time. 'I just hope you're managing.'

'I'm doing just fine,' Anthony said.

The mother turned to her only child and smiled sadly. 'Even if you weren't,' she said. 'You wouldn't tell me. You forget how well I know you.'

Anthony breathed a sigh of silent laughter. He knew that she knew he wasn't coping at all, he also knew that she knew he'd never tell her that.

'Did you talk to that Janine girl?'

'Oh yeah, I'd forgotten I'd told you about her,' Anthony chuckled, glad of the change of subject. 'I dumped her last weekend. She was a psycho.'

'You did right son, you're well rid of people like that,' Louise answered, trailing off slightly at the end when it was realised that both mother and son were now thinking about their ex-husband and ex-father.

You're well rid of people like that.

The silence ended when Anthony cleared his throat and kissed his mother's hand.

'So,' he said. 'How are you feeling today? You seem better than usual.'

Louise smiled a smile of a thousand tears and said: 'I'm not getting better, Tony.'

She watched his face drop. She knew of Anthony's naive view on life. She knew if she spoke to him as usual today, he would leave this hospital on a high. *Wow, Mam's getting better! She's not usually that talkative! She'll be home within a week at this rate!* He would spend the rest of his visit today telling her how his week had gone, they'd exchange pleasantries and then she'd die.

She'd die without talking to him properly about the things she wanted to say and Anthony would be out there in the world on his own, totally unprepared for it. She had known for some months now that she had to remove those child glasses from her son and put on the heavy adult ones. She didn't want to and the thought had crossed her head a thousand times just let him be a dreamer while he still could... but that wouldn't be fair to him in the long run. Her Tony was a deep boy and she could hear a million questions just wanting to be asked behind that silent mouth of his. She could see pain and fear in the eyes of the teenager who loved his mother more than he did any other human being in the world. She could physically see it, and he knew that she was dying, of-course he did, he just liked to *believe* otherwise. And because of that optimistic belief, he wouldn't want to say any of the final things to her because then he would be admitting to himself that he might never talk to her again.

'I won't be coming home.' The words she spoke seemed so cruel. She was so scared for him.

'Don't say that, Mam,' Anthony dismissed her. 'You'll be fine. You're a fighter, aren't you; you'll beat this.'

'Tony,' she urged. 'I won't be coming home. I've fought this all I can but it's taken over me.'

Her strong, beautiful son bit his bottom lip and looked irrelevantly over to the empty plastic cups.

'I had a dream about you last night,' she said, her voice as hollow as a tunnel.

'Oh yeah? What did you dream?' Anthony asked. He granted her eye contact for a moment before his eyes swooped away from his mother's face and down to the floor. He couldn't look at her for any longer through fear of crying and upsetting her.

'I dreamt you were a big movie-star.'

'I am!' Anthony made a joke of it to try to ease the sudden lump in his throat.

Louise smiled and continued: 'You were living in this big house in the country with a beautiful wife and lots of children. You'd really made it.' She paused then added: 'I'm so proud of you, son. You're going to have an amazingly happy life. You know that, don't you? You'll conquer everything that stands in your way and you'll grow up to be a wonderful man. I'm so proud of you and I love you so much.'

Anthony tried to stop it but he just couldn't. It started with his face reddening and contorting, then a tear from each eye, before finally a pained gasp left his lips and made him sit up straight and wipe his eyes quickly. He'd been holding it in for months and now, within three sentences of his mother waking up, he could hold it no longer.

'Don't be afraid to cry, Tony. Don't ever be afraid to show emotion. That's what makes a person real,' Louise said, her eyes filling up.

'You're not going to die,' he commanded, his voice breaking and high.

'I am, Tony. I wish I weren't but I am. I'm sorry.'

Anthony listened to his mother and put his hands over his face, sobbing deeply into them.

'I don't want you to die, Mam. Why did you have to get poorly?' he cried, his chest heaving.

'I wish I didn't, Tony. I wish I could be here for you forever. But I can't. That's the way life is. You know I'll always watch over…'

That's when Louise could not talk for tears. She held out her arms and Anthony leapt into them, crying onto her shoulder. She held her only child tightly.

'I'm so proud of you, Mam. You're the strongest person I know. I love you,' he sobbed.

'Anthony,' Louise pulled her son away from her just enough for her to look at him close up. He really was a compassionate, loveable kid. He was his mother's child. 'Talk to me,' she said, looking into her son's eyes, which were still streaming violently with tears. 'Tell me everything you've ever wanted to say. Ask me everything you've ever wanted to ask. Talk to me about how you're feeling. Do it now otherwise you'll bottle it up and carry it around with you for the rest of your life.'

Anthony stared back into his mother's eyes and saw something he'd only ever seen once before, on the day they fled Leeds: fear.

'Are you scared?' he whimpered, the crying hysteria finally calming down.

'Yes,' she nodded and bit her lip. 'I'm scared about leaving you all alone.'

'Don't be scared for me, Mam. I'll be fine. You know I will. I'll be alright.'

'I know you will, but I just… I just wish I could watch you grow. Look at you, my little lad, a man already. I remember when you were a baby, you were so quiet and smiley.' She broke off into a teary laugh and shook her head. 'Do you know, the night we left Manchester I'd come into your room in the middle of the night…'

As his mother was speaking, Anthony left her grasp and sat down in his chair all ears. Sure, she'd told him about his father, but never about that night. He couldn't remember, of-course; he'd been just three years old.

'…and you were sitting up in bed, already awake. You asked me what I was doing – you were constantly asking questions – and I said we were going on holiday. You asked if Daddy was coming and I said 'no, Daddy's staying here', and do you know what you said?'

'What?'

'You said: 'Good, Daddy a bad boy.' You were *three*, Tony, and you already knew the difference between the rights and wrongs of human nature. You're an amazing, sensitive person. I know that you'll always follow your heart. You always have.'

'I can't remember Dad at all, Mam. I don't even know what he looks like. I don't want to. If I ever met him I swear to God I'd kill him.'

'He wasn't always like that. When I met him he was wonderful. All the girls turned green and your grandma and grandad loved him nearly as much as I did. When we got married it was even in the paper, a picture of us both at the church. He was a true community hero.'

'On the outside,' Anthony nodded. He knew this bit.

His mother nodded sadly. That was it; they'd begun the 'dad' conversation that always left Anthony feeling distant and upset, yet there was always so much he wanted to know. He decided now to ask her the few main questions he'd never asked her, the big ones, the ones he'd never quite had the courage to say before.

'Why did you put up with it for so long?'

'I didn't want you to be fatherless. He never attacked me in front of you until the day before we left. That's when I realised if I didn't leave he'd kill me and then you'd be left with him. Everyone knew what he was doing to me. I was in and out of the hospital weekly but nobody batted an eyelid. It was a tough time. But, thanks to you, I kept on going. And look what's come out of it.' Louise smiled at her son.

'Why was he so violent?' Anthony asked.

'He was angry at the world. He couldn't see the good in anything, he only saw negativity. His father used to beat his mother and him after he'd been drinking. He was always so angry at his father for it yet he took after him completely.'

'Don't you want to kill him? I do,' Anthony said, unaware that he was clenching his fists.

'No. You may not understand this, but I want him to be happy,' she replied.

'What? Why?'

'Because his entire life is a misery. If he found happiness he'd stop being so angry at everything. Tony, your dad's life is a red mist of hatred and fear. I wouldn't wish that upon anyone.'

'But he ruined your life, Mam. I don't know how you can say that.'

'He gave me a beautiful child and bags of strength. I hated the man he became, the man he was, or is... I don't know. But, I took only positive thoughts with me when I left. I had to, otherwise I'd have just given up. Hard times and mistakes are just lessons for the next time, and as long as you learn from them, there's no bad in them. You move on feeling wiser and stronger than you did before.'

'I love the way you think, Mam. I wish I could feel like that about things.'

'You do, Tony. That is the way you think. You're just too young to realise it yet.'

There was a thoughtful silence and Anthony said: 'I'll make you proud, Mam. I'm gunna be a famous actor and I'm gunna think the way you think. This sounds corny but, you're my hero.'

'And you're mine, son. I love you.'

'I love you too, Mam.'

More silence, this time not uncomfortable, not sorrow filled, just silence.

'Tony, be a darling and go ask one of the nurses to fill my drip up,' Louise said after a minute or two.

'Okay Mam.'

Anthony stood up, kissed his mother on the lips, looked into her eyes, and then left the room to find a nurse. When he returned she was asleep.

She never woke up. She died peacefully a week later.

Anthony sat on the wet grass and stared beyond the grey marble that lay in front of him. He was staring into his childhood again when suddenly a voice from behind him interrupted his thoughts.

Anthony turned around to see a young boy on a shiny silver mountain bike holding a small bunch of flowers.

'Sorry, what did you say?' Anthony asked.

'I said, are you alright?' the skinny boy of about ten repeated.

'Me? Yeah, I'm fine thanks. Just, you know, thinking about things.'

'Is that your wife?' The boy nodded his head towards the gravestone.

'No.' Anthony looked to the gravestone and then back to the lad. 'It's my mother's grave.'

'Oh, soz. How did she die?'

'Cancer.'

'Oh.' The boy looked over to the far part of the cemetery near the road, then back to Anthony again. 'My sister is buried in the new bit round the front. I've brought her some flowers. She was run over last year.'

Anthony's face creased and he turned fully around to face the obviously well brought up kid, who instantly reminded him a lot of himself at that age; polite and full of questions, even to total strangers. 'I'm sorry. How old was she?'

'She was eight. Her name is Ann. What's your name?'

'My name's Anthony...' Our favourite man was just about to ask the boy his name when he started smiling excitedly and said:

'That's my name too! But everyone calls me T. Does everyone call you T?'

'No,' Anthony laughed, shaking his head.

'I'm named after a movie-star. My dad used to be bezzy mate's with him.'

'Oh yeah? Which movie-star?' Anthony asked, amused by T.

'Anthony Harden.'

Anthony's stomach did a flip and his eyes widened. He sure as heck wasn't expecting that one.

'What's your dad's name?' he asked.

'Bob,' came the answer. 'Do you know him?'

'Millis? Robert Millis?'

'Yeah! I'm Anthony Millis. My Mum is Jackie Millis.'

Whoa! Not only was Anthony talking, by complete coincidence, to his childhood friend's young son, but also Robert had even named the kid after him! Robert always doted on Anthony, he was his right-hand-man. But that means... *Jesus. That means Robert had a little girl that was run over and killed last year. Shit. That's terrible.*

'Yeah. Yeah I knew him,' Anthony said, almost daze-like, remembering his cheeky best friend. 'We used to ride bikes and play footy together. Wow, I haven't seen him in years.'

'He's bald,' T said seriously. 'And I'm better than him at fishing. I caught a massive one and he only caught a stickleback.'

'Is that right?' Anthony smiled.

'Yeah, and he let me drive his car last week!' he said excitedly.

'Really?' Anthony mused, grinning.

T nodded frantically and said: 'He let me sit on his lap and I even drove it round the corner on our street. It's silver like my bike. Silver's my favourite colour. What's your favourite colour?'

'Mmm... let me think. My favourite colour...? Blue.'

'Blue used to be my favourite colour too, but everyone copied me so I changed it to silver.'

Anthony laughed and the boy giggled.

'I've got to take these flowers for my sister now. My mum gets worried if I'm gone any longer than ten minutes. I get grounded when I'm late.'

'Okay then, take it easy, T.'

'You too, *T*!' The boy sat up onto his saddle and pedalled off shouting: 'See ya!'

Anthony watched the boy ride off, shook his head with a smile, stood up, and began his long walk home, his feelings about the world a little less harsh than when he set off.

After T had neatly filtered the flowers into the holes at the foot of Ann's grave and disposed of the plastic wrapping, he mounted his bike and set off back through the graveyard. Upon seeing that his dad's friend was no longer sitting at that grave, he stopped his bike next to it to see if he could work out how old that guy's mum was when she died, with that legendary morbid fascination that kids have for that sort of thing. Only, he didn't get to her age. His eyes stopped on the name: Denharden.

Denharden.

Anthony Denharden.

No way! That's who I'm named after! I was talking to a famous movie-star! I know his favourite colour!

T pedalled home at a more break-neck speed than usual and threw his bike down in the driveway, running into the house like wildfire to tell his dad.

Obviously, Robert didn't believe a word of it and thought his boy was either lying or had encountered some bizarre coincidence of mistaken identity. When T had managed to convince his father that he was in fact talking to a man in the cemetery, he was grounded by his mother for talking to strange men. Robert couldn't believe that Anthony Denharden would ever return back to Morley, not with the kind of life he had led since he left when he was fifteen. It was never

297

mentioned again. You'll be pleased to know, however, that Jackie ungrounded T five days earlier than she'd said. He was back out on his silver bike again after only forty-eight hours!

Looking into the future a bit now, T never forgot that one minute, fleeting encounter. He doubted and questioned himself more and more about it over the years. *Was it really him? Did it really happen? Was I lying?* But he never forgot the roots of it. He even told his own children about it, and when ever he was asked what his claim to fame was, that's what he referred to... well, that and having his forehead signed by Billy Joe Armstrong at a Greenday concert when he was sixteen.

The more steps Anthony took as he walked home, the more he thought about his mother's words and how great her outlook on life had been. He thought about T and Robert, and for the first time in many years, didn't feel so totally alone. Because, if he was totally honest with himself, he'd felt alone since the day his mother had died.

Lucy had been his wife and Anthony had tried to make her his best friend, but she never allowed herself to be. She loved him to Heaven and back, but he'd never been able to really talk to her about his feelings. She tried to listen, but there was always that distance. That's why, when the whole Alex tragedy happened, it drove a stake through them that had been there ever since. But, man, she was an angel all the same.

She wasn't in any way heartless or uncaring; it wasn't that she never listened. It was more that she didn't get it. But Anthony could live with that, as long as he had her. His mother didn't hate his father, even after everything he did to her; all the broken bones, the black eyes, the bruises. She didn't hate him. So why did Anthony feel like he hated Lucy? He loved her too, which was why he was in a constant state of confusion. He had never divorced her; she was still his wife. Unlike his father, she had beaten him thinking he was something else. His father had beaten his mother knowing full well the person he was punching and kicking was the same person he had promised to honour and obey. That's the big difference. Lucy was ill, his father was just sick.

Since he came round in hospital, Anthony's life had been lived out in almost a mechanical set of motions. Nothing had sunk in, he hadn't come to terms with what had happened to him and really, he was still traumatised. If Dr Nazir hadn't have been drafted in, and if the NHS hadn't have been so good to him, he couldn't even have guaranteed that he would be here now. His mother would have turned in her grave if she'd have seen her little boy and the darkness that had been following him. He wasn't half as much like her as he'd have wished. She'd have shaken this off and been living happily and normally by now. Look at Anthony; he's still a total mess.

For the first time ever since that day in the bathroom, he seriously considered and felt up to going to see his wife. But first he planned to apologise to Saima, and humbly ask her over for the session that he had screwed earlier in the day.

CHAPTER 14

It was a little over a week since the horrific drug-fuelled accident of the child star had occurred.

By this point forensic pathologists in the US had gathered some very interesting information regarding something odd that had been found during the autopsy on our old pal Jerry, and forensic toxicologists had been called in from several different states to get together over this gem of modern discoveries. It seemed, as heard at the inquest that journalists such as Nick Fowler were regurgitating four-thousand miles away, that the gelatin transporters of this particular batch of drug were not dissolvable, and twelve had been found in Jerry's body during screening. This was the pot of gold at the end of a rainbow for those in the medical field. This stupid little drug would not show up on any of the standard drug tests (urine, tissue, and blood), but it was waving at them as bright as day with a sign saying: 'Hi, I'm an illegal drug', once a scalpel was applied to the stomach lining. The drug was officially named d-Lysergic Acid Hypothylameth 70 (LAH). It was classified such a high Class A that it was considered lowering the classifications of certain other drugs. Marone had said it himself many moons ago: compared to LAH, other drugs were candy.

Toxicologists were able to determine when Jerry had taken each tab, and how his body had reacted to them. It appeared that with the more recent ones, Ole Jerry Boy had been taking up to three at a time; the high obviously not half as intense once his body had gotten used to them. All but one of the tabs still carried minute strains of LAH laced into them; even the oldest and most acidically battered one, which had been in his system for approximately nineteen months, still had faint traces of LAH on it.

However, one tab found didn't have any sign whatsoever that any drug had ever been in contact with it. In other words there were duds flying around Jerry's intimate circle of friends, and Jerry had taken one.

This didn't make the news, however. There are duds everywhere, aren't there? Kids who don't know better are fed vitamin pills and aspirins in nightclubs and charged £5 for the pleasure. Brainless clients of cowboy drug dealers will not be snorting pure cocaine; there'll be Ajax and talcum powder and God knows what else mixed in there so the dealer gets a better cut. Mmmm... anyone fancy a lovely snort of baby powder... any takers?

The same day that Anthony rang Penford Hospital's reception desk to find out visiting hours was also the same day that Sky News broadcasted a report on the latest findings on what happened to their golden boy and the drug inquest surrounding him.

Anthony did not see it and went to bed that night thinking only of his wife and his memories.

The next morning, however, was when the television was turned on. Anthony was up at 4am, unable to sleep due to the terror and excitement of seeing his wife again in only a few hours time. He had told the receptionist that he would be there for 11am today, to fit in with the hospital's visiting regulations.

Anthony made himself a coffee and sat on one of the two green leather sofas in his front room. He switched on the TV and flicked channels for a while until he came to a female newsreader with a picture caption on the right of the screen: a grinning image of Jerry Tilsey. Alerted, Anthony sat up and turned up the volume.

'...scientists in America have also found a way to detect the drug, only officially named yesterday – a drug that the media are calling 'The Hollywood Killer' – by way of a new high-tech camera operation. A small camera is inserted through the navel and into the stomach lining, using a specially formulated blue liquid to pinpoint the carrier. Toxicologists are now analysing a batch of undissolved carriers to find out more about the drug that has caused so much controversy over the past week. The drug has been named d-Lysergic Acid Hypothylameth-70, or LAH, and has been classified a class A* *hallucinogen. More information is thought to become available within the next 48 hours...'*

Well, well, well and would you believe it. They can detect it.

They can detect it and find it in my beautiful girl. They can find it, apologise, have the sentence lifted, get her the proper treatment she needs, she can come home, recover, then we can forget about this entire situation. We will be together again. *I'm getting my wife back.*

With a sudden burst of childlike inspiration, Anthony leapt from the sofa and walked briskly back through to his bedroom. Instead of the news report making Anthony concentrate on the drug or Jerry, it had simply given him hope of his wife better again. His thoughts were turned to how she used to be. The prospect of her being back like that filled him with that childlike, premature excitement Anthony tended to suffer from.

It was still pitch black outside so he turned on his bedroom light. The place was most definitely in need of a woman's touch. Jogging-bottoms, jumpers, underpants and old socks littered the floor. The entire room was painted a tired creamy brown; his bed a subconscious statement of singledom with a dark brown quilt strewn and tangled upon his mattress. It was a far cry from the lush master bedroom he had occupied not long ago.

Anthony removed a Nike shoebox from the bottom of one of his extensive wardrobes and sat down on the corner of his bed with it. He stared at it for a moment, brushing his hand over the lid and sending particles of dust dancing around his face.

When the removal guys had cleared his house out, they had packed a removal box full of what they thought might be sentimental items to do with the couple that was once the ecstatically happy Autumn Leigh and Anthony Denharden. Anthony had waded through the large bubble-wrapped box in this very room, throwing away most things in the heat of anger and tears, blinded by depression and confusion. He had kept only the things that he literally couldn't bear to part with. That had been one of his darkest days. He was in no way ready to face items such as his wedding album and stills from their first film together after only a few weeks out of hospital. As he is sitting here now, he wishes so much that he had not thrown things away so hastily and kept more of their pre September 1990 life together. But as it stands, our lad is now left with only a box worth of small items to prove that he was in fact married to the world's sexiest woman… once upon a time.

Anthony took a deep breath and removed the cardboard lid. He had not looked in here at all, not since the day he put them in there in the first place and banished it to the back of his wardrobe.

The first thing Anthony picked out was perhaps not the best; it was Alexander's birth certificate. Anthony quickly put that by the side of him and moved onto the next thing staring up at him from the box. It was a piece of tissue with a red lipstick phone number written on it… written on it by the beautiful young Canadian woman he was working alongside on a film many years ago. She had suggested they meet up alone to practice their scenes and 'here, call me'. Anthony had called her, and then had subsequently married her. The tissue was scraggy now and the number was barely recognisable, but holding it made him feel like he did when she had given it to him with a knowing smile back in 1985. It made him feel like the luckiest man in the world.

With a soft smile Anthony went for the next piece of memorabilia. A flood of nostalgia hit him once more and this time he laughed out loud. In this middle-aged man's hand was a wonderfully tacky fridge magnet of the Eiffel Tower.

Anthony and Autumn had been dating for only two weeks when a break in filming came up and Anthony had whisked his new love off to Paris for the weekend. The Saturday afternoon was clear-skied and beautiful. They had been walking towards the tower eating crepes and laughing about all the chintzy merchandise they had passed so far on stalls. Anthony had suddenly stopped walking and brought his hand up to his forehead.

'What's wrong?' Autumn laughed.

'I've just realised something,' Anthony said seriously.

'What's that?' still laughing.

A smile to confirm he was messing around graced the handsome young man's face and he continued: 'I've been dating the most beautiful girl I've ever seen in my life for a couple of weeks now, and I haven't even bought her a present yet!'

Autumn laughed and put her arms around him. 'Well, you should maybe think about sorting that out then,' she joked.

'It needs to be something special, something to really show her how ecstatic I am when I'm around her... I've got it! Hold this.' With that Anthony thrust his crepe into his lover's hand and ran off shouting: 'I'll be back in a minute!'

A minute it was and Anthony was back bearing a small white paper bag. He exchanged it for his crepe and as she was opening it he said: 'This represents you, this represents me, this represents the kind of heartfelt, generous bloke I am.' He then bit his lip and waited for the reaction.

Autumn pulled out the most badly made, cheap fridge magnet she had ever seen in her life. She so much wanted to laugh but instead played along and held it to her heart: 'I... I don't know what to say. It's... it's *beautiful!* Oh Anthony, with this gift you have really proved that you are the man of my dreams!'

They had both laughed and she rolled her eyes affectionately saying: 'Come on, you klutz,' and they continued their journey hand in hand.

The next thing drove a spear through Anthony's heart. It was his child's sixteen week scan. Alex was still alive in the womb when this still had been captured. His wife was a blossoming, glowing mother-to-be, and Anthony was the happiest man alive. Again, this reminder of Alex was quickly swept aside and, as he went for the next piece of his life in a box, something shiny and round caught his eye. Anthony picked it out, studied it for a bit, placed the box and the rest of its contents on his bed and walked through to the bathroom to get a clearer look at it. The lightbulb in the bathroom was powerful and bright, whereas his bedroom light was comparatively dim. The solid gold item almost swam in his hand with the crisp convex reflections of the room. It was his wedding ring.

While Anthony was studying his wedding ring and deciding whether it really did belong in a box or not, Mrs Denharden was caught in the breath of a twitchy, itchy dream. She had been dreaming vividly more often in recent times: of-course she did not realise this because she was, after all, catatonic. Her dreams had been getting clearer because Reality was getting closer. It could only manage it in her sleep but it saw her and, in her dreams, from time to time, she saw it back.

Reality has had help, mind you (It's the kind of demon that couldn't quit smoking on will alone, if you may) from group therapy and the courses of ECT she had some time ago. They didn't benefit her waking state but they softened the toughness of the meat when Reality bit in the night. Lucy would relive so much in her sleep, so many questions would be answered, she would get better... and then she would wake up and from the second she opened her eyes the timid mouse would hide and she wouldn't even be aware that she had been sleeping, never mind dreaming.

If the good people of this world were to view Lucy's dreams like a movie, the mystery surrounding what happened to America's favourite actress would finally be solved. But nobody sees Lucy's dreams, nobody feels the fear that Reality brings with it into her room, nobody even knows Reality is in the building. Lucy Denharden is still as dead to them as she has always been.

Reality came to her in the early hours of this dark and cold morning. It came to her with berries. When it entered her room, her arm was up again. This pleased Reality because it had been happening more and more of late. In the beginning, she wouldn't move a muscle no matter what it tried to do; she was so blocked and so numb she made Reality want to ring her neck sometimes, causing it to quickly tire and move onto a less difficult subject.

But this was a good sign; Reality's most difficult project for a long time was now moving limbs without it even having to be in the room. Reality was powerful and experienced; it knew it would get to her in the end.

Reality entered Lucy and she jerked slightly once it was inside her. Reality shape-shifted itself into the form of a man and he found himself in a forest looking at a mouse. The mouse was shaking and was obviously only seconds away from darting away from him quicker than he could ever move, so he had to work fast.

Reality held out a hand full of berries to the creature. The demon and the mind of a catatonic woman studied each other for some time. Reality was careful not to move an inch. The mouse saw berries. After what seemed like an eon for our demon, the mouse carefully moved closer. Its ears were pricked up and its fur was still shaking, but it was coming to him. Eventually the mouse was at the tip of his fingers. It sniffed them and put one of its tiny front paws upon his fingertip to make a closer inspection of the berries. What a vulnerable mind Lucy has, Reality thought: the kidnapper is offering her sweets from his car and she is eating them.

The mouse put its other paw on another fingertip, causing its little body to stretch from the two paws on the forest floor and the two paws in Reality's trap. Our demon decided around this point that the mouse was close enough now and he was too excited to wait for it to get its whole body onto his hand.

309

He grabbed it swiftly with his other hand and squeezed it tight enough to feel its insides pulse...

Autumn Leigh was in a corridor, a separate body to the shrivelled dirty girl looking down on her from a hospital bed in the early hours of the morning. Lucy could see herself clearly, yet it was like she was looking down on a former life. Although it was a dream, Lucy's head was filled with semiconscious, subconscious thoughts. She had been doing this in her dreams for some time now. If only there was somebody to talk back; if only one of the nurses could penetrate her mind in the way that Reality could. They were trying but failing. They should try bringing berries.

...And then the dream began. It started so suddenly, as if the Dream God had just pressed the play button (situated next to the much-used delete button) on Lucy Denharden's subconscious.

Lucy, in her mind, was wide-eyed and watching.

Autumn Leigh was in a dark, shadowy corridor. She was pressed up against the wall, her head rolling back and forth. Out of tune violins and melting double basses pierced the air around her; the sound they were making was sickening. Shadows were closing in and out, jumping and sliding around her like ghosts.

Lucy knew her former self was not in a good place. The whole dream was in greyscale, a flurry of misty blacks and seeping silvers. The only physical giveaway to Lucy's waking self that she was in a situation like this were the shallow, fast paced breaths inhaling and exhaling from open mouth upon the bed.

Autumn Leigh was scared. She was worn out and unhappy.

Lucy could feel her fear and sadness like a blow. *Was I ever really that person? Is it all in my mind? Have I always been here?*

And then it came. It came and it was not a dream. It was a memory. His face, his voice, open your mouth, it was you... it was Jerry Tilsey.

Lucy Denharden's limp, sleeping body jumped to life as every single nerve ending that she possessed jumped and stung as if been struck by mental lightening. Her dull eyes snapped open.

She knew. She remembered. It all came back to her to her as fast as banks breaking, the poison water of her life spilled over her brain and polluted it with memories. She had been at a party when he had done it. They were both dressed up and she had won an award and then, out of the blue, he had attacked her. He had dragged her by her hair into a back room and he had raped her as she lay unconscious... she remembered. She remembered now for the first time. Then the black dots had come, and the visions and the things that she thought were real that nobody else saw.

She had a husband. What happened to him? She remembered a monster in her house, in her bathroom... a fight, a body in the bath, tying the belt of her silk dressing gown around her own neck...

...am I dead?

Lucy was awake, eyes wide, looking up towards the ceiling but straight through it to her former life. *Oh shit, has all this really happened to me?*

Slowly, slowly, Reality withdrew from Lucy – happy with its work – and left for the night. Lucy's eyes began to drop shut again, the questions slowed down, the memories became distant and she fell back to sleep. Asleep to wake in the morning the way the nurses had always known her. Asleep to wake in the morning with no recollection whatsoever of the dream, the memory, of waking up, of the questions she had asked, of the answers she was told.

Penford was situated in Warwickshire, which would take Anthony a good hour and a half to reach by train from Leeds Central Station. He was at platform six bright and early at 8.30am with a ten minute wait. Anthony had taken his ring in his pocket and now had it out, fiddling with it and thinking

311

about the past and future while he waited. He had not slipped it back on his finger; he would take it with him to reunite with his estranged wife and, depending on the outcome, would either wear it forever more, or never look at it again.

The train had arrived on time and by 9am Anthony was staring out to rolling countryside, still playing with his wedding ring absentmindedly. *What's it going to be like seeing her again? Will she even register that I am there? Will she still be asleep with her eyes open? Will she look at me? Will I recognise her? What will I say? Will I say anything? Will she hear me? Is this really a good idea?*

The last time Anthony had seen his wife she had knocked him to the floor and beat him with a weapon he later found out to be a toilet brush (of all things). He had seen her eyes as she hit him, he had seen them through his own, barely open and swollen. Her eyes that day were someone else's. They were not the same eyes that would stare up to him as they made love; they were not the same eyes he would fall into every time she smiled. They were alien. As the train passed farmers' fields Anthony hoped her eyes didn't look the way that they did on that day; he hoped they were hers again.

The last thing he had said to the woman he adored, the woman he married, was: 'Get off me you crazy bitch'. Painfully and regrettably, he remembered it as if it was yesterday. These were the last images he had of the woman he loved and, if anything good was to come out of seeing her again at all, it would hopefully be that, although upsetting, today's events would replace those last images. Even if he was never to see Lucy again after today, at least he could feel better knowing that the last time he saw her she was calm and quiet. Not attacking him to the point where his heart stopped.

But Anthony was seeing that as the worst case scenario anyway. For today he would also go to whoever it was in that hospital that held power and arrange for her to have this new test done. Then it would be carried out; it would be proven that her mental health had not deteriorated naturally and she could get help. Everything was going to be okay again. That's

312

what Anthony was trying to tell himself, over and over, to calm his nerves about what lay ahead for him in only a couple of hours' time.

Nurse Lindle had briefed all four of the staff that would be on duty that day about Anthony's visit. Patients were usually only asked to visit after 4.30pm, to avoid interference with any therapeutic programmes, but Lucy wasn't given any plans for that day so Anthony could stay as long as he needed to. Staff understood the importance of this case and situation. Lucy had been bathed and Rose, the student nurse, had brushed and plaited her hair. She looked as nice as a catatonic schizophrenic woman could do.

At 10.50am a taxi pulled up into the grounds and the receptionist let Anthony in.

Nurse Lindle's internal phone rang and she picked it up from the desk in her office.

'Anthony Denharden is here, Alicia.'

'Okay, get him a drink. I'll be with him in a minute.'

The receptionist put the phone back down and said with a polite smile: 'Nurse Lindle will be with you in a moment. Can I get you a tea or coffee?'

'No thanks,' Anthony replied, his face a picture of seriousness and nerves.

'Okay, sir. If you would just like to sit down over there, she won't be long.' Anthony was pointed in the direction of four uncomfortable looking plastic chairs.

'Actually, a glass of water would be great,' he decided.

'No problem.' The receptionist smiled and got up to fix his request.

Anthony sat down and looked around. It wasn't at all like he'd pictured it, this place. He had expected something a little more, well, plush. Feeling slightly foolish now for assuming that, Anthony realised that he was in a hospital, as simple and plain as any other all around the country... and why shouldn't it be? The only difference being that this hospital was for

313

people with ill mentality, damaged minds, broken souls – as opposed to brains and hearts and lungs. Why the hell would Lucy get special treatment just because she used to be famous? She wasn't any longer, she was a patient detained by the Mental Health Act. Anthony felt naive and stuck-up that he had thought this would be some kind of hotel.

The receptionist returned with his water and Anthony took it with thanks. His mouth was dry with nerves and as he brought the glass up to his mouth he was visibly shaking. No sooner had the receptionist sat back down when he heard footfalls drawing near from one of the three corridors that branched off from the waiting area. A woman appeared and smiled at him as she approached where he was sitting.

'Mr Denharden, I am Nurse Alicia Lindle. We like to operate on a first name basis here, so just call me Alicia.'

Anthony stood up and shook the nurse's hand.

'Hiya. How you doing, Alicia?'

'I'm fine, thank you. How are you?'

'I'm good. Would it be possible to talk to somebody regarding Lucy before I see her?'

'Of-course, I have some things to run by you anyway. I'm Lucy's Named Nurse so I see to her needs day to day. I'm also the head nurse of this ward so hopefully I'll be able to answer any questions you need to ask.'

'Excellent.'

Alicia smiled then said: 'Follow me, please.'

Anthony followed the nurse back through to her office and sat down as she shut the door.

'How is she? I mean, how's she been?' Anthony asked as the nurse sat down behind her desk.

'Well, she's still catatonic, but she's in good physical health.'

'What about her mind?'

'No change as of yet, I'm afraid.'

Anthony fell into nervous silence so Nurse Lindle began to feed him information, hoping that a greater understanding would help him cope when he saw her.

'Due to her delusional background we treat her with cognitive therapy and neuroleptic medication more than we do psychological therapy. However, she does attend group sessions twice weekly along with two other patients with similar conditions. We have tried many different sorts of therapy but as far as we can see she hasn't responded to anything so far. She has undergone several courses of electric convulsive therapy but to no avail. We are presently deciding whether it would be worth trying another course.'

'Isn't that stuff dangerous?'

'It's a very good form of therapy, especially for catatonic patients. I have seen several people totally reformed after treatment.'

Nurse Lindle opened a brown cardboard file on her desk and scanned it as she spoke.

'Lucy has been here for fourteen months now. Within that time we have had no trouble from her whatsoever. Unfortunately, we haven't seen any improvement either. We feel we can help her, it will just be a matter of time.' Nurse Lindle looked up from the file and asked: 'Do you feel ready yourself for seeing her, Anthony?'

Anthony shuffled slightly in his chair and replied: 'Yes. I think so.'

'She is catatonic, but please don't let that put you off talking to her. I believe she can hear every word you say, even if she can't process it all fully. We have given you a little room down the hall, which you and Lucy will be alone in. Our student nurse, Rose, will stand outside for the duration, in case you need her for anything at all. You can stay as long as you like; visiting hours don't finish until this evening so please, don't feel rushed. Lucy has already eaten and used the bathroom so she should be comfortable now. Is there anything you want to ask me?'

Anthony leaned forward slightly.

315

'What do you think happened to her?' he probed.

'I can only go by what I've read from her files,' Nurse Lindle replied.

'And what do her files say?'

'Well,' Nurse Lindle leaned back slightly in her chair. 'They say she's suffered some kind of trauma that she has buried enough to build up into catatonia. It appears to have been building for some time, finally becoming too much for her in and around the month of September 1990. We believe her weak physical state combined with the pressures of fame could have been substantial catalysts.'

'What about drugs?'

'Illegal drugs are not documented... I understand all drug tests taken before and after Lucy was detained came up clear.'

Anthony sat back again and shook his head.

'*Did* Lucy use illegal drugs?' Nurse Lindle asked, not sure where this was heading.

'I believe Jerry Tilsey gave her that drug that they're all on about on the news – LAH. But I also believe she didn't know about it. I saw a news report this morning saying that a group of scientists in America have discovered a way to detect it using a new camera operation. I would like Lucy to have this test. Can you do it here?'

Nurse Lindle shook her head and looked apologetic.

'I'm sorry, Anthony, but Lucy is detained here. We don't have the facilities to perform any kind of operation and I sincerely doubt that the authorities would allow Lucy to leave the hospital.'

'But this test is vital to her treatment,' Anthony said as calmly as he could manage.

'Lucy's treatment, both medical and physiological, is already correct and the most beneficial available to her condition.'

'But you've seen no improvement, you said it yourself.'

'I'm talking about people who suffer from catatonic schizophrenia on the whole,' Nurse Lindle said.

'But what if this drug caused her to develop that?' Anthony stared the nurse straight in the eye as he spoke. Nurse Lindle held his gaze.

'That would be impossible, Anthony. Drugs don't cause catatonic schizophrenia. They don't *help* it, and they may induce more obvious schizophrenic symptoms... but they don't cause it.'

'Okay,' Anthony broke the stare and sat back. 'If, for instance, drugs like this one they're all talking about *were* found in her system, you'd change her therapy, wouldn't you?'

Nurse Lindle shook her head. 'We are already giving her the best treatment we can. She's catatonic, Anthony. That is what we're treating her for... and that is what we would continue to treat her for even if drugs were found. It would make no difference to her whatsoever, except for the disruption of having the test done.'

'But it's wrong. If LAH caused this whole thing to happen, you should know. It would change everything.'

'I've never heard in my life of any kind of drug doing this to someone, and I doubt any medic has.'

'But this is a new drug, no-one's ever seen it before...'

'No. But I *have* seen catatonic schizophrenia before. And I can assure you, that is what Lucy is suffering from. Drugs or not, it doesn't matter. She has catatonic schizophrenia now, and that's what we treat her for,' Nurse Lindle repeated.

'Can you not just *ask* the Home Office?' Anthony had resorted to pleading now.

'I know that they won't allow it and I can see why. I really don't think there would be any benefit from sending Lucy for this new test and it could do more harm than good.'

'So why did you test her when she was admitted then... if there's no point?'

'We test all of our patients upon admission. It's for their records.'

'So you need to know if she's had a harmless tug on a J but you don't need to know if she's been given a new Class A, mind altering drug that nobody knows anything about yet... suspected to have been taken in the very month she developed this?' Anthony challenged strongly.

Nurse Lindle looked down to her desk and then back up to her patient's husband.

'Okay,' she sighed. 'I'll write to the Home Office for you. But don't get your hopes up.'

'Thank you,' Anthony nodded gratefully. 'Please understand; I just want to know what triggered this. I can't rest until I know.'

Nurse Lindle nodded and after a moment said: 'Would you like to see Lucy now?'

The room was bare and cold, clinical to the point of discomfort. There was a fold-down mock-mahogany and steel table in the middle, with an empty chair at the closest side and a woman in a wheelchair facing him at the other.

Anthony was shown in by Alicia and Rose and was told to call if he needed anything. The door to the room opened for him to step inside and there she was.

Anthony stood. He stood and looked at her. Both nurses ushered him in gently and said, in soft voices, for him to sit down. Anthony did as instructed and staggered over to his chair, not taking his eyes off the woman sat facing him. The door shut behind him and then they were alone.

His sweetpea had her head lolled to the left and her eyes were staring unfocused onto the tabletop. Her body had wasted away to bones and her hair looked like wire. Her mouth hung slightly open.

Anthony brought his hand up to his mouth to muffle a shocked cry. Tears had sprung into his eyes without warning the second he had first seen her today and now ran down his cheeks and onto his hand. He quickly wiped them but more fell. Anthony took a deep breath and tried his hardest to restrain the lump in his throat from getting tighter but it didn't work and he let out a sob.

'Oh God,' he cried eventually. 'Oh God.'

Anthony brought both hands up and covered his face.

Alicia instructed Rose to go get a glass of water and some tissues and '…other than that, leave them alone. Let him cry his heart out if he wants, just don't disturb them.'

Rose did as she was told and within two minutes was placing the glass and a box of tissues next to Anthony on the table. He thanked her and composed himself a little.

Once the young student nurse had left the room Anthony took a tissue and blew his nose. This made him feel a little better and the tears stopped. He looked back up to his wife.

'God, Lucy,' he said in a sigh. 'I'm sorry. It's… erm, it's nice to see you again.' Anthony studied his wife but she didn't move or flinch one inch. He continued anyway: 'You look good. I like the plait, it suits you.'

Again, not one movement. Anthony was starting to think that, if anything, seeing her might scar him more than if he hadn't come here. He looked up to the ceiling feeling awkward. He felt like he was talking to himself and, aside from feeling a little silly and that talking to her was pointless, he also didn't know what to say. The feeling reminded him so much of when he was seventeen and would go and visit his mother. He couldn't find the words.

'Erm… I'm living in Leeds now… in an apartment. It's, erm, it's alright. The flat's a bit like the one I had in London… same sized rooms.'

'Oh wow! I *loved* your place on Gomez Street, it was so funky!' was what she *should have* said. What she actually said was… nothing. Anthony bit his bottom lip and took a deep, shaky breath.

When he looked back at Lucy he noticed a bit of dribble falling from the left-hand side of her mouth.

'Oh, here,' he said, picking a fresh tissue from the box and standing up.

He walked over to the side of her and squatted down, taking the tissue and dabbing it carefully on her mouth. To get the rest of it he turned her head towards him gently using his left hand under her chin. Once he had cleared it up he looked in her eyes, only they were still in the same spot they had been in since he had walked in.

Anthony put the tissue on the floor and, with his left hand still touching his wife's chin, ran the fingers of his right hand down her snowflake face. Her skin was still the softest he'd ever touched and he could smell her natural scent. He inhaled it deeply and a thousand memories were evoked. And while he squatted close to Lucy and thoughts of better times ran through his mind, so did the thought that he had stood up in a church only a few years back promising to stand by this lady through sickness and in health. She was still his wife. Just to be back up close with her like he was now; that changed everything. He realised just how much he still loved her, and that was all that mattered.

Anthony used to lie next to this woman and breathe in this woman every single night. The way he used to touch her, with such love, such affection... he would touch this woman gently the way he was doing now, but she would respond. He shut her mouth and it stayed that way loosely. The helplessness of her muscles stung Anthony with a painful jab and he tried to banish the feelings that *no, that time has passed now* and that *oh God I'm in love with a warm dead body*. No, her eyes didn't show that crazed look of murder anymore, they didn't show anything. Anthony couldn't decide which was worse. Tears of unfairness welled, but there were no tears of hate and no tears of resentment. He was still in love with his wife.

'I remember,' he whispered, still only inches away from his love's face; 'when you first came over to England and stayed over at my flat on Gomez Street, when we first made love. That was one of the best days of my life. I hadn't seen you for nearly a week and I couldn't think of anything else for the entire time. I'd never felt anything like it. I was crazily in love with you. You were... are... the most beautiful woman I've ever seen, Lucy. That night, when you fell asleep in my arms, I knew that I would marry you.' Without realising it, Anthony wasn't having to think about the things he was saying, it was coming to him as smooth as sea-eroded glass.

He was still whispering as he continued: 'You were wearing that white 50s dress that you said hurt under your arms. You looked like heaven on earth. Well, you know, to say you were jet-lagged and hadn't slept for thirty-six hours you looked alright,' Anthony laughed. Joking with her came naturally, even in times like this, it seemed.

And that's when it happened.

'Open your mouth,' she murmured.

Lucy's mind, the mouse, had not woken up that morning as the weather had been getting cloudier and colder in recent times and it needed to sleep deeper than it ever had before. The forest that gave shelter to the mouse was getting blacker and darker, the trees were growing twisted and stunted and the other animals were getting nastier and their teeth longer. More and more in recent times a jester would take a stroll through the forest. He would walk past weeping and his bells would leave the mouse quivering and cold. All the mouse wanted to do was hide from it; to crawl into a root of an old tree and stay there, away from the fear and the din and the other, bigger animals. Even just a few minutes ago the mouse was sleeping to escape the fear but then something new had happened, something that didn't feel scary or intimidating, something magical happened. A ray of light shone down upon the forest, straight into the mouse's lair and into its eyes. The mouse awoke with a start and pattered outside.

There was heat, proper heat! And sun! And, right before the mouse's eyes, berries grew and flourished! It was amazing!

Then the voice, the voice came from the sky and it was Anthony.

Slowly and comfortably, the forest and the mouse became fainter and Lucy's thinking mind took over. 'Open your mouth,' were the words she managed to get out. She didn't even particularly mean to say that, it was one of the many lightening thoughts running through her mind. They were jumbled and ghostlike, spinning and whizzing around her like signposts.

If you could put them into human sense they would go something like: *Anthony's here! Jerry raped me! I've got to talk to him! I was attacked! Arrest Jerry Tilsey! It **was** him! It was him, just like you said in that hotel! He said 'open your mouth' and he put his finger in my mouth. I passed out, I passed out but I remember! I remember him raping me! Oh God Anthony it was terrible! I couldn't move! I couldn't open my eyes or move my body but I could **feel** him, I could feel him inside me! Oh God it was terrible! Get the police! Get the police!*

Lucy's mind was waking up but her body and mouth remained still and silent. The second Lucy realised this she fell into a pit of blinding frustration. She had so much to say, so much to tell him but she couldn't catch a thought long enough to say it, and just like when she was attacked, she couldn't feel her body. When her voice activated out of the blue and caught the words 'open your mouth' they had come out distorted and deep. She wanted to scream them, she wanted to scream them so loud it would echo and swarm around her mind... then she would say everything else and she could get out of this forest forever and go back in to the real world. She knew Anthony was there next to her and she knew that he was talking but she couldn't hear the words, she couldn't hear his voice anymore. She could only sense him. She couldn't even look at him; if only she could focus her eyes, but she just couldn't. She was trying and praying for it but it wasn't happening. Her entire body felt apart from her, like she didn't actually have one anymore and her mind was controlled by some foreign machine. Only the machine was broken and nobody knew that the mind was still in there, wishing that the voice box hadn't gone haywire and was only working on rare occasions.

As Lucy was begging for Anthony to see that she was awake and alive, Anthony was doing other things.

He had been right up next to her when she had said it. She had said 'open your mouth' loud and clear. Okay, she had *mumbled* it but the words were distinct. Open Your Mouth. He jumped back and fell onto his arm when she had spoke. It had shocked him as much as it would you if you were standing over an open casket at a funeral saying your last goodbyes, and having the dead body open its eyes and say: 'I'm bloody starving. You couldn't fix me up with a sandwich, could you?'

Anthony scrambled to his feet and opened the door so fast it made Rose jump.

'She spoke!' he cried. 'She said *open your mouth*! Go get that other nurse *now*!'

Rose dropped her mouth and seemed stunned for a moment before running off down the hall.

Anthony watched her rush off then ran back down to Lucy's side. *She spoke! She spoke! She's not catatonic! Yes! YES! YES! YES!*

'Come on, Lucy. Come on, I heard you! Come on sweetpea say it again. You can do it.' Anthony spoke as close to her face as he could get, cupping her head with both hands, listening harder than he'd ever had to before. *Come on Lucy, come on Lucy, I believe in you, you can do it. Speak to me, come on. Speak to me!*

But she didn't. She didn't move, flinch, speak, breathe... she didn't do anything.

'Come on,' Anthony whispered through gritted teeth. 'Come on Lucy.'

More silence ensued before Nurse Lindle and Rose came busting into the room in a panic.

'She spoke?' Nurse Lindle asked, slightly out of breath, moving the table and darting between Anthony and Lucy.

'Yes! Yes, she did. I heard her! Is this good? Is this a breakthrough?'

'What did she say?' Nurse Lindle asked, now turning on a pencil torch and shining it in Lucy's eyes.

'She said open your mouth,' Anthony answered urgently.

'Are you *sure*? Is that *definitely* what she said?'

'Yes! Yes,' Anthony said giddily.

Nurse Lindle turned to the student nurse: 'Rose, go get Dr Morgan.'

Rose nodded once and darted off again. Nurse Lindle turned back to Lucy.

'What happens now? Do you re-evaluate her? Does this mean she's not cataton…'

'Shh,' Nurse Lindle ordered, trying to listen in case Lucy spoke again. Anthony quietened immediately.

'Come on Lucy. Come on girl,' she whispered.

She waited. They both waited. Still, nothing happened.

As soon as she sensed more people around her the thoughts and the sharpness went and Lucy was back in the forest running away from the bigger animals. The mouse didn't surface again that day.

CHAPTER 15

Anthony, with a wedding ring on his finger, had been calling the hospital every day for a week after his wife had spoken to him and changed everything. So it came to a bit of a surprise for him when he picked up his ringing phone to Nurse Lindle on this cloudy morning.

'I have some good news for you, Anthony,' she said. Anthony's heart doubled its pumping because he knew. He knew she'd spoken again.

'I've received reply from the Home Office…'

'The Home Office? Already?' Anthony interrupted. 'Shit. What have they said?'

Nurse Lindle sighed slightly to show mild displeasure at been interrupted then continued: 'They said she should have the extended LAH test.'

'YES!' Anthony cried. 'YES! YES! Thank you, Alicia!'

'She'll be escorted by Dr Morgan and I in an ambulance to Stainfield Hospital, which is the nearest hospital with the right facilities for her. The test will be carried out two weeks today at 10.30am under general anaesthetic. If the test *is* positive then the findings will be sent to the American Institute of Substance Research for analysis, and if it's negative then that's that.'

'Okay, great. That's great news! Will I be able to find out straight away?'

'I'll call you as soon as I know. I hope this will put your mind at rest.'

'Yes. Brilliant. Thank you. Thank you for doing this, Alicia.'

'Okay,' Nurse Lindle laughed. 'I'll speak to you in two weeks then.'

'Okay! Great! You have no idea how much I'll anticipate that call!'

'Righty-oh then. Goodbye.'

'Bye!' Anthony grinned and put down the phone. 'Yes! Yes! Yes!' he laughed to himself. 'This is it! This is *it*!'

•

The two weeks felt like two months, every single morning waking up, mentally crossing off another day. Anthony could think about nothing but getting Lucy better again. His psychology sessions were full of positive, bursting energy and ideas, and he made Dr Nazir laugh on several occasions telling her of past times when his wife was well and they were on top of the world. Anthony had even cut down on the TCA and MOAI drugs he had been taking for his depression, and this was adding to his bounciness. He could honestly say that he hadn't felt this alive since before this whole darkness had ever swept over him.

And then it came: the night before the big day.

Anthony, like a child on Christmas Eve, had gone to bed earlier than usual to pass some time. Of-course, this meant he had laid awake tossing and turning, thinking about a thousand things. Finally, after two long hours, Anthony's sharp thoughts became slightly rounded, and then dreamlike, and then dream...

Anthony was walking hand in hand with Lucy, with his mother to his left holding a young child with blonde hair and blue eyes in her arms. They were approaching a funfair at dusk. The fair was used and deserted. No rides were running, no men were operating them, there was not a single person around except them. And then they were on a hill approaching a rollercoaster, away from all of the other rides. Anthony was aware in his dream that the operating machine was at the bottom of the hill, and the rollercoaster far away and out of sight from it. Anthony and Lucy were to get on this ride and his mother and his son were to watch. Anthony sat on the rollercoaster seat, which was facing backwards to the direction of the ride, and began belting himself in. The belts were actually straps around the ankles and he got one on and then looked to his wife who was still standing up. She was smiling

328

in a serene, rested sort of way and not making any effort to climb in next to him.

'Come on Lucy, get in,' he said.

'I'm not getting in; you are. I'll watch.'

Anthony began to ask: 'Why aren't you getting in?' but the ride started moving, pulling him away from his wife and towards countless twists and turns of cold metal with only one ankle strapped in.

Anthony held out his arms for his wife to save him and she tried. She tried to strap in the other ankle but the ride was pulling him backwards too fast and soon he was out of reach.

And in his dream Anthony was seeing his wife slip away and he was entering certain death, arms still outstretched, knowing that this was it…

Anthony jumped up with a gulp of air. It took but two seconds to realise that he had been dreaming and he was in fact safe in his bed, and when this occurred to him he sighed heavily and glanced at his alarm clock. 11.08pm. *Is **that** all?* Anthony let his upper body fall back down heavily on to the mattress and looked to the ceiling.

*In twelve hours it will all be over. In twelve hours doctors will know what this drug is **really** capable of. LAH will no longer be regarded as some nasty Class A, they will see what it can really do. They will see that it is lethal. Then the world, the world will be told that this is why Lucy is like she is, that it isn't her fault, that it was the drug that caused her to do what she did. And people will want it sorted. People will back me when I campaign for further tests, further treatment, for the sake of their own loved ones. People all around the world will 'go mad' just like Lucy did if the authorities ignore it, so they won't ignore it. They won't ignore Lucy anymore. They'll find a way to get this drug out of her system and then she'll wake up from this coma she's been in and we'll put these fifteen months behind us, she'll act again, she'll be the most respected star on the planet. People will remember her name* *forever, she'll never die...* and with this Anthony fell into deep sleep.

•

Nurse Lindle and Dr Morgan were at Penford for seven in the morning. Sitting in her office with the electric heater on full and the day close to breaking, they were finalising arrangements for the drug, if found, to be flown over to the American Institute of Substance Research.

This whole thing had already cost Nurse Lindle hours and hours of unpaid overtime. All the correspondence to her boss, the institute, the Home Office, Stainfield Hospital and the several hard-to-find American medics that had taken up the case after the little find, had taken their toll over the past fourteen days. And boy, didn't she know how much more was yet to come if it turned out that Mrs Denharden really had been slipped this drug in the month of her breakdown.

With heavy eyes and cold skin, Nurse Lindle updated the doctor on the latest information regarding Mrs Denharden and her current situation. Dr Morgan, a fine medic with heavily wrinkled skin and patches of grey hair, took notes and asked questions as Nurse Lindle spoke. He as good as ran Penford and Nurse Lindle respected him more than any other medic in the field.

'Right,' Dr Morgan sighed, scanning his notes once Nurse Lindle had wrapped up. 'So the journey to Stainfield will take an hour and a half, the prep and operation about an hour in total, and the anaesthetic will wear off on the journey back. So we're thinking that we'll be back and able to ring the AISR Centre by 2pm at the latest. What time will it be over there?'

'They're six hours behind so we'll be letting them know either way by 8am. Dr Rooney, who's the head of the institute, will be waiting for my call personally.'

'Excellent,' Dr Morgan smiled, before glancing at his watch. 'We've got a couple of hours to go over things so shall we go out for a coffee, get out of this office?'

330

'Oh yes,' Alicia sighed. 'I've been beginning to think that these four walls are all that's left in the world.'

Dr Morgan laughed, the feeling by no means foreign to him.

Over a coffee everything seemed less formal and, although this would not be the way Nurse Lindle would hold meetings with her own staff, she enjoyed the change.

Files, folders and papers covered the table that they were occupying at the café and Nurse Lindle drank black coffee from a chipped mug. The place was just as bloody cold as the hospital, if not colder, and was made worse by a constant draught caused by the arrival and departure of builders and early starters buying bacon butties and breakfast-trays.

After Lucy Denharden had been discussed in detail again, the two Penford employees that had worked together for many years updated each other on how their wards were going, how their families were doing and how they were. The two employees spoke with mutual respect and a grounded friendship. And, after they had finished their second coffees, they bid farewell to the café staff and drove back to the hospital to prepare Alicia's patient.

The ambulance ride was a comfortable 30mph cruise and Lucy remained contented and still throughout. Upon arrival at the hospital Nurse Lindle and Dr Morgan were briefed and then left in a waiting area as Lucy was wheeled off in a hospital bed.

After an hour or so, once the conversation had died out, Alicia had picked up an old copy of National Geographic and was flicking through it disinterestedly while Dr Morgan was sitting with crossed arms looking stern and in deep thought. Only a few moments later a consultant popped his head around the waiting area door and issued them into his office. The two medics followed in anticipation.

'Well,' the consultant sighed, moving around his desk and sitting down, ushering Dr Morgan and Nurse Lindle to pull up

331

a chair each. 'The patient reacted well to the anaesthetic and it should be wearing off enough for her to travel within the next half hour.'

The two medics nodded and the female gave a polite smile.

'Considering this was the first time this operation has ever been performed in the UK, I am pleased to say it went without complication and the patient suffered no trauma. As for the result, we can confirm that we did indeed find a carrier in the stomach lining and my assistant is preparing it to be flown to New York as we speak.'

The female mental health nurse expressed mild surprise at the consultant's findings by widening her eyes and tilting her head as if to say *is that so?*

The male mental health doctor just nodded and stroked his chin.

'I will call the institute as soon as you leave and inform them that they can be expecting the carrier at some point this evening,' the doctor continued.

'If it's sent out immediately it should arrive at 9pm their time,' Nurse Lindle replied.

Dr Morgan shuffled slightly and said: 'Good. Well, thank you for agreeing to perform this procedure. I understand it was short notice and with it being new and virtually untested we both appreciate your willingness to help.'

'Don't mention it, Dr Morgan. As I say, it was a relatively easy procedure. All I ask is that, for the first week, try not to immerse the patient's stitches with water.'

'Of-course,' *...of-course I know that, you oaf!* Nurse Lindle smiled.

'And I understand the AISR will be contacting Penford Hospital direct with all further correspondence?'

'That's right.'

'Excellent. Do you need me to do anything else at all, Dr Morgan?' The question was directly aimed at the older male, as he was obviously the main person to be dealing with here. The older male doctors usually were.

'No, that will be fine, thank you. But thanks again for your help,' Nurse Lindle replied with a bemused smile.

At 3.15pm Anthony's heart skipped a beat, rose to his throat and then started pounding wildly. For at 3.15 his phone started ringing. He had moved it to the desk in his study and was filling in a crossword trying to take his mind off things, when it sounded.

Anthony placed his hand over the receiver and let it ring once more before he picked it up.

This is it...

'Hello?'

'Anthony, its Alicia.'

Anthony gritted his teeth and asked how it went.

'A single plastic carrier was found and has been sent to America to be analysed,' the nurse said, getting straight to the point.

' W-what? So she *did* have the drug in her system?'

'It appears so, yes.'

Anthony could not speak; he only let out a sharp, emotion filled breath.

'Please don't discuss this with anybody until we get the analytical report back from the research centre that's handling it now. We're expecting to have that sent to us within the next three days.'

'Then what?' Anthony was still trying to take the information in. Yes, he'd believed it all along, but that's all it had been; a belief, a hunch. But now it had been proven: now it was fact.

'Then I'll discuss things with you further.'

'Can I come down?'

'Sure. We can do it over the phone though.'

'I know, but I'd like to see Lucy again.'

'Okay, but make it on Wednesday after three if you could, please Anthony. The report is getting couriered over here any time up to midday on Wednesday and I'll have to go over it myself first.'

'Yep, no probs. See you Wednesday then. Christ, I can't believe I was right all along. I just can't believe it.'

'Okay, Anthony. See you soon.'

'Okay, thanks.'

And with nerves and mixed emotions Anthony put the phone down on her, without even particularly realising he'd just done it.

Once the phone was back on the hook Anthony stared at it, his hand still gripping the receiver.

At first, the urge to laugh was almost as overpowering as the urge to cry and, as it turned out, Anthony ended up doing a bit of both before calming down slightly and succumbing to rational thought. And when this came, there was definitely no laughter involved. In fact, he felt totally different to how he thought he would. There were no tears of joy, she'd been drugged. Why would there be tears of joy over that? All the optimism he had been feeling about getting her better again was pushed to the back of his mind for a few brief moments and all he could think about was...

*She was drugged. My sweetpea was **drugged** with the most lethal shit around and it has ruined our lives, our careers, everything. She was drugged! There's no way she would have taken it knowingly. Jerry... it must have been. I've thought it all along. That little bastard drugged my wife. Why? Why did he do that to her? Holy Christ she was found passed out in that storage room. I bet he was in there with her... doing what? Why did he take my wife into a dingy cupboard and drug her?*

The anger came now. Pure anger, nothing but.

*And he's dead, he's dead so he's got away with it. The fucking scum that he is, he can't be punished for it now... it can't even be proven now. That little fucker. If he weren't dead I'd go over to LA and make him fucking pay myself. Now it can't be proven at all, there's nothing to say she didn't go in there willingly and get high with him but I **know** her! I know* *she wouldn't... but no-one else does, and no-one else will even hear that she was slipped, especially not now that Jerry's dead and more loved than ever. As usual, Jerry comes out the hero when all along he's the villain. I hope you're rotting in Hell you fucking son of a bitch.*

Anthony glanced at the crossword he'd been working on, and pushed it away. Suddenly, what a three lettered sly animal was didn't seem so important.

CHAPTER 16

Mary was sitting on her bed organising her nail clippings collection when Sara burst into her room with such urgency it made Mary jump and nearly drop the small cigarette-tin in her hands, sending nail clippings sprinkling to the floor.

'Sara!' Mary cried, dropping to her knees to retrieve the two toenails and one fingernail off the hard vinyl tiles. 'You stupid, stupid girl! I've spent hours getting those in order and now it's all ruined!'

'Mary,' Sara panted, out of breath and fired up on adrenalin, totally ignoring her friend's chastising. 'Mary, that ginger woman, that one in the wheelchair… she's one of them too. She's one of them and she's after me!'

Instead of the usual ignorance, Mary actually stopped and listened this time. After putting the nail clippings back in the tin and then placing it carefully under her bed along with a few other carefully preserved collections, she sat upright and asked Sara what had happened.

Sara had been walking down the dorm halls towards the TV room when Nurse Steve Jones turned a corner and came into view at the other end of the hall, walking towards her, although still about twenty rooms away. Steve was carrying a mop and bucket and was making his way down to room number five where one of the patients had thrown up…

'And he was *there*! As soon as he saw me I could tell he was after me, so I had to run and get out of his way because he was carrying weapons concealed in one of the hospital buckets and he'd have killed me. But I'm *too smart for him*,' Sara tapped the side of her head and snarled as she stretched out the last four words: 'And I got away…'

As soon as Steve saw her it made him apprehensive. Of-course, he could not tell his boss this because she would think of him, the 'rookie' of only a year and a half, as weak – surely.

But, Christ on a bike, how he wished he hadn't been assigned Sara White. She *scared* him. And from the moment he had realised she was walking towards him, he was expecting more grief, more threats, more offers. Great or what; the first patient Steve gets assigned Named Nurse to and he can't handle her. She was dangerous, he was sure. But, again, he didn't want to tell the big cheeses that he didn't agree with their decision to put her in a general ward. His girlfriend, Angela, nagged him to speak up, but Steve had always been so shy, so eager to please, no hassle, no mess. Back seat for Mr Jones, please. So he told them the facts, the threats... but he kept his personal opinions to himself. So, Steve was pleasantly surprised when 'Scary Sara' – as Angela called her – disappeared into another patient's room. He did not interfere, he walked straight past.

'...I hid in the nearest room, which was that ginger woman's room...'

'What did she say to you?' Mary interrupted, desperate for a gossipy story about the woman that she had had experience with herself, that familiar urge to make it even more exciting creeping up on her.

'Nothing. I didn't even see her at first, Mary. I was making sure *he* didn't follow me into her room, but he must have been told just to carry on walking, someone else must have entered the...'

Mary sighed and dismissed Sara with her hand, she hated it when she started going on about Nurse Jones; it was simply absurd.

'Oh for goodness sake, who would tell Nurse Jones just to carry on walking, Sara?'

'He has an *ear-piece,* Mary.'

'No he doesn't. You're just paranoid,' Mary tutted. 'Now, what did that ginger-haired girl say to you?'

'You never listen to me!' Sara said in her panicky, high-pitched whisper, flailing her hands around. 'The Secret Circle have the most advanced technology in the world. They *design* the ear-pieces so you can't see them...'

'That girl you're talking about told me that she was part of them, tried to get information out of me, she did,' Mary interrupted again, stopping Sara in her tracks as intended.

'She...? Did you tell her anything?' Sara asked once she had processed the information, her eyes wide with panic.

'No I didn't, even though she tried to bribe me and she was using tactics. I didn't tell her who you were.'

There was no double blinking, no loss of eye contact, no clearing of the throat. In fact, Mary's skills at lying were so advanced they contributed highly to the long list of reasons of why she was confined to Penford. She had fooled nurses, doctors and officials many times; she could switch it on at will.

'She already knows who I am, Mary. They all know who I am,' Sara said as a fact rather than a doubt to Mary's story.

'Of-course she knows what you look like, even which room you're in. But she doesn't know who you *are*, does she? She doesn't know the *real* you, and that's what they're after now.' Mary pulled it back swiftly, leaving Sara in no doubt that that's what she meant in the first place and that it was Sara that had misunderstood.

'Don't you dare tell her. You tell her *anything* and you'll live to regret it, Mary; I swear. I know people, I could...'

'Well, what did she say to you?' Mary asked. Sara stood up from the bed and began scoping the room.

'I don't know. It was a mumble,' she answered while searching frantically around all four joints of the walls to the ceiling, looking for cameras and bugs.

'Well, that's just ridiculous. She can speak perfectly well, it's all an act.'

By now Sara was opening the wardrobe doors and feeling for spy equipment at the top inside ledge of the doorframe.

'Of-course it's just an act. She's not catatonic at all, she's part of them, sent here to find out as much as possible about me. Now I know her mumble was a warning to me... a way to

341

scare me without blowing her cover. But look how much smarter I am than they are; they thought I wouldn't find out. They underestimate me.'

Sara dropped to her knees after finding nothing hidden in the wardrobe and looked under the bed. 'Check your tins,' she ordered, already aware of Mary's collections.

Mary huffed then told Sara to pass them to her. After all, the more Mary went along with her the longer they could carry on this excitement.

Sara passed Mary all five of her tins and sat next to her on the bed, to double check Mary didn't miss anything when she opened them.

'I saw her talking into something as well once. I went past her room and looked through her window. As soon as she saw me she stopped and pretended to be mentally ill again,' Mary said as she opened the first tin, full of nail clippings.

'Check it properly,' Sara said, seemingly ignoring Mary's last comments.

'Oh for God's sake Sara, there's nothing in there except my collection.'

'Let me look.' Sara tried to make a grab for the tin but Mary pulled it away defensively.

'You do not touch these. These are mine. You'll only mess up the order,' Mary commanded in a dark tone.

Sara pulled her hand back.

Mary went through the other four tins, letting Sara look but not touch. But, guess what, no bugs, no cameras, no spy equipment whatsoever. Only five tins containing five different collections: nail clippings, cigarette-butts (picked from the hospital's grounds), lumps of slimy hair out of the shower-room plug holes, stones, and used sanitary towels taken from the hygiene bin next to the toilet Mary uses.

'Right,' Sara whispered, barely audible. 'They don't know I've been in here, they don't know you've blown that woman's cover and it's going to stay that way for now. This is serious, you must *promise* not to tell a single soul about this conversation... promise?'

'Yes.'

'I'm going to monitor her for the next few days to see where she's at, how much she knows. Don't say anything in session, I don't want the nurses sniffing around and spoiling things. I won't let on that it was you who informed me if you absolutely assure me you won't give her any information.'

'I won't.' The buzz Mary was getting out of this was off the scale.

'Right, I have to go before she starts suspecting there's something going on.' Sara got up from the bed, opened the door, then said to Mary over her shoulder: 'Not a soul.'

Mary tapped the side of her nose and, once Sara had shut the door behind her, smiled a satisfied smile.

CHAPTER 17

Nurse Lindle had to do a double take when she first read the information.

It hadn't quite sunk in when the phone on her desk rang internally. She picked it up and, once she had confirmed that the call could wait, requested no more calls for the next half-hour.

Alicia sat back in her chair, taking the first page of the report into her hand and sighing heavily. She hadn't expected this at all. If she had even thought that this might be the outcome she wouldn't have ploughed all those hours research in after the drug test had taken place. It was quite a surprise.

Anthony turned up at Penford dead on 3pm with flowers for his wife's carer. He had gone against Alicia's wishes by telling Dr Nazir about the outcome but Alicia didn't have to know this and he was glad he had confided in his psychologist anyway, because she had taken the edge off the bitterness and the anger.

Nurse Lindle greeted him in reception with a large smile over the flowers, a quick, friendly hug, then a face that made Anthony ask: 'What?'

'Come into my office,' was all she said.

'I received the analysis report this morning.' Nurse Lindle sighed heavily and continued: 'Anthony, there were no traces of substance on the carrier.'

Anthony shrugged, confused. 'What does that mean?' he asked.

'It means she never took the drug.'

'No,' Anthony shook his head. 'No. She did.'

'Anthony... It was *intended* for her to take the drug, but what she *actually* took was a carrier with no drug present on it.'

'But... that's impossible. It must have rubbed off.'

'I'm afraid not. Forensic Toxicologists found several carriers in Jerry Tilsey's stomach lining. One of those had no trace of LAH on it either, the rest – some much older – did.

347

There is no way LAH can leave the carrier once it's soaked in. It's either on it or it's not... and it's not. The report here states that Lucy took the carrier around the back-end of 1990, around the same time as Jerry Tilsey's earliest trace. Jerry Tilsey was ripped off it seems, and Lucy was too.'

'Lucy didn't take that shit intentionally,' Anthony snapped, offended.

'I'm sorry, I didn't mean it to come out like that. But the fact is she has never had LAH in her system. She never took the drug.'

'But what happened to her... that wasn't natural.' Anthony's mouth did not fully close after he spoke, it hung open in shock.

'Do you want my opinion?' Nurse Lindle leaned forward.

Anthony only nodded, dumbfounded.

'This isn't official so don't quote me on it,' she pointed out first. 'But I think Lucy has most probably had mild schizophrenia since childhood. I also think you may be right about her not taking LAH knowingly. You want to know why?'

Anthony nodded again, mouth still open.

'I think Lucy may have suffered from the documented panic attacks as a physical result of the schizophrenia. Whether she ever told anyone about the reasons behind her panic attacks I don't know, because there's nothing on her records – either that or I'm wrong about this – which I might be, bear in mind. You say she was sensible about stimulants and depressants and I can understand that because they act as a well-known trigger for attacks, which was probably why she avoided them. So, why would she take something she knows will show her up?'

'She wouldn't.'

'At the awards in September 1990 she was found in a back room after an anonymous call to 911, which in itself is odd. I think this may be when, remember – off the record – she was given LAH. I think she passed out of a mixture of shock and alcohol and... maybe something else.'

348

'Like what?'

Alicia shrugged: 'Something that traumatised her enough to accentuate her schizophrenia, giving her a panic attack so great she was unable to come around from it, before finally hiding from it completely with catatonia less than a month later.'

'What could possibly happen to her that would affect her that much... to the point of seeing and feeling things that aren't there?'

'I have no idea, and wouldn't even like to guess. Like I say, this is only my opinion and I may be completely wrong.'

Anthony wiped his hand over his face and scooped back his hair with both hands, exhaling deeply as he did so.

'So, what now?' he asked.

'Now we continue with her treatment as we did before.'

'What if she speaks again?'

'Then we'll review it.'

'Well you must be able to do something to encourage her to do it. Can't you hypnotise her or something?'

'Anthony, we will do what's best for her,' Nurse Lindle assured the troubled man sat across from her. 'You've got to trust us.'

'Right,' Anthony said, almost to himself.

'Would you like a glass of water or something?' Nurse Lindle asked the man who was now staring unfocused towards the carpet near the office door.

He did not hear her.

'Anthony,' Nurse Lindle said in a more forceful tone, causing him to snap his eyes up to her as if he'd been in a daydream. 'I said would you like a glass of water?'

'Oh,' Anthony replied, slightly embarrassed. 'No thanks. I think I'll just see Lucy for a bit and then set off back home.'

'Okay.'

'Um,' Anthony continued. 'Please could I have a copy of the report?'

'I'm afraid not, sorry. That report's confidential and for Lucy's records only. I'll type you up a detailed letter though, including everything you need to know about the results of the test. Would that be okay?'

'That would be great.'

Anthony looked the nurse in the eyes and smiled. It filled Alicia with sadness to look at him. There was no happiness to Anthony's expression and the eyes that were looking at her were exposing him for the man he really was. A man who was on the verge of giving up; a man who had had everything he'd ever loved taken away from him; a man who was trying and failing to help he woman he was in love with. Looking at him made Alicia's throat tighten. She smiled back a sorry smile, her eyes heavy with sympathy and concern.

'I'm sorry we can't do any more to help her right now,' she whispered, her smile fading to a tight frown, not speaking loudly for fear of her voice cracking.

'You're doing all you can,' Anthony replied.

'Anthony...' Alicia began then stopped, not knowing quite what to say. His eyes evoked a thousands words in our nurse's head, but none of them seemed appropriate. There was a shared silence of helplessness, charged feelings, compassion and empathy, their eyes still locked.

'I know,' he nodded eventually. And he did. He knew.

He knew from the way that she was looking at him, he knew that she was thinking g*ood God Anthony, don't give up.* He knew that she was wishing she could help more; he knew that she was pitying him. And he couldn't help but let her; he couldn't hide it. Because, let's be honest, what now? What now? Nurse Lindle couldn't force his wife to get better and neither could he. If she was right, if something unspeakable had happened to Lucy and if she did always have something waiting to consume her then the likeliness of her recovering from it was slim to none now. Like an egg, Lucy had cracked. And cracked eggs are hard to piece together again.

...and it was a dud. I was wrong all along, all the times I've told people without a shadow of a doubt that she was spiked. All the hopes I'd pinned on it been drug-related so that she'd be easier to 'cure', so that it wasn't her beating me to death –

350

so that it was the drug. And it wasn't. It was her mind. In her mind Lucy saw worms, Lucy saw monsters and God knows what else. My wife went mad and on top of that I now have to deal with the fact that someone tried to poison her with chemicals. Somebody tried to drug my wife and what if the nurse was right about something traumatic happening to her? What could... oh fuck, I don't even want to think about it. My beautiful wife. I'm not getting her back, not now, not ever. No miracle drug treatment, no full recovery, nothing. She's gone.

'Can I see her now?' Anthony asked, his voice devoid of the massive, crushing emotion that was making his head spin.

Nurse Lindle nodded slowly then said: 'There's still hope yet, you know.'

Anthony dropped his eyes to the floor. He didn't reply because he did not believe it, and he felt she didn't believe it either.

Nurse Lindle cleared her throat and stood up from her chair. Anthony followed, his whole body simply going through the motions of a person standing up, his mind breaking and shattering.

The hope and optimism that Anthony had fought to regain since that fateful day was lost again in one swift blow; his rose-tinted personality crushed, his wife gone forever.

•

A lost man with grey skin is kneeling down next to a lost woman in a wheelchair in a familiar white room, accompanied only by a mock-mahogany and steel fold-down table and one chair.

The man strokes the side of the woman's face and wonders what she is thinking, wonders what's going on in her mind. Wonders if *anything* is going on in her mind.

Are you thinking of me? Do you hold the answers to the mystery of what happened to you? Are you aware that this is happening to you? To me? Are you aware of anything? Does your mind still function? Do you know I'm here? If I

351

whispered, would you hear me? Can you feel me touching you? Are you asleep? Are you dreaming? Do you have a dead mind, trapped inside a pulsing body with a beating heart? Are you dead? Lucy, can you feel me?

'Lucy, can you hear me?' the man, who was once a seventeen-year-old boy being told he was going to rule the world, asks.

The woman, who was once a seventeen-year-old girl with dreams too big for a small community, does not reply.

'Lucy.' The man does not pose her name as a question, more an order.

We suspend these two adults as poetic statues now.

The man is looking desperately towards the woman, his hand placed gently on her face, cupping a pale cheek.

She does not look at him. Her eyes point to her right, whereas he is at her left side. Her head has been lolled towards him since he entered the room; it remains that way still, motionless yet warm.

The man's clothes are clean but his body is worn. He radiates vibes of grief and he stenches of loneliness. We zoom in closer now: his hair is a mop of grey and brown, his ears are alert, waiting endlessly for just one more word, just *one*, from the woman who used to speak and thrill the world. His mouth is tilted to a frown, an equal mix of misery and concentration. The heaviness of life weighs down his shoulders, and his colour is drained by mental poverty. Dark circles cage beautiful, desperate eyes and his dull skin unmasks and exploits the troubles of many years.

We zoom in closer still and we see through the creased skin and chocolate brown irises. We see Anthony's soul...

A great red dragon is trapped in a cage, in the dungeon of a world that was once brightly lit. Its tail and head are as free as a bird, but its body and wings are penned suffocatingly into the box of bars. Men only a fifth of its size stand on the outside staring in at it. At one point these same men used to

352

whip at it. They used to brand it with irons and throw darts through the bars; anything to tame its writhing, freedom-deprived body. But now they only look in because the dragon is exhausted, merely a twisted heap of silence in a cage. Its eyes are shut and its tail lays limp. Several bright red scales have crisped and fallen to the floor, and some hang off the dragon's body like loose slates on a roof. A single tear, suspended in time, has barely left its eye. Here, in the dungeon of a world that was once brightly lit, is a defeated soul.

It wasn't always that way. Once, the dragon would scour the colossal skies majestically; it would swoop and fly and kiss the clouds. It was respected and worshipped; looked upon like a rainbow, holding the world in its claws. The sun was always shining and the countryside it flew above was nourished and rich. Its eyes were a shiny midnight black speckled with flecks of summer yellow, its armour and scales a striking red, hard and glossy. It would squawk and scream with freedom and power in its lungs. It would dip into crystal waters and dive into endless fields of sunflowers. It was a beautiful world... but then the clouds came. They blanketed forests and grassland with cold darkness, the waterfalls froze and the animals died. The dragon was washed into a cave by hard rain after masses of choking, smoky fog descended and got too thick to fly through. It lay there for an eternity, getting its energy back. And, just as it had nearly repaired itself and started to recover, man discovered it and took it hostage. They tied it up and claimed it as their own; they hauled and dragged it to their layer, and then they encased it with steel bars and padlocks and tortured it. This is how it is still, only now it has given up the fight and is letting them win. It has lain down conquered with a solitary tear. It has folded and is now simply awaiting ruin, praying for death.

We leave the dragon crying in its cage now and venture back to the women's general ward of Penford Hospital, this time to concentrate on the lady of his affections.

She still assumes the same position; her eyes still staring blankly at nothing, her body limp in a wheelchair, her facial muscles slack.

Unlike the man beside her, her physical being does not radiate grief. It tells us nothing. Her eyes, unlike the man, show no passion, no anger, no sadness. They simply stare.

Still, we go in deeper, travelling through those lifeless pupils and into her soul…

You and I are standing on dead leaves in a forest. The air is heavy and damp, trees loom over us and trap what would be midday winter daylight, leaving us feeling isolated and cold. Crows squawk in the distance and there is a whole aspect of intimidation that strikes fear and unease into both of us. To our left is a hollow tree trunk in which a small mouse is hiding. We know it is there because we can feel its fear. Everything else in the forest is fighting; the crows, the animals, the insects, the trees… But this one little mammal does not have the strength or courage to fight; it hides like a bullied child. It hides and yearns for the terror to fade.

We crouch down to the opening of the tree trunk and hear rustling from inside, as the mouse feels our presence and backs away further.

Put your ear to the hole where it hides. Do it now – don't be afraid of scaring it. It's scared already.

I place my hand on your shoulder as you lower your head to the opening, blocking the light. We hear a faint squeak and more rustling as the mouse tries to back up further still. If only we had one of those little yellow translation fish from the brilliant *Hitchhiker's Guide* to convert its language into English for us. I'd imagine we'd hear something like *please leave me alone, oh God leave me alone. Why can't you all just go away and let me live my life. I let you live yours, oh God why do you all have to pick on me all the time? Please just leave me alone.*

But we don't have that little yellow fish, so we only hear a squeak.

You look up to me and say: 'Why are we doing this?'

'Mmm,' I sigh. 'It's not coming out, is it?'

You shake your head.

'Come on then,' I say. 'I have a feeling we're not wanted here anyway.'

You follow my eyes to a tree only a few feet away. It is now quilted with silent crows all watching us with poisonous eyes. Just before you have chance to gasp I sweep us both back up to the hospital room and out of that intimidating, crushing atmosphere.

Well, that was nice. Our nerves are shattered now.

We send Anthony and Lucy back into motion, although neither move and I panic for a moment that our powers have gone and that they'll be suspended in time forever. But then Anthony brushes his thumb over his wife's cheek and I relax a little. We stand and watch.

'Lucy, can you hear me?' Anthony repeats. But we know that mouse he's talking to; we know it's too frightened to hear anything other than its own heartbeat, never mind listen to the quiet words of a man in a different world.

'She's gone,' you say to yourself.

'I know,' Anthony whispers, startling us both.

He kisses her gently, straightens himself up, tells her that he'll never give up on her, sweetpea, and then leaves the room.

Still – the fair skinned woman does not stir.

CHAPTER 18

Sara put down the pen, looked around her room again and read her letter back to herself, keeping an arm protectively around the sheet of paper so that the spy cameras could not pick up on it. Not at this point of the operation anyway.

For the Attention of all Active Members of the Secret Circle,

After several days' careful observation, it has come to my attention that the Secret Circle has been increasing activity within the Penford Psychiatric hospital, monitoring both myself and my fellow patients for some time now.

I understand that there are two 'moles' in close proximity to my living quarters; one posing as a nurse (Nurse 'Jones') and another as a fellow patient ('Lucy Denharden'). I know not how long you planned to monitor me before taking me captive, and I am also am unsure how many of the Penford staff were cooperating with your organisation and its plans to prevent me from leaking more information, but what I do know is that it ends now.

It gives me great satisfaction to know that I posed as such a threat to you; that you felt the need not only to have me committed, but to also continue tracing my every step, even after the laughably see-through set up of the police incident leading to my sectioning.

You think you have had the last laugh, but I have been laughing on the inside for many years now. Your Secret Circle isn't so secret any more, and hasn't been for a long time. Information about your organisation has been available freely in literature since the late 1950s and this is an international problem that is only getting bigger for you. Tracking and killing me won't get rid of the thousands of other people that know of your plans to destroy your own race.

Now that I finally have the chance to voice my thoughts in person to you, I would like to enlighten you of my personal opinions – the reasons for which I am against you so passionately in the first place. What you are doing is wrong and sick. You are killing off your own people; children that are oblivious to the way the world's run, entire communities that are simply going about their own lives – and all along you are slowly killing them for your sadistic reasons. You say population is the problem but I know that is just a mask, it is power that you are after. But you will never accomplish your task and I hope this grates you, because I know my words are important... otherwise you wouldn't chase me like you do. I hope this letter causes an emergency meeting, as I am confident it will.

You think you rule the world but that is bullshit: we rule you.

You spend so much time and money tracking me and who knows how many other people and I know why now: fear. You are afraid of me and I will die tonight knowing that I have won. You are a weak organisation and you hold power only over each other. You are only as human as I am and I've been to the meetings of likeminded people – people just like me trying to educate the lemmings; people like me trying to save the world from your ways and, mark my words, it will happen. You will be defeated and I will be there in spirit to see it. And I will laugh.

By the time you are reading this you will know how strong I am and you will wish, more than you do already, that I had never been born.

So I leave you with this, my final words: you are the pawns on our chessboard. We play you.

Sara White

Happy that her message had been put across, Sara folded up the letter and placed it under her pillow. She then left her room for the last time, shutting the door quietly behind her.

The fake catatonic was the only one she could get to because the 'nurse' only worked days and she had the passion to end it now. Activity was increasing at such a rate that even this time tomorrow may be too late. If they were monitoring her as closely as she thought, surely they would know she was up to something by now. She had to act fast, because if she didn't, they would.

Lucy was in deep sleep. It was, after all, 3am. With her room silent, her heart beating, and her body motionless, Lucy's subconscious was working overtime as it always did at this time of night. Lucy's dreams were often related to the life she used to have, the life of fame and riches and admiration. In her dreams she was mighty again. In her dreams she was the person she once was.

Only every now and again a nightmare would penetrate and tear her apart. It was during her nightmares when her world would slide and Reality would get in there just enough to let her know that something had happened that had taken all that happiness away, and it was usually during her nightmares that she would raise an arm and, on occasion, kick out.

But tonight Lucy was dreaming...

And her former self was on a large rock in her homeland of Nova Scotia. She was standing in the fresh Atlantic breeze overlooking the vast, blue ocean. The gentle waves of the sea was splashing up against the rock and onto her bare feet. The water was mild and pure. It was a summer's day and Autumn Leigh was wearing a thin, white cotton dress. It was flowing and stroking her body in the direction of the warm wind. Her hair was silky and free, her skin glowing and her eyes alive. In her dream she was at peace, she was contented and happy. The pebble-smooth rock upon which she was standing was part of a valley of similar fallen boulders. If she were to walk up the hill, she would be faced with a dust track leading through

361

dense, rich forest. But she was happy standing right there; at one with the ocean, as free as a bird...

The door to the mole's room was, as always, unlocked. Sara let herself in on tiptoes and, as she was hoping, her enemy was asleep.

Of-course, this girl wasn't really catatonic, so if Sara was to do this right, she had to do it fast. Members of the Secret Circle were trained to defend upon attack so the plan was to get in, strangle her as fast and quickly as possible, and then progress into the toilets where she had been stealing and stashing prescriptions for five days now. She knew she had to take them to overdose because if she didn't, after she'd killed one of their 'men', they would torture her and then they'd have won. If she killed herself before they could get to her, it would be *her* outsmarting *them*.

A gust of wind swept down onto Autumn Leigh from behind, from the top of the hill, and the near loss of balance it caused broke her daydreams. It came from nowhere and was oddly cold, making the hairs on Autumn's arms prickle up off her skin. It was also from the opposite direction from the sea breeze. Once it had been and gone, Autumn turned her head to the top of the hill, but it stood no differently and she was still alone. So, after a moment's apprehension, she turned her head back to the Atlantic and continued looking out into the deep ocean, this time her thoughts a little sharper.

Sara approached the mole with shaking fingers and a pounding heart. She knew she was doing this for the right reasons but still, she knew it was murder and there was huge chance the mole would overpower her. If that happened, Sara would be at the mercy of the Secret Circle. She had never murdered or even physically hurt anybody before whereas she knew the

362

mole most probably had done and this only added to her uneasiness. If she had the choice, she wouldn't be killing anybody... but she didn't have a choice, she was doing this to save her own life and for the benefit of human nature itself. By this point, Sara was standing over the woman. She watched her sleep for only two of her deep breaths, and then held out both hands towards her.

After only a matter of seconds, the wind came again. But this time it was so strong, Autumn lost her balance. Time seemed to slow down and Autumn's feet disappeared completely from beneath her. As her eyes looked down into the direction into which she was falling, she was horrified to observe that the pleasant, shallow shoreline had gone. Instead, Autumn was seconds away from plunging 200ft into a creek with violent, cold waves crashing and pounding against it. Autumn had just enough time to skip a heartbeat and lose her breath before she was beginning to fall dramatically towards her death, from a height, towards the cold ocean...

Sara's hands fell around the mole's neck and from the very outset, began squeezing tightly.

The top half of Autumn Leigh's body was the first to be hurtled off the edge but as her arms instinctively spread outwards, a strong hand grabbed her from behind and pulled her back, hoisting her upright again and spinning her around all at the same time...

Sara continued pressing into her enemy's delicate throat.

The act of strangulation itself was surprisingly easy. Sara had been practising on her pillow and herself for a few days now but still, she expected the mole to struggle. The stress of spying must have worn her out; she must have been in an incredibly deep sleep.

It would have made Sara cringe if she had actually concentrated on the feeling of the grinding, compacting insides beneath the mole's reddening skin, so instead she shut her eyes as tight as possible and centred her focus on the fact that this would throw the Secret Circle into turmoil. That helped somewhat and enabled her to push her fingers further in.

'Anthony!' Autumn exclaimed as she fell into the arms of the man that had saved her.

He was smiling, looking straight into her eyes. For a moment, all Autumn saw were those eyes. The wind had gone, the sky had gone, the sea had gone. All she could see and feel were those amazing circles of chocolate; those deep, rich windows that she had fallen into thousands of times previously. Her body relaxed to the point where she was relying on him to keep her standing, she was lost in a whirl of awe. She was back in the arms of the love of her life and, oh Lord, she had missed his touch.

The ease of the murder pleased Sara to the core, and when the mole's tongue rolled out like a dry pink slug after about a minute of her squeezing, it simply made her press into her throat harder.

The simplicity of it all only proved to Sara that the Secret Circle was getting weaker, hiring breakable spies. There was a time when their spies were highly trained martial arts experts, the kind of people that would sleep with one eye open, if sleeping at all. Spies were supposed to be on duty twenty-four hours a day. Ha! Look at this! It was as good as a joke.

When Autumn did eventually yank herself back from the pull of those amazing eyes, the dream turned and was no longer a dream at all. It became memory.

Autumn Leigh and Anthony Denharden were dancing intimately, surrounded by all the living people they'd ever loved.

They were in the middle of a highly decorated hall, live music giving them rhythm; claps, tears and cheers making them laugh quietly into each others ears. Autumn was wearing her wedding-dress, Anthony a tuxedo. They had been married only seven hours and they knew, they knew they had their whole, bright lives ahead of them. It was a moment so amazing, so beautiful, that neither of them would remember it sharply in the months and years afterwards. It was so perfect, it was played out in a daze.

'I love you so much,' Anthony whispered to his new bride, stroking her luxurious, long ringlets as he spoke.

Autumn Leigh swayed with the music, held her love close and held back tears of joy.

'You saved me,' she whispered back.

At this, he held her tighter still and moved his head from his shoulder to look into her eyes.

At this point, the memory became a dream again, although the setting, the music and the moment remained the same.

'I've missed you,' Autumn said, her eyes suddenly filling with tears.

Sadly, in the real world, Lucy was being strangled and her eyes were filling with blood.

'Are you back now?' Anthony whispered, as the people and music in the background faded away and they were dancing alone.

'I've always been here, Anthony. I've always been thinking of you, I just couldn't tell you. But I'm back now and I'll be by your side forever.'

'Don't leave me again Lucy, please,' he pleaded.

At that moment, Autumn suddenly felt that she only had a few moments left in his arms. She couldn't possibly understand why she felt this strong, sad urge that she had to go, but an invisible soundless clock had begun ticking and she had no choice other than to accept it.

'I'll never leave! I love you more than I could ever tell you, Anthony,' Autumn cried, trying to get everything she had to say out at once, for fear that he would disappear at any second. 'I'm so sorry for hurting you. I didn't know it was you. I'm so sorry.'

'I love you, Lucy.' Tears were falling down Anthony's face now. 'My life is empty without you. Please, *please* just stay.'

'I love you!' Autumn cried as her love began to fade away. 'I'll stay with you! I promise…!'

And then Anthony dissolved and a bright light engulfed her.

The mole died easily and Sara left her with the only obvious evidence of murder being a red ring around her neck and a fat tongue lolling out of her mouth. Her eyes, although blood-filled beneath the lid, were closed all along and the whole act, from beginning to end, only lasted a few seemingly painless minutes.

•

With a frantic cry Anthony jumped from his sleep so violently he literally threw himself off the bed. His body hit the floor with a thud but he wasted no time scrambling to his feet and backing up.

Anthony stood in the dark looking at the bed he had been asleep in not twenty seconds ago, his chest heaving and bones shaking.

It had been a dream. *No, it had been more than a dream.*

As he played it though in his mind, standing in the darkness of early morning, his body began to shake more. He brought one hand up to wipe through his hair and when doing so he realised it was wet, wet to the scalp with cold sweat. It had been the most vivid, living dream he had ever experienced. He'd had some odd ones and some real ones throughout his life, especially of late, but this had been *real*. She'd been with him.

Knowing there was no way he'd ever get back to sleep, Anthony put on his dressing gown and proceeded to make himself a black coffee; all the time trying to rationalise with himself that it had just been an intense dream, and trying to put aside the feeling that he had really just seen her, she had really just been in his arms and telling him she was sorry and that she'd never leave him. *No, no, no. It's only because that's what I want her to say, it's been on my mind, it's always on my mind. The subconscious throws up things to help you deal with them, nothing more. Christ.*

Dr Nazir was coming for his session at 11am, but it was only knocking on 3.30am. *Great*, there's *hours* to go yet. Anthony couldn't wait for her to get here to hear her thoughts on his dream, to say the things to him that he was trying to convince himself over now, to say it was only a dream and no, Anthony, she wasn't really in your arms. No, Anthony, she wasn't trying to communicate telepathically with you. It was a dream. Dreams happen. Get over it.

The morning was bitter and the central heating hadn't kicked in yet, so Anthony had both hands wrapped around the coffee mug tightly. He was sitting at the black marble breakfast bar in his kitchen in silence, going over that dream again and again in rambled, confused order. He managed to do that for five minutes before it just seemed ridiculous to be sitting in the cold so he changed into tracksuit bottoms, socks and a jumper, flicking the heating on constant as he did so.

Another cup of coffee was poured as the central heating began to take the chill out of the air and Anthony took it through to the living room to sit in silence and think about what had just happened rationally.

His memories of the dream were broken up and distorted, faded for the most. Only one part of it was crystal clear, although he knew enough to know that the dream had been longer. He was with her, his bride, and they were dancing to the music of a beautifully arranged orchestra on their wedding day just as they had done all that time ago. The dream was an echo of that day with ridiculous accuracy; even the guests were wearing the same clothes and sitting in the same places. As they were dancing he had whispered that he loved her and she said *you saved me*. And as soon as she had said that he knew it was nor a dream or a memory… it was real. The love of his life then told him that she had missed him and within that second he was holding her for real, he was there, back in the dance hall. He could feel the satin of her dress against his fingers, he could smell her sweet, fresh perfume; he was with her. With this eerily new and foreign realisation Anthony had asked her if she was back now; his way of asking if this was actually happening. And she had said yes, and that she wouldn't leave him again. He then told her about how much he had missed her; that he'd been through such hell and she hadn't been there to hold him like she was now. After he had spoken, he suddenly got an urge to grab her so tight she would seep into him, and then she would *be* him and she couldn't get any closer or any further away.

But he couldn't do that, he could only savour the precious moments and the amazing feeling, a feeling that he could sense coming closer to ending as every second passed. The energy between them at that moment was almost glowing with love and when Lucy spoke again, almost frenzied with panic, it convinced him that she could feel him slipping away too. She was telling him that she loved him and that she was sorry and this made Anthony cry with desperation and he pleaded with her not to go, because now he could *feel* her being pulled away from him. Lucy had cried out that she loved him but, as she was promising that she'd stay with him, she had dissolved and Anthony was jolted from his sleep.

The dream had been sad but amazing all at the same time but most of all it had been real. Over an hour passed and Anthony was still lost in thought. It was only when he twitched his fingers against his cup when he realised his coffee was stone cold and decided to refill.

Once his cup was full of steaming hot coffee again, Anthony put down his mug and took off his wedding ring to study it. He had cleaned it all up a few weeks ago and it looked as shiny now as that brilliant day that she had slipped it on his finger with a tearful smile. Just as his eyes lost focus due to looking through the middle of it the phone began to ring. And that's when he knew for definite that it had been more than a dream: she had been saying goodbye.

Anthony lowered his ring slowly, his eyes remaining unfocused.

Each peal increased his heart rate that little bit more and gut instinct mixed with common sense told him that this was to be a phone call of considerable importance to him. No matter what, he had to answer it soon or it would ring off and he'd have a painstaking wait until whoever had phoned called back. Anthony got up off the couch and over to the window where the phone was.

He picked up the receiver with a certain amount of dread and from nowhere said, in an eerily matter-of-fact way: 'She's dead,' before whoever it was ringing him had even had chance to speak.

'Anthony?' Nurse Lindle's recognisable yet startled voice asked.

'Lucy's gone, isn't she?'

'Anthony, how…?' Nurse Lindle tailed off partly out of shock and partly because she was on her way to saying 'how did you know?' and that may well have turned out to have been one of the most tactless things she had ever said.

Anthony did not speak any further so Nurse Lindle began her well thought-out soft words, pretending to disregard what had just occurred, although that strange certainty and the knowing itself had thrown her somewhat.

'I'm sorry to ring you at such an ungodly hour. I'm afraid I have some bad news for you. It's about Lucy…' the nurse was thankful Anthony did not interrupt her and carried on carefully: 'I'm so sorry to have to tell you this Anthony, but I'm afraid Lucy was found dead this morning.'

Silence.

'Anthony, I'm so sorry.'

The news didn't even penetrate Anthony. It blanked his thoughts. He heard it, but he couldn't process the information. The nurse fell silent and Anthony continued with his blankness for around thirty seconds.

'Anthony, are you there?' Nurse Lindle eventually asked.

'Hmm-h,' he replied through closed lips.

'I'm so sorry,' she whispered again.

'What happened?' Anthony asked almost mechanically, not even believing this was real, not even registering what he was being told now that it definitely *was* real.

'We think...' Nurse Lindle stopped and sighed, wishing more than anything she didn't have to be telling him this. 'We think she may have been murdered. The police are here and they haven't confirmed it as definite yet, but that's how it's looking.'

Anthony nodded at the news in the same way you would nod if somebody was trying to teach you something but you weren't fully listening.

'Okay. Can I call you back?'

'Anthony, please don't... just, do you have somebody you want me to call... to be with you?'

'I don't have anybody,' Anthony replied factually, numbed.

'Do you want me to come up to Leeds?'

'No. No thank you.'

'I'll call you back in half an hour, Anthony. Do you promise you'll pick up the phone?'

'Yeah.'

'Okay Anthony, I'll...'

Anthony put the phone down and stood motionless. He had stopped shaking, his heart had stopped racing, his mind had stopped thinking.

A half hour later the phone rang, but Anthony didn't register it. He heard it, but it never occurred to him to pick it up. Half an hour after that there was a frantic knock at his door. This he did register as it shocked him enough to make his nerves tingle. It was the front door to his apartment. Whoever it was had got through the pin-numbered code of the complex. The knocking came again with a male voice this time.

'Mr Denharden? Mr Denharden, please open up; this is the police. You're not in any kind of trouble – we just want to make sure you're alright.'

Anthony walked zombie-like to the door.

'I'm fine,' he said.

'Mr Denharden?' the voice on the other side of the door asked, not as frantic this time.

'Yeah, yeah; I'm fine. Please just leave me alone.'

'Okay, sir. We were just checking. Your friend Alicia suggested we come round and make sure. Are you positive you don't want us to come in for a bit?'

'I'm fine.'

'Alright. Call us at Holbeck Police Station if you want us for anything, alright?'

'Alright.'

'Okay. Goodbye.'

'Yeah.'

Anthony slid down the door and pulled his arms around his head, sheltering himself from the world, still not allowing himself to think.

Something woke him from his daze and when Anthony lifted his head, it was light. Another little tap at the door filled his ears, a far cry from the pounding of earlier.

'Anthony? Anthony, are you there?' A sweet, familiar voice came from the other side of the door.

Anthony stood up, unlocked the door and opened it to Dr Nazir.

Dr Nazir was shocked when she saw the state of her client. She brought a hand up to the middle of her chest and said: 'Anthony, what's…?'

'She's dead,' he said. And then it hit him. She was. She was dead.

With a loud cry Anthony fell to his knees, his arms grabbing out to Dr Nazir's long winter coat. The doctor dropped her briefcase-bag and crouched to catch him, her arms reaching protectively out to him.

'Oh fucking hell!' he cried, screaming and sobbing on his knees, his arms now hugging her tightly to him.

Saima moved quickly and sat on the floor with him, repeating *shhh* over and over. She could only guess he was talking about Lucy and held him tightly with both hands rubbing and patting the back of his jumper.

He was wailing so loudly one of his neighbours opened his front door but Saima shooed him away without Anthony even seeing.

'Oh God, she's dead!' he was crying over and over.

Saima rocked with him and let him cry.

'She's dead, she's dead,' Anthony was repeating again and again, until finally, everything went black.

CHAPTER 19

So, that's all folks. That's the end... the end of our adventure. We have to part and get on with our own lives now, but don't worry; I won't leave you out in the cold. We both know the sun didn't stop setting after that moment, children didn't stop playing and the world didn't end. But that particular chapter in our characters' lives closed. So, I tell you what, before we say our goodbyes (for now?) let's fast-forward a few years and find out what happened after our time together finished. I owe that to you, my valued companion...

The manufacturers of LAH in Japan were tracked and busted the following spring. Since that was the only warehouse in the world that knew the make-up of the drug, it was never copied and the drug never became a problem. Yeah, yeah, to this day you will find cheap dealers offering you LAH but it's not LAH at all, it's just LSD with a higher price slapped on.

Marone Scott was arrested and jailed in the summer of 1992. He is still serving time now, and will be for a long time yet. His house was sold for three million dollars to the former drummer of *Toby's Wardrobe*.

Jerry's name lived on and he is now dubbed as one of the best young actors of all time – so tragically taken, what a waste. Only us and a handful of others know what he was really like because sadly, even those that knew he was a monumentally fucked up loser now will sing his praises and go along with the popular notion that 'yeah, I was lucky to know that guy.'

Carman's parents never got over the loss of their beautiful daughter and had split up due to the pain by 1993. Dwayne Connell never married Carman in 1999, as he would have done if she'd have been alive, and their daughter, Paris

Connell, never went on to be the interior designer she would have been because she was never born.

Sara White was buried in January 1992 after strangling a fellow patient and then committing suicide by overdose. The letter she wrote to The Secret Circle was the last addition to her file and over time her file was archived in the cellar of Penford, and the box it resided in became dusty and old.

Mary Cheeda missed her friend for only a few months before she found solace in a new patient, and from then on claimed that she hated Sara and that Sara had tried to strangle her once too but she had fought her off.

In April 1996 Alicia Lindle shed a tear in church for her eldest son, Jacob. Her only daughter was by her side, along with her devoted husband, while her youngest son was standing up front dressed in top hat and tails after being asked to be Jacob's best man on this, his wedding day. Only two years after that mild April day, Alicia became the mother of the bride and a grandparent to Jacob and Sharon's first child. Alicia still works at Penford and when she is not cooking big Sunday dinners for her extended happy family, she is overseeing the extensions and renovations of the hospital.

Nurse Steve Jones asked to be transferred to the men's ward, but after a particular vicious attack from a patient, he came out of nursing all together and set up a floristry shop with Angela. The business went on to be successful and by 2002 they had opened two stores.

Dr Saima Nazir continued improving the lives of many, many people and continued being recognised for it. She still meets up with Anthony for a coffee every now and again but these days it is not because he is her client... it is because he is her friend.

And Anthony? Well, let's just see it from a different perspective...

CHAPTER 20

The same three familiar homeless faces were sitting on the bench as she walked past. Of-course they were sitting on the bench – where else would they be at 10.30am on a Tuesday? Becka had got used to them by now. She worked for DLF Solicitors' on The Headrow and at seventeen years old, she was the 'gofer' of the employment department, chosen lovingly to fetch the solicitors' coffees every morning.

On only a few occasions the tramps would bother her, mainly just by calling out things like: 'Lovely hair'. She always smiled politely and simply carried on with her duties.

This June morning was sunny and warm. She wore her mother's short pastel summer dress and held £7.90 in her right hand and a half smoked Regal in the other.

Becka passed the three homeless men as usual, who were drinking Special Brew as usual, and waited outside the coffee shop to finish her cigarette as usual.

And that's when something totally amazing happened.

A handsome man and a naturally beautiful young woman walked straight past her and into the shop. Becka's heart rose into her throat and its rate increased tenfold. This was her moment but dare she? Dare she? *Yes,* she thought, *I'd kick myself forever if I didn't.*

So the Regal was forgotten and she followed the couple into the shop. Luckily there was a queue and the person she was after was at the back of it, holding hands and chatting happily.

'Excuse me, sorry,' Becka began as the two turned around. 'I'm sorry to bother you but… are you Anthony Denharden?'

The handsome man smiled and the pretty woman he was with grinned and let go of his hand so he could give this young stranger his full attention.

'Yeah, hi,' he said, smiling warmly and holding out his hand: 'Pleased to meet you.'

Becka had a moment of speechlessness before holding out her hand and shaking his vigorously, smiling as if possessed and wanting to laugh and cry at the same time.

'What's your name?' Anthony asked, genuinely interested.

'Becka. Anthony, I…' For a girl that couldn't usually shut up, she suddenly found herself totally and utterly lost for words. She had so much she wanted to say to her hero but now that it actually came down to it, the moment she had been fantasising about since she was thirteen, she was speechless. 'Um… sorry.' she laughed nervously.

Anthony and the lady he was with laughed with her in a way that made her feel totally at ease, and Becka was able to compose herself a bit.

'I just wanted to say how much I respect you. I think you're just… fantastic!' Becka now found that she couldn't stop laughing, a mixture of total excitement, happiness and nerves all mixed into one. 'I've read your book loads of times and I went to the cinemas twice to see *From Life,* and I just think you're one in a million.'

'Thanks, Becka,' Anthony beamed. 'What do you do?'

'Where do I work?'

'Yeah.'

'Oh, sorry! I work at a solicitors'; just getting their coffees. I'm just a junior.'

'Well, without juniors the world would collapse,' Anthony smiled.

Becka laughed far too loud and had to contain herself to stop.

'Oh, sorry,' Anthony said, turning his body towards the lady. 'I haven't introduced you. This is Chloe – my partner.'

'Hi,' Chloe smiled, shaking hands with Becka.

Becka knew who she was already. She'd seen her in pictures with Anthony many times, attending premiers and looking stunning. There'd even been a rumour over the past week that she was pregnant but Becka was too polite to ask.

'Are you gunna start acting again, Anthony? I'd love to see you in a film. You're such a good actor.'

'I would love to but I can't remember the lines unless they're written in front of me. Plus, writing and directing is alright, I suppose. I think I'm content to stick with that now,' Anthony said.

'Alright?! You're amazing! I'm sorry, you must hear this all the time,' Becka giggled. 'I write books, well, long stories, but I read yours and know I just can't compare... your work is life changing.'

'Are you a good writer?' he asked.

'My dad thinks so.'

'So if you're a good writer keep doing it. I'm sure one day I'll be boasting to my friends that I met that famous author in a coffee shop once. Believe in yourself and you can do anything, seriously.'

'Erm, I doubt it. I'm not that good.'

'If you want to do it – do it. You'll regret it if you don't.'

Becka blushed and brushed her hand as if to dismiss it.

'Are you living back in Leeds now?' she asked hopefully; silly visions of the three of them hanging out spinning round her head, making her heart race again.

'No, 'fraid not: just visiting. Chloe's never been to Leeds before so I'm taking her on a bit of a tour.'

Chloe smiled with diamond teeth, her dark skin glowing.

'Can I have your autograph?' Becka asked, afraid that she was boring them and taking up their time.

'Sure. Do you have a pen?'

'Oh, erm...'

'It's okay,' Chole smiled, opening her handbag. 'I have a pen and some paper.'

She handed the two to Anthony and he wrote: *Becka, it has been great speaking with you. Good luck with the writing. Don't give up. Anthony Denharden.*

He handed it over, and after Chloe had pointed out that there was nowhere to sit, he shook Becka's hand and said goodbye. He could have been the most average man in the world.

After everything he'd been through, the amazing highs and destructive lows, he still stood and spoke to a teenage girl like, for that moment, nothing else in the world mattered to him. He really was as inspiring and down-to-earth as the media claimed.

Anthony Denharden worked behind the scenes of films with the help of industry leaders as a sideline really. His main job these days was writing and his books had given hope to thousands of people all over the world, making him one of the most celebrated men of that time.

Along with several self-help manuals, he had also written a book about his life that had stayed as a number one bestseller for a whole year and had won awards for its sheer honesty and insight. The book was then made into the film *From Life* and you will find it in many people's list of top 5 movies. His story inspired millions.

And as Becka watched her hero walk out of the shop, she knew she had the power to do anything she wanted in life... and she did.

Becka became a published author and based her first novel around the man that had walked in and out of her life in a second and totally changed it. The book was called *Lucy's Monster*; you've just reached the end of it.

Okay, my friend, I must dash. It's been a pleasure knowing you and I want to thank you from the bottom of my heart for accompanying me on this journey. I tell you what, I'll make you a deal: if you promise me you'll continue to roll with the punches and use difficult times to simply make you stronger, I promise you the sun will shine the next time we meet.

Goodbye for now.

The End